Joyce Harrington

FAMILY REUNION

"There's never been a family, or a reunion, quite so terrifying...It's a major treat for mystery readers, who are faced with the twin questions of whodunit and what it was they did!"
—Edward D. Hoch, editor,
The Best Detective Stories of the Year

"FAMILY REUNION—shuddersome, compelling, stylishly written—delivers the goods."
—Stanley Ellin, author of
THE LUXEMBOURG RUN

"Superb suspense...chilling—a horror story about people who make you care."
—Dorothy Salisbury Davis, author of
SCARLET NIGHT

Other Avon Books by
Joyce Harrington

No One Knows My Name

FAMILY REUNION

JOYCE HARRINGTON

AVON
PUBLISHERS OF BARD, CAMELOT, DISCUS AND FLARE BOOKS

Design by Laura Hammond

AVON BOOKS
A division of
The Hearst Corporation
959 Eighth Avenue
New York, New York 10019

Copyright © 1982 by Joyce Harrington
Published by arrangement with St. Martin's Press, Inc.
Library of Congress Catalog Card Number: 81-14562
ISBN: 0-380-63099-0

The St. Martin's Press, Inc. edition contains the following
Library of Congress Cataloging in Publication Data:

Harrington, Joyce.
Family reunion.

I. Title.
PS3558.A6284F3   813'.54   81-14562
AACR2

First Avon Printing, April, 1983

WFH 10 9 8 7 6 5 4 3 2 1

For Doctor Mel
who supplied the power.

FAMILY
REUNION

CHAPTER
1

Sometimes at night I dream of River House, standing alone on the only high ground for miles around above the rushing brown water. The river is wide at this point and muddy with the silt washed down by years of winter rains leaching the fields upstream. There is always a memory of giant catfish. The house is empty in my dream, and empty in fact as I know from letters from home. Wendell never fails to mention it. Wendell is a cousin of some sort, second or third, a large, blustering man who sells sporting goods—hunting rifles, bowling balls—and has a quick pen for bad news. I have a photo album, a family treasure, which contains a yellowed studio photograph of a pinch-faced frightened baby in a christening gown. That's Wendell. My grandmother was the last of the family to live in River House.

River Road curves by the house, a thin strip of crumpled black macadam between the sheltering willows and the sour weedy slope down to the water's edge. Once the only road for travelers in this part of the world, it has been rendered redundant by the highway that roars half a mile away. Now its only traffic consists of puzzled angry drivers who took a wrong turn or secret nighttime lovers searching the darkness for a place to park and fumble each other. Or me, standing in my dream road gazing up at the tall narrow house, its clapboards gleaming silver in the moonlight, its shuttered windows brooding on past regrets.

The road is cracked and pocked with holes that would cripple a bulldozer and the county won't do a thing about it, so Wendell writes. He wants to hold a family reunion, open up the house, get everyone back for a week to renew family ties, have a barbecue on the lawn, pay our respects to those of us who are buried in the family graveyard behind the ruined apple orchard. I remember the taste of those apples, warm from the sun and tart and smelling as apples never smell after they've been picked and shipped to the city and wrapped in shiny plastic. I remember hiding from Wendell in the apple orchard when I was about nine, but I can't remember why—only that he was tall and frightening in his uniform (a Marine, I think he was), and the air in the house was moist with sorrow. Someone had died or gone away. I think it was my father. The apples were still green. I suppose I'll have to go to Wendell's reunion.

I haven't seen Wendell or River House in ten years. What brought me to the city was a Greyhound bus, sliding in the night through small towns strung along the highway like lonely birds on a telephone wire. Wherever we stopped, I awoke from my doze and looked out the window, seeing the same candy machine with the same candy bars slotted behind glass, the same bus station faces, weary and pallid in the thin, electric-blue light. By morning, though, the scenery had changed and there were rumors of the still-distant city in the widening of the highway, the clusters of drowsing suburban rooftops melting into the early mist. What made me board the bus ten years ago was a dreadful quarrel with my mother. Something about a boy I was seeing. No matter. My mother has gone on to other things, according to Wendell.

According to Wendell, my mother has contracted a mild form of lunacy. Not crazy enough to be confined, she prowls the town in tennis shoes haranguing people on the subject of floods. Apparently, she believes that all the rivers and oceans of the world are rising and will, one day very soon, cover the earth and drown us all. She wears a life jacket at all times. She has bought a small boat and keeps it stocked with food in the backyard. People have begun to call her Mrs. Noah, and both Wendell and the minister of her church have tried to reassure her that God will not destroy the earth a second time by water. Nevertheless, whenever it rains she sits in her boat in the backyard under a black umbrella waiting to cast off. Wendell has taken it upon himself to write me this news in pitying detail, just as he has written me over the years of the domestic trials of all the members of our numerous clan. He is our communications center. I wonder if he keeps them informed of the stingy tidbits of my life which I feel compelled to send him in return. To keep his letters coming. I always dread the sight of his precise handwriting on the plain cheap envelopes he uses, but I am careful not to discourage him from keeping in touch. I answer his letters with brief notes of my own, occasionally a picture postcard of a Manhattan view with a few cheerful, mysterious words scrawled on the back. "What a time we had last night! Party at Greg's place!" It pleases me to think of Wendell turning the card over in his moist, plump, bowler's hands, staring first at the gaudy colors of the building or bridge or statue on the front, then shaking his head over the message of wild and sinful delights on the back. In truth, my life is not so very wild. In truth, my life is rather tame and dreary. I go to few parties and I know no one named Greg.

Ten years ago, Wendell asked me to marry him. Our cousinship was far enough removed to make this union not only feasible but appropriate. My mother thought it was a great idea. "He'll take good care of you," she said. "You'll be set for life." Wendell was by then an established businessman and owned his own home in a newly developed tract of imitation half-timbered pseudo-Tudor houses northeast of the town proper. All he lacked was a wife. I did not leave home to escape Wendell; he wanted to help me escape my home with his offer. He subsequently married Bonnie Marie Warren, a nice, blond woman with short legs and a broad smile who worked in the County Clerk's office. Wendell's Christmas card each year is photographic proof that life is serious and good. Last Christmas, Bonnie Marie smiled broadly over the heads of Wendell, Jr., and Sally, while Wendell, Sr., stood solemnly beside her carefully avoiding looking at her hugely pregnant stomach. A birth announcement followed a month later. This year's card will include the twins.

Wendell thinks August would be a good time to hold his family reunion. He will make all the arrangements. He will even bear most of the cost, although those of us who want to and can afford it are welcome to contribute. He has been out to River House and found it in good enough repair, despite having been unoccupied for so long, to accommodate all of us from out-of-town. Unless, of course, I wish to stay with my mother in town.

Yes, all right, my note to Wendell said. I'll come to your reunion. I'll take my vacation in August. I don't think I should stay with my mother. It's been too long. We're practically strangers. I would like to have my grandmother's room at River House, the one with the tiled fireplace and the bay window overlooking the river. Am I remembering correctly?

There was a window seat in the bay window fitted with velvet cushions the color of plum jam. On visits to my grandmother, I always managed to slip away from the tea and gossip and curl up in the window seat, sometimes with a book I'd brought along, sometimes with the photo album that was kept on a lace-covered table beside her bed. This photo album, the very one that now has a special niche reserved for it in my bookcase, is bound in red plush and fitted with an ornate brass catch and hinges. It's very old, much older than many of the photos that cling to its brittle pages. On those afternoons in my grandmother's window seat, I held the album in my lap and turned the pages slowly, always starting from the beginning. The first few pages were filled with stiff unsmiling faces of people looking destiny square in the eye. The women, of whom there were many, wore their hair pulled into tight uncompromising knots and seemed carved of granite. The men had a softer look about them, as if their eyes might wander at any moment from the camera's stern focus to watch a bird in flight, their hair might escape the bonds of brilliantine and flutter in the breeze. The men, most of them, were young and their mouths were sensuous. The children, products of these long-dead unions, seemed serious and not inclined to play. I gave each page its due.

After about five or six of these pages, I came at last to a picture of a person I knew. My grandmother as a girl. I would not have recognized her as the slender pretty young woman in the white ruffled dress with her dark hair pulled loosely back and tied with a ribbon, but she came upon me one day in the window seat and pointed her young self out to me. But even with the softer styles of her youth, there was about her face a hard purposefulness, a heritage of the granite women who had gone before. She told me the picture had been taken a short time before her marriage and, indeed, on the facing page she sat in her wedding gown while my grandfather, pale-eyed and fair, his mouth hidden beneath a brushy moustache, stood possessively and proudly behind her. I never knew my grandfather. He died before I was born.

As often as I turned the pages of the album, as carefully as I followed the faces down the years, it was always a shock to come face-to-face with the man who was my father. He stood leaning against the hood of a car, squinting happily into the sun. The car looked new and shiny, which may have accounted for his happiness, and its wide chromium grill smiled beneath his proprietary hand. Someone, my grandmother perhaps, had by this time begun writing terse, crabbed captions beneath each photograph. This one said, "Raymond and his new green Pontiac. First car after the War." I don't remember the car, although he must have had it when I was born. My grandmother told me that when Raymond married my mother, he drove the car all the way to Myrtle Beach for a honeymoon and she was carsick most of the trip. There aren't many pictures of my mother in the album: the obligatory christening picture (The same white lace gown appears again and again throughout the album. Even I had my turn to wear it.) and a few fuzzy snapshots of a thin pinafored child unlovely in tight braids and dark stockings wrinkling around the high tops of her tightly laced shoes. I felt sad about those shoes. Perhaps if she'd had prettier shoes as a child, she wouldn't now be sitting in her boat on rainy days waiting for the deluge. I can afford to be generous now in thinking about my mother after ten years of silence on both sides, but I don't know how generous I will be when finally we meet again at Wendell's reunion.

There's a wedding picture, of course. The man named Raymond and my mother, a taller version of the pinafored waif, in a light-colored dress with what they called a sweetheart neckline and her hair tightly crimped beneath a silly band of artificial flowers. There was some reason why they didn't have a big church wedding; Raymond had no family to speak of or what he did have were not the sort that could be spoken to. My mother's face in her wedding picture is tentative and her eyes avoid the camera. She seems to be looking for something she's lost, but isn't sure what it is or even if she ever had it. The granite strain of the family's matriarchs has petered out in her. My mother's face is sand, shifting under the slightest impress, never the same from one emotion to the next. She waits to know what she should feel and then adjusts her face to suit. The only thing she ever did with any gumption was to marry Raymond, my father. And then he died.

She told me that he ran away and died. His grave is not in the graveyard behind the apple orchard, nor is it in Mount Olivet Cemetery on the hill beyond the park where the circus comes in August. I used to wonder, when I was a child, if the ghosts came down the hill and slipped through the canvas of the circus tent to laugh at the clowns and be frightened by the lions. If I were a ghost in Mount Olivet Cemetery, I would certainly come down to see the circus. But my father, Raymond, is not there. I know because I looked. And no one would tell me where to find him.

My mother told me lies. Different lies at different times. Did she think I would forget one lie, or like another one better? She told me he'd been lost at sea, that he'd been working on an oil tanker that foundered and he was not rescued. Another time, she told me he died of leprosy on an island off the Gulf coast of Mexico. Sometimes I think he didn't die at all. I think he ran off, and my sad mother was driven to inventing deaths for him, deaths she knew I wouldn't believe so that one day I would go and find him and make him come back to her. "He always loved you, Jenny," is what she used to tell me, as if he never loved her at all.

There are other relatives in the album, people whose older, changed versions will come to Wendell's reunion. There are aunts and uncles and cousins whom I haven't seen for ten years; some I've never met at all. There will be faces new to the family, young faces born into it since I went away, and those who married into it. I almost wish that I had married so that I could astound the family with my handsome, intelligent, wealthy husband. But I have no one in my life to fit that description, so I'll go alone to Wendell's reunion. They'll pity me in whispers behind their hands and perhaps I'll gaze with scorn at their awkward country ways. Maybe before the week is over, we'll be able to see beyond our accustomed masks. And maybe not.

The album stops when it is filled. The last picture is one of me dressed for a high school dance. The dress is an embarrassment in pink tulle and my hair is lacquered into an enormous pile of cotton candy puffs. The harsh color of the photograph had turned my mother's living room into a tilted greenish box filled with harmfully angled furniture and unpleasant lamps. I remember that just before the picture was taken, my mother had tortured my eyelashes with her eyelash curler and given my hair a final lavish cloud of hair spray. Afterward, a boy arrived, clumsy in his ruffle-fronted shirt, holding in both fists a white cardboard florist's box. I let him pin the gardenia to my pink dress but I can't remember his name. Nor do I remember who took the picture. I guess it was my mother. This was about a year before I left home. I'm sorry about all of that.

Wendell's reunion will be the third week in August. There is still plenty of time to change my mind.

CHAPTER

2

Ever since Wendell's last letter and my quick reply, I've been having constant dreams of home. Not just the one about River House where I am standing in the road looking up at its shuttered windows. That one I've always had. No. These are new dreams and some of them are frightening, like warnings. Stay away. Don't come home.

There's one in which I am sitting in my grandmother's window seat with the album in my lap. I am wearing a plaid pleated skirt and a pale blue sweater, just like the ones I had when I was twelve or thirteen. Falling leaves keep drifting past the window. My grandmother comes into the room. She is carrying her sewing basket. She says, "Jenny, you have a hole in your skirt. Let me fix it." I lift up the album and sure enough, there's a big hole in the middle of my skirt. I try to take the skirt off but I can't make the zipper work. The hole is growing bigger and bigger. My grandmother begins to work on the skirt with a huge needle and some coarse black thread. But no sooner does she stitch the hole closed than it slips free from its stitches and opens up again. At last she says, "It's no use, Jenny. You'll have to hide. You can't appear in public like that." And she opens up the window seat and makes me get inside. As she closes the lid, tears of blood run down her wrinkled cheeks. Then everything is dark and I can hear the click of a padlock close to my ear.

The window seat, as I remember, had no padlock, although it did have a lid that lifted up on a dark space within. I think there were old magazines stored there, *National Geographic*s slowly fading from bright yellow to sickly umber. My grandmother was a great saver. Every drawer, every closet, the spare rooms and the attic crannies of River House were filled with her treasures. I'd like to go there just to see what those treasures were. If they're still there. If Wendell, or some other well-meaning family member, hasn't cleaned out River House in the years since Grandma died.

Grandma. If she had lived I might not have stayed away so long. When I quarreled with my mother, Grandma wanted me to come and live with her. But I was angry as you can only be at nineteen and wanted to do something drastic to prove my rage for all to see. The only thing I could do was go away, and the only place I could go was to New York City. There was no doom in going to Pittsburgh or Indianapolis or even Chicago. Those were familiar, friendly names. People from our town went to those cities all the time. And came home safely. No point in going as far as California. There was a golden movie aura about the name and it was so far away, no one would worry about you or expect you to come back. They would only, on cold rainy January days, say to each other, "Hey, remember Jenny Holland? She must be lying on the beach right this minute."

No. To demonstrate the rightness of my cause, I had to take myself from the shelter of my mother's wings to the acknowledged Sodom and Gomorrah of our time. Of course, at nineteen I knew better. Didn't I read *The New York Times* at the public library? Sure there were terrible things that happened in New York. But terrible things happened everywhere. Even here at home. What about the time Junior Marshall shot his brother out in the woods and chopped him up into little pieces and then claimed the wild boars ate him?

It's odd how memories and dreams of home seem to be taking over both my sleeping and waking life. Fragments of half-forgotten incidents come between me and my present existence. Ever since Wendell started planning his reunion. Well, I don't have to go. I can write him and say, "Sorry, Wendell, I can't make it after all. Something has come up. Bucky wants me to spend a few weeks with him in Spain." Or, "Just got the word. No vacation until October. Big doings in the organization and yours truly is truly indispensable."

Indispensable, hah! Yours truly is indispensable only insofar as she knows the entire stock of Max's Secondhand Books from basement to the highest shelves reached only by rickety ladder, and can put an instant finger on anything from Marcus Aurelius to Harold Robbins. Without me, Max Stern would bumble along in his usual surly fashion, snarling at customers and letting them forage for themselves among the dusty shelves. He wouldn't mind, probably wouldn't even notice, my absence. Sometimes I think he keeps me on only out of sheer inertia. Once in a while, he asks me why I stay. "What are you doing for yourself, Jenny-girl? You're young, you're even pretty if you'd fix yourself up a little. What are you hiding from in my bookstore?"

To these questions, I merely shrug and smile and pass a dustcloth lightly over the accumulated years of city grit. I went to work in Max's bookstore about a year after I arrived in New York, a year in which I drifted around as a temporary officeworker while trying to find out what I could do with my life. I could have gone to college. My grandmother had stuffed the pages of the family album with twenty-dollar bills, exactly one hundred of them, and would have sent more if I'd asked her, but I couldn't and wouldn't and then she died. Wendell sent me some jewelry which he said she'd left to me in her will. There's an old-fashioned square-cut diamond ring, a pearl choker with a diamond clasp, a fine silver chain with an opal pendant set in intricate filigree, a child's gold bracelet studded with tiny flickering red stones which may or may not be rubies, and several pairs of earrings. I don't remember my grandmother ever wearing jewelry of any kind, except the wide gold band of her wedding ring. I suppose she was buried with that on her finger. But I do remember that her ears were pierced, although she never wore earrings and the indentations in her translucent old lobes appeared to have grown closed. My mother now owns River House but Wendell says she refuses to live there, preferring her small frame house in town. The house where I grew up. I wonder how Wendell persuaded her to open up River House for his reunion.

I could have sold my grandmother's jewelry and gone to college, if I'd had any idea about what to study. Instead, I wandered about the city, hitting the keys of typewriters in offices that ranged from solemnly splendid to dismally drear and watching the faces of the men whose universally tedious words I typed onto thousands of sheets of paper that glutted the mails and filled wastebaskets from coast to coast. None of them ever smiled as Raymond my father smiled with his hand on the hood of his new green Pontiac, although some of them smiled at me in a very different way and invited me out for drinks. And dinner. And a few of them, a very few, cried out in the night in the three-quarter bed that I'd bought on sale at Macy's with four of my grandmother's twenty-dollar bills.

I really preferred to read. That's how I came upon Max's Secondhand Books. I was a customer long before I became a fixture. Once I read a book, I like to keep it around. It becomes part of me and I need tangible proof that it exists, even if I never open it up again. I like to look at it, occasionally to stroke its spine as it stands captive on my bookshelf. I don't want to share it with anyone else. On the other hand, I don't like new books. There is something intimidating to me about books whose jackets are glossy and unscarred, whose pages have not been dogeared. I am comforted by the occasional smear of chocolate obscuring a paragraph or by the even rarer stray hair caught between the pages. I read pencilled marginal notes with great interest. I often browse in public libraries, but whenever I borrow books, I find myself owing enormous fines because I can't bring myself to return them.

Max's Secondhand Books was the answer to my dilemma. It was a dingy cavern of a store not far from my apartment that I discovered a few months after I'd settled in. Thanks to my grandmother's twenty-dollar bills, I was able to find myself a couple of reasonably clean rooms in the East Village, but not too far east. Max's became a regular Saturday afternoon stop and my reading took on a potluck quality, Tarzan to Captain Ahab, Thackeray to Ian Fleming, whatever leaped off the shelves and into my hands. It didn't matter, so long as there were enough pages to last me for a week. Max himself crouched in his tiny book-strewn office at the back of the store, a great gray bear in a shabby gray cardigan, ignoring me, leaving all customers to be dealt with by the thin young man with the red nose and lank black ponytail of hair who scowled in heavy concentration as he rang up sales on the ancient cash register.

But one Saturday, Max loomed behind the cash register as I approached with a mixed armload of science fiction, history, and a book on growing plants indoors. I'd bought a piggyback plant to brighten my windowsill and it wasn't doing well.

"Where's . . . um . . . ?" I asked. I'd never learned the young man's name.

"Quit," said Max. "Gone off. They all do."

"I'll stay," I said. I don't know what made me say it. In truth, Max frightened me a little, crouching in his lair like a fierce old wizard guarding the gates of ancient knowledge. I felt that he must know everything that lay between the covers of the books he bought and sold, and that made him powerful and menacing. It also made him far more interesting than the men whose flat unpalatable words flowed through the typewriters to which I dragged myself day after day.

He turned his slate gray eyes to me and said, "What do you mean, you'll stay? Who asked you to stay?"

"Nobody asked me. I'm asking you. I'd like to work here."

"Why?"

I shrugged. I had no answer for him. I couldn't tell him that the people in the books on his shelves were more real to me than the jostling crowds that surged along the streets, that my visits to the store had become the most important event of every week, that his hulking presence in the back room provided a kind of anchor for my life and kept me from drifting too far into the blankness of being young and alone in the city. Ridiculous? An overdramatized case of a schoolgirl crush on an older man? Yes and no. Max was not attractive to me in the way that might lead him to my Macy's three-quarter box spring and mattress. I felt no quickening in the pit of my stomach in his presence. He was certainly old enough to be my father, probably older than the long-absent Raymond would be if he were alive and I could find him. But from all the accumulated Saturdays that I'd been coming to the bookstore, never speaking a word to the gray presence in the back room, I'd carried away a sense of having found a safe haven. It was partly the store itself with its crowded shelves of secondhand lives, and partly Max, a surly patron saint of the used, abused, and mishandled.

"I've seen you here before," he said. "You come every Saturday."

"And I already know where everything is." The eagerness spilled out of my mouth, and my shoulders tensed under the revelation that he had noticed me.

"What's your name?" he asked.

"Jenny Holland," I told him.

"You're not Jewish?" he asked.

"No. Does it matter?"

"I don't know. I never had a *shiksa* working here. I never had a *girl* working here. What about shoplifters? Holdup artists? This is a rough neighborhood."

"I know. I live here. It's not so bad. Have you ever been held up?"

"No. But there's always a first time."

"Does anybody ever steal books?" I asked him.

"Sometimes. Not often." He smiled, broad lips parting in a round stubbled face. "If they want so badly to read, I let them. Better they should steal a book and learn something."

"So?" I asked him.

"So," he said. "Get over here."

He made room for me behind the counter and showed me how to work the cash register. He smelled warmly of pipe tobacco and dry cleaning fluid. His fat freckled hands revealed the mystic rites of wrapping paper and string. After watching me serve two customers on my own, he nodded grudgingly, said, "You'll do," and shambled back to his office at the rear of the store.

That was nine years ago. Nine years in which I spent six days a week in the store and the seventh at home reading. Oh, I went out occasionally, to a movie or an off-Broadway play, with young men who'd made the East Village a stopover in their lonesome wanderings and happened to drift into the bookstore in search of prophets. I sold them what they wanted, if we had it, and sometimes I would take one of them home with me (if he smiled) and feed him brown rice and shrimp, and hold him through the night, he sleeping, I awake, in my bed. To their invitations to travel on with them, I shook my head. The only way to find something that's lost is to stay in one place until it comes to you.

From my perch behind the cash register in Max's, I could watch the street and everyone who passed. I watched for ancient Pontiacs and a face that was capable of a wide proud smile. I hadn't planned what I would do if Raymond walked into the store. The possibility was remote. He undoubtedly was dead, as my mother had told me. But not in any of the ways she told me, and thereby rose the doubt. What if he came into the store in the guise of a young man, wispily bearded, gold-earringed, and shaggy? And he smiled his Raymond smile? And I took him home with me? What would Wendell and the rest of them have to say about that?

But, of course, he didn't come. The street, crowded with cabs and trucks and sky-blue Puerto Rican families on wheels, never produced Raymond's "first car after the War." It had probably rusted back into red earth somewhere, its windshield shivered, its tires become swings for children now grown up and remembering only sometimes that in their yard was a tree and from its branch hung a tire that they swung on or fell out of and broke a front tooth. And the young men came, and some of them smiled, but never like Raymond. Afterward, after they had left on their way to New Hampshire or Mexico or once it was Morocco, I always got down the family album to see if there was any resemblance. There wasn't.

When Wendell's letter came announcing the family reunion, I said to Max, "I'll be taking a vacation this year."

"About time."

"In August."

"Okay by me."

"A week, maybe ten days."

"Take the whole month."

"I don't need a whole month."

"Don't worry about me. I'll manage."

"I'll come back."

"Sure you will."

I'd never taken a vacation before. I had nowhere to go and there didn't seem much point in just staying home. But now

I was going and even though it was still months away, I began to think about how I was to get there. Should I buy a car and drive? I didn't know how to drive, but maybe there was time to learn. Buses certainly still traveled between here and there, but I didn't relish returning the same way I had left. Trains were a possibility, and I thought of the train station, grimy red brick, long and narrow and smelling of coal oil and stale urine, where we used to tease Crazy Emma who slept on the hard benches and lived on stale bread and cupcakes too old to sell even at the day-old bakeshop down beside the tracks. I couldn't go home that way, even if trains still visited the town, for fear of meeting Crazy Emma and seeing something in her mad eyes that matched my own. I would have to fly.

I called the airlines. No direct flights, of course. That didn't surprise me. Not many people from here would want to go there. I would have to fly first to Pittsburgh and then wait for the daily hop-skip-and-jump. So be it. I would fly. And Wendell would pick me up at the airport. I had forgotten, if I'd ever known, that our town had an airport. Just knowing it existed—concrete runways, a tower of some kind bristling on top of a square functional building, probably set down in the midst of soybean fields—made the distance seem less unconquerable. If I'd remembered about the airport, would I have stayed away so long? Would I not, in that first year, before Wendell married Bonnie Marie Warren, have called him and said, "I'm coming in on the two thirty-five. Please meet me." And all would be otherwise now. But I didn't remember.

Now, on the back of a picture postcard of the World Trade Center, I wrote, carefully and neatly, "Dear Wendell: Am flying in on August 19th. Will need a ride from the airport. Looking forward to getting away from this mad, mad city for a breathing space. Regards, Jenny."

CHAPTER
3

I went shopping for clothes.

I needed clothes to match my postcards. I couldn't go home in my Canal Street jeans, my wraparound batik skirts bought from street vendors at high noon between the hot dog cart and the sidewalk artist displaying photographs of cats. I took the last of my grandmother's twenty-dollar bills, five of them hoarded for years between the pages of the family album, raided my savings account, and went uptown. But first, I got my hair cut.

"Jenny, is that you?" Max popped his eyes roundly over his cigar and waved his hands in manic disbelief. I couldn't believe it myself.

For nine years, I'd done nothing about my hair but wash it when necessary and comb it once or twice a day. Sometimes I would ask one of my traveling young men to trim an inch or so off with my broken-pointed scissors. I'd even forgotten, or managed not to remember, that it was blond. But the hairdresser, a no-nonsense young woman with hands as light and swift as hummingbirds, sang its praises as she clipped and snipped. "My God!" she cried. "It's the color of dew in the morning. It's unreal!"

I glanced shyly into the great mirror facing me, terrified of seeing the odd creature reflected there. And odd it was, with its long bare neck rising from the slippery orange folds of the protective cape, the tiny serious face perched above, eyes huge, mouth wary, and the hair, all that river of hair falling to the floor and lying there in damp lifeless heaps. It was too late to scream, "Stop!" Nothing to do but let the slaughter continue. I closed my eyes.

When I opened them again, I saw someone I'd never seen before watching me triumphantly from the mirror. Her hair fell in a heavy shining sweep to her shoulders. Her eyes sparkled, their blue refreshed to the color of new lupines. As I watched, her mouth opened in wonder and she said, "Is that me?"

The hairdresser said, "You shouldn't use rubber bands on it. You had a lot of breakage." She gathered up the long strands of severed hair, tied them in a loose knot and stuffed them into a plastic bag. "Keep these," she told me. "You might want to have a piece made one day."

I left, carrying nine years in a pink plastic bag. When I had arrived in New York, my hair was puffed and teased according to the custom of my town. People stared at my head and smiled. For all I know, my mother still resembles a latter-day Madame Pompadour. Things were different in the city, and I'd had a lot to learn. I put the bag of hair on a shelf in my closet.

A few days later, I asked Max for some time off, put on my most presentable underwear, and went looking for clothes to dazzle the reunion. It would be hot in August in the river valley, and moist with dank-smelling vapors rising from the sodden ground. There would be thunderstorms and tornado watches. I bought myself a bright red nylon raincoat. I bought a sweeping green skirt and scant blouses and a romantic ruffled dress of blue and white gauze. I bought impractical high-heeled sandals and then, remembering the summer mud, a pair of red vinyl boots. A folding umbrella. A bathing suit because I didn't own one, and we might swim in the river. Presents. A scarf for Bonnie Marie, a funny barbecue chef's apron and hat for Wendell (he would wear them and laugh). For my mother, a box of chocolates because I didn't know what else. If she wouldn't eat them, someone would.

I stopped when the money I'd allotted for shopping was gone, but not before I bought a rust-colored imitation suede carryall to carry it all in. I still had the plaid canvas suitcase I'd left home with, but it wouldn't do for the reunion. Everything had to be new. New clothes, new suitcase, new me. The only old thing going home with me would be the family album.

I was packed and ready, my plane ticket bought and safely hidden inside a worn copy of *Look Homeward, Angel,* a week before it was time to go. I kept working at the bookstore, but the visions before my eyes were of horse chestnuts fallen beside a crumbling stone wall, ice crystals shimmering on bare branches at dawn, or the red-brick town with its hard edges softened by the gentle uprising of a river fog. So far, so good. Tender scenes of childhood. Pictures not found in any album. This wall, that tree, the turreted courthouse would all be there to welcome me home. I could read my ancient history in their placid abiding surfaces. But what about the people? Where do they fit in?

The people came at night in the dreams that played from first eye-closing to the cackle of the clock in the saving hour of the morning. No matter how I read or drank hot milk or swallowed sleeping pills left behind by an absent-minded insomniac who stayed three nights (his name was Richard, as I recall) on his way to Sri Lanka in search of composure; no matter how I exhausted myself, moved the bed around, slept in unaccustomed positions, the dreams insisted on playing themselves out, night after night. Miss Anna Grace, my fourth grade teacher, came back from her grisly death in a four-car pile-up on the Interstate, to pat my cheek with a hand that smelled of hard-boiled egg and Cashmere Bouquet soap and tell me that "one hundred forty-four square inches equal one square foot. A grave is only as deep as it must be. You must learn your twelve times table before getting married. Otherwise, your children will be deformed. Don't mope, Jenny. Keep your fingernails clean and stay out of deep water." Miss Anna Grace in my dream looked exactly as she did when I was nine and in her classroom decorated with travel posters of Spain and Greece and the Tower of London. She wore her navy blue and white polka-dotted silk dress with the round white collar. I knew it was silk because once in the terrible intimacy of the schoolroom she told us it was and that it was a thing of the past and in the future all of our clothing would be made of plastic. She died when I was a freshman in high school and we all went to her funeral. The coffin was closed. There were those (my mother among them) who said that she had caused the accident through her partiality to Southern Comfort. But we didn't know that for sure.

I didn't dream about my mother.

I dreamed I was standing in Market Street and the sidewalks were full of people moving steadily in one direction. They streamed past the Woolworth's and the J. C. Penney stores, past the Eagle Cafeteria (home cooking) and the Buford movie theater. There was something like tar stuck to the bottoms of my shoes and I couldn't move with the crowd. Wendell marched by carrying a rifle and then came a gang of kids I had known in high school. It seemed as if everyone in town—Dr. Barnes, the chiropractor; Minnie Lovins and her mother, inseparable because Minnie had never progressed beyond the mental age of four and even in middle age couldn't be left alone; Selma Swift in white cowboy boots twirling her baton; the Monkey Man, Ralph Dean Otwell, who got his nickname because he came around in the fall and for ten dollars would clamber up to your peaked roof and remove leaves and fallen branches from your rain gutters and downspouts—these, and it seemed a couple hundred others, drifted past me in the dream while my feet stuck to the tar in the middle of Market Street. When they had all gone past and the sidewalks on both sides were empty except for a thin yellow dog mooching in the gutter, I looked up the straight true length of the street and saw a man standing on the courthouse steps.

As soon as I saw him, he came down the steps and began moving toward me. He moved slowly and stiffly, his arms swinging at his sides like those of a battery-powered toy man. Even at a distance, his wide white smile flashed in his face like a searchlight. I wanted to run, but the dog was regarding me suspiciously and my feet were still stuck. The man moved closer. His double-breasted brown suit had a faint white stripe in it. His tie was broad and unpleasantly colorful. He wore brown shoes with pointed toes. His hands . . . were not hands at all. At the ends of his mechanically swinging arms, beneath the sleeves of his pinstriped suit coat showing just a fraction of an inch of white shirt cuff, hung two curved and shining blades. Like miniature scimitars of the sort flourished by turbaned warriors in desert films, his bladed hands sliced the air in Market Street. I watched myself watching him. His smile never flickered; his eyes were large and warm and sympathetic. Blue, I think, or gray. His right blade flashed up and down. My left arm fell off. His left blade flashed. My right arm. Then flash and flash and flash. Soon there was nothing left of me but a small round liver-colored object about the size of a hockey puck. The yellow dog mooched over and ate it.

In the morning, I wondered if this reunion of Wendell's

was making me slightly crazy. Only three more days until it would be time to go. I can always change my mind. Or the plane might crash. Or Wendell will call the whole thing off.

I bought a blow-dryer that day, so that my new sleek haircut would survive the dampness of the river valley.

CHAPTER

4

Wendell had changed for the fatter. He stood by the chest-high cyclone fence that separated the waiting area from the concrete apron where the planes deposited their passengers before sputtering off to other smaller airports. There'd been about twenty-five or twenty-six people who'd gotten on the plane at Pittsburgh, including a family of four whose whiny children made me grateful that we had the whole length of the small plane between our seats. I spent the next bumpy hour and a half reading and trying to remember if there were any prayers specifically designed to keep ancient DC-6's clear of the wooded hills and geometric fields that rolled by beneath us. Then we were landing, and there were eight, including me, who fumbled with their hand luggage and inched cautiously down the steep rolling flight of stairs that Casey Marshall (Junior's other brother who didn't get chopped into little pieces or eaten by wild hogs) and somebody else had pushed up to the door of the plane.

Wendell was waving like a windmill and I waved back while I said good-bye to the stewardess who'd lost all her lipstick and had a coffee stain on her perky scarf. "Have a nice day," she cried.

I scrambled down the steps and said, "Hi-dee," to Casey Marshall before I noticed that four of the other passengers were already clustered around Wendell making shrill and jolly noises. They were the man and woman and the two whiny long-legged tow-headed kids who'd made the front of the plane a battleground. I couldn't move very fast in my high-heeled sandals, so I took my time joining the group, walking slow and swingy with my new skirt flapping in the breeze. Wendell looked over the head of the kid who was climbing up his beer belly and grinned a big wet fat-lipped grin in his round blubbery face. "Jenny!" he shouted.

Everybody turned to look and I realized that the woman was my cousin Fearn, Wendell's sister, who had married an auto mechanic from Wilmington, Delaware, and had gone to live there and had two children, a nervous breakdown, and a hysterectomy in that order. Wendell had written the news. She seemed fine now, chubby and smiling, her hair dyed the color of ripe apricots.

"Jenny Holland!" she shrieked. "What don't I hear about you, living off in the big city like that!"

Her husband licked his lips and kept his eyes on my bright red toenails, painted the night before. He was tall and rangy, with big hands that kept flapping about aimlessly.

"We were gonna drive over," he muttered, "but the kids make such a fuss in the car. . . ." He shoved his hands into his pockets and began scanning the sky as if he were Randolph Scott looking for enemy bombers on the late show. His eyes were blue and squinty.

"Jenny, this here's my husband, Walter Proud. I don't believe you've ever met." Fearn conducted the introductions with her chest puffed out and a challenging frightened look on her face, as if I might find some fatal flaw in Walter or herself. "And over here is Billy and Millie, not twins but close enough to make no never mind. Just ten months apart, so two months out of the year they are the same age." And then she blushed, as if remembering the unseemly activity that gave rise to their close existence. "Billy's seven right now and Millie's six. Say hello to your aunt Jenny, kids."

The boy and girl swarmed off of Wendell and came shyly to stand before me. The girl obediently piped, "Hello, Aunt Jenny," with her round eyes, also blue, fixed greedily on my shoulder bag. Relatives, apparently, were a likely source of income. The boy crossed his eyes and let his tongue hang out of his mouth by way of greeting.

I said, "Hello, Billy. Hello, Millie," and was reprieved from saying anything else by Wendell's grappling me to his great sweaty chest.

"This little lady," he announced to the world, "is my most favorite cousin, and if she had any sense at all, she would have been my bride ten years ago."

I put my fists against Wendell's sport shirt and pushed, but it didn't do any good.

"Ooooh!" Fearn hooted. "Wait till Bonnie Marie hears about that! She'll cut you off and make you sit up and beg for it."

It was Walter Proud's turn to blush. He said, "Shut up, Fearn," and jerked his head toward Billy and Millie who were staring at the small struggle going on between Wendell and me.

"No fear! No fear!" Wendell boomed. "Bonnie Marie knows she's got me where she wants me. There's not a jealous bone in her body. But, oh!" He tightened his grip around my shoulders and pressed my head to his chest. A shirt button caught me painfully over the eyes. "How sweet it would have been!"

I tried going limp. I tried digging my chin into Wendell's breastbone. He held on tighter and his hand "accidentally" clutched my breast. I was about to grind my high heel into his Hushpuppy, when a thin voice whined, "Mama, I gotta go peepee."

Fearn took charge. "Wendell, you and Walter go get the luggage while I take these kids to the toilet. Jenny, you come with me."

"Yes, ma'am," said Wendell, smirking. "I'll see *you* later, little girl." He turned me loose with a pat on the rump.

I gave Walter Proud my luggage claim check and described my bag to him. Casey Marshall and his blue-coveralled companion were removing bags and bundles from the belly of the plane and piling them on a handtruck. I followed Fearn and the two kids into the cinder block terminal building and through the green enameled door marked "Ladies."

"Well, I don't know what's got into Wendell," she sputtered as soon as the door swung closed behind us. She dragged Millie into one of the stalls, undid her buckles and snaps and perched her on the toilet. Millie peered between her legs to watch her tinkling stream. "He's acting like a dumb old cock rooster in a yard full of pullets."

"It doesn't mean anything," I told her, but I was thinking about getting back on the plane and going on to wherever its next stop was. Billy was investigating the sanitary napkin machine, twisting its knob and shoving his hand up into its slot. "It's just been a long time since we've seen each other."

"Well, if you don't mind being pawed and mauled, don't let me interfere." She handed Millie a wad of toilet paper and told her to wipe herself. "But I don't think it's fair to Bonnie Marie or the reunion if he keeps on about how he wanted to marry you one time. Everybody knows you run out on him. You'd think he'd have a little pride."

"Fearn, I didn't run out on Wendell. I just . . . ran. There were other reasons. It had nothing to do with him."

"Billy, get your hand out of there and go pee." She buckled Millie back into her red overalls with a pair of fat bluebirds appliqued on the bib and hauled her over to one of the sinks. "Nothing, huh? That's not what your mother was putting around at the time. She told everyone in town that you run off to get away from Wendell because he got drunk one night and beat you up because you wouldn't put out for him until after the wedding."

I laughed. I couldn't help it. It was so far from the truth, and I'd been so far away from this sort of small-town big-family backbiting for so long, I couldn't take it seriously.

But Fearn did. She glared up at me from where she was bent over the sink washing Millie's hands. "What's so funny?" she demanded, and then turned on Billy. "Will you leave that alone," she screamed, "and go pee!"

"Don't have to," he answered. "What's this?"

He'd managed somehow to relieve the machine of a sanitary napkin and was carefully unwrapping it as if it might be a new kind of candy bar. Fearn snatched it from his hands and stuffed it through the swinging lid of the trash container. "Nothing!" she told him. "Nothing you need to know about. Now get on out of here." She herded the kids before her and continued scolding me over her shoulder.

"It wasn't so funny when Wendell was trying to live that story down. He couldn't show his face anywhere without getting teased about it and he had to give up being Scoutmaster until after he was a married man. The least you could have done was set the record straight."

"But, Fearn," I protested, "I didn't know anything about it."

"Well, you would have if you'd have come back once in a while and listened to what people were saying."

"But I didn't."

"No, you didn't," she agreed. "And I don't know why you've come back now. You don't belong here anymore. Anyone can see that. Anyone can see you carry nothing but trouble. You just better make sure you don't make trouble for Wendell."

I followed her out of the ladies' room. "It was Wendell who asked me to come."

"Sure," she said. "My brother doesn't always have the good sense God gave an addled duck."

Fearn put herself in charge of the seating arrangements in the station wagon for the ride from the airport to River House. Walter and Wendell in the front seat, she keeping an eye on me in the back seat, and Billy and Millie tumbled into the rear platform with the luggage. I looked out the window.

The airport was about ten miles outside of town, and now that we were rolling along the two-lane blacktop, I remembered that it had always been there. Not always, of course, but as far back as I could see. Only I'd never had occasion to go there. When folks traveled, they went by car or Greyhound bus, maybe by train, but hardly ever by plane. The airport was for the people who came to manage the chemical plants that sprawled along the river, and for the salesmen who came to supply the town with all the stuff we saw on television.

We rolled along, Wendell's station wagon sailing between the thick green fields of soybeans on one side and pig corn on the other like a great battleship through a calm sea. The first true landmark I saw that claimed a place in my memory was the Starlite Drive-In Movie where I'd gone to see *The Planet of the Apes* with Darnell Berry, captain of the football team, and we drank beer and ate hot dogs, and he tried to show me he was a real man but couldn't, and then drove like a maniac all over half the county until I was sure we'd crack up before I got home. He never asked me out again. The Starlite looked derelict and unused, and its marquee was bare.

Into the humming silence in the station wagon I asked, "Whatever happened to Darnell Berry?"

"Darnell Berry?" Wendell repeated. "Oh, Darnell Berry, big kid, used to play football? Seems to me he went to Vietnam."

"Did he come back?"

"Nope."

The silence settled in again except for the two kids in the back squabbling over who could crack his knuckles loudest, until Billy threatened to crack Millie's head and Millie bit him on the ear. Fearn said, "Shut up, you two," and tossed a couple of Tootsie Pops into the carnage.

After the Starlite, the landmarks came thick and fast. The hill where we went to cut straggly crooked pines for Christmas trees, the trailer park where once a man went berserk and killed his whole family of seven or eight children with a shotgun and hatchet on Easter morning, the roadside stand that still sold shining globes on pedestals and birdbaths and plastic ducks and deer to decorate your front lawn. My mother had once bought a purple-martin house, a large square box with many round windows on each side that looked like a housing project for birds. Purple martins were supposed to keep the mosquitoes down, but I can't remember if any ever came to live with us and do the job.

So memory dribbled back in tantalizing bits and pieces, events and people I had not thought of in many years. There were changes, too, along the road to town. The groundswell of brick and plasterboard had reached this far before petering out, and a rutted field was littered with unfinished rectangles set down on unpaved lanes beside a forlorn untenanted shopping center.

Wendell spoke up in funereal tones. "Jenny, remember old Jerry Joe McHenry, used to drive two blocks to church to show off his Cadillac car?"

"Uh-huh." Cissie McHenry wore a different cashmere sweater to school practically every day of the world, had her own little Triumph sports car by the time she was sixteen, and used to hold swimming pool parties for her cronies where, rumor had it, they drank vodka and swam bare-naked. She was Jerry Joe's only daughter.

"Well, poor old Jerry Joe lost his shirt on this one." Wendell jerked his head toward the desolate development. "He plain just never figured on the plants laying off and mortgage money drying up. Tried to commit suicide, but they pumped him out in time and now he's a permanent resident at the state funny farm." Wendell's voice oozed morbid satisfaction.

"What happened to Cissie?" I asked.

"Hoo, that Cissie!" Wendell's voice swiveled into a leer. "Cissie did okay by marriage, but she blew it all. Married some dude from Texas, one of her father's business buddies, a little bit older than her, say twenty years, but what the hell. He took her all over the world, gave her a charge account at Neiman-Marcus; nothing was too good for Cissie. And what does she do, the dumb little twit? Turns up here one day, drives right up to the Chancellor Hotel in one of them painted all over vans, high as a kite, and asks for a room for herself and this black gentleman, I use the term loosely, and a little yellow-faced baby. Well, needless to say, the Chancellor happened to be full up that day. So, our Cissie makes a scene you wouldn't believe, screaming and throwing things at the manager, even the nigrah had sense enough to be embarrassed. So what could they do but give them a room in the jailhouse until she calmed down. What a day that was!"

Some things never change. "Where is she now?"

"Oh, she's still around town, I guess. Maybe over on the south side. Seems I heard that the guy run out on her and she was working as a barmaid or some such."

While Wendell was relishing the fall of the house of McHenry, the station wagon had been grinding its way up a long steep hill. At the crest, I peered over Wendell's shoulder at the town spread out below. It was smaller than I remembered and cramped-looking with church steeples poking up every few blocks or so. I tried to find the courthouse as I had seen it in my dreams, but the view was barred by a tall brown glass-sided building blinking sullenly in the afternoon sun.

"What's that?" I asked before we slid down the slope and into the grid of streets and houses.

Wendell glanced at my pointing finger and hunched his shoulders in mingled pride and apprehension. "Oh, that's just our skyscraper. Fifteen stories, four elevators, restaurant up on top. Nice view. I guess you've seen a lot better."

I settled back in my seat, thinking I'd better make a list of things not to talk about, and caught Fearn looking at me purse-mouthed and prim. She said nothing, but her eyes shouted, "Go away and stop making us feel small and mean and stupid."

Walter Proud, thank God, was a quiet man and might

as well have been deaf into the bargain. He took no notice of the tensions zinging around inside the station wagon, but sat still and straight and spoke only when he had something to say.

He now said, "I'd like to pick up some cold beer and soda pop."

"No need! No need!" Wendell crowed. "That old Frigidaire out at River House is as full as can be. Couldn't fit another six-pack in. Don't think I'd let my dearly beloveds arrive thirsty, do you? And there's all kinds of cold cuts and potato salad and I don't know what all. Bonnie Marie's taken care of all that."

"Nevertheless," Walter insisted, "I'd like to contribute my share. Kids drink up a lot of Coke."

"Time enough tomorrow," said Wendell. "Your kind offer will sure be appreciated when everybody gets here. I expect there'll be thirty, forty of us, more or less. Never thought I'd see everybody all together at one time."

"It's a great idea, Wendell," said Fearn, "having a reunion. Just so long as everybody remembers that it's a *family* reunion and we're all here as equals and nobody's better than anybody else."

From the back of the station wagon, Billy groaned, "Ma-a-a, I gotta pee."

CHAPTER

We had to go through a section of town called Muley before we could get onto the old River Road. Muley wasn't exactly a geographic location, although it was properly equipped with streets, lanes, and alleys. It was more a state of mind. It wasn't quite the town ghetto, but a few blacks lived there. When I was a child a mysterious and numerous family of Chinese were to be seen slipping along in the shade, but no one knew exactly where they lived. Ralph Dean Otwell, the

Monkey Man, lived there in a garage with his truck and his ladders and rakes and long poles. The children of Muley went to school sometimes only to stare in amazement at the goings-on there, never to read or recite or figure on the blackboard. Their lunch boxes held strange misshapen chunks of gray bread, sometimes cold slimy bacon, never an apple or a Hostess Twinkie. The houses in Muley were small and shingled, with lopsided wooden porches and windows glazed with cardboard. Some of them still had outhouses perched at the far end of the backyards where a few chickens clucked and scratched. If you scooted through the back alleys of Muley (a short cut between home and the river), you learned to hold your breath. Sometimes a house in Muley would burn down, often with children inside, and then there would be great head-shaking and tongue-clacking about how the area ought to be demolished and something done for the poor folks who lived there. But nothing ever happened.

And nothing had happened in the ten years I'd been away. Muley drowsed in the afternoon sun. The women who sat on the crooked porches were either very thin or very fat and wore sleeveless printed housedresses of a kind not even Sears, Roebuck pictured in its catalog anymore. The children dabbling in the dust made games of bottle caps and stones, or tormented a cat, or dug aimless holes in the packed earth with a kitchen spoon. On the streetcorners, outside a fly-specked grocery store or a one-chair barber shop, the men herded together, hawking, spitting, telling the same old stories and barking their hard bewildered laughs. Their eyes were hurt and angry as they watched the station wagon roll by.

I was tempted to roll the window down and sniff the Muley air for old time's sake, but the station wagon was air-conditioned and Fearn was staring straight ahead at the creased back of Walter's neck and her jaw was rigid with distaste.

"Muley's the same as ever," I observed to no one in particular, remembering that the boy who'd caused the quarrel between my mother and me had been a Muley boy, serious and poetic and wanting desperately to get away. I wondered if he had.

"Trash is trash," hissed Fearn. "They don't even try."

"I give one of them youngsters a job in the store," said Wendell. "All he had to do was sweep up, keep the shelves stocked, and speak politely to the customers. Know what he told me? He said, 'Mr. Mears, this ain't no work for a man.' 'Well, what do you want to do?' I asked him. 'Want to drive a racing car,' he said. 'Good luck to you,' I told him, 'and good-bye.' I would have taught him the business if he'd shown any interest. But that's the way they are. One of these days, we ought to ship them all back into the hills and tear down all those shacks and build something worthwhile on that land. County's thinking about building a new courthouse. Could do it right there in Muley and have enough land left over for a new jail and a parking lot besides."

"What would you do with the old courthouse?" I asked.

"That old heap?" Wendell's scorn was almost tangible, bouncing off the windshield in loud snorts. "We're gonna have to hurry to tear it down before it falls down. Why just last spring, the ceiling in the County Clerk's office caved in right where Bonnie Marie used to work. Lucky it happened over a weekend, so no one was there to get beaned. Plus the place is such a barn, there's no way it can be air-conditioned. Can't get anybody to work anymore unless you're air-conditioned."

We'd left the last shack of Muley behind and were cruising along a new section of highway lined with used car lots, miniature-golf courses, steak and shake and burger and chicken and fish places, gas stations, and a roller skating rink. It seemed to go on forever.

"This is all new," I said.

"Yep. Things has really been booming out this way. Used to be nothing but mud and weeds. Now it's mud and money." Wendell boomed out a big laugh at his own joke. "I even opened up a branch of Mears' Sporting Goods out at the mall—that's about five miles down the road, I'll have to show it to you—and it's doing better than the old store in town. It's crazy what people will buy nowadays. Everybody has to have tennis rackets and everybody has to have water skis and everybody has to have running shoes. All this recession talk hasn't hurt Wendell Mears one little bit. Don't ask me why. I'm just sitting back enjoying it."

"Auto repair's doing pretty good, too," offered Walter. "People getting their cars fixed instead of buying new."

"Well, that's good news. That's what we like to hear. Say, maybe you could take a look at Bonnie Marie's clunker while you're here. Bought her this damn foreign car last year, damn Japanese beer can, and she says it makes a funny noise. Nobody around here can figure out what it is."

"Sure, be glad to," said Walter.

Wendell turned his attention to jockeying for a left turn off the highway and I recognized an ancient willow tree set back from a narrow road that dipped and twisted into green shadows. There used to be a board nailed to the tree with one bright red word painted on it. *Rabbits.* As we made the turn, I saw that the board was still there, but the word had faded to an unreadable pink smear. And the hutches that stood in an uneven row behind the tree were gone. For two years I had longed for a rabbit, but my mother said she didn't relish the idea of cleaning up rabbit turds, and still less skinning and stewing it when I got tired of it. Would a rabbit have made any difference? I guess not.

River Road. Now that we were on it, it was very different from my dream. The bareness of the dream was replaced by the lush reality of trees and undergrowth pressing fervently in on us from both sides. The river was somewhere ahead and to the left, but we couldn't see it yet. The road, as Wendell had written, was an obstacle course of potholes and dirt chunks fallen off the low crumbling banks. A large gray animal darted crazily in front of the car, froze, and scooted back the way it had come. A badger? Or a porcupine? Wendell drove carefully, muttering under his breath. In the rear of the station wagon, Billy and Millie crabbed at each other and kicked their heels against the back of our seat. Fearn threatened them idly and without conviction. She seemed subdued and not inclined to make conversation or even acknowledge my existence on the seat beside her. I began to ponder why I had come and what I had expected to find.

Fearn Mears had been two years ahead of me in high school. She was Wendell's baby sister and was always told that she was the beauty of the family. We had not been friends. She'd pranced through school in shiny vinyl boots and miniskirts, her bright brown hair a mass of lacquered ringlets. She spent all her allowance and babysitting money at the Merle Norman cosmetic shop just off Market Street and on magazines that told her what to do about a round face, a short upturned nose, slightly bulbous eyes and a full-lipped pouting mouth that seemed to rest on her face like cherry tomatoes on a plate. He deepest scorn was reserved for girls she regarded as "hippies —plain tall girls with long straight hair and shapeless clothe who did nothing at all about their bad complexions. She toler ated me because I was family and offered to "do my face" fo me, but I was never welcome in her group, a solid phalanx o six or eight girls who held slumber parties and traveled in giggling, perfumed hunting pack with Fearn leading them i their quest for boys. Fearn's greatest pride was that she weighe ninety-eight pounds and that the caption under her picture i the yearbook said that she was "Cutest" and "Most Popular."

Now, in the station wagon bumping along under sun speckled overarching branches, I glanced at her lime-green thigh and guessed her weight at about 140 and then fel ashamed of myself for taking pleasure in the blurring of tha long-ago girl under matronly rolls of fat. Fearn was no longe cute, but she still didn't like me much.

The car suddenly swooped into a dip in the road, caus ing the kids in the back to shriek and tumble and my stomach to cast loose momentarily from its customary place. When we crested the opposite rise, the tunnel of leaves was gone and the river flowed, broad and brown, just downslope from the road. I wanted Wendell to stop the car and let me out so I could go running to it and touch it and stare into its muddy swirling depths. Maybe this was why I had come back. Maybe, if you have a river in your life, you always have to return to it.

But Millie was crying and Fearn was hauling her over the back of the seat to cuddle and scold her at the same time and Billy was complaining loudly of a stomachache, so it didn't seem like a good time to ask everyone to wait while I indulged a sentimental notion of kinship with what was undoubtedly a polluted and unremarkable geographic fact. I contented myself with watching a barge labor slowly upstream, a line of laundry waving like signal flags, a young man in shorts sunning himself on a hatch cover.

"Not much further now," Wendell announced. "How's it look to you, Jenny-girl?"

"Fine. Just fine," I told him and left it at that. Wendell would think me silly if I tried to tell him how my heart was thudding in my chest, how excitement was rising from the soles of my feet aching to run bare through weeds and over rocks, how I felt on the brink of a revelation that might turn my life around.

"Your mama won't be coming out until tomorrow. Said she didn't know if she could stand the shock and wanted to do it by degrees."

"Would it be such a shock?"

"Well, you know how she is."

I didn't, of course, but Wendell was trying to be diplomatic and soothing. Fearn had no such compunctions.

"I should think it would be a shock, to see your only daughter after ten years of nothing. If I was your mother, I wouldn't travel twelve inches, let alone twelve miles to see you, even if you was dying in agony and screaming your head off." She cradled Millie's head to her breast as she spoke as if to demonstrate that her own daughter would never be so ungrateful.

"Now, Fearn," Wendell cautioned. "You don't know the whole story."

"Don't 'now Fearn' me," she spat. "I know enough of it to know that Miss High and Mighty here left her mother without a word all these years and now the poor woman is just a tad on the batty side. And if you can't put two and two together, I can." She turned to me with spittle spraying from her lips like stinging venom. "You drove your poor mother crazy with worry over you, Jenny Holland, and anybody here in town will be happy to tell you that. Anybody but Wendell, and we all know he's a little bit simple when it comes to you."

"No," I said before my throat closed up.

"Shut up, Fearn," was Walter's contribution from the front seat, with a stern look over his shoulder at his raging wife.

"Here we are!" shouted Wendell as he speeded up with total disregard for potholes and winter-heaved pavement, shot up the narrow dirt drive and braked to a shuddering halt in front of River House. Bonnie Marie was standing on the front porch with her arms stretched out in welcome.

I'd missed my chance to see River House from the road. During Fearn's tirade, I'd kept my eyes closed and let the sound of her fury wash over me like icy rain. Up close, I could only see the house in small disunited fragments. The peeling paint, the sagging porch steps, the gaunt windows opening onto a darkened interior, the coarse, sparse grass that had once been sleek lawn. Perhaps later tonight, if there was a moon, I could walk down to the road and see the thing entire, the way I saw it in my dreams.

Wendell leaped out and hurried around to fling open the back hatch. Fearn, all motherly and comforting, struggled out of her seat with Millie clutched sniveling to her shoulder. Walter unfolded himself and ambled around to help Wendell with the luggage, while Billy clambered over it and raced off in widening circles like a crazed wind-up toy. Fearn shouted after him, "You, Billy! Don't go too far and stay away from that river!" Bonnie Marie clattered down the porch steps, came shyly to the door of the station wagon and peered in at me. I put my hand on the door handle and she did the same from the outside. Between us, we opened the door and exchanged serious appraising looks. Then she smiled a broad, open, honest smile, and said, "Welcome home, Jenny."

I could have cried. I almost did, but somehow managed to swallow the urge and whisper, "Thank you, Bonnie Marie."

She took my hand in her small plump one, and I held it gratefully as I stepped from the car. I had expected earth tremors at least when I finally set foot on home territory, but the earth remained still and firm and the only tremors were in my own legs.

"You must be tired," she said. "Come on in the house."

I stood for a minute, breathing the warm fragrant air and letting the sun take the chill from my body. I'd been traveling since early morning and each stage of the journey had been in a temperature-controlled cocoon. I felt like a chrysalis emerging for its first taste of earthly wonders.

"Sun feels good," I said.

"Oh, my, yes," said Bonnie Marie. "We've had some scorchers, but today's just about perfect. Come on, dear, I've got your room all ready for you."

I let her lead me into the house, all my senses open to receive the magic of remembrance. Behind us, Fearn called out, "Ain't you even gonna say hello, Bonnie Marie?"

"Hi, there, Fearn," she called back. "We'll have some tea and chocolate cake in just a minute. Why don't you go on back to the kitchen and put the kettle on? There's some red pop for the babies and beer for the men. Help yourself."

We walked on into the shadows of the front hall, and

hoped that Bonnie Marie had not incurred Fearn's enmity on my account. Evidently Fearn was capable of nursing a grudge for a lifetime. But Bonnie Marie, from her next words, had already encountered Fearn's ill will and had her own ways of dealing with it.

"That Fearn," she chuckled. "You just got to beat her like a dinner gong at least once a day. Next best is keep her busy as a bird dog, and that I intend to do."

The first thing that struck my remembering eye was the pattern of the parquet in the wide front hall. The wood was laid in a herringbone design with a border of darker interlocking pieces resembling the links of a chain. I remembered staring at it as a child until I grew dizzy and the floor seemed to waver and rise up like engulfing brown water. Against the wall was an ornate piece of furniture, a combination of hat rack, umbrella stand, mirror, and bench. There was nothing hanging from its brass hooks now, but my memory saw it sprouting huge black umbrellas, long trailing scarves, hats that grew like odd fruit from its branching arms. There was in the hall a faint scent of mildew mingled with mothballs.

"Let's go on upstairs," Bonnie Marie urged.

"What happened to the rug?"

"The rug?"

"There used to be a rug here. A red rug with lots of little bits of blue and gold. I guess it was some kind of Oriental thing."

"Oh, gee, honey. I don't know. Maybe it got moth-eaten or maybe your mother took it over to her place. Ask Wendell."

I used to sit cross-legged on that rug and pretend it was my magic carpet that would take me anywhere in the world I wanted to go. My travels were not limited by my faulty knowledge of geography. I went to lands not mapped in anyone's atlas, to planets unheard of by NASA. The rug was gone and so was the child who traveled on it. I followed Bonnie Marie up the stairs.

She chattered as we went. ". . . five bedrooms on the second floor and three that we can use on the third. I'm putting Fearn and Walter in that big back room with the screened-in sleeping porch. That way, the kids can sleep on the porch. Then there's Wendell's uncle Ambrose from Gallipolis. He's driving over with Irene and Mike and their kids, but I don't know if

he can manage the stairs—they had to take his leg off, you kno
—so I'm putting him in the back parlor. Wendell's grandma
staying with us; she'll be glad to see you. She was migh
disappointed you didn't come for your own grandma's funera
but I told her you had your reasons and no one could kno
another person's heart. Aunt Tillie's coming down from Ch
cago; she's just retired from schoolteaching. And then there
Ambrose's boy Petey and his wife from Lexington. They've g
three or four teenagers, I forget which. And his other boy, th
one who never married, what's his name? Oh, yes, David. O
is it Donald? Oh, well, whatever. He's coming all the way fro
Tucson on a motorcycle. And, of course, there's Wendell's m
and pa, but they live right here in town, so that's no problem
And my own folks, too. And I can't remember now who all els
But it's sure going to be a swell reunion. I hope the weathe
holds. Here we are."

We stopped in the upstairs hall outside a heavy dar
door framed in an intricate wood molding. With my hand o
the scrolled egg-shaped doorknob, I paused to look back at th
faded wallpaper, the leaded glass window on the stair landing
the newel post with its fat wooden globe that my small hand
had loved to smooth and slide over, the wall brackets with thei
yellow light bulbs made to look like gas flames. I had neve
thought to see any of it again.

"Go on." Bonnie Marie was more eager than I. "Ope
the door."

I did.

And stepped into a room my grandmother might have
left only moments ago. Sunlight streamed through the three tal
windows that formed a bay. The window seat with its plun
velvet cushions waited for me to curl up with a book. The
four-poster bed was made up with the quilt she'd pieced many
years ago. She'd called it Delectable Mountains and she could
tell me the history and previous owner of each scrap of fabric
that made up the whole bright field. The heavy linen sheets and
pillow slips were slightly yellowed with age, but they'd been
ironed to a crispness that almost crackled beneath my hands.
On the dressing table, my grandmother's tortoise-shell dresser
set glowed in waves of amber and burnt sienna. I picked up the
hairbrush and pressed its soft old bristles against my cheek. The
comb still had all its teeth, but the chamois cover of the nail

buffer was worn and ragged. I lifted the lid of the hair receiver, half expecting to find it full of twisted strands of gray hair, but it contained only a tiny gold safety pin. The rest of the room was just as I had last seen it ten years ago, with the exception of the family album on the bedside table. The album would soon be restored to its place.

"Do you like it?" asked Bonnie Marie, bursting with pride in the doorway.

"Has it been kept like this ever since . . . ?"

"No. Everything was packed away. But it was all right here in the house, so it was no trouble to find."

"Then you must have done it."

"Like I said, it was no trouble. Is it all right?"

"All right! It's perfect! It's just the way I hoped it would be. Thank you, Bonnie Marie."

"Oh, it was nothing. I better scoot downstairs and make sure Fearn don't put arsenic in the tea. She gets so upset since her operation, but she can't help it, poor thing." She backed out of the doorway and closed the door softly behind her.

I was left alone in my grandmother's bedroom with lots to remember and lots to think about.

CHAPTER

Most of the apple trees were dead or dying, their twisted arms bare or tossing only a few stunted grayish leaves. A few were in fruit, but such fruit as would not tempt a latter-day, welfare state Eve, small sour-looking bird-pecked apples, only good for use as missiles in a child war, a summer substitute for snowballs. And not nearly as much fun.

I walked beneath the pitiful trees, rummaging in my mind for a day, a bright sun-kissed day when I flew among their leaves like a small chirping bird. I knew the joy and luscious fear of hanging between earth and sky, grasping at air, the leaves clattering amazement in my ears. How could it have been, I wondered now, gazing at the brown gnarled limbs, some no higher than my head. I sat under a tree amid the rubble of rotting fruit and last year's leaves. Somewhere a woodpecker tapped for his dinner, sounding like an urgent prisoner rapping out a secret message of distress. The humble buzzing of the insect world rose and fell in languid waves. From halfway across the orchard a red squirrel crouched upon a stump and eyed me boldly as if to say, "This is *my* domain. What right have you to sit there?"

What right? I'd given up my claim. I'd scorned all this and gone away. And yet I had the claim of memory, the elusive picture of a small girl tossing among the apples and the leaves. Tossing? Tossed. By whom? And then the voice of my mother, thin and quaking, "Don't do that, Ray. You'll frighten her." Oh, Mother! What could you know of flying? Of the sure, strong hands that gripped you and held you powerless, and then with a shout and a swoop tossed you high into the delirious air, and then while you shrieked for an hour-long second, grinned devilish white teeth in a hard brown face so that you couldn't be sure whether the hands would catch you or let you fall broken and dying on the orchard floor. The hands caught. The hands *always* caught. The hard brown face was smooth and smelled warm and spicy. The grinning mouth turned into smacking kisses on cheeks, eyes, forehead. And far away and faint, the deep voice said, "That's my bird. That's my little bird."

Oh, Mother, did he send you flying, too? Did he catch you and bring you safely back to earth? Or did he let you fall, crashing into fearfulness and disillusion? You never told me much about Raymond my father. Only that he died, and that in such a way that I was never sure. Wouldn't it be odd if he turned up at this reunion to catch us both in his strong arms and tell us his traveler's tales?

I got up and strolled among the tired trees, tired myself from the effort of remembering and somewhat disappointed that memory, when captured, was so commonplace. There was no magic in the simple act of a father throwing his young daughter into the air and catching her. Perhaps it was time to hurl myself back into the family fray.

I'd changed into my jeans and worn flat sandals, applauding my good sense in bringing some old clothes along, and escaped from Fearn and tea and chocolate cake. Smiling Wendell had brought my carryall into the bedroom with a great show of labor, puffing and grunting through his gritted teeth. "What you got in here, Jenny-girl? Gonna give us a New York City fashion show?" He meant no harm, I told myself, but only in his joking, clumsy way had prodded a tender nerve. Suddenly, my gift for him, the ludicrous barbecue apron and hat, seemed both appropriate and hurtful. And Bonnie Marie's scarf seemed woefully inadequate. I decided to hold off on the giving of gifts, at least until I saw what others might bring. He came and threw his fleshy arm around my shoulder and pressed me to his bulky side. He gave off a smell of soap and sweat and peppermint.

"You've changed, Jenny," he told me. "You ain't the scared little rabbit who ran away. You're looking good."

He pulled me around so that we were facing the tall oval mirror of my grandmother's dressing table. "Now, lookit there," he said. "Ain't that a picture? Me and you, just like we used to be."

"Stop teasing, Wendell," I said, holding myself stiff and awkward under his hands. "It was never you and me. Not that way. Not a bit."

"Shucks, Jenny." He chucked me under the chin as if I were ten years old. "I know that. And you know that. But everybody else around here thinks you run out on me and you know how it is in a town like this. If everybody believes something, then it has to be true. I don't mind."

"Fearn does." I tried to pull away from him but he held me in the mirror's frame.

"Fearn minds everything these days. Now come on and give your old cousin Wendell a great big kiss for old times' sake."

I couldn't believe what my eyes saw in the mirror. Wendell was grappling me to him and holding my face up to his. His wide, idiotically smiling lips were descending. The struggle was dreamlike, more real in the mirror than in my arms feebly trying to push him away.

"Wendell, stop!" I saw my lips move and knew what they said, but could hear nothing.

Nothing until I heard the voice shrilling from the door.

"Jenny Holland! What in God's name do you thi
you're doing?"

Wendell fell away from me and lumbered to the windo
seat where he collapsed. I stood, impaled by the voice, hot wi
embarrassment and rage, unable to move. The voice ranted o

"I knew it! I told him. Don't invite her, I said. Sh
nothing but trouble. And wasn't I right? Not five minutes in t
house, and she's up to her dirty tricks. That may be the w
they do it in New York, but that's not the way we do thin
here. Wendell, leave the room."

Wendell snickered. "Aw, Fearn, she didn't mean
harm. I guess it was mostly my fault."

"There you go, taking up for her. You are so dumb.
don't know how you manage to get from one day to the next

The two of them wrangled across the room as if I we
a piece of unheeding furniture. I got the feeling that this w
something that went on between them every time they met.
just had the misfortune of supplying the current argument an
getting caught in the crossfire. Still, I was annoyed with We
dell for creating the incriminating scene, and then not bein
man enough to stand up to Fearn's accusations.

"Fearn," I tried to get her attention. "Fearn, listen . . .

"I'd better leave," she stated to the chandelier. "I'd ju
better leave before I say something really tacky. But I'm just ne
used to walking into tacky situations."

"Maybe you ought to try knocking on doors before yo
barge in." Wendell's enjoyment of her rage was obvious an
gleeful.

"Next time, I won't come up to tell her that tea's ready
Next time, as far as I'm concerned, she can starve." She sti
refused to look at me.

I tried again. "Fearn, listen. You don't understand
Wendell, will you please explain?"

Wendell shrugged. "Who, me?"

"Oh, I understand all right." Fearn plowed on with th
righteous energy of a born-again bulldozer. "He wasn't goo
enough for you ten years ago, but he's fair game now for yo
to practice your big city whoring ways on. And him with hi
own wife in the house, working her fingers to the bone to mak
it nice for you. You ought to be ashamed, but I don't suppos
you know the meaning of the word."

"Oh, for Chrissake, Fearn!" Wendell eased himself off the window seat and slouched over to her. "You got the whole thing bass-ackward. In the first place, it was nothing but a little cousinly kiss. Nothing wrong in that. And in the second place, it was me kissing her, not her kissing me. Or at least trying to. She don't kiss too easy."

"I'll bet. I'll just bet." She glared at me, leaving the chandelier for a more vulnerable target. "You're just lucky it was me that walked in on your little kissing cousin act. Supposing it was Bonnie Marie. That'd be real pretty, wouldn't it? Well, don't think that you can get away with any more of it. I'm gonna be watching you. Like a hawk. Come on, Wendell."

She surged out the door with Wendell foundering in her wake like a stove-in dinghy. He turned his big face to me, grimaced helplessly and was gone.

I closed the door after them and this time turned the bolt. It was funny, if it wasn't so sad. Fearn was crazy. That was the only explanation. Her life had closed in on her and turned her into a suspicious bully. And everyone tiptoed around her in the interest of keeping the peace. And Wendell still fancied himself the irresistible make-out artist of his youth, which he never was in fact but only in the dance halls and motel rooms of his imagination. Well, it was none of my business. I had only to stay for a week, put up with their silliness with as good a grace as I could muster, and leave them to their weary battlefields at the end of it.

I opened my carryall, quickly changed clothes, crept down the back stairs and through the dingy warren of pantries and laundry rooms without attracting anyone's notice. From the back porch to the apple orchard was a natural although unplanned excursion. The evocation of Raymond my father was a total, but sustaining, surprise.

When I returned to the house, Wendell and Bonnie Marie had gone. Walter Proud sat in the darkened front parlor with both television and radio tuned in to a baseball game. The reception on the television set was none too good; the players lurked on a snowy field and the batter swung at an indecipherable ball. But the sportscaster on the radio, with the nasal frenzy of his kind, told in frantic bursts of hyperbole what was

happening on the indistinct screen. The combination seemed t
please Walter. He sat in my grandmother's rocking chai
gently swaying back and forth, at every third or fourth roc
tipping a beer can to his mouth.

I found Fearn in the kitchen, placidly washing up the te
things. Braced for another round of recrimination, I wa
stunned by her complete about-face.

"You should have some of that chocolate cake," sh
said. "Bonnie Marie's a wonderful baker."

I started to refuse, but realized that I hadn't eaten sinc
the soggy ham sandwich on the plane. I was hungry. Fear
didn't wait for my answer. She dried her hands, got down
plate and cut an enormous wedge of cake.

"There, now," she said. "Dig in. You gotta be hungr
The kettle's still hot. I can make you a cup of tea if you like.

"No, thanks," I said. "Is there milk?"

"Is there milk! My goodness, is there milk! I'll bet yo
haven't had milk like this since you went away. It's from Spa
key's Dairy. Remember?"

She ran to the ancient refrigerator and plucked out
familiar brown glass bottle. Dale Sparkey insisted that brow
glass was better for milk than either clear glass or plastic. H
cows browsed on a hillside just south of town, and he kept ju
enough of them to supply the needs of his regular customer
But since practically everyone in town drank Sparkey's mil
including the kids on the free lunch program at the schools, h
did all right. I'd once had a grammar school crush on Dale, Jr
until he wrestled me down in the schoolyard and put an itchba
in my underpants.

Fearn poured the milk into a cut-glass tumbler and s
it down in front of me on the old pine kitchen table. "Tas
that," she said, "and tell if that isn't what milk is supposed t
be."

I tasted. It was. Cold and creamy and harboring a fai
alfalfa sweetness. "Thanks, Fearn," I murmured, not knowin
how far I could rely on this new-minted good nature. "That
Sparkey's milk, all right."

The milk and chocolate cake at the kitchen table starte
another stream of memory. I ate hungrily and spoke thic
words sweetened with gobbets of frosting. "I used to sit at th
table and help my grandmother shell peas. She had a vegetab

garden out back and those peas were so sweet. I think I used to eat more than went into the pot."

Fearn sighed dramatically and plunged her hands back into the steaming dishwater. Over her lime-green pantsuit, she wore a calico apron that looked vaguely familiar. "Hardly anybody grows stuff anymore. I tried some tomatoes last year, but with all the work and the fertilizer, it's cheaper to buy them at the supermarket. Don't taste as good, though."

She emptied the dishpan, dried her hands and came and sat at the table with me, her short rosy finger absently tracing old scars in the battered pine surface. "What's it like, living in New York City? Ain't you scared?"

"Oh, no." I knew I couldn't really tell her what my life was like. That wasn't what she wanted to know. She wanted to hear horror stories of muggings and rapes and murder in the streets. Then, too, I had hinted in my notes to Wendell of glamorous nights and important days, and I was sure he'd passed those hints on to Fearn and the rest of the family, with his own embellishments. All I could say was, "It's not like that at all." And hope she would let the subject rest.

She wouldn't. But she was content to expound her own views, gleaned, obviously, from television and from the more lurid of the weekly scandal sheets. "Well, I just couldn't live in a place like that. I'd be terrified, all those people and never knowing who was going to pull out a gun or a knife and go crazy."

"Fearn," I said, scraping the last of the frosting from my plate. "Doesn't Wendell sell guns in his store? Knives, too?"

"Well, sure," she said, pitying my ignorance, "but those are for hunting. That's different."

"Don't hunters go crazy sometimes?"

She thought that over, then grudgingly admitted, "Sometimes they have accidents. But it's still different. It's not like every time I go out my door I have to look over my shoulder to make sure I'm not going to wind up dead in the gutter. And what about the kids?"

"What about them?" I carried my plate and glass over to the sink, washed them and stacked them in the draining tray.

"Well, you can't tell me that it's a good place to raise children. I'd have to be watching them every minute. And I'd be afraid to send them to school."

I thought about the kids who played in the street outside my apartment. Skinny brown boys, bright-eyed and wise-mouthed, racing in and out of traffic. Girls who clustered in shrieking knots on stoops, casting precocious glances and crudely tantalizing remarks at the boys. No, it probably wasn't a good place to raise children. But I wasn't going to let Fearn get off on that one.

"Where are Billy and Millie now?"

"Oh, they're outside somewhere, playing."

"Well, suppose some weirdo comes driving along. It's a lonely road. Nobody much uses it anymore. And Millie is out in front picking daisies. What's to keep him from picking her up and stuffing her into the car? She'd be gone before you knew anything about it. Or what if Billy decided to go down to the river for a swim? The river looks nice and smooth. But it's deep and the current is strong. They might not find him for days, if they find him at all." Cruel, I know, but she hadn't been any too nice to me over the Wendell business.

She laughed weakly. "Shush, Jenny. Stop trying to scare me. You don't have children, so you don't know how a mother worries. Anyway, it's time they came in and took a nap. Tomorrow's going to be a big day. Lots of excitement."

She went out on the back porch, and I heard her calling their names. Her voice was high and anxious. Dissatisfied with myself, I wandered back into the front parlor. Millie reminded me uncannily of myself as a child. The pale, blond hair, the small, wistful face. She was lucky to have Walter for a father, just as I'd been lucky, for a while, to have had Raymond. Something niggled at my memory, but the television and radio were still tuned in to the baseball game and the sudden cheering for a double play drowned the vague thought. Walter had fallen asleep in the rocking chair and missed the action. I tiptoed across the room and switched off both receivers. Walter snuffled softly, but didn't stir. The clock on the mantel tinnily dingged the quarter hour. I stood in the middle of the quiet room, waiting for an inspiration about what to do next.

I could go up to my room, my grandmother's room, and finish unpacking. I could explore the whole house before the rest of the troops arrived and filled up the bedrooms and the halls with their bodies and their cries of recognition. I could go back outside and walk as far as the old cemetery. Wendell, I recalled, had written that my grandmother was the last of the tribe to be buried there. No more room, but she'd had her piece of ground picked out since her husband died long before I was born. I could go down to the river and dabble my feet in the brown water as I'd wanted to do on the way from the airport.

The air in the front parlor was heavy with Walter's sleep and with the heat of the afternoon. The velvet drapes were closed against the slanting sun, probably an attempt by Walter to improve the television's faulty reception. The shadowed pieces of furniture surrounded me, wallowing like hippoes in the dim hot air. In the silence, the stray memory crept back. It was something about a rainy day with the house hushed as it was now, a game of checkers, and then going up the stairs, up and up, to the very top of the house, where there was . . . what? Goosebumps sprang up on my arms and a clammy dampness slickened my hands as I rubbed at them. In the mirror over the mantel, my face showed wan and large-eyed. I clutched at the memory, but the patterned wallpaper intervened, its thick vines and pallid flowers curling and beckoning.

There was no sound except the clock's flat impatient ticking and Walter's occasional snuffle. And a distant ringing in my ears. I glanced down at the floor. My feet seemed to have receded and become alien objects seen from a great height. The blue and gray swirls of carpet became a vast expanse of turbulent ocean. A cordon of pain came from nowhere to wrench at my astonished organs and suck the strength from my legs. Doubled over, I groped toward what must have been my grandmother's velvet sofa. The heaving waves of the oceanic carpet drew me down into their depths.

CHAPTER 7

Floating. Motionless and at peace, borne unresisting on a tide that flows placidly to an unknown destination. There is no sky, no earth, no time to be up and doing. Only the warm unhurried water and complete surrender.

Somewhere a voice says, "Jenny."

And another voice says, "Hush. Let her be."

Yes. Let her be. Let her float undisturbed. Let her rest. In peace. Let her not look down and see the faces staring up at her. Drowned faces with gaping mouths and bulging eyes. Let her not feel the cold hands plucking at her arms and legs. Let her not find the one face out of all those thousands that swims closer, smiling, offering chilly kisses and long bony comforting arms. Let her not hear her own voice echoing out over the water. "Daddy!"

The other voices are closer, more insistent.

"Jenny, are you all right?"

"Maybe we should get a doctor."

Suddenly, there is a shoreline, white, cold, snow-covered. The tranquil water becomes a swift-moving torrent. The submerged faces shrink back into the endless depths, all calling, "Jenny, Jenny, Jenny." The water rejects her, casting her out onto the frigid beach. She watches herself, lying naked in the snow.

And then she opens her eyes.

"Oh, thank God! What did you do to yourself?" Fearn hovering with an enamel basin filled with ice cubes.

"Shut up, Fearn. Let her rest." Walter, on the other side of the bed, holding something hard and cold against my head.

There was a pain. Not like the one that gripped my body —how long ago was it? No, this was a dull thudding ache on the side of my head. A headache.

"What happened?" Was that feeble croak my voice?

"That's quite a goose egg you got on your head." Fearn sounded proud of my accomplishment.

"Woke me up when you hit the floor. Thought it was an earthquake. How you doin'?" Walter, in his taciturn way, seemed concerned.

I put my hand up to the ache. My hair was damp beneath the ice pack that Walter lifted out of the way. The swelling was about the size of a prune, but smooth and very, very tender. When I took my hand away, I examined my fingers for traces of blood. There wasn't any. The dampness was only ice melting through the dish towel that Walter now replenished from the basin that Fearn held out to him across the bed.

Someone had carried me upstairs. Someone had taken my sandals and jeans off and covered me with the Delectable Mountains quilt.

"You must have fainted." Fearn obviously liked her diagnosis. Fainting meant I was weak and vulnerable, inferior.

"I don't faint."

"Well, you sure hit your head on something. I suspect it was the arm of that sofa. Solid mahogany. Maybe you just tripped and fell." Walter replaced the ice pack, sending cold trickles down my neck.

"How long was I out of it?"

"Oh, ten, fifteen minutes. Something like that."

"Did I say anything?"

"Groans and moans. Nothing anybody could make any sense of. Just enough noise so we could tell you were alive."

Alive. So I was. And likely to remain so, despite the dream that was still very much with me. Death had rejected me. The comforting waters had cast me back onto the cold inhospitable shore of the living. I closed my eyes but could not conjure back the drowned face of Raymond my father. Did the dream mean that he had drowned all those long years ago? And why would I want to dream of myself floating into oblivion? For that matter, what had made me keel over like that? Fearn's practical tones interrupted my reverie.

"Well, if she's all right, I've got things to do. Those kids'll never take a nap if I don't go put them down."

I opened my eyes. "I'll be fine. Thanks a lot, Fearn."

Still she couldn't leave. "Maybe Wendell ought to take

you to the doctor tomorrow. I don't know what we'd have done if you'd been hurt bad. No telephone and no car. Somebody would have had to walk over to the highway."

"Truly, Fearn. I'll just rest for a while, and then I'll be up to give you a hand with supper."

"No need. No need. I can manage. You should take some aspirin and go to sleep. I'll see if I can find some."

She scurried out, carrying the ice basin with her. I looked up at Walter, whose impassive face was turned toward the door.

"Thank you for the ice pack."

"Had enough?"

"Yes, please."

He took the ice pack away, holding it loosely between his strong mechanic's hands. "Don't mind Fearn," he said. "She feels cheated. I never know how it's going to take her."

"You're very kind."

"No, I'm not. I only do what needs to be done." He walked away from the bed, then turned and came part way back. "You did faint, didn't you?"

"I guess so. I'm not sure. It never happened before."

"Why?"

"Why did I faint? I don't know. I just felt disconnected from myself and the air was so thick. And then there was a pain."

"Reason I ask is, I was sitting there with the baseball game and I started to feel like I couldn't move. I thought it was the beer and just being tired from the trip. But I'd never been tired like that before. It was like something was pressing down on me. The last thing I remember before dozing off was that my ears got all plugged up. I couldn't hear the radio. All I could hear was that clock ticking away. Funny."

"I heard the clock, too."

"Funny," he repeated. "Well, I guess I'll go see if Fearn's got anything for me to do. Can't stand being idle."

He moved to the door and opened it. Fearn bustled through with a glass of water in one hand and a bottle of aspirin in the other.

"Here we are," she announced. "I found these in the bathroom. And you'll never guess what else I found. Some real old-fashioned shaving gear. A straight razor and a strop and one of those lather brushes and even a cake of shaving soap. Wendell thinks of everything, doesn't he? But I don't know anyone who shaves with a straight razor anymore. Not even Uncle Ambrose. Here, take a couple of these, Jenny. Sit up so you don't choke."

I sat up obediently and took the aspirin tablets from her hand. The pain in my head thumped sickeningly at the movement. She stood over me until I placed the tablets in my mouth, and then held the glass of water to my lips. I sipped and swallowed.

"There, now. You just lie back and get some sleep."

"Yes, Fearn."

And I did lie back, gratefully, but not to sleep. I closed my eyes and watched through the fringes of my eyelashes as they tiptoed out the door and eased it closed behind them. I sensed rather than heard their whispers in the hall. I waited until there were no more creaks of dry, aged floorboards, smoothing with my fingertips a path through the Delectable Mountains. Here was my mother's first school dress, a faded plaid of navy blue and red, and here my grandmother's lilac calico apron. A scrap of checkered shirting and some stripes that might have been a pillow tick. The quilt was, itself, a kind of family album, each piece a talisman of days and people gone or changed beyond redemption. Here was a vibrant diamond of red sprinkled with tiny yellow flowers. Who had worn it bravely on a summer day to a picnic or on a stroll down Market Street catching all eyes and reveling in its gypsy brightness?

I tossed the quilt aside and crept cautiously from the bed. The ache in my head, muffled by aspirin and feather pillows, lay low and kept a chancy peace. My carryall crouched open on the window seat, and from it I took my ancient summer bathrobe, a disgracefully threadbare object of blue and white striped cotton. I put it on and listened at the door. There was no sound in the hall. Fearn and Walter must have gone downstairs. Perhaps they were sitting on the porch looking out over the river. Or maybe Walter had gone back to his baseball game and Fearn was finding things to organize in the kitchen. I opened the door and slipped barefoot out into the hall.

The only light filtered up from the leaded glass window on the landing, a confused dim glow of amber and green and mauve. The hall itself was confusing, being shaped roughly like a swastika, with short arms branching off in three directions and down the stairwell. The bathroom, as I remembered, was just across the hall from my grandmother's room, and had another door opening into the back bedroom where, presumably, Billy and Millie were napping on cots on the screened porch. It was not as old as the house. The house had been built before the Civil War when bathrooms were rare if not unheard of. I knew—someone had told me—that the bathroom had been a wedding present to my grandmother from her husband's family. It had once been a small sitting room attached to the back bedroom.

For a bathroom, it was large. And magnificent with a kind of overdone, turn-of-the-century, middle-class opulence of marble and mahogany. It held, in addition to the usual although outmoded accommodations, a vast carved mahogany dresser with a pink marble top and a wide mirror framed in a garland of wooden flowers. In one corner stood a pale marble maiden, modestly draped, supporting on her shoulder a slightly top-heavy water jug. I remembered, from my childhood, wondering what would happen if she threw down the jug and stepped down from her pedestal, and being slightly afraid that she might. But it was the objects on the dresser that I had come to see, the shaving set that Fearn had mentioned with mingled awe and amusement.

The china mug, indeed, held a partially used cake of shaving soap. There were tiny craters on its surface where bubbles had burst and dried. The ivory-handled brush stood upright beside the mug, its bristles showing signs of wear. The strop, a long, flat snake of black leather, badly cracked and buckled, hung from a brass hook set into the wainscoting. And the razor, again ivory-handled, lay folded on the pink marble waiting for me to pick it up.

I did. It felt weighty and important in my hand. Both the razor and the brush, I noticed, bore on their handles oval silver plates engraved with ornate monograms. After a moment's concentration, I deciphered the curving script. The initials were REH. Was that what I had come to see? Raymond Earl Holland. Had I known it would be so? I had no memory of Raymond my father shaving with this razor or any other. I picked up the shaving mug and raised it to my nose. It smelled faintly spicy and familiar. Puzzled, I glanced into the mirror.

It showed me a woman with a pale face and lank disheveled hair. The hand holding the mug set it down with a sharp click on the marble surface. Then it gripped the razor and slowly unfolded it. I watched in the mirror as the blade shone and danced in the woman's hand. First, she pressed it against the thumb of her other hand and took it quickly away. A line of blood appeared. The woman in the mirror put her thumb into her mouth.

There was a salt taste on my tongue, and the air in the bathroom darkened and grew thick. I thought of my dream of drowned faces and wondered if there might be something in this house, some elusive memory, that was pushing me toward self-destruction. It was crazy, but I couldn't seem to help myself. I shook my head, trying to clear away the morbid thought, and looked again into the mirror.

The woman in the mirror raised the blade to the side of her head. She gripped a lock of hair in her free hand and sliced at it with the other.

I dusted the hairs from my numb fingers and they scattered like blown dandelion fuzz across the pink marble. I wanted to drop the razor and hear it clatter harmlessly on the marble, but my fingers refused to obey the command.

The woman in the mirror raised her arm, wrist bared, and pressed the flatness of the blade against it. Her eyes met mine with a fearful question. What could I tell her? What answer did she want from me? She waved the razor at me and smiled. Courage, she seemed to say, it's not as bad as all that. It's peaceful and quiet and there are no bad dreams. And then she bared her wrist again.

I watched the blade in one hand move closer to the thin white wrist, and while I watched I heard from far away, from that vast distance on the other side of the bathroom door, a thump, a howl, and then an aggrieved sobbing. I folded the blade back into its sheath, not daring to look into the mirror again, and placed the razor carefully at the back of the dresser top. Out of the way of children. Then I opened the door leading into the back bedroom. The sobs came, as I suspected, from the screened porch. Millie had fallen out of her cot and lay on the floor in a heap of misery. I picked her up and held her to my shoulder. She wrapped her legs around my waist and nuzzled damply into my neck. She was, I thought, more of a comfort to me than I was to her. She had brought me out of my trance and back to commonplace concerns. I hugged her gratefully. When Fearn came into the bedroom, Millie had quietened down and was murmuring about a big dog that had chased her and was going to bite her.

Fearn scolded. "See what you did, you bad girl. You woke up Aunt Jenny. You ought to be ashamed, crying like a big baby."

"She couldn't help it, Fearn. She fell out of bed."

"Well, she didn't have to sound off like a fire engine. Put her down, Jenny. No sense in babying her. If I picked her up every time she howled, I'd have her hanging around my neck twenty-four hours a day."

Millie clung tighter and started to whimper. Billy sat up in his cot and said, "Can I get up now?"

Fearn groaned.

"I think she had a bad dream." I patted Millie's back and she quietened down again. Bad dreams were something I could understand.

"She's always having bad dreams. I think she makes them up just to get attention."

"Can I get up now?" Billy's plea was turning into a fretful whine.

"No!" Fearn glared at him and he ducked beneath the covers, wriggling like a puppy.

"Why don't I take them down to the river? It's too nice to stay indoors."

"What about your head?"

"Oh, it's all right. Just a little sore."

"Well, if you're sure you want to."

"I'm sure. I was going to go down there anyway. They might as well come with me."

"No swimming."

"No. We'll just skip some stones and watch the boats go by."

"Well."

"I'll keep an eye on them, Fearn."

"They're pure mischief."

"They'll be good. Won't you, kids? For me?"

Millie's head nodded into my shoulder and Billy poked his out from under the covers and shouted, "Yeah, man!"

"Well," Fearn drew out her deliberation to the aching point. "Well, all right, then. It'll give me a chance to get us unpacked. Put your shoes on, Billy. Millie, get down now and stop being such a crybaby."

Millie jumped down from my arms and ran to get her shoes. I started back to my room to get dressed, but stopped in the doorway.

"Oh, Fearn," I said, as offhandedly as I could manage. "I don't think you should leave that straight razor lying around in the bathroom. One of the kids might get hold of it."

"Oh, you're absolutely right," she said. "I'll put it away."

"Have you any idea where it came from?"

"No. I've never seen it before. Maybe Wendell picked it up in an antique shop. He's all the time picking up junk."

"You think Wendell put it there?"

"Well, he must have. Him or Bonnie Marie. Just trying to make the place look nice and old-fashioned, I guess."

"It has my father's initials on it."

"Does it? Now, isn't that interesting?" She bent to tie Billy's sneakers. "Well, I'll put it away in a safe place. But I'm going to leave that razor strop handy. No telling when we might want to use it on the seat of somebody's pants."

I went back to my room, my grandmother's room, eager to get dressed and out of the house where forgotten ghosts of memory shimmered on the edge of consciousness.

CHAPTER

The river. Now that I was on its bank, gazing off across its broad brown ripples, I truly felt at home. Isn't that silly and sentimental? I asked myself. New York has a river, lots of rivers, and a bay and an ocean to boot. And sometimes on summer days, after work in the bookstore, I would go over to the South Street Seaport and walk out to the end of the pier and watch the gulls swooping over the garbage scows on the East River. But it wasn't the same. There weren't weeping willows leaning over my shoulder, or sassy red squirrels grabbing up sycamore balls from practically between my feet. When you look out across the East River, all you see is the other side. But looking out over this river, and squinting just enough to blur the present, you can almost see sunbonneted women and men with long rifles floating downstream in flatboats with their babies and their baggage, looking for home. And on the opposite shore, isn't that a Shawnee canoe waiting silently in a sheltered cove, the men in it watching and wondering what business these strange creatures have in the wilderness? Home is the place that you have stories to tell about.

"Billy, if you dig, you might find an Indian arrowhead."

"I seen a movie on TV; this Indian chief killed lots of soldiers. But they all got killed in the end."

"They used their arrows for hunting, too. And sometimes they camped right here on the river."

"Yeah? Where are they now?"

"Gone. It was a long time ago."

"Did they have to eat oatmeal?"

"I don't think so. Why?"

"I went to camp and it was terrible. They made us eat oatmeal. It had lumps."

I smiled. The oatmeal of childhood always has lumps. There's some kind of lesson there if I wanted to puzzle it out. But Billy was racing off making *ka-pow* noises, probably in pursuit of Geronimo. I turned to Millie, who was hunkered down staring at the ground.

"What is it?" I asked her.

"Ants," she said. "A million of them."

She'd found an anthill and its inhabitants were busy. They were large black ants and they formed two disciplined lines, one moving away from the anthill, the other coming home carrying or dragging morsels of food. Millie was fascinated with watching ant after ant struggle up the slope of the anthill and plunge into its round mouth, while others wriggled out again and marched off to rejoin the endless food brigade. I followed the double line of marchers with my eyes to where it disappeared in a patch of pokeberry bushes. Now I was fascinated, too. I wanted to find out what it was that they were so industriously carrying home, bite by infinitesimal bite. I left Millie to her vigil and sauntered toward the pokeberries. The ants ignored me; they had important business to attend to. The bushes grew shoulder high. I pushed my way among their broad leaves and hanging clumps of bright red berries, always with an eye on the ground for the moving trail of ants.

I should have smelled it, but I didn't. Perhaps my city-abused nostrils had grown insensitive. Or maybe it was freshly dead and hadn't yet begun to decay. It was a kitten. A very young, black and white kitten, its fur wet and matted, its lips drawn back to reveal the tiny buds of milk teeth. The ants were working industriously at its belly and around its eyes. As I watched, one of them crawled out of its ear. There were flies, too, buzzing helpfully around. Had someone tossed it from a passing car to wander on the river bank and slowly starve to death? Or was it one of an unwanted litter that had escaped drowning only to collapse on the shore? It was pathetic, but no more than that. The ants would return it bit by bit to the ongoing stream of life.

I'd forgotten about Millie, or assumed that she would remain entranced at her observation post. I didn't hear her creep up behind me. I felt her small hand on my thigh as she peered through the pokeberry leaves. Instinctively, I dropped my hand over her eyes, but not soon enough. She had seen. She gurgled softly and broke away from me. I ran after her, but she was quick. She ran to the anthill and kicked it over. Then, weeping and choking, she stomped on its remains and on the ants that, despite the destruction of their outer portal, attempted to hold their ranks and continue the supply line.

I pulled her away. She shrieked and struggled. Billy galloped up to see what the excitement was all about. When he saw the tumbled anthill and the ants bravely trying to restore order, he grabbed a stick and began poking it down into the exposed nest.

"Billy, stop!" I cried. "Leave them alone."

"Aw, shoot," he muttered. "They're only ants." And he continued prodding.

"Let's go up to the house now."

Millie writhed and kicked, a tiny fury with vengeance distorting her streaming face. It was all I could do to hold on to her.

"Billy, you kill them!" she screamed. "You kill them fuckers! You hear me?"

Out of the mouths of babes. I wasn't shocked. I'd heard it before on the city streets. But somehow, I hadn't expected to hear it here on the banks of the peaceful river with the high clear sky vaulting overhead and off in the trees the raucous comical call of the blue jays.

"Let's go," I said again, and began dragging Millie up the slope toward the house. Billy swept his stick half-heartedly across the straggling line of ants and followed, complaining.

"You're no fun. You're just as bad as my mom. She won't let us do anything."

I dragged Millie across the road and up the dirt drive-way to the house. She wept and struggled all the way until, at last, we both collapsed on the porch steps. I tried to hold her close to me for whatever consolation I could offer, but she wrenched herself away and, trembling and tear-stained, she screamed, "I bet you killed it! I bet you threw it there and killed it! I hate you!"

Billy, who had meandered up, still swinging his stick, stood watching with grave interest.

"Killed what?" he asked.

"That kitten," Millie roared. "That little dead kitten down there."

"Where?" Billy mouthed, and then streaked off back the way we had come.

Fearn opened the screen door and stood, stern and annoyed, with one hand on the doorknob, the other on her broad hip.

"What's going on out here?" she demanded.

I started to tell her. "Millie's a little upset. She saw a . . ."

Millie ran to her mother, babbling and clutching. "Ma, I seen a dead kitten, Ma. The ants are going all over it and Aunt Jenny killed it."

Fearn glanced at me curiously, then bellowed out down the slope. "Billy! Billy, you get your ass back up here! Right now!"

Billy ignored her and disappeared into the stand of pokeberry bushes.

"Fearn, I didn't . . ." I protested.

She shook Millie roughly. "Are you telling me lies, young lady?"

Millie buried her face in Fearn's apron, shaking her head and crying. Fearn plucked her away. "Stop that," she commanded. "You're getting snot all over me. Go inside and wash your face. And stop that howling."

She pushed Millie through the screen door and closed it behind her.

"She makes things up," she told me. "She's always trying to be the star of the show."

"But it's true, Fearn. There is a dead kitten down there. Millie saw it and I think it frightened her. It wasn't a pretty sight. The ants were eating it."

"Did you kill it?"

"No. Of course not."

"Well, then. She's got to learn to stop telling lies." Fearn sighed. "I swear, I don't know what to do with her. I beat her till she's black and blue and she still makes up stories. Well, she'll get it this time, but good."

"Fearn," I pleaded. "Don't beat her. She wasn't telling a lie. She just got a little confused. I was there and the kitten was there. She made the wrong connection."

Fearn stood over me, looking down from the height of her motherhood. "How many kids have you raised, Jenny?"

I shrugged and looked away down the slope. Billy appeared on the bank of the river, swinging something in the air over his head. It wasn't his stick.

"Well, if you ever have any," Fearn lectured on, "just remember that you can't let them get away with anything. Not anything. Once they start telling lies, you just have to beat it out of them. Why, if I didn't give Millie a few good whacks over this, she'd think she could just keep on making up stories about you. You wouldn't like that, would you?"

I had no answer for her, none that she would listen to. I thought of Millie, cowering in the house, waiting for the beating that was better than no attention at all. If anything, it would confirm in her young mind that I was a merciless killer of helpless kittens and God knows what else. On the river bank,

Billy whirled a small dark object over his head and with a lurch launched it out over the smooth flowing stream. I watched it sail in a high wide arc and plunge into the river with scarcely a splash. Billy stood motionless on the shore, staring after it.

"Did you see that?" I asked Fearn.

"See what?"

"Billy just threw the kitten in the river."

"Well, good riddance." She dusted her hands together righteously, as if cleansing them of sin. "I can't stand cats, anyway. I hope there aren't any more around, dead or alive."

Billy came trudging back up to the house, a small thoughtful figure with his hands crammed into his pockets and a frown troubling his brow. Fearn watched him come with pride and apprehension mingling on her round face. He reached the porch and looked up at her.

"I'm hungry, Ma," he said.

"Tell me something new." She retied her apron strings as if she were girding for new battles. "Go wash your hands."

She pulled open the screen door and stumped away into the house. Billy sat down on the lowest porch step and began picking splinters out of the worn wood.

"Threw the cat in the river," he said.

"I know."

"Well, it's better than getting et up by those dumb ants."

"I think you're right."

"Millie is a wimp."

"What's a wimp?"

He looked at me with pity and scorn. "You know, it's like Millie. Dumb and crying all the time."

"She was frightened."

He considered that, and then agreed. "Yeah. She's a wimp and a scaredy-cat. I seen a dead person once."

I wondered if Billy made up even better stories than Millie did. "Where did you see that?"

"Oh, it was just my grandma when she died. They made me and Millie go up and kiss her in the coffin, but Millie wouldn't. She screamed and all, and Ma had to take her outside and smack her. I didn't mind. It wasn't no worse than holding a frog, only I never kissed a frog."

"My grandmother died, too."

"Did you have to kiss her?"

"I didn't come to the funeral."

Billy looked at me in awe. "Ain't you scared?"

"Of what?"

He lowered his voice to a whisper. "My ma said if we didn't go to the funeral, Grandma would come back and haunt us. Does your grandma come back and haunt you?"

"No." I shook my head, more in wonderment over Fearn and her child-raising methods than to reinforce my disbelief in the return of dead grandmothers from the grave. "There are no ghosts."

"Oh, yes, there are." Billy's superior wisdom shone from his eyes. He had, by now, accumulated a small pile of gray wood splinters and he began arranging them in a circle like a tiny bonfire. "This house is haunted. That's why nobody lives here. I'm gonna stay awake tonight so's I can see the ghost."

"Billy, truly," I insisted, "there are no such things as ghosts."

"My mom says."

Fearn's voice came shrilling from the back of the house. "Billy! Did you wash those filthy hands yet? Supper's almost ready."

He got up, reluctant to leave me unconvinced. "You wait," he said. "That ghost'll come. I bet it'll make Millie wet her pants."

I got up and followed him into the house. He strutted away toward the kitchen, turning once to wink at me over his shoulder. I headed upstairs. In the bathroom, the straight razor had disappeared from the dresser top. From the other side of the connecting door to the back bedroom, I heard Millie sobbing mournfully. I hesitated at the door, wondering if there was any comfort I could offer her and then decided I would only make things worse. Fearn would not appreciate my meddling in family matters. I washed quickly and went to my bedroom to put on my new green skirt for supper.

There was no skirt to put on. I hadn't unpacked yet but had left my carryall unzipped on the window seat. My new skirt and my fancy new blue and white dress had been lying on top. Now they lay on the bed, sprawled on top of the Delectable Mountains, slashed into shreds. The ivory-handled straight razor nestled in the midst of the destruction, its blade clean and gleaming. Millie, I thought. It must have been Millie. It was a childish act of revenge, but nevertheless it hurt. I'd worn the skirt only once, and the dress not at all. I picked them up to see how bad the damage was. The skirt, a bright full sweep of emerald green, was beyond saving; there were jagged slashes across the front that no amount of careful needlework could repair. The dress had suffered less damage, one long slash down the back and a sleeve dangling loose like a broken wing. I might be able to rescue it with tiny stitches hidden in the intricacies of its dainty floral print. But not now. Not right now.

Now I would go down to supper and say not a word about what had happened. Poor Millie, I thought. She has enough trouble. If I mentioned this to Fearn, Millie would undoubtedly suffer the consequences. But wait. What if it wasn't Millie? What if Fearn herself, in a rush of rage, had lashed out at me by destroying my clothes? It had been fairly obvious in the car that she had no liking for me or for my presence at the reunion. Then she had about-faced and shown kindness with milk and chocolate cake, and with ice and aspirin for my aching head. She was erratic and unpredictable. She could have done it while I was down at the river with the children. If she had, I wouldn't give her the satisfaction of mentioning it to her. Not even to the extent of asking her for a needle and thread.

The walk to the river and the business of the dead kitten had taken my mind off the pain in my head. But now it flared up again, dull and insistent. I dropped the damaged clothes back onto the bed and sat down beside them. Weary and dismayed with the first day of the reunion, I could have slept. Fearn had left the bottle of aspirin on the bedside table, and there was a swallow of water left in the glass. I took two, and then two more, hoping they would get me through supper. If Fearn *had* slashed my clothes, I wanted to give her the chance to wonder why I chose to keep silent about it. And if she hadn't, if Millie had done it, it was better that Fearn should never know. It was inconceivable that Walter could have had anything to do with such pettiness. And Billy had been outside with me at the time it must have been done. It must have been Fearn or Millie.

Of course, Billy would probably insist that it was the ghost. In a way, he would be right. There was a ghost at work here. The ghost of old family animosities, rattling its chain down the years and into the next generation. I should not have come.

But here I was. I went down to supper. But first I locked the door of my grandmother's bedroom and slipped the old iron key into the pocket of my jeans.

CHAPTER

9

"I know it's only a cold supper, but I *could* use a little help." Fearn scurried between the kitchen and the dining room carrying platters of cold cuts and bowls of potato salad and cole slaw.

"Tell me what you want me to do."

"Well, if you can't see . . . oh, all right. Bread, pickles, mustard, mayonnaise, milk. Everything's set out on the counter. All you have to do is carry them in. Billy, did you wash those hands yet?"

"Yep."

She paused for inspection. "Well, wash them again and scrub those fingernails. You look like a coal miner."

Billy groaned and slouched over to the kitchen sink. I followed Fearn's directions and carried an assortment of dishes and jars to the table. As we passed each other, I glanced at her face. It showed nothing but concentration on the job at hand. She didn't avoid my eyes, but her own were distracted.

"What about Millie?" I asked her. "Do you want me to call her?"

"No, ma'am." Her lips tightened. "She gets no supper. And she knows what she's going to get afterward. You can call Walter if you want to. He's out back somewhere."

"Fearn." It was on my mind to ask her why it offended her so much to have me here. But she looked at me impatiently with a plate of carrot sticks in her hands. I said, "I'll wash the dishes tonight."

"I should think so," she snapped, and turned away.

I went out the back door. The back porch was not as wide or as grand as the front. A rusted washline pulley dangled from one of the squared off columns that supported the porch roof. One end of the porch was trellised, and I remembered that rambler roses had once grown there. Nothing grew there now, and through the spaces in the latticework I saw Walter prowling among the ramshackle outbuildings that lay scattered on half an acre of barren ground a fair distance away from the house. The stories of my childhood held that these had once been slave quarters. They might have been, but this side of the river had been free territory in those bad old days. The shacks, six of them, had fascinated me when on visits to my grandmother I had been allowed to roam freely outdoors. Despite the cautions of my mother that they were infested with deadly brown recluse spiders, I had been drawn to peer into their dark ill-smelling interiors. They each had a small stone fireplace and a single unglazed window in the rear wall fitted with a wooden plank shutter. The floors were of packed earth; most of the doors had fallen off their hinges or were about to do so. They were all empty although once, while exploring, I had come upon a man sleeping in one of them.

Now, as I watched Walter moving from shack to shack, I was reminded vividly of that heart-stopping moment years before when I had looked in expecting nothing but spider webs and seen the length of him sprawled on the dirt floor beside the cold fireplace. This was sometime after my father had died or run off or whatever it was he had done, and I thought for a moment that I'd found him. I said, "Daddy," and the man sat up, instantly awake. He was not my father; he had a stubble of beard on his face which my father never had and a hard, nervous look about his eyes. His clothes were wrinkled and ragged and there were holes worn through the soles of his shoes. I said, "Excuse me."

And he said, "Come here, little girl." His voice was soft and blurry, and he smiled when he spoke like a dog grinning after a rabbit. I ran.

Back at the house, my mother and grandmother were sitting at the kitchen table talking. The radio was playing.

"Well, I hope he doesn't turn up around here," my mother said.

"Who?" I asked.

"The man in the moon," my mother said. But I listened to the radio and heard that a prisoner had escaped from the county prison farm. Then my grandmother switched it off.

"Go outside and play," she told me.

"Can I have some cookies?"

She gave me some of my favorites, oatmeal raisin, and an apple. I left. My mother called after me, "Stay close to the house."

A prisoner. It occurred to me for the first time that maybe my father was a prisoner in a jail somewhere. Maybe at the very same county prison farm that this one had escaped from. Maybe he could tell me where my father was, especially if I gave him the apple and the cookies. I ran back to the shack. The man was gone. I looked in all the shacks. There was no sign of him. I ran down to the road. Nothing. And there were no boats on the river. I sat down, then, on the dock that used to be there and ate the cookies and the apple and threw the core into the river. I never told anyone about the man in the shack.

"Walter!" I sang out.

He turned and waved, and I motioned him to come up to the house.

"Supper's ready!"

Obligingly, he came shambling toward me. I decided to wait for him and not risk Fearn's wavering moods without his presence as a buffer. The late afternoon sun sprinkled the raddled apple orchard with gold and glinted on the smooth headstones in the family cemetery beyond. Tomorrow I would find some flowers and pay a visit to my grandmother. Tonight I just wanted to get through the evening as peacefully as possible until I could lock myself into the bedroom and sleep. Walter hove into speaking distance.

"Seems like somebody's been camping out in one of them cabins."

"Oh, yes?"

"Ashes in the fireplace. Bunch of tin cans heaped up in the corner. Could be old. Could be fresh. I couldn't tell."

"Maybe he came back," I murmured, my mind still dwelling in the past with the escaped prisoner who might have known my father.

"Who?" said Walter, looking at me curiously.

"No one. Must have been a backpacker. Some kid traveling through. Fearn says supper's ready."

"Well, good enough." Walter squinted at the sky. "Clear as a bell," he pronounced it. "Wendell couldn't have ordered better weather for his reunion."

Walter. Tall, ordinary Walter. He seemed so sane and solid. What would he say if I told him about the slashing of my clothes? Would he want to know that his wife or his young daughter had used that sharp razor in that way? Would he even believe me? In the calm early evening, I didn't want to believe it myself. Perhaps I had imagined it. Perhaps if I went back upstairs now I would find everything whole and the razor safely hidden away from destructive hands.

"It's a fine evening," I agreed. "I hope it stays that way."

From the kitchen window, Fearn's voice shrilled at us. "Are you two aiming to stand there all night gawping at the sky?"

"Coming, Fearn."

Walter loped up to the back porch with his long gentle strides and I followed him, content to let him precede me into Fearn's firing range. But other than urging Billy to drink his milk and remember to use his napkin, she had little to say throughout the meal. She ate sparingly, nibbling at a sandwich and poking at a deviled egg. When Walter commented on the excellence of the potato salad, she merely stared at him, and when he inquired as to Millie's whereabouts, she grimaced and jerked her thumb toward the ceiling. Walter subsided into silence. I ate my food in silence, too, content to enjoy my first meal in ten years in my grandmother's dining room.

This room, too, was fitted with a bay window but, unlike the one in the bedroom, this one looked out toward the willows and the fields at the side of the house. As I ate, I watched the long shadows cast by the setting sun, flickering dark shapes plunging across a golden sway of tall dry grass. The last meal I had eaten in this room had been the night before I'd boarded the bus for New York City. My grandmother and I had sat at this table over plates of roast chicken and new peas. I'd been too excited, too angry, too hurt to want to eat. But she'd patiently coaxed me into mouthful after mouthful, and told me she'd be pleased if I would live with her until things were patched up between my mother and me. I told her I saw no hope of that, that the town was too small to contain the two of us, that my mother was narrow-minded and provincial, and that if I had to give up my poetic Muley friend (whose name was Vergil, I now recall), I certainly wasn't about to marry Wendell who even then was putting on weight and had joined the Elks. There was nothing for me to do but leave. I spoke with all the drama and adamant cruelty of youth. I believe I even flooded my plate with self-pitying tears. My grandmother endured the scene without ridicule or recrimination. In the morning, she drove me to the bus station in her old Packard, a car she kept for state occasions, weddings, funerals, and visits to her doctor or her banker. She told me I was always welcome to return; there would always be a room for me in her house. I shook my head, granted her a scanty good-bye, and ran from her into the bus station. I didn't even thank her for her kindness. By the time I came to my senses and realized that I probably had given her a terrible hurt, she was dead and the doors she had held open to me were closed.

And so, this evening, in this dining room, in the silent company of my unhappy cousin Fearn and her family, over sandwiches and potato salad, dear Grandmother, I send you my thanks, ten years too late. Your sideboard is here, your table and chairs are here, and here your treasured china rimmed with fragile flowering bands of blue. And here am I. Tomorrow my mother is coming. Will we be able to find, in your house, a way to close up the deep wounds each of us has nurtured all these years?

The disturbance reached us first as a tinkling of the crystal drops of the chandelier. We all looked up, and in that fraction of a moment, the ceiling resounded under a thunderous blow from above. Walter leaped from his chair and ran to the stairs. The screams began before the rest of us had risen, thin, tight screams that ended in a wail of, "Ma-a-a-a!"

Fearn turned pale and whispered, "Millie." And then she, too, bolted for the stairs. Billy scurried past her, the light of adventure gleaming on his avid young face. I followed, hoping that poor Millie had not gotten herself into more trouble and a further dose of Fearn's displeasure.

When I got to the top of the stairs, Walter had already gone into the back bedroom and turned on the lights. Fearn and

Billy were just going through the door. I stopped for a moment and glanced around the hall. All the other doors were closed and the only sounds to be heard were the shrieks that came, apparently, from the sleeping porch. I joined the others in the back bedroom.

There was no light on the sleeping porch except for that which filtered through from the bedroom and the purple glow of the deepening twilight. It was enough to see that both cots were empty. While the others crowded out onto the porch to find Millie, who was still shrieking although not so loudly as before and with every indication of running out of breath, I glanced around the bedroom for the source of the thump that had shaken the chandelier and startled us all. I hadn't far to look. Someone had overturned a tall walnut highboy. It lay face down across the floor just inside the door. Someone. There had been no one upstairs but Millie. Would she have had the strength to do it? And if she had, why? It was the same kind of blind malicious mischief that had slashed my clothes.

Walter carried her, kicking and squalling, into the bedroom and laid her on the high double bed. "Hush, hush," he soothed. "It's all right now. Daddy's here."

Fearn followed, scolding. "I don't know why you always want to baby her like that. It's getting so she thinks she can get away with murder as long as you're around. Screaming her head off and scaring the wits out of all of us, and then hiding under the bed. And will you look at that!" Fearn had caught sight of the toppled highboy and hurried over to inspect the damage. Then she went back to the bed, pushed Walter aside, and stood glowering down at the whimpering child. "Millie, look at me," she demanded.

Millie, as if hypnotized, gazed up at her mother and held her breath.

"Why did you knock it over?"

"Didn't."

"Don't lie to me, young lady. Why did you knock it over and cause all this commotion?"

Millie despairingly began to shake her head rapidly from side to side and clutch at the bedclothes.

Walter intervened. "Leave her alone, Fearn. Can't you see she's frightened?"

"She'd better be frightened!" Fearn exploded. "She's really going to get it for this."

Walter sat down on the bed and stilled Millie's shaking head with one large hand. With the other, he gathered both her small ones and clasped them together on her heaving chest. When she had quietened down, he began to talk to her.

"That was sure a big bump, wasn't it?"

She nodded.

"Made my teeth rattle around in my head."

She giggled.

"Millie-baby, did you make that big bump?"

She shook her head and whispered, "No."

"Then who did? You can tell Daddy."

Millie squeezed her eyes shut and shivered.

Fearn snorted. "You won't get anything out of her but lies," she declared. "You'd do better to help me get this highboy back on its feet."

Millie opened her eyes for a moment to glare at her mother, then quickly closed them again.

"In a minute, Fearn. Millie's gonna tell me exactly what happened and then we're all gonna have some ice cream. I think I saw some chocolate chip in the freezer downstairs."

Billy, who had been hanging over the foot of the bed watching his sister's misery, said, "Can I have mine now?"

No one answered him. Walter gathered Millie up in his long arms and set her on his lap. She curled herself into his warmth and tugged a wisp of her tow-colored hair into her mouth.

"Now, Millie," he coaxed, "you tell me what made you start howling like that."

"I seen something," she mumbled.

"And what did you see?"

"I seen a lady."

"Hah!" said Billy. "I bet she thinks she seen a ghost. She's such a wimp!"

"I did, too, Billy." She struggled out of her father's arms to crouch on the bed and face Billy's challenge. "I seen a ghost. She was all hairy and old, and she come creeping into the room and went all around, and then she knocked over the . . . the thing, and then I yelled, and then she went away." Millie scrambled back onto Walter's lap and hid her face in his chest.

"Well," said Fearn. "What did I tell you? Now it's ghosts. She's just a born liar and she's never going to stop it if you keep on coddling her."

Billy looked at me with secret knowledge in his eyes. "Maybe it's your grandma's ghost," he said.

"That's enough, Billy," said Fearn. "There's no such thing as ghosts."

"But, Ma," he protested, "you said . . ."

"Never mind what I said. What I'm saying now is that there are no ghosts. Now you get on out of here and leave Aunt Jenny alone."

Billy stomped out, muttering, and I heard his footsteps racing down the stairs. Obviously, chocolate chip ice cream took precedence over arguments pro and con the existence of ghosts. But someone had tipped over the highboy and slashed my clothes, and if it wasn't Millie or a ghost, there had to be someone else in the house. And if there were any truth in Millie's story at all, that someone was a hairy old woman who crept about doing mischief.

"Maybe we should search the house," I suggested.

"What for?" asked Fearn. "You won't find anything. Or anybody."

"I think we'll do it," said Walter. "Just to be on the safe side. Fearn, you take Millie downstairs with you and give her something to eat. Keep her and Billy in the kitchen. Jenny and I will take a quick look around."

"Oh, so now it's Jenny and you. Isn't *that* cute?" She jutted her round chin at me belligerently. "I hope you *do* find something. I hope you find exactly what you deserve, and in case you don't know what that is, I'll be only too glad to tell you."

She would have gone on, but Walter's voice, low and firm, interrupted her. "Move it, Fearn."

She moved it. She hauled Millie off the bed and marched her out of the room. Millie looked back forlornly at her father, but went along without a murmur. Fearn, stiff-backed and flushed, had not a word or a glance for either of us. Away down the stairs they went, while Walter and I watched from the bedroom doorway. When their footsteps had reached the bottom of the stairs and faded away toward the kitchen, Walter turned back into the bedroom.

"Might as well pick this thing up," he said.

He went to one side of the fallen highboy and I went to the other. Together, we lifted it and set it back in its place against the wall. The damage was slight; a drawer pull was bent askew and the finish on one corner was marred. The hardwood floor had suffered a deep gouge where the corner had struck. I picked up the embroidered dresser scarf and replaced it, and against the leg of a chair Walter found a small white hobnail glass vase still intact with its bunch of strawflowers none the worse for the fall. While we worked, Walter maintained a brooding silence, but after we had restored order, he spoke, addressing himself to the vase of flowers which he had placed dead center on the embroidered scarf.

"Doctor says she's likely to have a hard time of it for a while. Says if it gets too bad, she should go see a psychiatrist. But she won't. She says she's not crazy, only that she wanted to have more kids and now she can't, and there's nothing crazy about that. I sure hope she straightens out soon. Don't matter to me if we don't have more kids. Billy and Millie are just fine. Except they're starting to get a little nervous, especially Millie. Fearn's just too hard on her." He gave the vase a final minute adjustment and walked to the door. "Guess we better look around a little. I was thinking that maybe whoever was camping out in that shack got into the house."

"Could be," I said, although I doubted it. I was debating whether to show Walter what had happened in my room. I'd have to, if we were going to search all the rooms on this floor and the next. Fearn wasn't the only one likely to need a psychiatrist; if Millie and not the "hairy old lady" were responsible for the damage, she needed help, and quickly. And Walter needed to know about it. "I want to show you something," I told him, and led the way across the hall to my room.

I fished the iron key out of my pocket and unlocked the door. The room was dim with the misty darkness of summer dusk. I could just make out the looming shapes of the four-poster bed, and the trees that rustled just outside the bay window. I pressed the light switch and flooded the room with harsh overhead light. My carryall was just where I had left it on the window seat, but of the ruined clothes that had been strewn across the bed, there was no sign. Nor was the razor anywhere to be seen.

"What did you want to show me?" Walter asked.

"It's gone," I told him. "It's all gone." I moved swiftly about the room, opening drawers and peering into the wardrobe. Nothing. I told him then what I had found when I'd come upstairs to change clothes before supper. I told him, too, that I had at first suspected Millie of having attacked my clothes with the razor because she connected me with the death of the kitten on the river bank, and then that it might have been Fearn in one of her erratic moods. But now, it seemed that it was neither one of them. Fearn certainly hadn't tipped the highboy over, and neither Millie nor Fearn could have gotten into my locked room to take away the slashed clothes. And the razor.

Walter stood quietly listening to all I had to say. There was pain in his blue eyes, and I hated having been the one to put it there. When I finished, he asked, "If it is one of them, what should we do?"

"We don't know who it was. At this point, I'm inclined to believe Millie's story about the 'hairy old lady.' At least, I think there's been someone in the house playing malicious tricks on us. I think we ought to continue the search. I would like to find that razor and lock it up. I don't like the thought of someone creeping around the house with a weapon like that in his back pocket. Or hers."

We searched the two upper floors then. The three remaining unoccupied bedrooms on the second floor, and the three smaller ones on the floor above. Bonnie Marie and Wendell had spared no effort in getting the house in shape for the reunion. All the beds had been freshly made up and there was not a speck of dust to be seen, as might be expected in a house that had been closed up for almost nine years. Some of the furniture would fetch good prices on the antiques market, and I wondered why my mother chose to keep it all, and the house itself, when she could easily sell it off and live quite comfortably on the proceeds. But I knew nothing of my mother's financial position. Wendell had written only of her eccentricities. Perhaps she was already comfortable enough to suit her state of mind. In any event, we found nothing in any of the rooms to indicate the presence of an intruder. The attic storerooms, where someone might have been hiding, had escaped Bonnie Marie's attention. They were filled, as they had been in my grandmother's time, with a welter of objects that had outlived their usefulness—china dolls and tattered quilts, crippled chairs with frayed cane seats, a porch swing, old steamer trunks, and hanging lonely in a shallow closet, a moth-eaten sailor suit. And over all, an undisturbed layer of dust. No one had been hiding among the castoffs. The razor, and my clothes, had disappeared as if they had never existed.

We went downstairs. Fearn and the children were in the kitchen, seated at the table playing Old Maid. Half-finished bowls of ice cream stood melting at their elbows. Millie was stirring hers into a chocolate-studded mush. "Billy's got the Old Maid. I know he does," she taunted.

"Have not," he grumped, scowling at his cards. He had only four left.

"Then give me your farmer."

He threw his cards face down on the table. "This is a dumb game. I don't want to play anymore. I'm going to watch television." He took his dish of ice cream and ran out of the room.

Millie snatched up his cards. "I knew it," she crowed. "See, Billy had the Old Maid and he quit so I win. He's just a sore loser."

She sat staring at the picture of the raddled crone on the face of the Old Maid card.

"Put the cards away, Millie," said Fearn. She rose from the table, untying her apron. "And help Aunt Jenny with the dishes." She turned to Walter, who was helping himself to ice cream. "Did you find anything upstairs?" she asked.

I held my breath. I hadn't asked Walter not to tell her about my razor-slashed clothes. If he did, it would surely send her into another fury and possibly bring down more recriminations on poor Millie.

He concentrated on scooping ice cream into a dish and said, "Nope. Not a darned thing. Want some ice cream, Jenny?"

"No, thanks," I breathed.

"She looked like this." Millie's voice trembled. She still sat at the table, clutching the Old Maid card and staring at it with tears brimming in her huge blue eyes.

Fearn snatched the card from her hand and quickly gathered up the other cards from the table and stuffed them back into their box. "Don't be silly," she said. "Nobody looks like that. Now you get busy, Miss, and do whatever Aunt Jenny tells you to do. Show her what a good little housewife you are. Don't make me ashamed of you."

Millie turned her tearful blue gaze on me, and I smiled in what I hoped was an encouraging fashion. I'd never been around children much, and from what I'd seen so far of Billy and Millie I doubted that I could ever comprehend them or win their confidence.

"Well," I said, "shall we get to work?"

"Yes, ma'am," said Millie.

A poor beginning, but it seemed to please Fearn. She smiled and nodded to Walter. "I think I'll just put my feet up for a bit. Coming?"

Walter followed her out of the kitchen, carrying his heaping bowl of ice cream. At the door, he turned and looked back at me, seemed about to say something, then changed his mind, shrugged his shoulders, and left.

Millie and I were alone in the kitchen among the dirty dishes. My grandmother had never had a dishwasher installed; she didn't believe in them, she said, and did quite nicely with her dishpan and bar of brown soap. I looked under the sink. The white enamel dishpan was there in its usual place. I got it out and began filling it with hot water. Fortunately, the bar of brown soap had been replaced by a plastic bottle of detergent. I squirted some into the pan. Millie watched my every move. I felt awkward and couldn't think of anything to say to her.

At last she spoke. "Do you want me to dry?"

"That would be nice."

She came over then and took a dish towel from the rack beside the sink. She wrapped it around and around both her small fists until she looked as if she were wearing a muff, still watchful and tense. She reminded me of a small hunted creature, a rabbit or a raccoon, curious but ready to bolt at the slightest hint of danger.

I splashed some dishes into the soapy water, waiting for her to make the first move. I didn't have to wait long.

"Billy never has to dry dishes."

"Why not?"

"He's a boy."

"What difference does that make?"

"My mom says . . ." She made a stern, ugly face, in disrespectful imitation of her mother. We laughed and left the issue of shared housework, having established a tentative communion of minds, and worked for a few minutes in a companionable silence. Then she spoke again.

"I felt sorry for that kitten."

"Me, too."

"It was really dead, wasn't it?"

"Yes, it was."

"I don't want to be dead and have the ants eat me up."

It was hard to find a response to that. I had no idea what children—or this particular child—thought about death, whether it was a remote concept or an immediate threat. I tried to evoke my own feelings when, as a child, I was told of my father's death. But all that came was the sour taste of green apples; anything else eluded me. I could only try to be honest and treat her concern with respect.

"Everyone dies, but most people get very old first."

She nodded wisely. "Like my grandma."

"Yes."

She smiled up at me and dried a few plates and then, still smiling, asked, "Did you kill that kitten?"

"No," I said. "I didn't."

"I didn't think so. Not really. Maybe Billy did."

"No," I told her firmly. "He didn't. I don't know how the kitten died, but I'm sure that no one here had anything to do with it."

"Okay," she said, and seemed content.

Having established this much of a rapport with Millie, it was more difficult than ever to conceive of her as running amok with a straight razor or tipping over heavy pieces of furniture. She was, after all, only six years old and, although she might be confused by Fearn's alternating protectiveness and wild accusations, she seemed far from being a casebook example of psychotic hostility. But I was no child psychiatrist and for all I knew she could be adept at hiding her feelings beneath a facade of disingenuous directness. I was still wondering whether to bring up the subject of the strange events in the house, when she saved me the trouble.

"There really was an old lady in the room."

"There was? How did she get in?"

"Through the door, silly. How else would she get in?"

"What did she look like?"

"Ugh! Witchy and ugly and she smelled bad, too."

"You mean she got close enough so you could smell her?"

Millie nodded soberly. "She came right up and whispered in my ear."

"What did she say?"

Millie motioned me to bend down so she could whisper to me. I knelt on the floor beside her and put my arm around her. I felt the soft puffs of her ice cream-scented breath against my cheek as she babbled the chaotic words into my ear. I froze with the malevolence of the message. I'd heard Millie explode into street language down on the river bank, but this was something so vile, so full of ancient evil, that it could not have been conceived in a child's mind. Not even in the mind of a very sick and twisted child. She had to be repeating something she had heard.

I held her close and looked hard into her round innocent face. "Do you know what that means?" I asked her.

She shook her head.

"Did you tell your mother?"

"No. I didn't even tell Billy. It's bad words, isn't it?"

"Well, it's not good." I hugged her again and got back up on my feet. "I'll tell you what. Let's finish cleaning up the kitchen, and we'll keep this a secret between the two of us. We won't tell anyone. And I'll try to find out who this old lady is and make sure she doesn't come sneaking around anymore. Okay?"

"Okay."

We finished up the dishes in ten minutes, during which Millie told me all about how much she liked going to school even though her first grade teacher was fat as an elephant and went around the room spying for candy and took it away when she found it and never, never gave it back.

I listened to her prattle, glad that I had succeeded in getting her to open up to me and wondering how on earth I was going to be able to keep my promise.

CHAPTER

10

I stood in the road and looked up at the house. The round full moon sailed low in a starless sky and seemed about to impale itself on the weather vane atop the octagonal turret that crowned the gingerbread pile. All the windows were dark and the house gave the impression of being uninhabited. A wind rose, sweeping up from the river and carrying with it the scent of sour mud and damp vegetation. The willows rustled, rubbing their slender leaves together like hundreds of dry grasping fingers. I felt glad to see the house in this way, at night, alone, with the bright moon shining on us both. But at the same time, I was aware of an animal prickling of my skin. I could see nothing to be alarmed at, but my body was setting up distress signals. I looked behind me. The road curved away empty until it was lost in the darkness of the trees.

When I looked back at the house, a light had come on in the small turret window. It seemed to be candlelight; it flickered and glowed now yellow, now orange, and was the only spot of color in the moon-silvered and shadowy scene. Someone must have climbed to the turret using the narrow rickety pull-down ladder that I had always been forbidden to climb. The light grew brighter.

A silhouette appeared in the turret window. It was nothing more than a head and an upraised hand; the window was too small to admit more of the figure than that. It seemed to be a man or, perhaps, a woman with short-cropped hair. The light spilled around it, giving it the effect of being haloed, all the while growing brighter and redder until at last it burst through the window and leaped forth into the silvery night. The figure in the window uttered a single cry in a voice both harsh and dreadful, and then crumpled back into the flames. It had cried my name.

The house was on fire and I stood in the road, unable to move. I knew I had to do something: run, shout, wake up the sleepers and get them out before the flames reached them. I could feel the heat of the blaze; sweat broke out on my forehead and ran down my face. Or was it tears? I struggled to move my legs; they were weak and failed me. I opened my mouth to scream, but could manage only a muffled groan. The house was crackling with fire, the flames gushing out of every window. Helpless, I closed my eyes.

When I opened them, I was in darkness. My legs were tangled in the Delectable Mountains quilt and my pillow was damp beneath my cheek. I raised my hand to brush loose strands of hair away from my face; my head was soaked and my hair lank and slippery. A dream! Oh, God, it was only a dream! I reached out to switch on the bedside lamp.

The room came into being in the soft light. Everything was exactly as it had been when I'd gone to bed. From the open window came the gentle creaking of branches and the furtive scurrying of nocturnal animals, normal country sounds that had probably been interpreted by my unaccustomed and sleeping mind as the crackling of a raging fire. There was no breeze and the night air hung hot and heavy around the bed and my sweating, trembling body.

I got out of bed. I knew I wouldn't be able to sleep again until I had looked around enough to belie the dream. My thin cotton bathrobe was lying across the foot of the bed. I put it on and, barefooted, tiptoed out into the hall.

A single fixture glowed on the landing casting my shadow before me as I crept cautiously toward the arm of the oddly shaped hall that contained the stairway to the third floor. The stairs creaked as I trod them and I hoped that Walter and Fearn were sound sleepers. The third-floor landing was in darkness. I found a switch and a feeble light came on. It was enough to light my way to the narrow attic stairs. I wished I had a flashlight, but I had none in my room and didn't want to search the kitchen for one. Walter and I had not bothered to look into the small turret room on our earlier search. Walter hadn't known about it, and I, perhaps I had forgotten or was still acting under the rule laid down to me in childhood: never go into the turret room. Something about the flooring being rotten and unsafe. And anyway, it had always been locked.

The attic was lit by a naked bulb that hung swaying on a long cord from the ceiling. The turret was reached by a stepladder that folded up against the ceiling when not in use. It led to a trapdoor barely wide enough for a person to squeeze through. I tugged at the rope that dangled from the ladder and it glided down and came to rest at my feet. I peered up at the trapdoor and wondered whether to climb up and see if I could open it. The turret was located at the far front of the house, and the light from the single bulb did a poor job of illuminating this portion of the attic. I couldn't tell from below if the trapdoor was locked.

I put a hand on the ladder and felt gritty dust beneath my fingers. In the gloom, I looked to see if mine were the only recent disturbances of the dust. It was hard to tell. There was dust on some of the steps and not on others, nothing as distinguishable as a footprint or the marks of other fingers. Cobwebs clung to the sides of the ladder in fragile festoons. I climbed, watching each step carefully for evidence of recent passage.

When I came within reach of the trapdoor, I stopped and gazed at it with enormous relief. I could go no farther. It was securely locked with a sturdy hasp and padlock. There could be no one hiding up there; Millie's "hairy old lady" could not have locked herself in with the padlock on the outside. Just to be sure, I tugged at the padlock. It was a heavy one, of bright steel, and it stayed locked. Good. Maybe I would ask Wendell for the key tomorrow, and maybe I wouldn't.

I clambered back down the ladder and pushed it back up to its position against the ceiling. At least my dream had been only that; there was no fire starting at the top of the house. I could go back to bed and sleep for what was left of the night. Perhaps a glass of Sparkey's milk would help me get back to sleep. I left the attic and tiptoed down through the silent house. I heard the mantel clock in the parlor chime the quarter hour, but a quarter after what I wondered.

When I got to the kitchen I saw by the clock over the gas range that it was a quarter after three. A fine time to be wandering around an old, almost empty house looking for dream fires or figments of a child's imagination. The refrigerator hummed, a cozy, companionable sound, and I opened it and got out one of Sparkey's brown bottles. I put it on the counter and opened the cupboard above to get a glass. I'd opened the bottle and begun to pour when a slight insistent tapping at the kitchen window caught my attention. A branch, I thought, not wanting to look, a trapped insect, a loose shutter. The tapping continued. I looked.

The face leered in at me: shriveled lips drawn back in a hideous grimace over snaggleteeth, a hooked and crooked beak of a nose, small deep-set eyes gleaming and wet with malice and around it all a ropy tangle of snarled gray hair. It was the face on the Old Maid card, Millie's "hairy old lady."

I must have screamed. I only heard the echo of it ricocheting through the quiet house. Sparkey's milk bottle crashed to the floor and suddenly my feet were wet. The face disappeared from the window and I ran for the back door. When I got out onto the back porch, there was no one in sight. I stumbled down the steps and out into the dark yard. Unlike in my dream, there was no moon, no silvery light to make things clear. Only the high, cold, unfriendly stars, no help at all. Anyone, a dozen anyones, could be hiding a few yards away among the trees and I would never see them.

"What's going on?" Walter stood on the back porch squinting sleepily out into the darkness. "Who's out there?"

"It's me. Jenny." I picked my way back to the house, trying to avoid the stones that had bruised my feet on the way out. "There was someone outside. I saw a . . . face at the window." I was somehow reluctant to tell him the kind of face it was. It seemed so unbelievable, a caricature of a face.

"Hey, what's this?" he said, and crossed the porch to pick up something from beneath the window. "Well, I'll be damned!"

It was the first time I'd heard Walter swear. He came to me as I climbed the porch steps and showed me what he'd picked up. "Is this what you saw?"

I nodded, mute with astonishment and doing my best to suppress a rising tide of giggles. What Walter held out to me was a mask, a rubber Halloween mask and a cheap nylon wig. It was the classic witch's face, warts and all, and it was laughable lying collapsed in Walter's big hands.

"Well, I guess we won't be seeing her around anymore." I was gasping with relief and flushed with the embarrassment of having been scared out of my wits by a child's plaything. "I must have been somebody's idea of a joke."

"Yes," said Walter, "but whose?"

That sobered me, and I glanced back out into the dark yard. "I don't know." I remembered the eyes that had glared at me out of the mask. They hadn't been the eyes of someone enjoying a joke. They could be watching from the shelter of darkness, and waiting. I shivered. "Let's go inside."

In the kitchen, Fearn, belted into a hot pink and purple paisley dressing gown, was grumbling over the broken milk bottle.

"Watch your feet," she scolded. "I honestly don't know why we have to have messes like this at three o'clock in the morning."

"I couldn't sleep. I came down for some milk. And then I saw . . ." I gestured at Walter.

He held up the mask. "She saw this at the window. I think I'd have jumped out of my skin, too."

"Well, she could have put the milk bottle down first. Now I have to clean it up."

"Let me help," I offered.

"Not in those bare feet. Now, get out of the way," she ordered, "and let me get finished." She bent over and began sopping at the spilled milk with a sponge. I backed off, feeling like a guilty child.

"Fearn," said Walter, "I think this means that Millie really did see someone in the bedroom. I think someone's been playing jokes on us."

"Not very funny, if you ask me," she muttered, picking the shards of brown glass out of the puddle of milk. For once, I agreed with her. "It's nice to know," she went on, "that Millie tells the truth once in a while. I think you ought to put that thing away and show it to the police tomorrow."

"The police?" I echoed.

"Well, what else do you do about prowlers? Invite them to come in and have a cup of tea and throw the furniture around and murder us all in our beds? Walter, make sure that all the doors and downstairs windows are locked."

She was right, of course. The police *should* be told. But this was no ordinary prowler, if any prowler can be classified as ordinary. This prowler knew his or her way around the house and had keys. How else could my clothes have disappeared from a locked room? This prowler had a purpose, one that went far beyond ripping up my clothes and frightening Millie. What could the police do? Try to get fingerprints off the witch's mask? And then what? They couldn't watch the house day and night. They would only tell us to be careful and report the next incident.

The next incident. We wouldn't see the "hairy old lady" again, but I felt sure we hadn't seen the last of the person behind the mask.

We went back to bed. My feet and legs were sticky where the milk had splashed and dried, and I washed them before I climbed back beneath my grandmother's Delectable Mountains quilt. And there I lay, propped up on two fat pillows, staring into the darkness, afraid to close my eyes lest the dream should come again revealing something to me it was better not to know. I'd always had dreams of River House. They'd been disturbing because of the aching loneliness that stayed with me when I woke from them. But they hadn't been frightening. Now, suddenly, in the weeks before the reunion and here in the house itself, my dreams were visions of death. My own, the legend of Raymond's, and of the destruction of the house and all in it. What was it all about? If I slept, would I sleepwalk and set fire to the house? Or was it something about the house that was lost in memory and trying in my dreams to return? The dreams were horrible. Sick, frightening, and crazy. Did they mean that I was losing my wits? The first signals of a mind gone haywire? And memory. What was I to make of the bits and pieces of my childhood that had begun to trickle back? Times and places and people I hadn't thought of for years. I'd hidden from them all behind a barricade of books, the ones I'd read and the ones I tended in Max's store. Now I'd come out from behind the barricade. What would I find waiting for me? What had been waiting for me all these years in River House?

Or was I nuttily imagining the whole thing? No. It couldn't be that. Walter had held the Halloween mask in his hands. My clothes were really slashed. Well, then, if I'd managed so successfully to hide from my memories of the past couldn't I just as easily hide from something I'd done only yesterday? Maybe I ought to start keeping track of every hour of every day, just to be sure there weren't any blank spots, times I couldn't account for. If I were crazy, I wanted to be the first to know it.

The darkness lightened gradually, and somewhere in those restless hours before the dawn, it occurred to me that the padlock on the turret trapdoor was brand new.

CHAPTER

11

Morning. The early light was intense and promised a day of heat and brightness. I was out before any of the others were up, searching in the weedy plot that had once been my grandmother's flower bed for some survivors to take to her grave. I found only a few straggling day lilies and left them where they drooped among the nettles and the poison ivy. My grandmother, I was sure, wouldn't mind if I came empty-handed.

The old graveyard was small and many of the stone markers had sunk into the soft earth. A few had toppled over and one had split across, its top portion lying behind the jagged stump. It marked the grave of one Henrietta Mears Allinson, beloved wife of Joshua, mother of Henry, Susannah, and Rachel, 1833–1901. "Her earthly work is over. She rests in Paradise." Henrietta must have been one of the granite-faced matriarchs in the family album.

I wandered among the stones, stooping now and then to peer at a dim inscription, not really searching for Grandmother's grave—I knew I'd find it sooner or later—but simply letting myself be drawn by shapes and shadows. The grass here grew long and lush, unlike the ruined patchy lawn around the house, and I didn't let myself think too deeply on the reason for its luxuriance. Instead, I made myself a mental note to see if I could find a scythe in the old barn and sometime during the week do a little trimming.

The newest stone, whiter and taller than all the rest, stood at the far corner of the plot, shaded by a slender gray-barked beech tree. A cardinal, regal in his brilliant red plumage, eyed me arrogantly from one of its branches. I remembered Miss Anna Grace telling us in the fourth grade that there were more cardinals in the state than people. We believed without question—it was a pretty thought and we'd all seen plenty of cardinals—but now I wondered if Miss Anna Grace had based her statement on a bird census or on her private view of how things ought to be. The cardinal in the beech tree offered no opinion but continued to watch me as I stood admiring him.

"I won't be buried here. There's no room and it's too lonely."

The voice came from behind me. Despite its familiarity, it gave me a jolt. I gasped and whirled to see who was there, even though I knew who it would be. From the corner of my eye, I saw the cardinal rise from its branch and flap away over the trees.

"Mother." I don't know whether I said it aloud or merely thought it. My mouth was dry as sand and my heart thumped achingly.

"You're thin," she said. "And short. I thought you would be taller."

I couldn't say how she seemed to me. Her hair was gray, grayer than when I'd last seen her, and rigidly sculptured into a structure of fussy curls. Her face was still the face that I remembered, but it had slipped and sagged as if the flesh had lost its mooring to the bone beneath. She wore white slacks and a strange loose smock of a stiff dark blue fabric that fell almost to her knees. Beneath the smock, her body looked oddly deformed until I remembered that Wendell had written of her habit of always wearing a life jacket. I glanced at her feet, half-hidden in the long grass. She was wearing clean white sneakers.

"I couldn't sleep," she said. "I thought you'd be sleeping. You always liked to sleep late."

"No more," I said. "I have a job. I get up early." How odd that we should be talking blandly in the bright morning. Should I open my arms to hold her? I didn't know what to do.

"Yes," she said. "That's true."

The truth she found in what I'd said was apparent only to her. Perhaps it was what I hadn't said—that sleep was no longer a blessing, that dreaming made it a prickly comfort at best—that struck a chord in her. Did she have dreams? Did we share something, some secret knowledge, that we'd denied all these years?

"It won't rain today," she said.

I looked at the sky. The sun, pale yellow, had crested the tops of the beech trees and there was nothing else above us but high blue distance.

"Not a cloud in sight." I promised myself to be agreeable, to say nothing about her strange habits. It was only for a week.

She shook her head as if in sorrow, staring at the ground. "But you never can tell. I have an umbrella in the car. These storms can come up out of nowhere. Can you swim?"

"I think so. It's been a long time, but I brought a bathing suit. I thought we might want to swim in the river."

She looked alarmed and then quickly produced a sad, sweet smile. "No one does that anymore. It's not safe. But I suppose if you want to, no one will stop you. Wendell has a swimming pool."

"Yes," I said. "He wrote me." I moved a step closer to her. She held her ground for a moment and then retreated a step, turning as if to look back toward the house. I let the distance between us remain.

"Would you like coffee?" I asked. "Have you had breakfast?"

"I haven't been out here since . . ." She turned again and gazed at the white stone at the edge of the graveyard. She shivered and her voice was faint. "I never liked this place. There's too much . . . weight here. Too much watching."

"The dead don't watch."

"No. Of course, they don't. They only lie there. It's you that does the watching. You, me, everyone, all the time, watching. And through us, they see. Why did you come here?"

"To visit Grandmother's grave."

"No. Why did you come back? Are you watching me? She always did. Yes, I would like some coffee."

She was disturbed, shaking. I wanted to put a hand on her arm and guide her back to the house. But I was afraid she would shrink, scream, or even hit me. Wendell had written me only of her eccentricities. Hadn't he noticed her terror? Or had he been sparing me the news, knowing how difficult it would have been for me to come home with only her madness to greet me? Was this whole reunion a scheme to get me back here to witness what my leaving had done to my mother? Oh, Wendell!

"Come on, then." I led the way and she followed, down through the barren apple orchard and across the yard where last night I had peered into darkness searching for the owner of the hideous face that had glared such hatred at me through the kitchen window. In daylight, with my unhappy mother trailing behind me, it seemed that I must have invented the hatred and the person in the witch mask was only playing a silly prank. If, indeed, there had been such a person.

Fearn was busy in the kitchen when we entered. The coffee was already brewed and Billy and Millie were greedily scooping up cereal at the kitchen table. Fearn smiled and greeted my mother with a hug. I noticed that my mother didn't shrink from her touch, and that Fearn saw nothing out of the ordinary in her manner.

"Well, you're an early bird, Aunt Elizabeth," she chattered. "How about some scrambled eggs? I was just about to put them on and I can just drop a couple more in." She cracked more eggs without waiting for an answer while my mother, all smiles, sat down at the kitchen table without a hint of the distress she'd shown me in the graveyard.

"Thank you, Fearn," she said. "That would be very nice."

Fearn beat vigorously at the eggs in a brown crockery bowl and cast a pointed glance at me. "Well, don't just stand there, Jenny. Get your mother a cup of coffee. It's the least you can do."

I did as she told me, while Fearn and my mother chattered quite normally about who would be coming to the reunion and how hard Wendell and Bonnie Marie had worked to make it a success. As I set the brimming cup down before her, my mother glanced up at me with a bright smile and put her hand over mine.

"I'm so glad my little girl has come home," she said. "That's why I came out early. I couldn't wait another minute to set eyes on her."

There was no trace of the frightened, frightening woman who'd claimed the dead were watching her. There was, of course, the ungainly bulge of the life jacket beneath her dark blue smock, but apparently Fearn and everyone else chose to ignore it. It was my turn to cringe. I wanted to pull my hand away from hers but couldn't with Fearn watching and nodding her approval of the filial scene. Instead, I sat down beside my mother. At close range, I could see the fine wrinkles radiating from her eyes and scoring her fallen cheeks. Fearn poured the eggs into a frying pan and called out for Walter to hurry up. And then my mother said something that shook me to the core.

"I wish that Raymond could be here. He'd surely love to see his little girl all grown up."

"Ain't that the truth?" said Fearn, giving all her attention to the golden mounds of egg forming in the pan.

Did she feel my hand tremble as she held it pinned to the table? I hadn't heard my father's name spoken except in the fortress of my own mind for more years than I had been gone. I'd learned, while I was growing up, never to question her about him. At first she'd told me different versions of his death, and then refused to speak of him at all. And she'd warned me, with threats of dire punishments, not to mention him to anyone in the family or even in the town. I'd learned to keep him, and any questions I had about him, to myself. And now here she was, speaking his name quite openly across the breakfast table, and Fearn giving it no more significance than a mess of scrambled eggs.

I pulled my hand away, giving as my excuse, "I think I'll have a cup of coffee, too."

I pushed back my chair and went to the cupboard for a cup, and then to the stove where the old graniteware coffee-pot squatted on a low warming flame. By exercising enormous concentration I was able to pour myself a cup of coffee without spilling any or dropping both pot and cup. Thank heavens Fearn believed in strong dark coffee. I stood beside the stove and sipped.

Walter came in, pink from shaving and full of good cheer. "Well, well," he said. "Look who's here. Good morning, Aunt Elizabeth. What's the forecast for today? Flood or fair weather?"

My mother laughed—it was a girlish giggle, really—and treated Walter to a flirtatious flickering of her eyelashes. "We'll be fine today. No guarantees, of course. You know what the Boy Scouts say. Be prepared."

Walter sat down in the chair I'd vacated and Fearn

began dishing up scrambled eggs. At the foot of the table, Billy and Millie, finished with their cereal, had begun spitting orange juice at each other.

"Here, here, kids," Walter chided. "None of that. Go on outside and play."

They squirmed off their chairs and ran out the back door. Fearn shouted admonishments after them, not to wander off, not to play by the river, not to get dirty.

Amazing. It was all so normal. They could even joke about my mother's flood phobia. Even *she* could joke about it. And not a word said about the face at the window or the pushing over of furniture. Of course, only Walter and I knew about my slashed clothing, and he hadn't actually seen it. And only Millie and I knew about the words spoken by the "hairy old lady" in the dim bedroom. Did Walter believe me? For that matter, did I believe Millie? I sat down again, this time with the width of the table between me and my mother, and began eating scrambled eggs and toast.

Before we had finished, there was the sound of a car laboring up the dirt driveway and the happy rhythmic beeping of its horn. In a few moments, Wendell rolled into the kitchen with a tall aluminum coffee urn in one arm and a folding playpen under the other.

"Borrowed it from the church," he said, setting the urn down on the counter.

Bonnie Marie followed, her arms full of the twins, now six months old and dressed only in diapers and identical cotton T-shirts that read, "I'm a little stinker."

"Put the playpen on the back porch, Wendell," she instructed.

Behind her came Wendell's mother, my aunt Augusta, carrying a huge pan of fried chicken.

"Hello, everybody," she said. "There's more of this in the car. Where shall I put it?"

Fearn bustled; Walter held out his big hands helpfully; my mother laughed; the babies cried. The reunion had begun.

CHAPTER
12

By noon, the lawn in front of the house was beginning to resemble a parking lot. Aunt Tillie, a tall, lean, intelligent woman, caused a flurry of excitement when she arrived at midmorning, expertly guiding her crimson Porsche to a halt at the side of the front porch. Wendell goggled at it and clamored to know how a retired schoolteacher could afford such a car.

"It was a gift, dear child, from a beau," was all that Tillie would tell him, with a mischievous sparkle in her eyes. Wendell patted the car reverently and licked his lips, while Tillie opened the trunk and hauled out a wicker hamper that clinked faintly when she set it down on the ground.

"What's that?" Wendell asked, eyeing the hamper suspiciously, as if it might contain a bomb.

"My contribution to the festivities," she told him. "When you carry it indoors, carry it gently. It's only a modest domestic vintage, but it deserves kind treatment."

"Wine?" asked Wendell.

"Wine," said Tillie.

"Wine!" echoed Fearn from the porch. "Well, I never!"

"But you should," said Tillie. "It's quite civilized and not nearly as fattening as beer."

Fearn stalked into the house, slamming the screen door behind her. From that moment, I liked Aunt Tillie. She stood as tall as her sister, Augusta, who now came around from the back of the house to greet her. There was a strong family resemblance between the two, but where Augusta was as sturdy as a farm wife, Tillie was as lean as a fashion model. They held each other at arm's length for a moment, each searching the other's face, then laughing, fell into a close embrace. From my observation post, half-hidden by the down-swooping branches of a willow tree, I watched their joy in each other and felt a stirring of submerged regret that I had never had a sister.

"Where's Mama?" Tillie asked.

"Dan's bringing her out later," said Augusta. "She's pretty frail these days. Eighty-seven come October."

Under the tree, I pondered the complex relationships that brought all these people together today. Tillie and Augusta's mother was my own grandfather's sister. Tillie had never married, but Augusta had married her second cousin, Daniel Mears. His brother, Uncle Ambrose, had married a girl from Gallipolis who had given him three sons before dying of pneumonia in one of the mildest winters on record. He'd married again but lost his second wife to a driver of moving vans who'd come to Gallipolis carrying the goods and chattels of the new Methodist minister. She'd actually gone off with him in the empty van. All of this happened before I was born, but was part of the family history told to me by my grandmother. In my mind, the stories had taken on the quality of myth, the characters less real than those I read about in the books I took home from Max's Secondhand Books.

Another car drove up, this one a sedate gray Buick, befitting a banker or an insurance salesman. I came out from beneath the tree, knowing that if I didn't, Wendell or Fearn would come searching me out to make sure I was being a part of things. I didn't feel a part of things.

The doors of the Buick glided open and an entire family in white shoes stepped onto the straggling grass. The woman held a small white dog, a poodle, in her arms.

"We just had to bring Mimosa along," she said. "She gets so nervous when we leave her in the kennel. I hope you don't mind." She set the dog down and it stood trembling and showing the whites of its eyes to the crowd gathering around.

"Petey!" cried Aunt Augusta. "Arlene! My goodness, you're looking prosperous."

"Well," said Arlene, "I can't say that Peter's exactly in the poorhouse." She tugged at the dog's pink leather leash so that the sun glinted off the rings that decked her manicured fingers. She and Mimosa wore the same shade of nail polish.

Petey stood tall in his shiny white patent leather tassle loafers and breathed deeply and seriously so that the small alligator on his red polo shirt alternately crouched and sprang.

"Doing just fine," he said, trying hard not to smirk. "Never have to worry about hard times in my business."

I'd joined the jabbering circle around the gray Buick and quickly realized that this was Uncle Ambrose's son from Lexington. I knew nothing about him; he hadn't figured very prominently in Wendell's letters and I couldn't remember ever having seen him before, even as a child. "What *is* your business?" I asked, just to be sociable.

Petey's children, two teenage girls and a bespectacled adolescent boy, burst into fits of nervous giggles. The rest of the company made prim mouths and looked everywhere but at me. It was left to Fearn to whisper angrily, "You little idiot! He's a mortician."

Petey came over and put a long white hand on my shoulder. Despite myself, I shuddered. Petey grinned down at me. He was tall and thin and, now that I knew his trade, cadaverous. It was illogical; I hated myself for feeling repulsed, but I seemed to be able to smell dank floral arrangements in his presence and hear lugubrious music.

"Don't be embarrassed," he said. "It takes most people like that. And the kids have to take an awful ribbing in school. But it's a business like anything else, and a damned good one. I really wanted to be a doctor, but . . ." He shrugged, and in that shrug I read old disappointments and acceptance of the compromise that had given him a good life and a place, however distasteful to others, in the community.

"I'm sorry," I muttered.

"It's all right." His voice was melodious and soothing and I supposed, with a further rush of embarrassment, that it was part of his stock in trade. "Now, since you're here," he went on, "I presume you're part of the family. But which part? I don't believe I have the honor of knowing your name."

I opened my mouth to tell him, but Fearn leaped in to give him a capsule history with a typically Fearn-style bias.

"She's Elizabeth's girl, the one who ran off to New York ten years ago and only now decided to allow us all the pleasure of her company. Jenny Holland."

"Oh. So you're little Jenny," he said. "I distinctly remember the time we all went to the county fair and your daddy pretended he was going to throw you into the hog pen. Held you up over the railing, he did, and the sow just rolled her eyes and grunted while you wriggled and screamed like Kingdom come."

"I remember that," said my mother, who'd come out of the house and knelt on the grass to scratch the poodle's ears. "She was only three or four at the time. He told her that pigs ate little girls."

"Be careful," said Arlene. "Mimosa's very high strung. It's getting so I can't keep a maid. She bites them."

"Well, she won't bite me. Will you, you sweet little puppy, you honey little doggie?" My mother picked up the quivering poodle and held it tightly against her blue smock. The poodle struggled to get free, scrabbling frantically with its painted claws. But my mother's life preserver protected her and she hugged the poodle closer to her armored breast, crooning soft syllables as if to a fretful baby. The poodle lifted its upper lip showing small, sharp, yellowish teeth. Its eyes rolled nervously.

"Better put her down, Elizabeth." Aunt Augusta stood over my mother, a look of patient exasperation on her broad kind face. "And you're getting grass stains all over your knees."

"Doesn't matter. It'll wash out. This little doggie and me are going to be best friends."

As she held the poodle up to her face to kiss its nose, it released a hot yellow stream that showed dark on her blue smock and trickled onto her white slacks. She threw the dog away from her with a cry of disgust and sat back on her heels, helplessly watching the spreading stain. The dog ran, yipping, in crazed circles, its pink leash whipping along behind it like the tail of a Roman candle.

"Mimosa! Come back here!" Arlene pleaded, while the dog ran in ever-widening loops across the weedy field. "Peter, do something! She'll hurt herself. She'll get ticks."

Peter blew a shrill two-fingered whistle which only spurred the dog on to greater speed. She was by now a white blur lolloping in the distance. He waved his children into the chase and they all fanned out across the field, followed by Billy and Millie, happily shrieking and running in circles of their own. Arlene collapsed against the hood of the Buick, moaning, "I can't watch this. I simply cannot watch this."

Aunt Augusta helped my mother to her feet. My mother stood with her arms held stiffly out from her body, peering down at the yellow stain on her white trousers. "I'm all wet," she moaned. "I'm all wet."

"Don't worry, dear." Fearn bustled up and took her arm. "Come on in the house and we'll find something of mine for you to put on while I wash these things out."

"I never could abide poodles," said Aunt Tillie, with a withering glance in Arlene's direction. "Give me a good honest mongrel any day."

The four of them trooped into the house, leaving Arlene drooping beside the car. Despite her claimed reluctance to watch the scene, she was stealing glances out over the field, shuddering whenever the dog eluded its pursuers. Wendell came out of the barn carrying a portable barbecue, followed by Walter with a sack of charcoal on his shoulder. They turned toward the back of the house where Wendell had set up the picnic tables.

I retreated to my haven under the willow tree. So Raymond my father had once threatened to throw me to the pigs. I'd never heard that story before and had no memory of it. I wished that Peter hadn't mentioned it. It didn't fit in with the few memories I did have of my father, but now I would never be able to forget it. He must have been smiling as he held me out over the grunting sow. I tried to picture his smiling face, to smell the hot rank odor of the hog pen. I saw myself small and struggling, frantic to escape the great rolling beast beneath my feet. Pigs ate little girls. Would he drop me? Or save me, holding me close in his long strong arms? And what was my mother doing while all this was going on? Perhaps I would ask her. Would she tell me?

From across the field came a shout of triumph. I peered through the green curtain of the willow branches and saw that the army of dogcatchers had congregated in one spot. Against the red of Peter's polo shirt a small white bundle lay still in his arms. They began to walk back to the house. Arlene dragged herself off the car and went to meet them. As she passed within a few feet of the willow tree, I heard her muttering to herself.

"I knew we shouldn't have come. They're all crazy, and that woman's the craziest of the bunch. God only knows what's going to happen next."

I crept out the other side of the willow's circle of shelter and walked away down the hill toward the river.

CHAPTER
13

I must have fallen asleep. The roaring sound came out of nowhere and stopped before I could figure out what it was. I opened my eyes and saw the empty river sluggishly rolling by. My head felt thick and my shoulder ached where it was resting on an uneven hump of ground. I lay there, wondering how much time had passed and what it was that had awakened me.

"Pretty."

The voice came from behind me. I twisted my head around and saw a pair of scuffed black motorcycle boots planted on the slope about four feet behind me. Above the boots, the usual Levi's went up and up and up; this was one long-legged rider. Between the Levi's and the beard, which was the next thing I noticed, was a black T-shirt and a vest of leather patchwork. The beard was full and wiry and bronze; it was met by hair that was long and sleek and sun-streaked. Somewhere in there was a face. Eyes glinted down at me like chips of turquoise, and wide plummy lips made a slash in the beard. A leftover from another decade, he reminded me of the young men who stopped off at my place on their way somewhere else.

"The scenery, I mean. But you're good, too."

"Well, thanks." I sat up and looked beyond him to find the source of the noise that had awakened me.

His motorcycle, a battered black monster that looked as if it had been cobbled together from parts of other dead cycles, squatted at the side of the road. It was fitted with a sidecar. He saw me staring at it.

"Malachi is sleeping."

"Malachi?"

"My kid. I brought him along. I thought he ought to know about his family. Who are you?"

"Me? I'm Jenny Holland. I guess you're David from

Tucson. They said you were coming on a motorcycle, but they didn't say anything about Malachi."

"Yeah. Well, I guess they don't know about him." He grinned. Lots of white teeth behind those juicy lips pushing through all that beard. "I hope my old man doesn't have a stroke when he finds out."

"Why should he?"

He looked at me pityingly, as if I were deficient in reasoning power. "Well, for one thing, Malachi is part Indian. And for another, he's a bastard. His mother and I never got around to getting married. And if that isn't enough, I've been raising him up to know bullshit when he stumbles into it. He tends to be a little bit mouthy."

"Where's his mother?" I don't know why I asked. It really wasn't any of my business, and I could feel the redness creeping up my neck. I was relieved when David merely shrugged and gazed out across the river.

"I'd forgotten how soft and mellow this part of the world can look. There's every kind of green imaginable. It's a blessing to the eye."

"Are you an artist?" I seemed to be specializing in dumb questions, but there was something about David that brought out the clumsy in me. Maybe it was his absolute and unselfconscious maleness combined with a sensitivity that most people would regard as feminine. It made me too much aware of my own lack of grace and wholeness. He shook his head.

"No. I tried that, but things never got down on canvas the way I saw them in my head. And I never could draw worth a shit. I gave it up before it made me crazy. Now I just keep old Malachi and me in pinto beans and blue jeans by selling books to the few remaining Tucson earthlings who are willing and able to read. I sell a lot of science fiction."

"Hey! Me, too! I mean I work in a bookstore in New York. Max's Secondhand Books." I was excited all out of proportion to the significance of the coincidence. It meant exactly nothing that David sold books in Arizona and I did the same two thousand miles away. But I needed an ally for the duration of the reunion, someone who wouldn't look upon me as a defector from the good life and the cause of all my mother's woes. David would make a good friend.

"Come on, Jenny Holland," he said, giving me a hand

to help me to my feet. His hand felt warm and calloused in mine. "Let's go face the dragons of River House together."

He led me up the slope to his motorcycle. I looked into the sidecar and saw a dark head of feathery fine straight hair and a soft round cheek the color of milky tea. The rest of the boy was wrapped snugly in a bright woven blanket.

"Isn't he hot all wrapped up like that?"

"It gets pretty windy on the road. Hop on, and we'll pull up in style."

He straddled the machine and kicked it into sputtering life. After a moment in which I wondered how I would keep from falling off without getting closer to David Mears than I was ready to, I climbed onto the pillion and put my arms around his waist.

"I can't believe you're Peter's brother," I shouted over his shoulder, small talk to distract me from the quivering of the machine beneath me and the lean, hard feel of David's body in my arms.

"Pious Pete," he shouted back. "He'd like to think that I fell off the edge of the world. Hang on! Here we go!"

The shuddering, jolting, racketing ride lasted less than a minute but it seemed to me like a year, a year in which I placed my life in David's keeping. It was an odd sensation for me, both the ride—I'd never been on a motorcycle before—and the absolute trust required of the passenger. I wondered how Malachi managed to sleep through it all. We pulled up at the foot of the front porch. There was no one in sight, but I noticed that an enormous station wagon had been added to the other cars parked on the straggly lawn.

"Hey, there!" David shouted. "Anybody home?"

"They must be around back," I told him. "Wendell was setting up the barbecue back there."

I got off the motorcycle, my legs quivering from the brief ride. David silenced the machine and got off, too.

The boy in the sidecar stirred. "David," he murmured, "are we there yet?"

"You bet we are. Come out and see how this bunch of your ancestors lived."

The boy sat up and stared solemnly at River House. His eyes, shaded by long black lashes, were exact replicas of David's but everything else about him—the wide cheekbones apparent even under the baby roundness, the small but finely modeled nose, the thin brownish lips—bespoke his mother's heritage. David watched his son sizing up the territory. I wondered if he realized how much pride and love his beard failed to conceal.

"What do you think, Malachi?" he asked.

"Are we going to sleep here?"

"For a few days."

"I like sleeping on the road."

David turned to me. "Malachi never makes snap judgments."

It was my turn to be subjected to the boy's solemn scrutiny. David introduced us as he would two adults.

"Malachi, I'd like you to meet Jenny Holland. Jenny, this is my son, Malachi Mears. Jenny is part of that family I told you about. A cousin, I think."

"Distant," I was quick to add, and again felt the flush creeping up my neck.

David gave me an odd look and then nodded. "A distant cousin. Family's full of first, second, third and twice removed. I never could keep track of it all."

Malachi clambered out of the sidecar and came over and took my hand as if he were claiming me as a newly discovered territory. "I have cousins in Arizona, too. They live on the reservation. I don't get to see them much." He looked to be about four or five years old and his voice was unformed and childish, but his manner and conversation were serious beyond his years. I wondered if he ever ran and shouted as other children did.

Fearn stuck her head around the edge of the screen door, took one look at David and Malachi, and drew it back in again. I don't think David saw her, but if he did, he chose to ignore her swift disappearance. He began to unload the motorcycle. I helped him pile the bulging saddlebags and bedroll on the porch. Malachi pulled his blanket and a knapsack from the sidecar. After a moment, Wendell came hurrying around the side of the house, followed by Peter and a tall fattish man in tan chinos and a red, white, and blue plaid sport shirt. Although I'd never seen this man before, I had no trouble figuring out that he must be David's other brother, Michael.

Wendell hailed me as if I'd been missing for days instead of an hour or so. "Jenny! Where've you been? We looked all over for you." He pounced on David and shook him over-heartily by the hand. "Welcome! Welcome to the reunion. I'd recognize you anywhere with or without all that face fuzz. You been gone from your folks even longer than our Jenny-girl. I see you've already made her acquaintance and isn't she a sweet little lady?" While still wringing David's hand, he eyed Malachi and reared back in mock surprise. "Now, who can this little fellow be? Somebody's been keeping secrets. I never got no wedding or birth announcements. You been holding out on us, young David, my friend, but we're all just as pleased as punch that there's one more of us to carry on the family name. Ain't we, boys?" Wendell nodded vigorously in the direction of Peter and Michael, who were keeping a grim-faced distance from the motorcycle. Behind the screen door, Fearn's white face shim-mered like a curious moon. Peter was the first to speak.

"Hello, Dave. Long time. You look . . . just fine. Glad to see you." His words came out as if they gave him toothache just passing through his mouth.

David sighed and, taking Malachi by the hand, walked across the few feet of shriveled grass that separated him from his brothers. "These are your uncles, Malachi. I told you they'd be here. This is Peter and this is Michael."

Michael, stone-eyed, spoke over Malachi's head. "He don't look like none of us. Bit on the dark-complected side, ain't he? But I guess you get a lot of sun out West."

"Uncle Michael," said Malachi, "you don't look much like my father, but I guess you're my uncle all the same."

David grinned and said, "Mike, you haven't changed a bit. You're still an ignorant shithead and I bet you can still arm-wrestle anyone into the ground."

Michael obviously didn't know whether to huff with anger or puff with pride. But the tension was broken, and Peter inserted himself slickly into the gap. "Dad's around back, rest-ing up from the drive over. Try not to get him too excited. He's been asking about you ever since he got here. Nothing like the return of the prodigal to perk up an old man's interest in life. To say nothing of another grandson. He really is yours, isn't he?"

"He really is."

"Not adopted?"

"Not adopted."

"Well, let's get this over with."

They trooped back around the house, Wendell in the lead, David and Malachi just behind him, and Peter and Michael marching grimly along at the rear. Fearn's face had disappeared from the screen door, so I guessed she had scampered through the house to find herself an observation post for the momentous meeting of Uncle Ambrose and the newest member of the family. It was an occasion I felt I could well afford to miss.

I sat down on the front porch, content to let my body soak up the sunshine and my thoughts wander over the events of the past two days. Fearn, who in the early hours before the dawn had wanted to call in the police, now seemed to have forgotten all about witch-faced prowlers and toppling furniture. Maybe it was just as well. Surely with so many of us gathered at River House, no prowler would dare try his tricks. Still, I wondered who it could have been. An enemy of Wendell perhaps; no one could live in a town this size without attracting enemies, and Wendell seemed more likely than most to have his share. It could be anyone from a business rival to an old and still-jealous suitor for Bonnie Marie. Wendell would undoubtedly have spread the news of the reunion around town. If some vicious practical joker bore him a grudge, disrupting the reunion would be a likely revenge. I wondered if Fearn had told him about last night's intrusions.

From the side of the house leading down to the ramshackle cabins came the sound of children laughing. It was a happy, uninhibited sound, nothing to be alarmed about, yet I craned forward for a clearer view of what was going on. Billy and Millie led the pack. There were two other children whom I hadn't seen before but recognized from Christmas cards—Wendell, Jr., and Sally. Malachi ran with them; apparently he'd been accepted by the tribe. And stumbling awkwardly behind, running two steps and walking three, not really part of the group but obviously detailed to keep an eye on them, was Peter's boy whose name I did not yet know.

They ran around the cabins, quietening as they peered into gaping doorways, then tumbling backward in a burst of squeals and giggles. They did this two or three times, then disappeared into the next cabin and became very quiet. I was reminded of Walter's discovery the night before of the signs of someone having camped out in one of the cabins, and of my own heart-stopping encounter years ago. I didn't believe that the children would find anyone lurking in the cabin; yet, apprehension drew me to my feet and I began walking down the slope toward the barren half-acre which in my childhood had been forbidden ground.

Before I reached the cabins, I heard the singing. The voice was piercingly sweet, a boyish soprano, and the song was yet another memory, this one of restless Sunday mornings earning enough gold stars to be awarded a Bible—"Onward, Christian Soldiers." It was accompanied by a tinny rhythmic banging and, as I drew closer, the soft stomping of small sneakered feet.

Peter's boy led the procession out of the cabin. He was singing and keeping time with a batonlike object with which he sliced the air in a precise pattern. Behind him came small Sally, draped in tattered green which fell from her shoulders like a cape. Wendell, Jr., wore a strip of the green tied around his head, its ends hanging down over one ear. Millie was next, daintily picking her way along and holding up the skirt of my flower-sprigged dress so that it would not sweep the ground. Malachi and Billy followed, each banging on a tin can, one with a bent spoon and the other with a rusty can opener. As they marched toward me, the sun bounced off their leader's glasses, obscuring his eyes, and slanted richly on the ivory handle of his makeshift baton.

"Stop!" I called out.

The singing stopped, but they continued to mark time to the tinny banging from the rear of the line. I reached out for the razor, but the boy whipped it swiftly behind his back.

"Give it to me," I said.

His jaw set mulishly. His eyes were still blinding circles of glass.

"Do you know what it is?" I asked.

"It's mine," he said. "I found it."

"Please stop that banging," I called out over his head. The other children broke ranks and stood eyeing me in a wondering semicircle. "What's your name?" I asked the older boy.

"Luke."

"Well, Luke," I said, "you may have found it, but it doesn't belong to you. It was stolen from the house last night."

"I didn't steal it," he mumbled. "I found it with a bunch

of old rags and junk. Back there." He jerked his head toward the cabin and the other children nodded in serious agreement.

"Will you show me?"

He deliberated, still holding the razor behind his back. Then he shouted, "Sure!" and ran back to the cabin. The other children whooped and followed, and I ran along behind them.

The cabin was the same one, I was sure, in which I had found the derelict or escaped prisoner so many years before. The stone fireplace held ashes, just as Walter had described, and beside it was a chipped enamel saucepan crusted with the remains of a meal of baked beans. Walter hadn't mentioned that, nor had he mentioned the kerosene lamp on the stone mantel or the jumble of musty blankets and old clothes against the back wall.

I groped my way into the cabin—it was dim inside even in the middle of a brilliant summer afternoon—and fumbled among the bits and pieces of clothing, searching for a clue to their owner. The children clustered just inside the doorway, silently watching and sensing something awry. I pulled a sleeveless sweater out of the heap; it was a coarsely knit green wool raveling at the bottom edge. Next, I picked up a pair of men's trousers of brown shiny gabardine. They were badly creased and discolored along the fold lines, but otherwise in good repair. From their size, I judged they had been worn by a tall slender man; from their style, he must have worn them a long time ago. There was a jacket to match; wide lapels, double-breasted, a stained lining of a slick sleazy fabric, possibly rayon. As I was about to put it aside and continue probing through the heap, my hand brushed the inside pocket and felt a bulge there.

I slid my fingers into the pocket and pulled out a worn brown leather wallet. The first thing I saw when I opened it was a photograph. My mother. Not my mother as she was now, but much younger. Sitting in a lawn chair under a tree. The tree had large white blossoms and cast a shadow over her face, but I could see that she was smiling. Standing by her shoulder, in deeper shadow, was the figure of a child. White-blond hair, a single frightened eye, and the printed pattern of a summer dress I once loved. Giant strawberries against a green background. There was nothing else in the wallet.

I closed it, put it back into the jacket pocket and turned

to the children. "Put everything back where you found it," I told them, "and go back to the house."

The girls quickly took off their marching finery, edged past me as if I might at any moment turn into a dragon or a witch, and tossed the ruined skirt and dress onto the heap of old clothes. Then they skittered out of the cabin and disappeared. Malachi and Billy hurled their tin cans into the corner and left, too. Wendell, Jr., lingered for a moment, curiosity shining on his round fat face, then he, too, plunged out the door and shouted for the others to wait for him. Luke alone remained.

"Give me the razor, Luke," I said.

"Razor?"

"That's what it is, you know. Give it to me and I'll show you."

"No."

"Why not?"

"Finders keepers. I found it, so it's mine."

He was an unattractive child, not only because of his thick eyeglasses. His face was lumpish and sullen, and his hair mud-colored and greasy-looking. He wasn't heavy, but gave the impression of being composed of pale dense flesh, suety and moist. His hands were soft, the fingers thick and clumsy. He began fiddling with the razor and seemed surprised when the blade sprang open and sliced his hand. The blood that streaked across his palm and dripped onto the earthen floor looked black in the dim light.

He dropped the razor and stared at his hand. The only sound was a gagging whimper that forced its way through his clenched teeth. I scrabbled through the heap of old clothes, looking for something to use as a bandage, at least until we could get back to the house and do a proper job of cleaning the wound. I found an old white shirt. Luke's natural pallor had become tinged with gray and beads of moisture were forming on his forehead and running down his face. He held his injured hand stiffly away from his side as if trying to disown it, but it shook with the same tremors that racked his body. The blood continued to drip onto the floor.

"Hold on," I told him as calmly as I could, and I tried to tear the shirt into strips. The fabric, old as it was, refused to tear. I snatched the razor from the floor. The blade bore a single streak of blood, thin and wet. I hacked at the sleeve of the shirt; it came away with only two strokes of the razor. I wondered who had honed the blade to such a killing edge, and why. The boy was weaving back and forth and looked as if he might collapse. I threw the razor and the remainder of the shirt down on the pile of clothes and began binding the sleeve around Luke's bleeding hand. The blood soaked through the cloth as quickly as I wrapped each layer over the one before. Luke looked once at what I was doing, then turned away and vomited. I'd no idea how deep the cut was, but obviously it wasn't going to stop bleeding without better care than I could administer here in the cabin. I'd have to get him back to the house.

"Can you walk?" I asked him.

He groaned and shook his head. The sour stench of vomit filled the tiny room. I was beginning to feel queasy myself and debated whether to rush outside and call for help or try to move him the few feet to the door. He was much too big for me to carry. Before I could do either, a shadow blackened the doorway.

"What's going on in here?"

Luke straightened up, shook himself loose from me and cried, "Uncle Wendell! Help! She cut me!" Then he fell insensible at Wendell's feet.

CHAPTER 14

"Of course, I didn't."

Luke had been rushed to the hospital, his cut stitched and bandaged, and he was now enthroned in a garden chaise at the head of one of the picnic tables being fed apple pie and ice cream by his mother. Wendell and I stood apart from the feast, now in its final overstuffed phase, discussing Luke's accident.

"Well, now, why do you suppose he said you did?"

I shrugged. "Who knows? Maybe he was mad at me for trying to get the razor away from him. Or maybe he was afraid to let his parents know he'd been playing with it. What does he say about it now?"

"Only that it hurts. And that he can't remember how it happened because he fell down and hit his head. Only the doctor didn't find anything wrong with his head, not even a bump."

The women had begun gathering up the paper plates and stuffing them into huge plastic bags. Aunt Tillie, who insisted that her wine be drunk from real glasses even if she had to wash them herself, passed by on her way to the house with a tinkling tray of empties.

"I'd like to get my hands on that young toad," she remarked. "Arlene's turning him into a marshmallow. Your mother's really enjoying herself, Jenny. She appreciates a nice bottle of wine."

I looked across the picnic tables and found my mother sitting in one of the rocking chairs that Wendell and Walter had hauled out of the house to supplement the benches. She was dressed in an ill-fitting peach-colored outfit of Fearn's and her face had flushed to an unhealthy purplish tinge. In her hand she clutched a wineglass; on the table, within easy reach, stood a bottle. I couldn't tell how much wine was left in the bottle, but as I watched, she refilled her glass and drank from it. My mother was drunk and getting drunker.

I struggled with the shock. After all, why shouldn't she take a drink? She had certainly passed the legal drinking age. But in all the years of my childhood and adolescence I had never seen her take anything stronger than a sip or two of near beer and then she made a face over it. Maybe Wendell hadn't written me the whole story of her decline; maybe he'd held back on the information that her flood phobia came out of secret bottles emptied in solitary nighttime rooms. I looked up at him.

He seemed just as surprised as I, but evidently not at her condition. "Well, I'll be hogtied and fried for breakfast!" he exclaimed. "I never thought your mammy would cozy up to a hippie like he was the Second Coming."

Years ago, I'd learned that whenever Wendell pulled his cornpone yokel act, he was really thinking of something else, usually to someone's disadvantage. But what he said was true. My mother, animated and flushed in her rocking chair, was directing all of her chatter and girlish giggles at David Mears, who was sitting at the picnic table beside her. During the meal, he and Malachi had sat at one of the other tables with his father and brothers, but now the old man was dozing under a tree and the children had followed Bonnie Marie indoors for their helpings of ice cream. I hadn't noticed whether David had sought my mother out or she had called him to her. As I watched, she refilled his wineglass and said something that made him throw back his head and laugh. I couldn't remember my mother ever having said anything funny. Not to me.

"There are no more hippies, Wendell," I told him. "David runs a bookstore. He's a businessman, just like you."

"Like me! Hah! You want to be a businessman, you got to sell something folks want to buy. Books! Hah! Why, Jenny-girl, in a few more years, there's goin' to be branches of Mears' Sporting Goods all over this whole entire state. That's because I find out what people want and I sell it to them. They want running shoes, I sell 'em running shoes. They want guns, I sell 'em guns. You wouldn't believe the business I do in guns. If they ever decide they want gold-plated knuckle-dusters, Wendell Mears will have 'em in stock. Now, you can't tell me that peddling books is anything like the kind of business I do."

"No. I guess not." I considered for a moment, then asked, "Wendell, would you sell me a gun? Or lend me one?"

I had told Wendell roughly what had happened in the cabin and shown him the razor. But in the haste to get Luke to the hospital, there hadn't been time to tell him anything more. After he and Peter and Arlene had driven off with Luke sprawled in his mother's lap, I'd gone back to the cabin and gathered up all the old clothes, the razor, and my ruined dress and skirt, and taken them up to my room. There I'd gone through the clothes carefully, searching for some sign of their owner. But outside of the wallet, which I'd already found, there was nothing.

While I was examining the clothes, I heard footsteps on the stairs and Fearn's voice angrily calling my name. I hadn't been much help in getting the meal ready, and I suspected that she was determined to put me to work. I crammed everything into the dark recess under the window seat and when she banged wrathfully on the door, I called out to her to come in. She did, at full spate.

"I don't know what makes you a princess and the rest

of us your slaves. You surely have the knack of disappearing whenever there's work to be done, and even if nobody else minds, I do." She stood with her fists planted on her broad hips, glaring at me.

"I'll be right down, Fearn. But first, tell me what you think about the things that have been happening here. Last night, you wanted to call the police."

"That was last night. Now if you don't mind, we've got about three dozen people to feed."

She turned to leave, but I ran to the door and closed it before she could get away. "Don't go yet," I whispered. "I want to talk to you."

"I've got rolls in the oven. They'll burn." Her voice had changed; it was quavering, low-pitched. And the anger in her eyes had turned to something else. Fear? Of me?

"What changed your mind about calling the police?" I asked her.

Her eyes shifted around the room. Her face was pale above the lilac-sprigged apron. "It was a lot of silliness. I didn't see any prowler."

"Did Walter tell you that my clothes were cut up?"

"Yes, he did. He told me what you told him. But he didn't see them. And he didn't see any prowler, either."

"Well, what about Millie? She saw someone."

"She did *not!* I finally made her tell me the truth. She knocked that bureau over herself and then made up a story just as I suspected. She does things like that when she's upset. And you got her frantic over that dead kitten. I'd thank you to keep away from her. Now, let me out of here. I've got work to do."

She made a half-hearted attempt to push me away from the door, but I held my ground.

"What about the face I saw at the kitchen window?"

"You saw it. I didn't. And neither did Walter."

"And the Halloween mask?

"How do I know? Maybe you threw it there yourself."

So *that* was what she thought. And presumably she'd convinced Walter that I was behind all the disturbances.

"And what about the razor? I suppose I put it in the cabin so the children would find it and Luke would cut himself on it?"

"You said it. I didn't. We'll find out when they get back

from the hospital and Luke can speak for himself. But I'll tell you something, Jenny Holland. I'm not going to let you or anyone else spoil Wendell's reunion. And if you're not out to spoil it, then you'll come down to the kitchen right now and pitch in with all the rest of us. Your mother's been asking about you and you owe it to her to try to make up for all those years. At least she knows how to behave at a reunion. She's making an angel food cake from your grandmother's recipe. And I've got to get those rolls out."

"One more question, Fearn. And then we'll both go down. Have you told Wendell about any of this?"

"Of course not. Oh, don't worry. He still thinks you're Miss Wonderful. Sometimes I think he dreamed up this whole reunion just to get you back home. I don't know how Bonnie Marie puts up with it. That woman is a saint."

I moved away from the door. Fearn went through it like a shot and I followed wondering if there was any point in locking it behind me. Whoever was playing diabolical games had a key to this room and probably to all the others. Could it be Wendell himself? But why? There didn't seem to be any rhyme or reason behind the pranks. And no one had been intentionally hurt. Luke had cut himself through meddling with something that was no concern of his. Those clothes had been put there for someone else to find. And the razor. For me to find. As I followed Fearn down the stairs, the thought that I'd been fending off sprang into full flower in my mind. The clothes, the old-fashioned, out-of-date clothes made to fit a tall, slender man, had once belonged to Raymond my father. That was the significance of the wallet with my mother's picture in it. The picture of my mother and me. Who else would have carried a wallet with that particular picture in it? What other clothes would have been folded and stored away all these years, only to reappear at a family reunion? Was not my father part of this family? Had my mother, in some quirky desire to have him present, brought along his old clothes and hidden them in the cabin? Did I dare ask her? Or at least show her the wallet and the picture and see what her reaction might be?

The hallway of River House reeled with the good smells of food cooking. All the rooms that we passed were empty; everyone was either in the backyard waiting for food or in the kitchen preparing it. Except, of course, Luke and his parents and Wendell who would soon be coming back from the hospital. Fearn plunged into the heat and bustle of the kitchen and made straight for the oven, which she jerked open. Her rolls were safe and golden brown. She scowled at me and jerked her head toward a mound of lettuce and a huge salad bowl. I picked up a knife and got busy.

"Happen I got a gun in the wagon. Never go anywhere without one. But what do you want with a gun, Jenny-girl? You planning to shoot up this reunion?" Wendell kept his eyes fixed on David Mears as if he'd like to use him for target practice.

"No. But we had some trouble here last night, and I'd feel better if we had something to protect ourselves with."

Wendell smiled down at me. "Trouble, Jenny? What kind of trouble? Fearn didn't tell me about any trouble, and you know she tells me everything."

"She doesn't want to spoil the reunion for you, and besides she claims she doesn't believe it happened the way I know it did." I told him then about everything that had happened the night before—the slashed clothes, the toppled furniture, Millie's "hairy old lady," and the face at the kitchen window. I even told him the whispered words that Millie had babbled into my ear.

He tsk-tsked and frowned and shook his head, but didn't seem any more inclined to believe me than Fearn did.

"There's something funny going on here, Wendell," I insisted. "Something ugly and evil and frightening. I'd feel a lot safer if there was a gun in the house. You don't even have to give it to me. Let Walter keep it. He's not likely to go shooting at phantoms."

"Walter didn't ask for it. I doubt if he'd want it, what with all the kids around the place. Bad enough Luke got tangled up with that razor."

"But don't you see, Wendell, that's precisely why we need to protect ourselves. To make sure something like that doesn't happen again. Someone has been prowling around playing malicious pranks. How do we know he won't turn dangerous? You'd feel pretty awful, wouldn't you, if that razor had been used on someone's throat? Where did it come from, anyway? Did you put it in the bathroom?"

Wendell looked staggered. "Me? No way! I never saw

that thing before it turned up out in the shack. In your hand. With Luke's blood all over it."

I started to protest, but Wendell held up his hammy hand.

"Just hold on a minute, Jenny. I'm not saying that you had anything to do with Luke's getting cut up. I don't believe that for a minute. But I do read the newspapers and I know that people who live in big cities have a tendency to get very suspicious-minded. It's only natural, what with all the mugging and killing that goes on there. Now this is just a little old peaceful town where nothing much ever happens. Could be you're making mountains out of molehills and seeing spooks under the bed. And you know where that leads. Straight to the funny farm. You just got to relax, Jenny. Relax and enjoy the day."

"Relax!" I exploded. "Enjoy the day! When some lunatic has been cutting up my clothes and has a key to my bedroom? Are you going to give me that gun or not? If you won't, I'll get one somewhere else. Or I'll get some other kind of weapon, a pitchfork from the barn or a carving knife from the kitchen. But I'm not spending another night alone in that room with no way to defend myself. I'll sleep with that razor under my pillow if I have to."

Wendell laughed at me. "Still a little old hellcat, ain't you, Jenny-girl? Your mama's looking at you like she'd like to take a peach switch to your legs. Well, come on around to the wagon and I'll give you what you want, and even throw in a few lessons on how to use it."

I glanced across at my mother, but if she had been looking at me, she wasn't now. She was resting her head on David Mears's shoulder and her eyes were closed. David was taking the empty wineglass from her limp fingers. Wendell took my hand and led me around the house to the front lawn where the cars were parked. He pulled open the door of the station wagon and the stale accumulated heat blasted out at us. The glove compartment, when he opened it, spewed forth an avalanche of road maps, hard candy, and catalogs of sporting equipment. Wendell reached in under all the junk and pulled out a gun.

It was bigger than I thought it would be and, when he handed it to me, heavier than sin. I held it cradled in both hands, running my thumb over the long barrel. It glistened at me in the slanting path of the late afternoon sun, blue as distance, black as memory.

"It's a revolver." Wendell's voice was hushed and reverent; he might have been in church. "A Smith and Wesson."

"Yes," I said, fingering the words on the barrel, the grooves in the cylinder where the bullets hid. "Why do you carry it?"

"Well, Jenny-girl," he was blustery and important again, "a man like me, a businessman, has to be careful. There's a bad element in this town, no use denying it, and everybody knows I carry real money with me just about every day. A man's got to protect himself."

"Did you ever have to?" I asked. "Protect yourself?"

"No, ma'am." He swelled with pride. "Because everybody also knows that Wendell Mears can shoot the spots off a polecat with its tail on fire. I get my picture in the paper every time I win the sharpshooter competition, and that's every year for the last five or six. I don't like to brag on myself, but I'll be glad to show you my clippings and the trophies I got cluttering up the place. Now come on down to the graveyard and I'll show you how it's done." He pulled a yellow cardboard box out of the glove compartment, checked its contents and slammed the door of the station wagon.

We skirted around behind the barn, Wendell stopping to pick up an armload of empty beer cans from the pile that was growing in the old horse trough, and reached the graveyard without running into anyone. Wendell set six beer cans up on one of the tombstones and paced off what seemed to me an impossible distance. He motioned for me to give him the gun, and I did, butt end first.

"It's loaded, you know," he remarked.

I backed off, snatching my hand away and almost dropping the gun before he had a firm grip on it.

"Don't be nervous," he said. "You're the one who wanted to do this."

He whirled around, set his body in a bent-kneed, straddle-legged crouch, his broad rump protruding like a khaki-covered sofa cushion, and fired off six shots that merged into a single crackling anthem of sound. The beer cans all disappeared.

I had resisted covering my ears with my hands. Now I

forced myself to breathe in the stinging acrid air that floated over the quiet graves.

"Your turn," he said. "Go set up some more beer cans."

I did as I was told, wondering if I really wanted to go through with this. Talking about guns was a lot easier than holding one in your hand and seeing what it could do. Scattered around on the ground behind the tombstone, some of them twenty or thirty feet away, the dead beer cans flaunted their open jagged wounds. I trudged back to where Wendell was standing, a smug smile splitting his round sweating face.

"Think you could do that?" he asked.

"No," I said. "But I'll try."

He showed me how to load the gun and pointed out all its parts. He spoke knowingly of grip and stance and recoil, and of easing off on the trigger instead of jerking it back and sending a shot into the wild blue yonder. Then he put the gun into my hand and marched me closer to the beer cans on the tombstone, cutting down his distance by half. The beer cans still looked impossibly far away.

He stood behind me, his bent knees pressing into the backs of my legs, and urged me into an imitation of his shooter's crouch. I felt ridiculous and clumsy. His hot breath tickled my neck. He held my arms extended and showed me how to cup my left hand under my right. The barrel of the gun wavered and sank. If I weren't careful, I'd be shooting into one of my ancestor's graves. I raised the gun, squinted along the sights, and pressed very gently on the trigger as Wendell had told me. Nothing happened.

"Just a little harder," he whispered moistly into my ear. "Slow and easy."

My hands were sweating and the gun felt as live and slippery as a fish that might squirm out of my grasp and flip over onto the grass, gasping for its natural habitat. It was an unnatural object to me and seemed to know it. I squeezed the trigger harder.

The explosion, when it came, knocked me back into Wendell's waiting arms and jarred me to the core. I was trembling, but my hand still held the gun. I'd closed my eyes and when I opened them was disappointed to see six beer cans on the tombstone. I hadn't hit any of them.

But Wendell was smiling. "Not bad," he said. "You

knocked a chip right out of that tombstone. This time, try a little higher and to the left."

"I don't know . . ." I began.

"Sure you can. You got five shots left, and a whole box of ammunition to play around with."

Again, he kneed me into position, and again I raised the revolver. I shifted it to my left hand and wiped my sweaty right one on my jeans. Then, without giving it a lot of thought, I gripped the gun the way Wendell had shown me, aimed it at the third can from the right, sighted and fired. This time, I kept my eyes open. And I saw the can on the end, not the one I'd aimed at, leap spinning into the air and drop to the ground.

"Good girl!" Wendell exulted. "You winged him. Not bad for a beginner. Do it again! Get the next bugger right in the gut!"

Wendell's excitement was contagious. I felt a stirring in my stomach, very much like the almost painful yearning by which I recognized a likely candidate for comforting in my Macy's three-quarter bed. I sighted and fired again. The beer can opened like a rose and went sailing off among the graves. The soles of my feet tingled from the shock waves and my whole body was suffused with warmth. I was beginning to understand something about guns.

"Jenny."

The voice came from behind us, flat and disappointed. I whirled around, the gun still in my hand, pointing. Wendell pushed my arm down so that the muzzle was aimed safely into the ground. Then he hugged me to his side and said, "Hi, David. Like to pop off a few?"

David stared at us, his eyes opaque and contemptuous. "Gun freaks," he said. "They sent me to find out what the racket was all about."

"Just a little target practice," said Wendell.

"So I see." His eyes met mine and I cringed at what I read there. "Jenny, they had to put your mother to bed in your room. No way she can drive back to town tonight."

He turned abruptly and walked away.

"No! Wait!" I called after him. "You don't understand."

I would have followed; somehow it was necessary that David realize I wasn't doing this for a lark, that I wasn't what he said, a gun freak. But Wendell held my arm.

"I might have known," he muttered. "We got some of
is kind here in town. Soft-headed. Pansies, most of 'em. I got
ne fired from the high school. He wanted to disband the riflery
lub. Can you imagine? Called us a bunch of gun-toting Fas-
ists. You gonna shoot anymore?"

"I . . . yes . . . no . . . it's getting a little dark. Maybe
ought to go see what's wrong with my mother."

Wendell shrugged. "Suit yourself," he said. "Seems like
he was just having herself a good time. She'll be all right in the
orning."

I didn't know where to put the gun. If I carried it openly
a my hand, someone, probably Fearn, would be sure to see it
nd ask questions. I wasn't even sure I wanted it. David's
ontempt had brought me down from the high I'd experienced
n hitting two out of three beer cans. It seemed faintly ridicu-
us now. And surely the prowler, whoever he was, wouldn't
e able to play any tricks with the whole house full of people.

Wendell must have sensed my hesitancy. He took the
un and said, "Run along, Jenny-girl. I'll bring this up to the
ouse later on." He smiled knowingly. "Wouldn't want old
earn to get all hot and bothered now, would we?"

I ran through the graveyard and back to the reunion,
aving Wendell to clean up the beer cans and the spent
artridges.

CHAPTER
15

We sat on the banks of the river and sang. Walter Proud,
turned out, possessed a fine rich baritone and a repertoire of
miliar songs everyone thought they had forgotten but remem-
red after the first few bars. A guitar appeared from the trunk
someone's car and David pulled a harmonica from his
ocket. When Walter led us into the "Tennessee Waltz," Bon-
e Marie kicked her shoes off and dragged Wendell to his feet.

Together, slipping and sliding on the grassy slope, they danced in the moonlight. The words of the song pierced my memory and I knew that once Raymond my father had held me high off the floor and whirled me around, dipping and swaying, while others looked on and brightly colored lights flashed. My mother wasn't in the memory and there was crying under the music but I couldn't remember why.

The small children had been put to bed, except Malachi who drowsed in the haven of David's long legs spread on the grass. David had ignored me since he delivered his terse message in the graveyard. I had tried to catch him alone to explain why I felt I needed the protection of a gun, but he kept himself occupied playing tag with the children, discussing education with Aunt Tillie and motorcycles with Walter, and having a mock-serious argument with his brothers over whether to put Uncle Ambrose in a nursing home. Although I lurked nearby and sent the occasional pleading glance his way, David continued to be unaware of my existence.

Wendell, however, sidled up to me before the singing while I was helping Bonnie Marie move the playpen indoors for the twins to sleep away from the noise and chatter outdoors. He carried a canvas zipper bag and made extravagant motions for me to follow him upstairs. Bonnie Marie laughed and said, "I hope you two won't be making a lot of noise in the house. The babies are cranky and need a nap."

"No fear," Wendell whispered. "Me and Jenny thought we'd look in on Aunt Elizabeth, see how she's doing, and tuck her in for the night. Right, Jenny?" He waggled the canvas bag at me suggestively.

"Right, Wendell. Be with you in a minute." I followed Bonnie Marie into the parlor and set up the playpen in front of the empty fireplace. The babies, one in each of Bonnie Marie's motherly arms, were alternately howling and taking greedy pulls at the nipples of their plastic milk bottles. She handed one of them to me as casually as if it were a sack of flour and bent to settle the other one down on the padded floor of the playpen. I'd never held a baby before; they didn't come into Max's Secondhand Books often. I was surprised by the weight of it and repelled by its sour smell. The baby was none too pleased with me, either. It goggled at me over its milk bottle, then convulsively spat the nipple out, threw the bottle on the floor, gripped my hair in its sticky hands, and screeched. I almost dropped it.

"Cut that out, baby," said Bonnie Marie. She took the squalling infant from me, patiently disentangling its hands from my hair. "One's worse than the other," she said by way of apology, "and they egg each other on. And to top it all off, even I can't always tell one from the other. Dwayne's got a birthmark on his left bottom cheek and Wayne doesn't, but who's got time to look? Come on, now, baby, hush up."

The baby hushed up as soon as he was put down in the playpen and given his bottle and a scrap of faded flannel to hug. Wendell beamed down at them for a moment, said, "Ain't they cute?" grabbed my hand, and dragged me after him up the stairs.

In my bedroom, the velvet drapes were closed and the air was hot and thick with the smell of too much wine taken. The Delectable Mountains quilt covered a small mound huddled on one side of the bed. I tiptoed around to look at my mother. She was sleeping. Her hands were closed into small liver-spotted fists tucked under her chin. She looked like an aged baby. I touched her forehead. It was slick with perspiration.

Wendell stood in the middle of the room mouthing words at me. I gathered that he wanted to know where to put the canvas bag. I tiptoed back around the bed and over to the bay window. The room needed some fresh air, especially if I was going to have to sleep there later in the evening, sharing my grandmother's four-poster bed with my mother's secondhand wine fumes. I pulled open the velvet drapes and raised the center window of the bay. The breeze off the river seeped into the room carrying the mingled scent of damp vegetation and distant wisteria. Below us, on the sloping river bank, the reunion was gathering to watch the sunset and toast marshmallows. Walter Proud carried a watermelon on his shoulder. I felt Wendell breathing conspiratorially behind me.

"Where do you want me to put this?" he whispered.

I opened the window seat and indicated the dark interior space. The clothes I had carried up from the shack were tumbled into the bottom of the cubbyhole.

"What happened to all the *National Geographic*s that used to be in here?" I asked.

"Bonnie Marie took 'em home for the kids to look at."

I nodded. It made sense. Somebody should be looking at them. At Max's, the aged *Geographic*s were most often bought by mothers of schoolkids with reports due on exotic parts of the world. Wendell opened the canvas bag and handed me the gun and the box of cartridges.

"I reloaded it," he whispered.

Behind us, a long shuddering groan and a creaking of the bedsprings made us both start and turn. My mother had rolled over in the bed and now lay on her back with her tiny clenched fists pressed into the pillow. A trickle of purplish saliva ran down her chin. Her eyes were still closed.

"Let's go." Between Wendell's breathy whispering and my mother's restless wine-soaked sleep, the room was intolerable to me. I fled across the ancient braided rug, not caring whether or not Wendell followed. I ran down the stairs and out the wide front door to join the other members of the family—my family—trooping down to the waterfront to pass the evening doing normal American family things. *What is wrong with me?* I wondered as I ran. *Why did my own mother, sad and helpless, evoke such a feeling of revulsion?* All she'd done was drink a little too much. I'd seen drunks before, even helped one or two of my wandering boy-lovers recover from weeping jags brought on by wine and pot and the terrifying anxiety of being young in a world gone haywire.

There was none of that here. Here there were watermelon and sunset on the river, people who *knew* that life was safe and good. They could accept my mother and her eccentricities because for them the center held; they prospered and their children flourished. If sickness came, they saw a doctor. They went to church on Sunday, to the dentist twice a year, to the barber often enough to keep hairy anarchy at bay, paid their life insurance premiums and were not disquieted. A heavenly reward would be theirs at some distant unthinkable time, but in the meantime the earthly rewards were sufficient. Cousin Peter, of course, knew the darker side of things but only in a business way. He could wash his hands of death and go home with a cheerful countenance and a new car every year. And David, David was different. He'd gone out searching and found something that pleased him. I wanted to ask him what it was, if he would talk to me, and tell him that the gun was not an idle whim.

The gun. But what if Fearn was right? What if the disturbances were of my own doing? Could I have slashed my own clothes and not known I was doing it? I'd had a bad knock on the head. Was it enough to make me do something crazy and not remember it? Had I really seen the horrible face at the window? I must have. How else account for the Halloween mask thrown down on the porch? Or did I do that, too? And if I did, where did I get it? I certainly didn't bring it along in my luggage. No. But it was convenient for Fearn to believe that I was the source of all the trouble. It suited her notions of good and evil. Home folks were good; the big city was evil. Didn't Jenny Holland leave the good old hometown behind and run off to the big city? What could be worse than that? Now she's come back bringing the taint of evil with her to trouble and plague the reunion.

No! Please let it not be true! But what if it *was* true? It could be that by returning to River House I'd disturbed some layer of the past, long buried in my memory, and the disturbance was prodding me to acts that were alien to my nature. So alien that I couldn't remember doing them. But that would mean that I'd been sleepwalking or moving in a kind of trance, and I didn't like to think of that. It was frightening enough to have fallen into a kind of semitrance before the bathroom mirror with the open razor in my hand. If I'd completely lost awareness of who and where I was at that moment, I could have done something irrevocable. Like slicing my wrists. No one else knew of that silent confrontation between me and the woman in the mirror. *She* could be the one causing the trouble. *She* could be the one that Fearn suspected. But *she* was *me,* and thereby rose the doubts. I vowed to keep away from mirrors and lock the bedroom door when I went to sleep. It might not do any good, but it certainly couldn't hurt.

I joined the group on the river bank. Walter had cut the watermelon and was handing out slices. Luke's sisters were prissily picking up twigs for the bonfire while Luke sat clutching plastic bags of marshmallows in his good hand and holding his bandaged one stiffly before him like a raised scepter. I accepted a slice of melon and sat down on the grass next to

Aunt Tillie who was dipping chunks of fruit into her wineglass and eating them with purple-stained fingers.

"Like some wine?" she asked. The wine bottle, corked, lay on the grass beside her. "I've got another glass around here somewhere."

Across the way, Fearn scowled and spat watermelon seeds over her shoulder. Wendell ambled down the slope with a sweating six-pack in either hand. The rest of the family formed an uneven semicircle around Walter and the watermelon, Arlene sitting primly on a plastic cushion with Mimosa coiled nervously in her lap, Uncle Ambrose installed in his portable wheelchair, his empty trouser leg pinned up over his stump, and the others sitting or sprawling about on the tough grass.

I declined Aunt Tillie's offer of wine and asked her, "What do you remember about my father?"

The question surprised her. She choked on a melon chunk, managed to swallow it, and groped for a handkerchief before she answered me. "Only met him once or twice," she told me. "What do you want to know?"

"Anything. All I know is that he died and what he looked like. I have two snapshots of him."

"They never told you anything else?"

I shook my head. "Not really." My mother's several versions of how he died didn't count.

"How old are you, Jenny?"

"Twenty-nine."

"Well," she said, "it's time you knew a thing or two. This crowd can be so damned close-mouthed whenever they're not being the biggest gossips in four states. First of all, you were what they like to call a premature baby, born five months after the wedding. Nothing puny about you, though. I happened to come home that Christmas to recuperate from a bout of bronchitis and a broken engagement, and I'd see your mother strolling you around town in a fancy baby carriage."

I felt a twinge of pride in my mother. She'd broken the small-town rules and flaunted the evidence in their disapproving faces. "But what about *him*?" I asked. "What was he like?"

Aunt Tillie sighed. "Ray Holland was about as handsome as they come, blond hair and blue eyes, a bit on the gaunt side, hungry-looking. Made all the girls want to take care of him. Your mother was no exception. Except that he married her. Your grandmother didn't like the idea very much, but she had to go along with it." She refilled her glass and sipped.

Across the river, the sun had disappeared behind the rolling blue hills, leaving in its wake a gaudy persimmon sky where a lone hawk wheeled in majestic circles, higher and higher. I wanted to soar with him, above the river, above the reunion, and look down on these small concerns. What did it matter the kind of man my father was? Would it do me any good to find out? Everything I had learned about him so far threatened my cherished notions of who he was. The man was dead; why bother resurrecting his youthful misdemeanors? And yet, my need to know overcame my yearning for detachment. The hawk disappeared beyond the hills.

"Why didn't my grandmother like the idea?"

"Well, honey," Aunt Tillie made a face indicating disapproval of ancient injustice. "Ray was a Muley boy and that's one thing you can never live down in this town. Oh, he was smart and presentable and ambitious. He wanted to rise above his beginnings. A lot of people held that against him. He'd been in the Navy and gotten an idea of the outside world. Don't know why he came back, but he did, and got himself a job of some sort and a car, and set out to break all the susceptible hearts in town."

"It was a Pontiac. A green Pontiac."

"H-m-m?"

"The car. I have a picture of it."

"Oh. Well, it wouldn't surprise me if that green Pontiac saw some pretty heavy action up until the time he married your mother. Maybe even after. I seem to remember hearing that he was picked up by the police once. A little girl was raped, or close to it, down by the freight yards and she mentioned a thin blond man and a green car. Apparently it wasn't Ray, but he had that kind of reputation. Not a rapist, but a girl-chaser and kind of mean if he didn't get his way. And besides, he was from Muley. In those days, the police always picked up the Muley boys first whenever they had a crime to investigate. I bet they still do. Anyway, it didn't make your grandmother love him any better."

"But he settled down, didn't he? After they were married? After I was born?"

I wanted to know more, but I didn't like what I was finding out. I didn't mind the Muley part. Raymond my father could have been a Hottentot for all I cared. But I wanted him to have been a *father*, someone who cared about me, not the town Casanova.

Aunt Tillie glanced at me and then down into her wineglass. "I'm talking too much," she said. "I suppose he did. I don't really know. I went back to Chicago after the holidays and didn't come back home again until a year or so after he died. You'll have to ask someone else."

"What about *his* family? Are there any Hollands left in Muley? Why aren't they here at the reunion?"

Aunt Tillie shook her head and drained her glass. I got the feeling that she was sorry she'd told me as much as she had. When Walter began singing "Sweet Betsy From Pike," she was the first to join in, loudly chanting the chorus and humming when the words eluded her.

I sang, too. We all did. We sang the persimmon color out of the sky and welcomed the first stars of the evening. A barge floated by downstream and saluted us with a blast of its horn. We acknowledged its passing by launching into "Shenandoah," but only Walter knew it all the way through and he finished singing solo. David lit the bonfire and between songs we gobbled toasted marshmallows and listened to Uncle Ambrose's tales of ancient floods that inundated Market Street, blizzards that buried the entire town, and the tornado that deposited a cow on top of the courthouse. It was a fine conclusion to the first night of the reunion. Tomorrow was Sunday and there'd be church for those who cared to go and sleeping late for those who didn't. My questions would keep. The night was too peaceful to disturb with ugly speculation about my father. I would put it all out of my mind and perhaps tomorrow my mother would tell me what I wanted to know.

It must have been close to midnight. The bonfire had burned down to glowing embers and Luke was whining that his head hurt and his hand hurt and he was thirsty and wanted some soda pop. Everyone was sung out except for Walter who softly started in on "Goodnight, Irene." We all listened drowsily, content to let the gentle night breeze and Walter's song drift over us. The river washed hypnotically at the shore. I could almost believe in peace in the bosom of my family and the triumph of simple pleasures.

The first shot cracked into Walter's plaintive chorus; the second reverberated into a stunned silence. The screams split the night like the howl of a dying animal.

CHAPTER
16

I ran toward the house, stumbling up the slope and tripping over unseen rocks. Behind me, in the dark, I could hear lumbering footsteps and heavy breathing. It must have been Wendell. Only he and I knew where the shots could have come from. The others asked excited questions and Fearn began to shriek hysterically about Billy and Millie and all of us being shot dead in our beds. The poodle, Mimosa, set up a frantic yipping. Above it all, the screaming ululated, inhumanly, mechanically. It seemed to envelop the earth.

I reached the front porch and pulled the screen door open. Wendell was right behind me. There were lights on in the hall, dim lights that sent grotesque shadows dancing across the walls and tall furniture. I ran to the stairs, pausing at the first step to listen. The screams were muffled inside the house, but there was no doubt that they came from somewhere above. I started up with Wendell jostling along beside me, trying to get there first.

"Better stay back, Jenny-girl," he muttered. "No telling what we might find."

I had no intention of staying back. If my mother had tried to kill herself with the gun that I'd hidden in the room, if she were lying there wounded hideously and screaming in pain, then I wanted to be the first one at her side. I elbowed Wendell sharply in the stomach, heard him gasp, and ran on ahead. The door to my bedroom—my grandmother's bedroom

—was closed. But the screams were definitely coming from the other side of it.

Wendell was yelling, "Wait, Jenny! Wait!"

But I couldn't wait. I gripped the doorknob and pushed the door open on darkness. It was dark for only a second. The flash came just before the sound. It illuminated a staring terrified face. In the split second before the bullet streaked over my head, I memorized the panic in my mother's eyes. Then all was dark again, except for the lightning bolts behind my closed eyelids as I hit the floor. The screaming had stopped. The room was full of thunder. Both my knees hurt where they'd hit the parquet before the rest of me.

"Ma?" I whispered. "It's me. Jenny."

There was a sigh.

From the hall came another whisper. "Jenny? You all right?"

"I think so. Can you turn on the lights?"

The lights came on. I looked over my shoulder to see Wendell's arm snaking around the doorjamb, his finger just leaving the light switch. The rest of him was safely out of range on the other side of the door.

My mother was slumped on the floor, her back propped against the window seat. The window seat was open, its plum velvet cushion tossed aside. My mother's arms hung limp at her side, her hands open, palms up. Beside her right hand, the gun rested innocently on the floor. She was crying. Not sobbing or screaming, just letting the tears run down her face.

"Ma," I whispered, "what happened?"

No answer but tears.

I crept across the floor, slow and easy, not wanting to startle her into picking up the gun again. After the shot reverberated into silence, the house became preternaturally quiet. I could hear Wendell breathing in the hall and the cautious whispers of those who had gathered on the front porch. The old house creaked and the floor trembled as I made my interminable way across it. My mother didn't move except to raise her wet face to the ceiling and open her mouth in a soundless howl. All the screams had been wrung out of her. Tears dripped off her chin.

I reached the gun after what seemed like a year of crawling across polished wood and braided rug. She made no protest when I picked it up, didn't even seem to notice. I sat back on my knees and called out to Wendell to come in.

"Is it all right?" he asked. "Are you all right?"

"I'm not shot, if that's what you mean."

He tiptoed into the room, awkward in his curiosity and more than a little ashamed of his lack of heroism.

"You shouldn't have barged in like that, Jenny," he scolded, trying to regain his natural sense of superiority. "You could have got killed."

I ignored him. The gun was still warm in my hands and smelled acridly of quick biting death. I got up and put it on the dresser where it lay incongruously amid the embroidered daisies and forget-me-nots of my grandmother's dresser scarf.

"Help me get her up," I said.

Together we lifted her—she weighed very little but her arms and legs flopped uselessly—and managed to carry her to the chaise longue. She still wore Fearn's peach-colored trousers and tunic, now wrinkled and stained with wine, and her body was still distorted by the bulky life preserver underneath her clothing. She didn't seem to be injured. There was no blood anywhere and her eyes, although red from weeping, seemed otherwise normal. When we moved her, she gave no sign of being in pain.

I sat on the chaise and took her hands in mine. They were cold and still and slightly moist, reminding me of the clammy yellow claws of dead chickens. In the hall outside the room, the rest of the family had gathered. I could sense their hushed expectancy. It was Fearn who crossed the threshold and put it into words.

"Is she alive?" Her face was strained and avid, and I knew she was asking if my mother were dead.

"She's alive." I wanted them all to go away. I wanted to be alone with my mother to find out what she had been shooting at, what had frightened her so badly. "She's not hurt, but she's cold," I said. "Maybe some tea."

"Of course," said Fearn. "Don't know why I didn't think of it."

She hurried away. Wendell brought the Delectable Mountains quilt from the bed and we wrapped my mother in it. I wiped her face with a corner of the quilt. She'd stopped crying and lay back on the chaise gazing at the ceiling.

Walter poked his head in the door and said, "Do you think we ought to search the place again?"

I didn't think it would do any good. If last night's prowler had returned, he certainly wouldn't stick around to be shot at again. But it would give them all something to do and leave me alone with my mother. "Good idea," I told Walter and he began organizing the men into search parties. The women still hovered in the doorway. Arlene, disapproving, asked loudly, "Is she drunk or crazy or what?" I motioned to Wendell to close the door. He did, and came back to where I sat smoothing the quilt over my mother's shivering body. His hoarse whisper echoed my own thoughts.

"What the hell was she shooting at?"

"Not crazy." The words blubbered from my mother's lips almost incomprehensibly. But I caught them.

"Ma. It's me, Jenny. What happened?"

"I know it's you. I'm not crazy and I'm not blind." As if to prove it, she glared at me, opening her eyes wide and then blinking back another rush of tears. "I wasn't even drunk. Only a little tired. That's all."

"All right. All right." I soothed her as if she were my hurt child, and she relaxed back onto the sloping chaise.

"I saw you, you know. Both of you. You thought I was sleeping, but I wasn't. I wanted to see what you were up to, so I pretended to be asleep. And I saw you hide that gun. Fearn thinks you're up to something."

Wendell huffed over and began to defend himself. "That Fearn's a troublemaker. All I've done is treat this little girl to a little cousinly attention. Nothing wrong with that."

"Shut up, Wendell." My mother's directness surprised me, and I realized I knew almost nothing about the kind of woman she was. When I'd left, I'd been little more than a child, with a child's view of the person who'd directed my life until then. I'd given no thought to the forces that had shaped *her* life. And I'd accepted the news in Wendell's letters of her increasing eccentricities at face value. My mother was a little odd but harmless. Every small town has it share of gentle loonies. They become part of the landscape, like the decaying courthouse or the legendary giant catfish in the river. And nothing is ever done about them until they become a menace. My mother, shooting up the night, had maybe turned the corner.

Wendell had retreated out of the line of fire and sat sulking on the bed. There was a sharp knock on the door.

"Come in," I called.

It was Fearn with a tea tray and a frown. She was followed by Bonnie Marie and Aunt Tillie.

"Where do you want this?"

Fearn was outdoing herself in ungraciousness. I indicated a small inlaid table beside the chaise, and she set the tray down with a thump that almost sent the milk pitcher toppling.

"Arlene wants Petey to drive them all back to Lexington this very minute," she reported. "She says she's not going to spend the night under the same roof with a crazy woman."

My mother turned her face to the back of the chaise.

Aunt Tillie, looking as if she'd like to smack Fearn, said, "Stop exaggerating. All she said was that if there was any more shooting, she'd just as soon not be around when it happened."

"Well, that's what she meant." Fearn's voice was loud and defensive. "And I don't blame her. And if I'm not being too inquisitive, what's that gun doing here anyway?" She turned her attention to me. "Did you bring it with you? Is it one of your famous New York City Saturday night specials?"

I glanced at Wendell. He and Bonnie Marie were holding a whispered confabulation seated side-by-side on the bed. He looked up when the pause that followed Fearn's question got too weighty to ignore.

He said, "Bonnie Marie's just reminded me that it's getting kind of late, and we ought to be driving back over to our house. Anybody wants to can come over for a swim after church tomorrow."

"I asked a question," said Fearn. She stood, scowling and mulish, in the center of the room with her hands on her broad hips, her feet firmly planted on the braided rug. "I'm not moving until I get an answer."

Wendell played dumb. "What was the question?" He obviously enjoyed getting a rise out of his sister. He succeeded.

"The gun!" she screamed. "Where did it come from?"

My mother's shoulders began to shake. I couldn't tell if she was alarmed or trying to subdue a fit of laughter.

"Well, I guess it's mine," said Wendell.

"Oh, you guess it's yours," Fearn mocked him. "Well,

if it's yours, you can just take it away with you. Haven't we had enough trouble without inviting more?"

"The gun stays here," I said. I wasn't about to let it go until I found out what my mother had been shooting at. If she'd seen the person who'd slashed my clothes and frightened poor Millie, I wanted to be able to stop him from doing anything worse.

Before Fearn could argue any further, David Mears appeared in the doorway carrying a dark bundle.

"We've been all over the house," he said. "There's no one here who shouldn't be here."

My mother raised her head. "From top to bottom?" she asked him.

"From attic to cellar." He shook out the bundle he was carrying and held it up for all to see. "We found this in the old coal bin."

"A sailor suit," said Aunt Tillie. She went over for a closer look. "Full of moth holes. Must be old as the hills."

"Submarine," said my mother. "Submarine sailor."

"In the coal bin?" I asked stupidly. "Are you sure it wasn't in the attic? I saw one up there yesterday."

David favored me with a scornful flick of his eye. "In the coal bin. Downstairs. I know the difference between up and down."

"David," I pleaded, "all I'm asking is whether or not there's another sailor suit in the attic. If there isn't, then somehow that one made it down to the cellar and I don't think it got there all by itself."

David considered. "I don't think there was another one up there. I don't remember seeing one, but I'll ask the others." His manner was still stiff, but at least he was looking at me with something one step up from contempt. His dislike was hard to take, but I could stop feeling like something that lived under a rock.

He started to leave, but my mother called him back. "Davey," she said, "bring it here."

He carried the dark bundle to her, while I wondered how she had gotten on such cozy terms with him. She took the bundle and cradled it in her arms, stroking and patting it as if it were alive and in need of loving. Had she ever held me so, I wondered. If she had, it was so long ago I couldn't remember

I couldn't bear to watch and turned away to close the window seat and straighten out the cushion. It was Aunt Tillie who asked the question.

"Wasn't Raymond a sailor when you met him?"

"Oh, yes," my mother answered. "Submarine sailor. Bang, bang. He's dead."

"Of course," said Tillie, "but could that be his uniform?"

"Sure it is," said my mother. "I saved it." She held up the jumper and poked her finger through a moth hole that would have rested right over the wearer's heart. "Bang, bang. I killed him."

"Don't be silly, Elizabeth." Aunt Tillie had spent too many years in the classroom. She spoke to my mother as if she were a giddy girl student unable to come to terms with fractions. "But now that you've brought it up, what *were* you shooting at? You gave us all a fright."

"Don't you be silly, Aunt Tillie." My mother cocked her head and grinned wickedly, her face creasing into a wrinkled mask of sly humor. She chanted, "Silly Aunt Tillie, silly Aunt Tillie, silly Aunt Tillie. I was shooting at the moon. Go away and leave me alone." She bundled the sailor suit beneath the quilt and turned her face, once again, to the back of the chaise.

I was sitting in the window seat wishing, like my mother, that they would all go away and leave us alone. Wendell prowled the room restlessly, while Fearn sulked in the doorway and Bonnie Marie sat patiently on the bed. The old house murmured with the activities of the others. Overhead, there were thumps and faint laughter; all the older children were dormitoried on the third floor and apparently were too excited by the shooting to settle down. David still stood beside my mother, gazing sadly down at her. He took Aunt Tillie's arm and said, "Let's go. Let her get some sleep. We'll talk about it in the morning." He glanced over at me, his face neutral, and said, "You'll take care of her?"

I nodded.

From the doorway, Fearn broke in. "What about that tea? Is she going to drink it or not? It's probably cold by now. I swear I don't know why I bother."

Placating words were on my lips, but I was interrupted by Wendell's discovery.

"Hey!" he cried. "Look here! Damn if it isn't a bullet hole! And here's another!" He was pointing eagerly at two spots in the flowered wallpaper, both to the right of the doorjamb and somewhat above his head. "Well," he smiled at all of us, "at least we know she was aiming high. But what was she aiming at? Must have been some kind of tall pink elephant. Or maybe it was a pink giraffe. Hah! Come on, ladies. Let's get going. Time we get home, it'll be damn near time to get up, and I got to usher at church in the morning. See you all there."

He prodded Fearn out the door, and Bonnie Marie followed, waving good night and blowing a kiss at me. David shepherded Aunt Tillie along behind them. At the door, he turned and looked back at me, a long, slow, questioning look, and then closed the door softly as he left. I waited a few seconds, then crossed the room quickly and locked the door with the key I took from the pocket of my jeans. My mother still lay huddled on the chaise, her face hidden, her body a mound under the Delectable Mountains quilt. I walked over to her.

"Ma," I whispered. "Do you want some tea? It's still warm."

"Jenny?" Her voice was weak and quavery, an old woman's voice. "Have they gone?"

"All gone, Ma. Do you want me to go, too?"

She twisted around to face me. "No, Jenny. Don't you leave." Traces of the panic I'd seen earlier returned to give her the look of a frightened trapped animal.

"Okay. I'll stay."

Fearn had provided two china cups on the tray along with the milk and sugar. The earthenware teapot was warm to the touch. I poured. The tea looked strong and overbrewed. I added two spoons of sugar and a generous dollop of milk.

"Come on, Ma. Drink this. You'll feel better."

She sat up and reached for the cup. But before she took it, her eyes fastened on my face.

"I shot at you, didn't I?"

I nodded and looked away. What can you say to your mother after a statement like that?

"Jenny, I'm sorry. I didn't mean to shoot at you. I thought it was . . . I thought he'd come back." She covered her face with the quilt and began to sob, dry hacking sobs that sounded as if they would break her in half.

"Ma. Stop it, Ma." I put the teacup down and stroked her tousled gray head. Her stiff curls had sprung apart like broken watch springs. "I guess I'm just lucky you're such a lousy shot."

She peeped at me over the quilt. Her voice was muffled by the portion of it, faded blue and white calico, that she held against her lips. "You don't hate me for it?"

"No." I thought about it. "No. I don't hate you." How could I hate the creature that lay trembling and half-crazed on the chaise? Even if she weren't my mother, I'd want to help her. If I knew what to do for her. "Come on, Ma. Let's get you undressed and into bed. You'll be more comfortable there."

She was like an unresisting doll in my hands. I pulled the quilt away and began to undress her. Her arms and legs were thin, the skin bluish white and puckered in places as if it were meant to fit a larger person. When I began to unbuckle the life preserver, she clutched it to herself with frantic scrabbling fingers.

"Ma," I crooned to her. "Ma, you don't need this. Honestly you don't. You'll sleep better without it. It's not going to rain tonight." I stroked her clutching hands and waited for her to loosen her grip.

"It might," she whispered. "You never can tell."

"It won't," I tried to reassure her. "Believe me. Anyway, I'm here. You won't be alone. If anything happens, I'll take care of you."

"That's right." Her hands loosened a fraction. "I won't be alone. I've been alone so long. But now you're here, and you won't let me drown. Will you, Jenny? Will you?"

"Of course not."

Her hands came away and she let me unbuckle the life preserver and take it off. But what was I promising? Not to let her drown? Easy. There was no danger of the river rising and inundating the second floor of River House. But she was drowning in something else, some fear or guilt about which I knew nothing. How could I save her, keep her afloat, if she foundered in her own deep waters? I doubted if even she knew what it was that prompted her to seek symbolic safety in the life preserver.

I tossed the thing aside and went to get my nightgown from beneath the bed pillow. She sat on the chaise, vulnerable

126

in nothing but her underwear. I'd never before seen my mother undressed, almost naked. I tried to keep my eyes averted; it seemed so much like a sacrilege. The secret parts of my mother's body were not for me to see. I shook out my night-gown and held it before me, a sheltering curtain between the two of us.

"Here," I said. "Put this on."

"Is it yours?" she asked. "What will you use?"

"It's all right. I have my bathrobe."

She took the nightgown. I turned away, pretending to straighten pillows on the bed and listening to the soft rustling sounds she made.

"It fits," she said. "It's a nice nightgown. Soft."

It was only a cheap nylon thing I'd picked up on Canal Street, but it was white and plain and I was inordinately glad that she liked it. I hadn't put much pleasure into her life.

"Come on to bed now."

I went back to help her across the room. She leaned on my arm, and that made me glad, too. I felt as if our roles were reversed; she the child, and I the mother. I wondered if she had once known the same kind of protectiveness about me as I now did about her. She lay down on the bed with a sigh. I covered her with the top sheet and went to get the quilt.

"Will you sleep here, too?" she murmured.

"Sure."

"That's good."

I turned off the overhead light, leaving on only the dim bedside lamp on the night table. She had closed her eyes and was smiling. After I spread the quilt over her, I turned away and quickly got undressed myself. Just as I was reluctant to see her nakedness, I didn't want her to see me bare. I belted my cotton bathrobe tightly and crept into the bed beside her. Her breathing was steady and calm.

I said, "Good night, Ma."

"Good night, Jenny."

I turned off the lamp. The room was dark except for faint starlight that spattered the bay window. The house was quiet. If any of the others were still awake, they were thinking their own thoughts or whispering softly to each other. I could hear the river moving, a deep, lulling, heavy rhythm of old songs and stories and cold, deep secrets. I closed my eyes.

Her voice came to me in the darkness on the edge of sleep. "Jenny."

"M-m-m?"

"I didn't tell you who came to visit me tonight."

"Who, Ma?" I wanted to know, but yet I wanted to sleep, to forget everything that had happened, and wake up in the morning cleansed and refreshed to a day that would hold no surprises.

"Raymond came."

"My father?" *No!* my mind screamed. I'm not hearing this. I'm dreaming. He didn't come to her. He wouldn't. He would come to me. Only to me. I've been waiting so long. My voice spoke coolly in the night. "But he's dead, Ma. You told me he died."

"Yes, I know. Imagine how surprised I was. Frightened. That's what the shooting was all about. I'm afraid I killed him. He looked so strange. I thought he was going to hurt me. Where is he now, Jenny?"

She gripped my hand beneath the covers. I wanted to pull away, tried to, but she held tight. I opened my eyes to stare into darkness, but my lids were heavy, so heavy. I could see nothing. There was nothing to see.

"Go to sleep, Ma." My lips clung to each other. I had to force the words out. "Raymond is dead."

Her words went with me into my own deep sleep. Or was I already sleeping and dreaming that she spoke? "Yes, Jenny. But he looked so young standing there in his sailor suit. Until I saw his face, Jenny. That's when I knew I had to shoot him. He'll stay dead now. You're safe."

Safe? From what? Drowsily, I pondered the question. Now was the time to ask her. It almost seemed as if she wanted me to. But sleep cemented my lips and cast a pall of blankness over a niggling tidbit of memory. I drifted into a dream of ladders dancing crazily under the apple trees.

CHAPTER
17

The tapping at the door woke me. It was still dark in the room, but the open window framed a luminous kind of gray, almost tangible. It must have been close to sunrise. I glanced at my mother. Her features were indistinct, but she didn't move. Still sleeping. The tapping came again, and a low voice called my name.

"Coming," I answered.

I slipped out of bed, pulling tight the belt of my bathrobe which had come undone during the night. At the door, I hesitated. What would I do if I opened it upon a young man in a sailor suit holding a straight razor in one hand, a look of eternity upon his fleshless grinning face? My dreams had been turbulent.

"Who's there?" I whispered to the locked door.

"David Mears. I need to talk to you."

I unlocked the door and opened it a crack. The night light in the hall revealed that it was indeed David standing on the other side. He loomed, tall and shaggy, dressed only in his jeans. My apprehension disappeared in a rush of gladness at his words. I needed to talk to him, too. He was the only one in the entire family I felt I could trust. I had no reason for my feeling, except that he was the only one beside myself who had completely broken away and wasn't bound by ties of blood and convention to blind himself to what was going on. Not that *I* knew what was going on. Only that there was something dreadfully wrong and that my mother was at the center of it. The others wanted to keep up the charade that everything was normal and my mother slightly batty. They could discount me as an unnatural daughter and a troublemaker intent on wrecking their small-town serenity. David was not entirely acceptable to them either, but he managed to ignore their disaffection.

"What's wrong?" I asked him, opening the door wider.

"Come with me."

I looked back into the bedroom. As far as I could see in the shaft of light from the hall, my mother hadn't moved and was still sleeping soundly. I pulled the key from the keyhole, slipped out into the hall, closed the door, and locked it from the outside. David watched me curiously.

"Why?" he asked.

I put the key in my pocket. "Just to be safe."

He took my hand and led me to the stairs.

"Where are we going?"

He put a finger to his lips and mouthed, "Outside."

I let him lead me down the stairs and out the front door. On the porch, he began whispering to me.

"After I got Malachi bedded down, I couldn't sleep. I tried reading for a while and I guess I dozed off, but something must have waked me up. The house was still, except for the noises that old houses sometimes make. Creaking sounds, mice running around in the walls, that sort of thing. I tried to get back to my book, but I was restless. It was about three-thirty. I decided to take a walk."

He was leading me down the dirt drive as he talked. I hadn't bothered to put on shoes, and the pebbles in the road diverted my attention from his story. It was just barely light enough for me to spot the worst of the sharp stones before I stepped on them.

"I walked down to the river and followed it for a while, down to where there's an old rotten pier falling into the water. I sat there for, oh, about fifteen minutes or so, maybe more, just listening to the night, watching the river, letting myself drift. It's good to do that once in a while, you know. I heard an owl hoot three times and then I decided to come back."

He stopped walking and I waited for what came next.

"It was when I reached this part of the drive. I looked up and—" He took me by the shoulders and turned me around to face the house. "—and I saw a light in that window."

I followed his pointing arm. It was slanted upward in a straight line toward the turret window. There was no light on now. His arm dropped.

"The turret," I said. "There's no one up there. It's locked."

"I know," he said. "I went up to the attic and found the trapdoor. There's a padlock on it. I felt pretty foolish knocking on the trapdoor in the middle of the night as if I thought somebody was locked in up there. There wasn't a sound from the other side. Do you know what's in that room?"

I shook my head. "I've never been up there. It's funny. I had a dream the other night. I guess it was last night, but it seems longer ago than that. There was a light on in the window. Like a candle. And there was someone up there. And then the light turned into a fire and the whole house was burning. And whoever was up there called my name. I was supposed to save everyone in the house. But I couldn't. That's all. I woke up."

David listened to my dream without comment. He continued to look up at the window as if waiting for the light to come back on. "It's right over my room," he said. "The room where Malachi and I are sleeping."

"And your room is right over my room, my grandmother's bedroom. Why did you wake me up? Why tell me about lights at the top of the house? Why not tell your brothers? Or Walter Proud?"

He took my arm then and led me up the drive to the porch. He sat on the top step and waited for me to do the same. I did, leaving a careful six inches of weathered plank between us. The sky had turned from gray to amethyst, and the river slid by between its banks like a broad rippled strip of silver ribbon. A cardinal flew out of the still-indistinct blur of willow trees, swooped over the dew-spattered cars parked on the front lawn, and perched inquisitively on one of the tilted poles that carried the electrical line from the road up to the house. He stared down at us, his scarlet presence glowing in the pale dawn. I was reminded once again of Miss Anna Grace's contention that cardinals outnumbered people in this part of the world, and I wished it were so. But there was only one cardinal, and the man beside me with his red beard and his golden hair, talking quietly in the still morning.

"When we searched the house last night, none of them thought we would find anything. Oh, Walter, maybe, was willing to give it more than a quick once-over. But then he got caught up in the prevailing attitude that your mother had been seeing things and that there wasn't much point in looking for a crazy woman's wine-soaked bogeyman. Do you think your mother is crazy?"

I stared down at the dirt drive, and then up at the cardinal preening himself atop the pole. Now that David was giving me a chance to open up and spill all the events and worries of the past few days and nights, I was reluctant to begin. There was so much I didn't understand. I didn't want him to think I was stupid or insensitive or trying to justify my own behavior, either here at River House or over the past ten years. Nor did I want him to get the idea that I shared my mother's illness, something I'd begun to worry about myself.

"Well," he prompted, "do you?"

I shrugged, fidgeted, and shook my head. "No. I don't know. She does crazy things."

"Sure she does." He took my hand. My first instinct was to pull away, and I did manage a feeble tug. But his grip was strong and his hand was warm, and I needed a little strength and warmth to be going on with. I let my hand stay where it was and even returned the pressure a little. With his other hand, he turned my face so that I was forced to look him straight in the eye.

"Look, Jenny," he said. "I spent some time yesterday talking with your mother. I don't think anyone's taken the trouble to talk to her or listen to her in years. Now, I'm not blaming you. I know you went away because you felt you had to. I did the same thing. But something is bothering your mother. She's frightened. It may be all in her own mind, or it may just be that she's lonely and getting old. I think it has something to do with River House. She said yesterday that she was glad to see it full of people and lively again, but that she'd be just as glad to see it and everything in it burn down to the ground. Sounds like your dream, doesn't it?"

"She thinks she saw my father," I blurted. "That's what she was shooting at. She thinks she killed him. David, my father's been dead since I was a child. Why is she bringing him back now? And shooting at him? At his ghost? Isn't that crazy? Maybe they're right. Maybe I ought to get her to a doctor before she really hurts somebody. What should I do?"

I didn't realize how I was babbling and trembling until he put his arm around me and pulled me close. Tears tried to come but I refused them. I couldn't, wouldn't, cry on his shoulder. I knew that he felt the tremors that swept through me; he stroked my hair and murmured my name soothingly. Little by little, I grew calm. I opened my eyes—I'd screwed them shut against his chest—and turned my head to see broad fingers of gold slanting across the weedy grass and the river beyond. The sun was up. The cardinal had gone about his business. It was Sunday morning.

I told him then, as briefly and unemotionally as I could, everything that had happened at River House since I'd arrived. I left nothing out. I even told him how Fearn had hinted that I was behind the disturbances and wondered aloud if it could be true, if the knock on the head I'd received when I fainted in the parlor could be causing lapses of memory. My head was still tender where the swelling had not completely gone.

He listened attentively, and, when I completed my story, he asked two questions.

"Do you believe you did any of this yourself?"

"I don't know what to believe."

"Do you think your mother did? Do you think she was up in that turret with a flashlight at three o'clock in the morning?"

"I don't think so. But I don't know. It could have been anybody. It could have been me, and I don't remember doing it. Maybe it was just a reflection of the moon."

"Maybe."

He stretched and yawned, and I was reminded that he'd had only a few hours' sleep. Although I'd had only a little more myself, I wasn't tired and I felt that I was keeping him from his bed. It was still very early. Maybe he was one of those people who liked to sleep until noon. And now that I'd told him everything, my own words came back to me like the ramblings of an impoverished soul trying to seem important. Like my mother. Like mother, like daughter. I got up quickly, my face flaming with embarrassment, and headed for the front door.

"Hey, where are you going?"

I muttered disjointed phrases having to do with coffee and Sunday morning and getting ready for church.

"Yeah," he said. "The coffee sounds good and I could do with a shower, but I'll give the church part a pass. Malachi and I get nervous in church."

I laughed. "Me, too. But Wendell will be counting noses."

I went into the house and David followed. We walked together up the stairs. On the landing, he paused and whis-

pered, "I'll be down in ten minutes for that coffee." Then he
went up to the third floor, taking the steps two at a time. I
unlocked my bedroom door, eased it open, and slipped inside.
My mother was sitting in the window seat gazing out the open
window.

"I wanted to go to the bathroom," she said, "but the
door was locked. I couldn't get out." She didn't look at me.

"Sorry, Ma. I didn't want anyone creeping in on you."
I wondered if she'd heard any of our conversation on the front
porch.

"Well, I'll go now, if it's all right with you."

She glided across the room, tiny and frail in my sleazy
Canal Street nightgown, and went out without favoring me with
a glance. I remembered from my childhood that she acted this
way when she was angry. It used to be scary; the freeze, the
overpolite manner of speaking, the eyes fixed anywhere but on
the object of her wrath, usually me. It used to make me feel
dirty, guilty and sick, whether or not I knew why she was
angry. Most often, I didn't know but that only made it worse.
It meant that I was stupid as well as bad, that I had done
something terrible but was too dumb to know what it was. As
a child, I had shriveled when she turned on the chill. Now, I
felt only pity for her weakness.

While she was gone, I searched for something to wear
to church. I couldn't wear jeans; an old skirt and blouse would
have to do. I laid them out on the chaise. The moth-eaten sailor
suit still lay there where she had left it. I bundled it into the
window seat along with the other old clothes I'd brought up
from the shack and my late lamented skirt and dress. If the
ghost of Raymond my father was prowling River House, he'd
be doing it stark naked. All his clothes were in the window seat.
I giggled at the silly irreverence of the thought, but stopped
when I noticed the yellow cardboard box of cartridges for
Wendell's gun.

The gun was still on the dresser where I'd left it the
night before. Not a good place for it. I'd have to hide it somewhere else. Someplace where neither my mother nor anyone
else could find it. The room didn't offer much in the way of
hiding places. The closet was shallow and bare except for my
few belongings; the dresser drawers were too easily searched.
The fireplace was a possibility, but I doubted if I would have

time to investigate the flue for a suitable ledge or niche before my mother came back. I snatched the gun from the dresser and stuffed it and the box of cartridges under the mattress on my side of the bed. When my mother returned from the bathroom, I had made the bed and was brushing my hair before the oval mirror that hung above the dresser, being careful not to look directly at my reflected image.

She was dressed in her own clothes, the white slacks and blue tunic that she had worn yesterday. The life preserver was noticeably absent. She threw my nightgown down on the bed.

"Will you be going to church?" I asked.

"Not like this," she answered. "I'll have to go home and change."

"Would you like me to go with you?"

"Whatever you like." She was still giving me the freeze treatment. I wanted to tell her it wasn't working, but more than that I wanted to find out why she was doing it. Was it just because I'd locked the bedroom door, or was it something else that had turned her cold and withdrawn after confiding in me in the darkness last night? She must have overheard David and me discussing her on the front porch. It was all I could think of. And I knew it would do no good to try to draw her out.

"I'm going to get dressed now," I told her.

She took the family album from the bedside table, sat down in the rocking chair, and began thumbing through it.

"I haven't seen this in years," she said.

"No. I've had it with me in New York. Grandma gave it to me when I left."

"Yes. She told me. She wanted you to have a link with home. She hoped it would make you want to come back. But it didn't work. It was one of her little tricks that didn't work."

"Tricks?"

"Go get dressed, Jenny. I don't want you to be late for church."

I left the bedroom, feeling about ten years old. My mother could still do that to me.

CHAPTER 18

The hot water wasn't very hot, barely tepid. But it was just as well. I'd promised David coffee in ten minutes, and there wasn't time for a long, hot soak. I was out of the tub in five and dressed in another three. When I got back to the bedroom, my mother was gone and the family album lay open on the floor next to the rocking chair. Not, as I might have expected, to the page where Raymond smiled and leaned on his new car, but to the pictures of my grandmother as a girl and a bride. I closed the album and put it back on the table, wondering why she had left it open at just that place.

I went down to the kitchen. David and Malachi were already there, and the coffee was perking away in the old graniteware pot. David presided over a pan full of sizzling bacon.

"Good morning again," he said. "Feeling better?"

I was feeling neither better nor worse, but I nodded and sniffed appreciatively at the coffee- and bacon-scented air. I hadn't known I was hungry, but now food prepared by David raised an appetite that was almost an ache. Malachi eyed me somberly over a glass of milk.

"Have you seen her?" I asked.

David nodded toward the back of the house. I looked out the kitchen window. My mother was walking back and forth in the tall grass beyond the deserted picnic tables. Her head was bent, but every few yards or so she would straighten up, shade her eyes with her hand against the morning sun, and scan the horizon. She seemed to be looking for something.

"Should I go out to her?"

He answered my question with one of his own. "Who's Louisa?"

"I don't know."

When I looked out the window again, my mother was bent over tugging at something hidden in the grass. I ran out the back door and across the yard. She was red-faced and sweating, both hands wrapped around a rusted iron staple set into a heavy round of concrete about two feet in diameter. She set her feet and pulled again, but the concrete plug refused to budge.

"What are you doing?" I tried to loosen her fingers from the iron staple, but she clung to it and shouldered me away. I went sprawling into the grass.

"Get help!" she gasped. "Louisa!"

"Who's Louisa?"

She glared at me over her shoulder. "I left her out. She's gone. I think she fell in. Or someone threw her."

"Fell in?"

Memory came. A dank, scummy smell. Darkened, water-logged boards that never dried out. Mud that oozed and squished between bare toes and small frogs that hopped out of nowhere and landed clammy on your feet. Spiders. And the hollow sound of pebbles dropping forever until they struck bottom with an echoing splat. My mother's voice. *Stay away from that well, Jenny! I wish you'd cover it up, Mother. You don't need it. You've been on the town water for years.* The dented bucket that went creaking down and came up leaking brownish water alive with small odd creatures. The rotten board that cracked and split beneath your weight, sending you tumbling fortunately backward into the grass and not the other way. The old well. I'd forgotten.

"Oh, Jenny." My mother blinked at me and let go of the staple. "That's you, isn't it, Jenny?"

"Yes. And that's the old well. When did it get covered up?"

She straightened up, smacking her hands together to remove the flakes of rust. "A long time ago. You remember. It was after . . . there was an accident . . . someone . . . oh, maybe I didn't tell you. You were too little."

In the hot morning sun, I felt a chill prickling at the back of my neck. "Ma. Who fell into the well? Who's Louisa?"

She laughed. "You'll think I'm an old silly. Louisa was my doll. A sweet little china-faced doll with a cloth body. She belonged to your grandmother before me. I left her out one night on the rim of the well. In the morning she was gone. We dipped for her with the bucket but she never came up. She must still be down there. I guess I had some kind of brainstorm from looking at those old pictures. Thought I was a little girl again, looking for my Louisa." She stepped onto the concrete well cover, stamped on it a few times and smiled at me. "No danger of anyone falling in there now. It's sealed for good."

I got up from the grass where I'd landed when she'd shoved me aside. No damage, only a slightly bruised rump. "But what about the accident?"

"What accident?"

"The one that happened just before you covered up the well."

"I didn't cover up the well. It was your grandmother who did that. She said it was all for the best."

"What was?"

"Why, covering up the well, of course." She moved away, heading back to the house.

I followed her, grabbed her arm, made her stop. She twisted, making squealing noises in her throat, but I hung on. "Who fell into the well, Ma? Was it my father? Is *that* how he died?"

Amazed! There was no other word for it. She stared at me amazed. And her voice was rich with the righteousness that was one of the things that had driven me from home ten years ago. "Why, no, Jenny. Whatever gave you that idea? As I told you long ago, your father went to California to work in an aircraft plant. Lockheed, I believe it was. He was going to send for us, but unfortunately he was drowned while swimming in the ocean on his first day off. A great pity. I think I would have liked California."

I was dizzied by this version of my father's demise. But I held on to her arm and questioned her further, as I would never have done ten years ago.

"Did you go to his funeral?"

"Well, no, dear. I was too distraught. And besides I had you to take care of. Anyway, they never found his body. It was as if he'd disappeared off the face of the earth."

Too many lies. When I was a child, I'd had no choice but to believe her. Or try to. But even then I must have suspected something false about what she told me. Had I asked her questions then? I couldn't remember. My mouth filled with the taste of sour green apples.

"He always loved *you*, Jenny."

There it was again. That was what she'd always said. In exactly that tone of voice. Sad, bitter, envious. What did she mean? What was she hiding? A thought came, so bizarre, so unnerving, so utterly at odds with reality that I tried to deny it space in my mind. But it came and it stayed. It was the old well. There was something in the old well, and it wasn't the doll, Louisa. It was Raymond my father, and my mother had put him there. My mother had killed my father out of jealousy of his love for me and hidden his body in the old well, and had lied and lied and lied about it all these years. And that's what was troubling her. No!

Fearn had called me an unnatural daughter and she was right. How could I think such a thing about my own mother? I had no reason to think it. I had no right. She told me lies about his death, but she was telling herself those same lies. It isn't a crime to lie; it isn't killing. However he died, she simply couldn't accept it so she invented distant romantic deaths for him. That's how the lying began, and she kept it up over the years until she no longer knew truth from falsehood, and her fears became imaginary ones. My leaving when I did probably didn't help matters, but the seeds of her illness had been planted long before.

But I had a right, too. I was his daughter and I had a right to know the truth about his dying. Why and how and when and where. No more lies. And only she could tell me.

"Ma, Aunt Tillie told me my father was a Muley boy."

"Aunt Tillie should mind her own business."

"Well, was he?"

"No. Of course not. Do you think I would marry a Muley boy? Even if I'd wanted to, your grandmother wouldn't have let me."

"Not even if you were pregnant?"

"Who told you that? Tillie, I suppose. Well, it's a vicious lie. I don't know why she wants to bring up these old lies. You were born a few weeks before your time, but that was because I fell down the stairs. Nothing wrong with that. It happens all the time. You shouldn't have come home if all you're going to do is raise up old ghosts."

She twisted away from me again, and this time I let her go. She plodded away across the yard, a small, sad, tormented figure, clinging to her threadbare fictions. I didn't know how to reach her. Last night, when she'd whispered to me in the dark, I hadn't wanted to hear. This morning, she was entrenched behind her barricades. I followed her back to the house.

David was dishing up breakfast, but I'd lost my appetite. Not so my mother. She was digging into hot cakes and bacon as if it were her last meal on earth, and telling Malachi the story of the time the oil barge hit the bridge and the explosion blew out all the windows in town. Wendell had written me of the disaster in lurid detail and sent newspaper clippings. It had been the biggest event in the town's history since the blizzard of 1911. I poured myself a cup of coffee and sipped it standing next to the counter where David was beating eggs into a grainy looking yellow dough.

"What's that?" I asked.

"Cornbread."

"You like to cook?"

"Like to, have to. I like to eat, and so does Malachi." He handed me a blackened baking tin. "Here, make yourself useful and grease this for me."

I took the pan and plunged my fingers into the can of shortening that stood open on the counter. My fingers left deep gouges in the white slick grease and when I ran them over the inside of the pan, there were wavy white trails against the blackened metal. Gouges and trails, wounds and scars. Everyone was wounding everyone else. We couldn't make a move in this world without leaving our mark on someone. My mother was right; Fearn was right. I shouldn't have come back here. I was gouging and wounding left and right. Maybe I should just go away today, while everyone is at church, and let them have their reunion in peace, without me trying to dredge up a whole lot of things that were best forgotten. David could take me over to the airport on his motorcycle and I would just sit there and wait for the next plane out. And forget about trying to find out anything at all about my father. David had been talking softly.

". . . and once they've all gone to church, I think I can get that trapdoor open if I just unscrew the hasp. That pan ready yet?"

I handed him the greased pan and washed my hands at

the kitchen sink. He spooned the batter into the pan, smoothed it out, and put the pan into the oven. I could feel the heat when he opened the oven door.

"So what do you think? Will you stay and help me?"

"What do you expect to find up there?"

"Probably nothing. Dust, cobwebs, bats, the family skeleton." He ran hot water into the crusted mixing bowl. "I'm beginning to doubt that I ever saw anything in that window. Daylight has a way of making spooks seem ridiculous. But I'd still like to take a look. Things don't get padlocked for no reason."

"My grandmother always said it was locked because the floor was rotten."

"That's a reason. But is it the real reason? That padlock is fairly new. Who do you suppose has the key?"

I looked at my mother. She was mopping up the last trace of syrup with a piece of bread. The house was hers. If anyone ought to know about keys, she was the one.

"Ma, that trapdoor in the attic, the one that goes into the turret room—"

"What about it?"

"Well, it's locked."

"I know."

"Do you have the key?"

She shook her head. "Lost it."

"Does Wendell have it?"

"Now what would Wendell be doing with it? I told you I lost it. There was only one, and I lost it a long time ago. That was a good breakfast, David. Thank you. Now I'm going home to my own house and change my clothes and go to church. I never miss church. Are you coming, Jenny?"

I was curious to see my old home, the house where I lived and grew up until I was nineteen years old. But I was even more curious about the room at the top of this house. And to be honest about it, I'd far rather have spent the morning alone with David at River House than with the rest of my family listening to sermons and singing hymns. I could see my old home another time.

"I think I'll stay here."

"Suit yourself." She rose from the table and carried her dishes and silverware to the sink.

"Just leave them, Ma," I told her. "I'll wash up later."

"That's a good girl." She looked vaguely around the kitchen. "Now, where did I leave my pocketbook? Oh, it must be up in the bedroom. I'll just go get it."

After she left, David smiled at me. "I'm glad you're staying. Even if we don't find any skeletons in the attic, we can have the place to ourselves for a while. You don't mind being left alone with me, do you?"

"And me," said Malachi. "Can we go fishing?"

"I think so," said David. "How about it, Jenny?"

"Sure. If you like catfish. Personally, I hate them. But I'll be glad to watch."

There were sounds on the stairs, many footsteps and bantering young voices. The teenage contingent from the third floor marched into the kitchen. There were five of them, including Luke who cradled his injured hand in his other arm and arranged his pale pieface in lines of suffering. His lips were pursed and his eyes wary. His two sisters and their cousins, the tall, gangly sons of Irene and Mike, walked cautiously, as if treading lines that would keep them from touching each other, but just barely. The girls held their heads high while their eyes made furtive forays in the direction of the boys. The boys kept their eyes fixed on their large shoes and swung their shoulders in a swaggering way. They were glad to find David in the kitchen, and crowded around him asking questions.

"What was all that shooting last night? Nobody'll tell us anything."

"Boy, am I hungry. What's for breakfast?"

"This place is haunted. I heard a ghost walking around last night." This from Luke, who snatched a strip of bacon from the platter and crammed it into his mouth.

"Sorry to disappoint you, Luke, but that was me." David ruffled the boy's lank hair and turned his attention to the others. "Virginia and Georgia, find some plates and set the table. Sammy, get out some eggs and start cracking. Eddie, go wake up your grandfather and see if he needs some help."

There were groans and protests, but they did as they were told. By the time the others came downstairs, breakfast was ready and the long dining table bristled with David's cooking. I'd helped, too, but it was David who'd done the job. Fearn bustled into the kitchen ready to take over, but David shooed her out again and made her like it. I stayed in the kitchen, sipping coffee and nibbling on a chunk of cornbread.

My mother didn't return. I assumed she found her pocketbook and left by the front door to drive home and get ready for church.

Arlene wandered through with Mimosa on her pink leash on her way to the backyard. The dog's painted toenails clicked on the worn linoleum and she nipped in passing at David's sandaled feet. Arlene said, "She's just a bundle of nerves. Neither one of us got a wink of sleep last night."

David smiled.

Over the rattle of silverware in the dining room, I could hear the voices of the family but not what they were saying. Whatever it was, it was causing Fearn to emit squawks of protest and David's brother Mike to laugh boisterously. I was content to remain in ignorance of the discussion; they could have been talking about me or my mother. David, too, showed no inclination to join the group in the dining room. He sat down at the kitchen table, where Malachi still lingered tracing fork trails in the syrup remaining on his empty plate, and started to eat his own breakfast. I refilled my coffee cup and sat down across the table from him.

I'd never known anyone quite like David. To outward appearances, he looked like any of the thousands of young men who'd slouched through the last decade, bearded, long-haired, casually if not sloppily dressed. There weren't many of them left anymore; most of them had exchanged their beads and jeans for neckties and safe jobs. David had found what most of them claimed to have been looking for, a way of life that didn't compromise his human values and personal dignity. He had to be well over thirty even though he was the youngest of the three brothers. And, like me, he was an outsider in this family. He, too, had gone away and lived in a way they couldn't comprehend, a way that offended them. But unlike me, he appeared content with himself and what he had achieved, and he seemed impervious to the family's scarcely concealed contempt. He treated them all with courtesy and kindness, while I longed to shake them out of their complacency, to what end, I wasn't quite sure. But the ties of family were making themselves felt. On the one hand, I was beginning to be afraid that I wouldn't be able to leave when the reunion was over, that I would be caught in my mother's awful web of loneliness. And on the other, I felt myself more and more drawn to David's generous nature and I dreaded the inevitable day when he would mount his motorcycle, with Malachi in the sidecar, and thunder away to the West. I sighed.

"They'll be gone to church soon."

"Yes. And they'll think the worst of you and me staying here alone."

"Does that bother you?"

"No. I don't know. They can be so filthy-minded." I was thinking of Fearn and her inevitable comments once she found out that David and I had spent the morning alone. But then I realized that I was entertaining about David precisely those thoughts that I found reprehensible in Fearn. I raised my coffee cup to hide my confusion.

"Maybe you ought to go along with them."

Arlene came back through the kitchen with Mimosa in her arms. "I think she's picked up some ticks. Someone should have cut that long grass. It's full of all kinds of bugs." She shuddered elaborately and went into the dining room.

"No, thanks," I told David. "I'll stay. Maybe I'll find time to cut the grass."

In twenty minutes, everyone had left. Fearn looked surprised when I turned down her invitation to ride along with them in Bonnie Marie's little Japanese car that had been left behind for their use. But for once, she said nothing. Aunt Tillie climbed into her red Porsche and roared down the road before any of the others had stepped off the front porch. Luke whined for a window seat in the funereal gray car and got it. Uncle Ambrose hobbled around on his crutches humming an old dance tune, until Irene told him he'd do better to get himself into a Sunday frame of mind, whereupon he shifted to a lugubrious rendition of "When the Saints Go Marching In." At last, they were all gone. David, Malachi, and I stood on the porch waving at their dust.

"Can we go fishing now?" asked Malachi.

"In a little while. We'll need some worms."

Malachi yelped and ran off to the rear of the house where the earth in the old barnyard was likely to yield some fish bait. David went to his motorcycle and, after groping around in the bottom of the sidecar, pulled out a khaki-colored canvas sack.

"Tool kit," he said, swinging it heavily at his side. "Shall we go upstairs?"

CHAPTER
19

River House was quiet with more than a summer Sunday morning gone-to-church stillness. There was a feeling of vacancy and relaxation after the sudden onslaught of visitors. The house was folding back into itself, retreating into its broken slumber of almost ten years. We passed the shadowy front parlor where the mantel clock ticked loudly in the gloom. It seemed to be hurrying time along, with each tick treading on the echo of the one before. Our footsteps echoed, too, on the hardwood floor and as if by common agreement, we went more softly through the hall and started up the stairs.

On the first-floor landing, I motioned David to wait while I looked into my grandmother's bedroom. I knew my mother had left; her car was gone. But she might, for reasons of her own, have doubled back to lie upon the chaise and read the pages of her life in the family album that had startled her into looking for her long-lost doll. She wasn't there, of course, and the album was just where I had left it on the table beside the bed. I was tempted to call David in and show it to him, show him the smiling photograph of Raymond my father and the earlier ones of my mother in her sad, ugly shoes, but that could wait. Lying on the floor at the foot of the chaise was my mother's life preserver, a gray arrangement of harness straps and bulky canvas-covered sections of cork. I was pleased that she'd left it behind and hoped that my coming home had helped her abandon her flood phobia.

I closed the door and we continued to the stairway to the third floor. This was a much narrower stairway than the one we had just climbed, and we had to go up single file. David went first. It was an inner staircase with no windows to lighten the interior gloom. As we ascended, the silence grew even more profound. Even the air seemed to thicken into an almost tangible substance, filling mouth and nose and pressing in upon eardrums to set up an internal vibration that thrummed beneath the stifling soundlessness. The flat slap of our sandals on the stairs came muffled through the dense atmosphere. I clung to the rounded handrail and hauled myself along, following David endlessly upward. A trickle of wetness crawled down my neck. I slapped at it, at first believing it to be a spider or an insect, but when my hand came away wet I realized that my head, face, arms, and my whole body were covered with sweat. It must have been hotter than I thought.

We reached the top at last. On the third floor, the ceilings were lower and the rooms smaller. There was light from dormer windows set into the slope of the roof at either end of the central hallway. But the thrumming silence persisted, and I swayed slightly as I struggled to follow David to the final stairway, little more than a ladder really, that led to the attic.

He started up, and I set my foot on the first riser. A weakness attacked me, a draining of energy starting somewhere in the deep middle of my body and sapping the will from my arms and legs. I sat down abruptly. It was odd. I wasn't dizzy. I didn't lose consciousness. I simply couldn't go on. I was aware of David crouched over me on the stairs. I knew I was blocking the way so that he couldn't get down. I heard his voice clearly, asking me what was wrong, but I could find no words to answer him. After a while—it couldn't have been long—the weakness passed and I got up. David looked at me strangely.

"What happened?"

"I don't know." I didn't want to admit to weakness. I was sure that David would have no patience with women who drooped and fainted. *I* had no patience with my own failing. "It was nothing. The heat. Let's go on."

"You're sure?"

"Of course, I'm sure." I hadn't meant to snap at him and tried to soften my answer by adding, "I came up here the other night and managed to survive. I'll be all right."

He turned and went on up the stairs without a word. The thrumming in my head was gone and the air had cleared.

My hair and my shirt were still damp, but the sweat that had been pouring from my body had dried leaving me cool and lightheaded. I was eager to see what lay on the other side of the trapdoor and wondered if it would all look familiar to me. I couldn't remember if I'd ever been up there. It seemed a natural place for a small lonely child to explore on boring visits to grandmother and play pretend games of princesses imprisoned in towers. But if I had, the memory of it was gone.

We came out onto the attic floor. There were closets here and oddly shaped small rooms with sloping ceilings all crammed with the dusty debris of generations. Dust motes swam in the air currents that we set in motion by our passing. David switched on the single light bulb. It swung on its cord sending long shadows swaying across the floor; our shadows danced while we stood still.

"Well," said David, "are you ready?" His voice was hushed, almost a whisper, as if he were afraid of being caught trespassing. I felt the same, although it occurred to me for the first time that, unless my mother had made other arrangements, one day this house, my grandmother's house, would belong to me. I was both pleased and dismayed at the thought.

"Ready," I said, loudly enough to banish all hesitancy, and walked across the dusty boards to the dim corner where the folding stepladder roosted snugly against the ceiling. I tugged on its dangling cord and down it came, smoothly and without jar or protest from its hinge and spring mechanism. Its sections unfolded and locked into position with scarcely any help from me. David went up, his canvas tool bag dangling from one hand.

I waited below, ready to be helpful, to hold the bits and pieces as David dismantled the sturdy iron hasp. When he called, "Here! Catch!" I expected him to toss me the first of the several screws that held the hasp in place. Instead, I caught the padlock itself. "Guess what?" he said. "It was open."

I looked up. David was swinging the trapdoor down and away. Through the rectangular opening a gray light filtered and I could see the canted roof beams that supported the ornamental tower. The view was blocked as David hoisted himself through the opening. I scrambled up the ladder and he reached down to help me crawl through the narrow space. We both found ourselves kneeling on the floor of the turret room.

I had expected dust, grime, and cobwebs. These we found in abundance. What I had not expected was the small table and the pair of tarnished silver candlesticks, each containing the guttered remains of white wax candles; the filthy pallet on the floor; the small straight-backed chair, its needlepoint seat frayed and tattered.

"I wasn't dreaming," David whispered. "I did see a light."

He got to his feet and picked up one of the candlesticks. I got up too and started prowling the room. There were other evidences of occupation. A coffee can half-full of cigarette butts; a yellowing stack of newspapers against one wall; a well-used deck of cards; a gaudy box that had once contained chocolates, now full of dried, gnawed apple cores. A stained china chamber pot, sweetly decorated with painted roses on the outside.

A row of nails had been pounded into the wall at one side of the room. They were all empty except one, and from that one hung a calendar. It was of the current year and the page was of the month of August. The date of the beginning of the reunion, the nineteenth, was circled in red.

My eye was caught by a flash of color amidst the grimy tumbled bedding of the pallet. I went to it and pulled it out, catching as I did a whiff of stale unwashed sleep. It was a ragged strip of green cloth, a limp remnant of what had been my new skirt.

"David," I said, "look at this."

He had put down the candlestick and was thumbing through the topmost newspapers in the stack. "Funny," he said. "Some of these are fairly recent. Daily papers for a week or so, then nothing for months or a whole year. What did you find?"

"This." I held the strip of cloth out to him. "It's part of the skirt I told you about. The one I found cut to shreds in my room."

He took it from me and gazed around the small uninviting room. "What I can't figure out," he said, "is how he could manage to lock himself *in.*"

"Who?"

"Well, I think you have to agree that someone's been living, if you could call it that, in this room. And for quite a long time, too, if these newspapers mean anything."

"Yes. Of course. But who is it? And why? And what was

a piece of my skirt doing in that bed?" To call it a bed was giving it a relationship to human needs it didn't possess. I looked again at the heap of dingy, foul-smelling sheets. There was a pillow, too, and on it I seemed to see the impress of a head. But what head? What kind of person could lie in such animal squalor? I knew that poverty could create far worse conditions than these, but there was about this strange room the taint of prison. Yet where had the prisoner gone?

Suddenly I wanted to be gone, too. I wanted to leave the room and lock it and never see it again. I knew that if I went to the window—there was only one—I would be able to look out over the tops of the trees to the river beyond. I would see the road curving away in both directions. And then I would feel a hand on my shoulder and I would turn and laugh because we had a secret hiding place, and then . . .

"Jenny! Jenny! Snap out of it!"

My eyes swam back into focus and I saw David's worried face hovering over me.

"Where were you?" he asked. "A million miles away by the look of you."

"Let's get out of here," I mumbled.

I scrambled down the folding ladder, careless of the knocks and bruises that peppered my shins in my haste. At the bottom, I called back, "Close it up! Lock it!" But I didn't wait to see whether he did or not. I ran.

Down the three flights of stairs, past the rooms that held today's suitcases and yesterday's memories. There was no one in the house but David and me. But I was afraid to stop at any of those closed doors to peer inside and find, lying on one of the beds, the displaced tenant of the turret room. I ran out onto the porch and clung, panting, to one of the fluted columns that gave the place an air of faded grandeur.

Malachi came around the side of the house carrying a coffee can.

"I think I have enough now."

"That's fine." I tried to make my voice sound normal.

"The man said to put some dirt in. That way they won't dry up before you get ready to use them."

"Good."

"He said the best place to fish is past the old dock where there's a big rock that's almost an island. He said he fishes there all the time."

"Who said? What man?" Everyone had gone to church. Who had told Malachi where to fish?

"The man who showed me where to dig for worms. He was right, too. I got a lot."

David came onto the porch. Malachi ran up to him and held out his coffee can.

"Look, Davey," he piped. "Can we go fishing now?"

"Where is the man now?" I asked Malachi. "Where did he go?"

"Back in the barn. He said there was a fishing pole in there."

I peeled myself off the column, ready to give chase. "Come on, David," I shouted. "It's him! Malachi, you stay here. David, did you lock that trapdoor?"

"I closed it, but you've got the padlock."

I unclenched my left fist. There blinking in the sunlight was the shiny steel padlock, its loop hanging loose in my hand. I tossed it to Malachi.

"Hang on to this," I shouted. "And stay right where you are. Come on, David."

I ran around the side of the house, not waiting to see if David was coming, too. The barn loomed, gray and weather-beaten, behind the house. The five-barred gate hung loose on its hinges and whole sections of the fence that had once enclosed the barnyard had fallen in. I dashed through the gate and up to the gaping door of the barn.

The door was wide and tall enough to accommodate a hay wagon heaped high with fragrant hay. But there'd been no hay in this barn for many years, no sweet-smelling mountains of golden grasses that would cushion you and make you sneeze if you climbed to the rafters and leaped. There was a wedge of sunlight that penetrated for perhaps five feet. After that, the barn was dark.

I stood in the light and called, "Come out! We know you're in there. Come out right now!"

Far in the depths of the barn, there was a sound. I thought of Wendell's gun, safely tucked away beneath the mattress in my grandmother's bedroom where it could do no harm. Or any good. Just inside the barn door, a rusty pitchfork leaned against the wall. I inched over to it and let my fingers close around its worn shaft. There was another sound behind me, and I whirled clutching the pitchfork.

"What is it?" David stood in the barnyard just outside the door, watching me intently.

"He's in there. Malachi saw him." I turned back to face the black interior of the barn. "Come out!" I called again. "Come out or we'll call the police!"

There was a clanking from deep in the blackness, metal striking metal, and I held the pitchfork before me awkwardly, like a broom. The barn could hold other tools—scythes, axes, even a hoe or a spade could be deadly. There was silence for a moment, then an uneven shuffling sound. I strained my eyes to peer into the vast dark interior. Beside me, David took a step forward and then another, crossing the boundary between light and dark.

"We only want to talk to you," he called, his voice deep and confident, almost seductive.

I moved up to stand beside him just inside the area of darkness. Once there, the darkness ebbed slightly and I could make out the vague shapes of horse stalls and complicated old machinery. Far in the back, a pale oval bobbed in the gloom and the shuffling sound drew nearer.

He came out into the light blinking and smiling, carrying a fishing pole in both hands as if it were an aerialist's balancing rod and he needed it to keep himself upright. He wore bib overalls, faded from much washing, and a plaid cotton shirt buttoned tightly up to his thick, short neck. The sleeves of the shirt stopped long before his wrists began, wrists that seemed to have an extra joint so that the hands could flop in any direction. His face was large and smooth and pink, disturbed by no trace of beard or eyebrows. The smooth pink skin continued over the roundness of his skull with only sparse patches of fine silky yellow hair lying in limp strands. It was impossible to tell his age; his eyes were bright blue and innocent, but there was something ancient in his stance. He spoke in a kind of gobbling bark with an earnestness that pleaded for understanding.

"Knew I'd find it back in there. Here 'tis." He offered the fishing pole to David, then changed his mind and tried to hide it behind his back. "I don't be thievin'. It's for the kid. Where's he?"

"Who are you?" I asked.

He eyed me and then the pitchfork which I still held

with its tines pointing in his direction. Then he licked his lips and gazed off over David's head to the sky beyond. I lowered the pitchfork but still held onto it. Whoever he was, his arms were long and strong-looking and his shoulders the size of hams.

"Who are you?" I asked again.

"Donny," he barked, still gazing off into the sky.

"Donny," said David. "Have you been in the house?"

That brought him back to earth or, rather, to an odd kind of pleading posture with his shoulders hunched and his eyes fixed on the ground.

"Uh-uh. I ain't *never* been in the house. Wouldn't go there. She told me not to, and I don't. Been a lot of folks in there, but not Donny. Donny don't go in the house. There's that kid. I showed him worms."

I glanced back out into the barnyard. Malachi was hanging on the five-barred gate, his coffee can balanced on the gatepost. He waved at Donny.

"Who told you not to go into the house?" I asked.

He sighed and continued to stare at the ground, but I saw his eyes shift slightly in my direction.

"She told Donny to watch. She pays me three dollars. She says Donny is the watchman." He raised his head and there was pride in his eyes. "So I do that. I watch."

"What do you watch for?"

He shook his head and his round jaw jutted stubbornly. "She says never tell anybody. I have to go now." He thrust the fishing pole at David and brushed past him into the barnyard.

"Donny! Wait!" David called after him. "Where do you live?"

Donny moved swiftly across the yard, his lurching gait making it apparent that one leg was shorter than the other. We started to run after him but realized the futility of questioning him further.

"He's frightened," said David.

"Yes," I replied, "and simple."

We watched him clamber over a broken section of fence and hare off through the trees that surrounded the family graveyard.

"Donny, the watchman," I mused. "I think I'd better ask my mother about her security arrangements. Maybe he's just supposed to discourage people from using the place as a lovers' lane. How would you feel if you were parked with a girl and found that face mooning in at you?"

"Could be," said David, "but we still have the question of who's been living in that room."

"Yes. And I think my mother might be able to shed some light on that, too. She and I are going to have a long talk. And this time, I'm not going to let her evade the questions or make me feel like a nosy impertinent child. Will you help me, David?"

"Is it time to go fishing yet?" Malachi had picked up the fishing pole from where it had fallen when Donny had bolted. "Why did the man run away? I thought he was going with us. He said he could show us a good place."

"Well," said David, "he had to go home. But we'll go anyway. Right now. Coming, Jenny?"

David was obviously uncomfortable evading Malachi's questions and I thought, This is how it begins, innocently enough, wanting to shield your child from an unpleasant fact. Was this how my mother's long career of deception had begun? What unpleasant fact had she tried to shield me from? Was it something I couldn't have understood, or that she couldn't bear to let me know? Was Malachi capable of comprehending that Donny ran from us because, in his simplicity, we represented a threat to his continued employment as watchman?

"I'm sorry he can't come," said Malachi. "He's nice. But kind of dumb."

"Yes," said David. "But he probably knows more about fishing than I do. Let's go."

"I'll come along in a few minutes," I told them. "If Fearn comes back from church and finds the kitchen a mess, she's likely to have a fit and lose all her Sunday sanctity."

David looked alarmed. "Are you sure you want to be in the house alone?"

"I won't be long," I assured him. "If I don't come in twenty minutes, you can send in the militia."

"I don't like it. What if Donny comes back?"

I laughed. "Please don't be protective. I'm not used to it. Anyway, Donny seems harmless and he's dead set against going into the house. All I have to do is stay inside."

"Come on, David," Malachi urged. "I bet I catch a bigger one than you."

David smiled helplessly. "If you're sure you'll be all right . . ."

"I'm sure. I'm used to being alone. Off you go, and if you want to find the rock in the river, just go downstream past the old dock a little ways. You can't miss it. I'll meet you there. Good luck."

I watched them go off, tall golden David and small dark Malachi, father and son. David carried the pole and Malachi retrieved his coffee can from the gatepost. I found myself wondering about Malachi's mother, how she could have left him, and David, and what reason she had for going off. And above all, how she could have neglected to marry David who seemed to me the sanest, most decent sort of man I'd ever encountered. He'd said nothing to me about Malachi's mother except that she was an Indian and that they weren't married. I began to invent reasons for their present state—her people objected to David for a son-in-law; she was already married to one of her tribe; she intended to marry as soon as she could get her family's consent or a divorce, whichever applied; she had died and left David with the infant Malachi.

Nuts, I said to myself, you read too many books, Jenny Holland. Life isn't nearly as romantic as the stories you stuff your head with. Let's go wash dishes and get back to grim reality.

Grim reality manifested itself in an array of sticky, syrupy plates with an army of flies buzzing in happy possession. I immersed myself up to the elbows in hot water and detergent and methodically disposed of both dishes and flies, all the while indulging myself in a slightly off-key warbling of all the hymns I could remember from childhood. It was, after all, Sunday morning and though I was neglecting church, I gained great moral superiority over the dishpan by fervently raising my voice in praise.

I was just wringing out the dishcloth when I heard a tapping on the back door.

Well, now. I wasn't expecting any visitors. Members of the family who'd defected from church wouldn't bother to knock. Nor would David if he'd returned from the river. Door-to-door salesmen wouldn't be making their rounds on Sunday morning and River House was a bit off the beaten path even for Jehovah's Witnesses who seemed fully capable of knocking on every heathen door under the sun. In the city, they always found me sleep-stunned and irritable. I peered through the kitchen window over the sink, but could see only a small section of the back porch. The rapping came again.

I dried my hands and went to the door. Through the glass panes, a pink oval bobbed and smirked. It was only Donny, returned for some arcane reason of his own. I swung the inner door open and pushed the screen door ajar, conscious of an obscure feeling of relief.

"Hi," I said. "Come on in."

He wagged his head, grinning. "Nope," he said. "I brought that. For you."

"That" was a bushel basket brimming with ripe tomatoes. It sat on the porch behind him, and he stood back to regard it with admiration.

"Picked 'em my own self."

The pungent fragrance of the tomatoes drifted into the house, and a few of the flies that had escaped drowning or swatting buzzed out to investigate. I stepped out onto the porch myself and bent to examine Donny's gift. As I did so, I sensed a small furtive movement behind me. I turned in time to see Donny whip his hands behind his back. What had he been about to do? Grab me? And then what? I decided to pretend I hadn't noticed.

"Thank you, Donny. Will you carry them into the kitchen for me?"

"Nope." He stood there grinning.

Well. All right. The tomatoes could stay on the porch. And if Donny wouldn't come in, I could stay on the porch, too, long enough to get some more information out of him. If that was possible.

I let the screen door slam and went to perch on the porch railing. Donny didn't move except to let his hands swing loosely at his sides. I looked him over, wondering how to begin. He shifted uncomfortably on his huge feet and grinned ever wider. At first I had thought him to be a boy, an outsized feeble-minded, but basically good-natured teenage boy. But his grin showed me teeth that were stained brown, probably from years of chewing tobacco, and I realized that Donny was closer to my own age.

"Where do you live, Donny?" I asked.

He waved vaguely westward and answered, "On the farm."

I knew that years before there had been small farms fringing the river bank. My mother and I had sometimes driven out that way to buy fresh sweet corn from roadside stands, and we'd always gotten our Halloween pumpkins there. Presumably at least one of those farms had defied the development spreading from the highway of which Wendell was so proud, and was still in existence.

"Do you live alone?"

"Nope. Ma and Grandpa. Ma and me does the work. Grandpa just sits."

I had a swift mental image of a grizzled shrunken version of Donny sitting in senile stupefaction outside a tarpaper shack, while a raddled woman in a sunbonnet hoed endless rows beneath a broiling sun. I banished the image; no sense in growing sentimental over what was undoubtedly a cliché brought on by early reading of Erskine Caldwell.

"What's your last name, Donny?"

He gazed at me as if the question made no sense.

"Name's Donny."

"Yes, but don't you have another name? A family name?"

He hung his head. The grin had vanished and his pink face grew even pinker. I had obviously touched some chord of shame. When he spoke, I could barely hear him.

"Ma calls me Dummy."

"Oh. I'm sorry. I didn't mean that." I felt my own face growing red in sympathy with his embarrassment. I offered what I could by way of recompense. "My name is Jenny."

"I know that. She told me."

"Who? Your mother?"

"Nope." He laughed, clutching his stomach and bending double under a tidal wave of mirth, as if I'd said the funniest thing imaginable. "Not her!"

"Who then?"

"The lady. The one who comes here."

Now we were getting somewhere. The "lady" was obviously my mother, and for some reason, she'd been discussing me with Donny.

"What did she tell you about me?"

"She said . . . she said you was pretty." The sudden gleam in his bright blue eyes told me he agreed.

"What else did she say?"

"She said you was too smart for your own good."

Did she indeed? And what was *that* all about? In a way it was a compliment. My mother had never thought highly of all my book reading, a vice I'd acquired early in life and indulged in to the detriment of my social life. I'd suffered through countless lectures on the general topic of "No man wants a bookworm for a wife," with variations ranging from "You'll ruin your eyesight," to "I don't want you getting ideas."

Well, Donny certainly wasn't one to "get ideas," but I still didn't understand why he'd been posted as watchman or what he was supposed to watch for.

"How long have you been watching the house, Donny?"

He pondered that and finally struggled through to an answer. "Long time."

"How long? Weeks? Months? Years?" I was beginning to grow a little impatient.

Another long silence, and then, "Since when the house burned down."

"Whose house? Yours?"

He nodded. "Then she give us the trailer."

"Who did? The lady?"

Another nod, and the grin was back in place. "It's nice. Got an indoor privy and everything. Only Ma won't let us use it."

We seemed to be veering off the track. A house-proud or trailer-proud, Donny wasn't getting me any closer to the answers I craved. One more try, and then I'd have to be getting down to the river where I hoped David and Malachi had failed to catch a single catfish. I hated the sight of the beasts, slick and vicious-looking with their long mouths and their stiff pointed whiskers.

"What have you been watching for?"

I'd overstepped his boundaries. His grin vanished for good to be replaced by a sullen shifty-eyed expression, one that I would hate to encounter in a dark forest at midnight.

"I be goin' now," he muttered, and did so at once, stomping down off the porch and making his way unevenly across the yard. I watched him go, wondering if I would be favored with yet another opportunity to question him. He seemed willing enough to part with information, such as he had or such as it seemed to him, up to a point. Interpretation of the information was more or less up to the hearer, and I still didn't know what to make of most of it. On an impulse, I shouted after him. "Donny! Thanks for the tomatoes."

He stopped dead, turned around and shouted back at me, "You're welcome. Don't be afraid. I be watchin'." Then he scurried on his way.

CHAPTER
20

When I reached the rock in the river, about a quarter of a mile from the house, there was no sign of the fishermen. Malachi's coffee can stood on the grassy bank, the damp black earth within it squirming with earthworms. The fishing pole lay beside it. The rock rose from the swirling water like the great gray back of a prehistoric beast. It was possible to reach the rock by leaping from the bank if you were long-legged and spring-heeled enough and didn't mind the chance that you might miss your footing and tumble into the river. You could also wade across if the river was low and you'd already resigned yourself to getting wet. When I was in high school and we'd visit my grandmother, I'd often used the rock for sunbathing.

It was funny how so many memories of my younger days were tied up with visits to my grandmother. We must have spent a lot of time at River House, my mother and I. By comparison, I couldn't remember much at all about the house in town where we had lived since I was born. Oh, I knew where it was all right, and how the rooms were furnished, but I couldn't remember ever *doing* anything there. All the important things seemed to happen at my grandmother's house. And always the two of them sat huddled over the kitchen table, sipping tea and talking in low voices. And sending me away to play, but not too far and don't get dirty.

The midmorning sun gleamed like a slice of lemon in a pale lemonade sky. It was hot and growing hotter, and somewhere upstream, closer to town and out of sight around the curving point of land, the distant buzz of speedboats argued fretfully of Sunday morning water-skiing. I wondered whether I would find old schoolmates skimming up and down the river and if they would remember me. But of course they would. According to Fearn, I'd been a nine-days' scandal when I left, and even though there'd probably been other and more interesting scandals since then, a small town never forgets. Well, I wasn't about to start renewing old acquaintances; I'd never been very popular in school and had no really close friends.

I wondered where David and Malachi had gone. Probably off exploring, soon to return with a giant toadstool or a couple of chipped flint arrowheads. Kids were always finding arrowheads along the river, but no one really knew what had happened to the people who'd made them. There were ancient mounds a few miles away, and the public library in town cherished some dusty relics in a locked glass case. But the mound people themselves had disappeared long before the Shawnees and the first settlers came to quarrel over the rich river valley. Now it was all changed, but here in this quiet spot, if you closed your ears to the buzzing speedboats and squinted your eyes against the high white jet trails that connected distant cities, you could imagine yourself in another, purer time. I unbuckled my sandals, left them side-by-side on the grass, and leaped for the rock.

I made it. The tail of my skirt got soaked as it trailed behind me when I landed in a crouch. The smooth surface of the rock was warm to my bare feet and hard beneath my body as I lay on my stomach and cradled my head in the curve of one arm. I let the other drift over the side of the rock until my fingers touched water. Cool and living, the river soothed my hand like a poultice that could cure all woes. I closed my eyes.

"Jenny!"

The voice calling my name was more a whisper inside my head than a sound from outside. I told myself I was imagining it and didn't look up.

"Jenny!"

It was a strange voice, not David's, and certainly not Malachi's. Nor was it poor Donny's distinctive bark. I opened my eyes, resentful of the intrusion, and without raising my head looked at the grassy shore just a few feet away.

"Jenny!"

There was no one on the bank, at least not in the clearing that rimmed the water. Further back, the trees grew thickly, saplings struggling for space and light among their taller, older fellows, the ground a tangle of creeping vines. I raised myself up on my elbows and stared at the green wall of vegetation. Nothing moved. There was no wind to ruffle the leaves. If there were small animals in the thicket, they were keeping very still. The sun shone in my eyes, making it difficult to keep an unremitting lookout. I blinked and wiped way the moisture from my eyes with the back of my hand.

"Jenny!"

"Who's there?"

"JennyJennyJennyJennyJenny!"

The voice was exultant, crazed, rising in pitch, terrifying. Crouched on the rock, I realized I had nowhere to go. If I leaped ashore, I would be leaping closer to the source of the voice. To go the other way meant throwing myself into the swift current of the river. I could swim but hadn't for many years, and I'd never tested myself against anything deeper or stronger than the old walled-off swimming area near the public campgrounds on the other side of town.

"Jenny! Don't be afraid. I want to show you something."

The voice was wheedling now, coaxing, and even more frightening than before. But still I couldn't see where it was coming from. There had to be someone hiding among the trees, someone who knew me, some member of the family. But the voice meant nothing to me. It was grating, harsh, almost metallic, and unlike any I had ever heard before. I crouched on the rock wondering which way to jump, if it came to the point that I had to jump at all.

I'd forgotten the distant buzzing of the speedboats, unseen around the bend of the river. But one of them had apparently detached itself from the swarm, its motor sounding nearer and its white prow nosing its way past the point of land where the old dock sagged into the stream. It was still too far away for me to distinguish its passengers, but I stood up on the rock and waved and shouted at them. It was fairly ridiculous to have to be rescued from a rock within a few feet of land, but behind me the voice cried my name again, this time oozing disappointment.

The boat was veering in my direction. I took one last look into the thicket. Leaves were fluttering, branches swaying. If there was any sound it was drowned in the roar of the approaching boat. I caught a glimpse of something white moving through the undergrowth. Then it was gone and the leaves lapsed into stillness. The boat pulled up near the rock and its motor sputtered and died.

"Hi, Jenny."

Malachi was at the wheel looking dazed and delighted. Wendell lounged beside him, ready to lend a helping hand to the steering. In the stern, David sprawled, loose-limbed and barechested, his shirt wrapped around his head like a turban.

"Can we give you a lift, lady?" Wendell guffawed at his joke and tried to improve it by adding, "I don't usually pick up hitchhikers."

David sat up when he saw my face and mouthed, "What's wrong?"

I shook my head and grabbed for the rope Wendell tossed me. He pulled the boat closer to the rock and helped me clamber aboard. "Why aren't you in church?" I chivvied him. "I thought you'd be shoving the collection plate under all those holy noses."

"Well, I should be," Wendell drawled, "and that's a fact. But it looked like a good day for talking to God from this here pew on the river." He slapped the side of the boat. "So I headed on down this way and found these two river rats just about to bait hook, but I convinced them there wasn't nothing worth catching when you could be zipping along with the wind in your face. Right, Malachi?"

"Right, Uncle Wendell. Can I steer some more?"

"Sure. We'll take your aunt Jenny for a quick trip as far as the railroad bridge and then back again. Steady as she goes, Captain."

Malachi gripped the wheel proudly in his small brown hands and stared firmly ahead through the windscreen. Wendell nodded at David, who tugged the engine into noisy life.

That done, he folded my hand into his and kept his peace. Wendell, after casting a single significant glance at our joined hands, did the same. It was impossible, in any case, to converse without shouting over the roar of the motor. And so we sped away, leaving behind the rock, the can of worms, the fishing pole, and the voice that had called my name from the thicket. At least I knew the voice did not belong to Wendell.

CHAPTER
21

My nose got sunburned. It glowed in the mirror like a traffic light when, after Wendell had brought us back to River House, I went upstairs to comb my hair. It was whipped into snarls by the wind on the river and it took me ten minutes of concentrated brushing to get it to look nearly normal. I heard a car drive up while I was smearing some cream on my nose and other less scorched but still pink portions of my face, and went to look out the bay window. Petey and Arlene were getting out of their huge gray car, apparently in the midst of an argument. The girls and Luke dragged themselves sullenly out of the back seat. Luke's fretful whine drifted up through my open window.

"But I wanted to go swimming."

"Shut up, Luke," snapped Arlene. "I don't care what you want."

Luke tried another gambit. "My hand hurts."

"Go upstairs and pack your bag." Peter issued the order in a tone that brooked no insubordination. "You girls do the same."

Luke stomped onto the porch, with Georgia and Virginia trailing along behind, whispering to each other. Petey and Arlene followed them into the house.

I quickly wiped away the excess cream from my face and left the bedroom. On the way downstairs, I passed Luke and the girls trudging up. Luke shot me a killing glance and the girls giggled behind their hands. Arlene's voice, angry and determined, resounded through the hall.

"I was never so mortified in my life. I told you we shouldn't have come. Even Mimosa has better sense than most of your family."

Her husband was placatory but there was an edge to his soothing words. "All right, all right, Arlene. I agreed to leave and we'll do it. Now just let the whole thing drop."

When I appeared at the foot of the stairs, he looked away and muttered, "Is David around?"

"I think he's out back with Malachi," I answered. "What's the matter?"

"Nothing," he said, and shouldered past me toward the back of the house.

"Nothing, my foot," said Arlene, glowering at me. Her veneer of graciousness had cracked, but her wrath was slightly ludicrous as she stood there with the poodle's curly beribboned head rising inquisitively out of her straw handbag. "You should have been there. You, of all people, should have been there. Your mother threw a fit in church, disrupted the whole service and had to be carted away to the hospital. I've never seen such goings on in my entire life. And now, if you'll excuse me, I've got packing to do. As far as I'm concerned, this reunion is nothing but a gathering of lunatics."

She started for the stairs. I blocked her way. "What do you mean?" I demanded. "What kind of fit? Is she ill?"

"Ill!" she exclaimed. "That woman is sick. A real sicko. Anybody who would run up and down the aisle during the sermon tearing her clothes off and shrieking some kind of crazy gibberish ought to be locked up. Not only that, but as soon as she realized what she was doing, she pretended to go into a trance. Threw herself down right at the foot of the altar with her eyes rolled up in her head and her tongue hanging out, twitching like a bug on its back. It was disgusting. They had to have four men carry her out."

Arlene was relishing the telling of the tale. Her eyes sparkled and her mouth delivered the words as if they were pearls of great price.

"And they took her to the hospital?" I prompted.

"That's what they said. I didn't stick around to see her

go. She's not *my* mother. My mother would be aghast to know that her grandchildren had witnessed such a scene. I managed to put my hand over Luke's eyes, so I don't think he saw anything he shouldn't have."

"Thanks, Arlene. You're a real Christian." I moved out of her path and started out to look for David. Perhaps he would take me to the hospital on his motorcycle.

Arlene couldn't resist a parting shot. "Real Christians don't behave like *that*. And real Christian daughters don't let their crazy mothers run around loose."

She hurried on up the stairs with Mimosa yipping back at me like a tiny malignant scold. Maybe she was right and maybe she wasn't. With all the strange things that had been happening at River House, cutting and running looked very much like the better part of valor. But I couldn't run now, not with my mother in the hospital and no explanation for the inhabitant of the turret room.

David came running through from the back of the house with Malachi scampering along behind him.

"Petey just told me what happened. Come on. I'll take you to the hospital. Malachi, run upstairs and get my boots, please."

"Okay!" The boy ran up the stairs and David gathered me into his strong bare arms.

"Petey's pretty sure she'll be all right. He thinks it might have been a touch of heatstroke. They took her off in an ambulance, and Fearn and Walter went along."

I looked up at him. "You know it wasn't heatstroke, David."

"Yeah." He nodded gravely.

"She's got something preying on her mind. I'm tempted to let myself wallow in guilt and believe that my coming home has set off some kind of reaction in her. But I don't really think it's that at all. Seeing me again after all these years may have had something to do with it, but the real reason goes back a lot further. And it's got something to do with this house. I'm almost sure of it. It's that room up there at the top and something that happened a long time ago. I mean to find out what it is."

Malachi thundered down the stairs, carrying David's huge black motorcycle boots. He gazed soberly at the two of us,

David with his arms around me, and me obviously pretty comfortable with the arrangement. I broke away. David sat down on the bottom step, took off his sandals, and shoved his feet into the boots. I looked at the T-shirt that was still wrapped around his head, turban-fashion.

"Maybe you ought to wear your shirt a different way. They might think you'd cracked your skull and put you to bed before you know what hit you."

David clapped a hand to his head. "Oh, yeah!" he exclaimed. "I forgot."

He wriggled into his shirt, checked his pockets for keys and wallet, and stooped to plant a small peck of a kiss on my cheek. His beard tickled and I backed off automatically, laughing as I did so to show I meant no ill will. We trooped out to the motorcycle, Malachi leading the way. On the front lawn, Petey was fussing around his car with the trunk lid raised and all the doors open. When he saw me, he found something important to attend to inside the trunk.

"So long, Petey," David called out. "See you around."

Petey raised his head. "Yes, well, I guess we'll be gone by the time you get back. Arlene just can't take this sort of thing. She's high-strung."

"It's all right, Petey," I told him.

"I'd take you down to the hospital," he continued, "but she wants to leave right away. You know how it is."

"It really is all right. I've been dying to ride on this monster, anyway."

"Have you?" said David. "Well, climb aboard."

Malachi scrambled into the sidecar and settled down, looking like a papoose in a cradleboard. David mounted the machine, and I climbed up behind him, keeping my nervousness well concealed, I thought, behind a smile and a brave show of anticipation for the ride. Malachi handed me up a yellow helmet from the depths of the sidecar. I eyed it dubiously. If this means of transportation was dangerous enough to warrant wearing a crash helmet, it was dangerous enough to avoid entirely. I thought about walking or hitchhiking. David turned and smiled at me.

"Put the helmet on, Jenny. And don't worry. I know this bike as well as I know anything in this world. I practically built it. And we've never had an accident." He put on his own black helmet and disappeared behind its dark visor.

The news didn't reassure me as much as it was intended to and I was tempted to utter a feeble reminder to the effect that there was always a first time. Instead, I put the helmet on my head and my arms gingerly around David's waist. In a few moments, we were thundering off down the dirt drive. When we reached the road, David put on speed and my tentative grip around his middle involuntarily came to resemble that of a boa constrictor around its lunch.

The dips and curves in the road gave a decidedly unsettling quality to the ride. My stomach and possibly a few other vital organs became unmoored and jounced around inside me with remarkable abandon. Hell existed, I decided, and it was an endless country road and a motorcycle that never needed refueling. When we reached the highway, the ride became smoother although the shuddering of the heavy machine never ceased. But the Sunday morning traffic posed another threat. Everyone, it seemed, was out driving somewhere and doing it at speeds that bore no relation to the posted limit. David nosed into the stream of traffic and we rocketed along, keeping pace with all the other demons of the road. I closed my eyes, pressed my head against David's back, and hung on for dear life.

Forever is a long time, say twenty minutes of unparalleled, gut-wrenching fear. I felt the machine go into a long curve, slowing as it went, and finally come to a stop. The engine still thrummed. David's voice came faintly into my helmeted ears.

"Petey told me to take the first turnoff after the roller rink. Where do we go from here?"

I opened my eyes and looked around. The landscape was achingly familiar. Across the street was the red brick elementary school I'd attended where Miss Anna Grace had expounded her cardinal population theory. Its grassy yard was deserted and it seemed small and shabby, not at all the towering fortress of recalcitrant fractions that it had been in the sixth grade. Three blocks away, down a tree-lined street, was the house where I'd grown up. In the other direction, the worn cobblestones swooped steeply up to Rattlesnake Hill. That wasn't its legitimate name, of course, but generations of school children had passed on the lore of the deadly snakes coiled in crannies of the rocky cliff that formed the highest point in town.

We knew it by no other name, and once in a while, often enough to perpetuate the legend, a snake was indeed found and killed on the hill. Usually a harmless garter snake. The hospital sat on top of the hill, screened from the road below by an ancient stand of hickory trees whose green-husked nuts would rain down on the schoolyard in the fall, providing ammunition for rowdy boys to fire at coyly shrieking girls.

"Up the hill," I told him, motioning to the steep slant of cobblestones, "and around to the right. You can't miss it. I think I'll walk from here."

I started to get off the motorcycle, but it was already in motion so I had no choice but to renew my hold on David and hope that the ascent of Rattlesnake Hill wouldn't tip me off to go bumping and rolling down the cobbles. This time I managed to keep my eyes open.

The hospital had changed. The central building was still the same, but it was flanked on either side by new low modern additions. The town's ubiquitous red brick had been used in the expansion, but where the new buildings glowed rosy in the sunshine, the bricks of the original hospital were blackened and stained, as they had been when I'd had my seven-year-old tonsils removed, from the coal dust and smoke that had once been an ineradicable ingredient of the town's atmosphere. A large blue and white sign directed us into a newly paved driveway and the emergency entrance. We found the parking lot and the ride was over.

I managed clumsily to get myself off of the motorcycle and stood on shaking legs waiting for my inner portions to recover from the assault. Never again, I swore. I'd find some other way to get back to River House after we'd seen my mother.

"You can take the helmet off now."

David was standing beside me trying hard not to smile at my obvious case of the shakes.

"It takes a little getting used to," he said. "Next time it'll be easier. You might even get to like it."

I shook my head and handed him the helmet. Then I stalked away with as much dignity as I could muster on trembling legs and knees that threatened to buckle at any moment. A concrete ramp led up to a shiny metal door in which a small rectangular window was set. I pushed through and into the smell of hospitals everywhere: one-third disinfectant and two-thirds pain and fear. We left Malachi in the waiting room and found my mother by the sound of Fearn's voice raised in argument.

"If she's not sick, why do you want to keep her here? You doctors are all alike. Once you get your hooks into someone, you never let go until you've done as much damage as you can. I ought to know. I'm as damaged as a woman can be. All because of doctors."

We stood in the open doorway and took in the scene. Fearn, flushed and tear-stained, was berating a thin dark-haired man in a white coat with the usual stethoscope dangling from his pocket. Walter Proud was hovering helplessly and making shushing motions which his wife ignored. And my mother was propped up in bed looking frail and frightened as her eyes darted from Fearn to the doctor and at last came to rest on me. She smiled then and let her head fall back on the pillow.

The doctor turned to see what had distracted her. His face was closed and stern, his eyes dark and angry. Before I could introduce myself, Fearn attacked.

"Well, it's about time you got here," she bleated. "Your poor mother lying here at the mercy of these quacks and you off gallivanting with this . . . this hippie." She glared at David and turned to the doctor. "This is Mrs. Holland's daughter. She'll tell you the same thing. Tell him, Jenny. Tell him you want to take your mother home."

"It's all right, Fearn. I'd like to talk to the doctor. Why don't you and Walter wait out in the hall?" I shot a glance at David and he understood. He took Fearn's hand and started leading her to the door. Walter caught on and put his arm around her on the other side. Between them, Fearn had no choice. She twisted her head around and fired a parting shot at me over her shoulder.

"It's all your fault, Jenny Holland. She's finally gone off the deep end. It never would have happened if you hadn't come back and started picking away at old scabs. Why couldn't you leave us all alone?"

The door swung closed behind her. My mother lay quivering in the bed, her eyes closed and tears running down her ashen cheeks. I looked at the doctor. He'd turned away and was looking out the window, obviously waiting for us to settle our own family squabbles. There was a small box of tissues on the nightstand beside my mother's bed. I plucked one out and dabbed her streaming cheeks with it. Her eyes fluttered open.

"Jenny," she murmured. "I'm so tired."

The doctor's voice, soft and reticent, came over my shoulder. "We gave her a sedative. She'll be asleep soon."

I looked up at him. The anger had left his dark eyes. He seemed only slightly sad and infinitely patient.

"I'm sorry about my cousin. She lashes out at everyone these days."

He shrugged. "We get all kinds."

"What about my mother?" I asked. "What's wrong with her?"

Again he shrugged. "Nothing physical," he said. "As far as we could tell from a preliminary exam. Of course, the tests aren't back yet. But she seems pretty healthy to me. Apart from the anxiety . . ." His voice trailed off inconclusively.

"What does that mean?"

He motioned me away from the bed. My mother's eyes were closed. The tears had stopped and she seemed to be asleep. We sat on the two visitors' chairs and spoke in whispers.

"I'm no psychiatrist," he said, "but it seems to me that she's under some kind of mental strain. I understand that you've been away for a while and just returned. Have you quarreled with your mother?"

"No." I thought over what *had* gone on between my mother and me since yesterday morning and decided I was being truthful. We hadn't quarreled. But I wasn't sure I wanted to tell him about her shooting at phantoms in the middle of the night, or looking for her lost doll that may or may not have fallen into the well more than fifty years ago. Perhaps she *did* need to see a psychiatrist. If so, he'd be the one to talk to about her bizarre behavior. I thought of the filthy pallet in the turret room at River House. Could *she* have been the person who lay there? Could she, with some twisted idea of going back to her childhood, have created a nest for herself at the top of the old house, a safe haven from the memories that tormented her in the house in town where she'd spent the few years of her marriage with Raymond my father? I felt tears prickling behind my eyes at the thought of her creeping through the old deserted house to the prisonlike room in search of peace. "No," I repeated. "We haven't quarreled."

"Well," he said, "I'd like to keep her here for a while. Give her a chance to rest and pull herself together. She'll probably sleep through the rest of the day and maybe all night. And we do have a staff psychiatrist. I could ask her to talk to your mother when she comes on duty tomorrow."

"I don't know." I looked across at my mother lying motionless in her drugged sleep. "I don't know if she'd be willing. In this town, folks would rather die than admit they needed *that* kind of help. And they'd rather lock their crazy relatives in the attic than have them openly visit a shrink. I don't imagine your psychiatrist is very busy."

"No, she's not," he admitted. "She's set up a mental health clinic and a hot line for suicides and battered wives. She gets a lot of crank calls from Bible-thumpers threatening judgment if she doesn't leave their women alone and stop putting ideas in their heads, and the occasional high school kid about to run down and jump off the bridge because he didn't make the football team. But she's convinced that people are just as disturbed here as they are in the big cities, so she keeps at it. Are you staying in town long?"

At first I thought he was inquiring on behalf of my mother, to know whether she would have someone to look after her when she went home. But he was smiling at me, his eyes gleaming and hungry, in the way those men used to smile, not a Raymond smile, when they wanted to go home with me after a couple of drinks and a mediocre dinner in an out-of-the-way restaurant. I got up and moved over to the bed, pretending I'd noticed my mother twitch in her sleep.

"Not long," I muttered. "No, not long at all. A week or so. That's all." I bent to adjust the coverlet over my mother's thin chest.

"Well," he said, "she'll be all right now. Rest and no excitement. And I'll send Doctor Marks in to see her in the morning."

He went to the door. I watched him go. Before he pushed the door open, I called after him.

"Doctor!" I didn't know his name. "What do you think is *really* wrong with her?"

He turned back, his dark eyes once more sad and pa
tient. "I'm not sure," he said, "but when they brought her in
she was terrified."

He left.

CHAPTER

22

I would have left, too, but I wasn't ready to face another
round with Fearn, who was probably waiting to pounce on me.
I stood beside the bed, my hand resting on the coverlet, my eyes
fixed on the door that had just swung shut behind the doctor.
Any minute now, Fearn could come barging in; David could
come to tell me it was time to go back to River House; Bonnie
Marie would certainly come to see if there was anything she
could do. I didn't want any of them. I wanted to be alone with
my thoughts and with my mother. My terrified mother.

Terrified. All right. I'd seen for myself the evidences of
her terror. It had caused her to make a spectacle of herself in
church. But by doing that, she'd at least been able to get herself
to a safe place, this room, where she'd get the care she needed.
Because surely her terrors were all in her head. She'd been the
one who slashed my clothes, she'd been Millie's "hairy old
lady," and the person in the Halloween mask who'd peered in
the kitchen window at me. And it was she who locked the world
away up in that turret room because there was no one else to
do it for her. Oh, I realized she couldn't lock herself in. But she
could lock out the rest of the prying world when she wasn't up
there reading her old newspapers by candlelight in the middle
of the night. It all hung together with craziness of the life
preserver and the rowboat in the backyard. But why?

What was there in her mind or in her past that sent her
on these terrible excursions? Perhaps Doctor Marks could find
out. Not quickly, not easily. But I'd certainly do everything I
could to help before I went back to New York.

The cold claw grasped my wrist and my heart lurched as I instinctively tried to pull away.

"Jenny. Don't leave me." Her voice was reedy and her words were slurred. Had she been reading my mind?

I looked down at her. Her eyes were slitted open, straining to remain focused on me.

"I thought you were asleep, Ma."

"Not sleeping. I heard him. You. Don't let them send me away."

Her grip slackened and her eyes closed. I tried to ease my wrist out of her fingers, but she roused herself again and gripped harder than before. Her nails dug into my flesh.

"Relax, Ma. All you have to do is rest. Everything will be all right." I realized the emptiness of my soothing words. Everything wasn't all right and wouldn't be for a long, long time.

"Stay, Jenny. I need you. I need you to help me. I can't do it all alone anymore."

She was drifting again, her words fading. Her eyelids fluttered with the effort to stay conscious.

"I'll stay, Ma. For a while, anyway."

I meant to be reassuring. I wanted her to do exactly what the doctor had ordered. Rest and recover. I wasn't ready for the reaction my words provoked.

She sprang up in bed, her eyes wide open and bulging with fear. "No!" she screamed. "No, no, no! I can't let you do that! You've got to go away. Right now! Oh, Mother! Can't you do something? Why did you leave me with this?"

I didn't know whether to ring for the nurse or run out into the hall and try to find the doctor. I couldn't do either; she clung to my arm with both hands, staring into my face as if she would memorize it.

"Jenny," she gasped. "Go away. You were right to go when you did. I missed you, but I never minded. You did the right thing." Her voice turned bitter. "I had my own mother for company. We were a fine pair. She managed things. Much better than I've been able to. She kept everything under control. The only thing she couldn't make me do was move out to River House. Oh, no. She couldn't get me to live out there. But then she died. Did you know she died, Jenny? Do you know *how* she died?"

I dredged up an answer from my memory of Wendell's letters. "She had a heart attack and fell down the stairs, didn't she? Wendell wrote me the news."

She sank back onto her pillow and closed her eyes. "Oh, I'm so tired," she moaned. "So tired of it all. Go away, Jenny. Go right away. Today. And never come back. This place isn't good for you."

"I won't go until I know you're all right," I told her.

But she didn't hear me. Or at least she didn't answer. Her hands fell away from my arm and I was free to go, to run for the doctor. But now she truly seemed to be sleeping. I shook her gently, my hand flinching away from the boniness of her shoulder under the hospital gown. She didn't move.

"Ma," I whispered close to her ear. "Ma, can you hear me?"

She slept. I tiptoed to the door and pushed it open. It sighed on its heavy oiled hinges. Down at the end of the hall the relatives congregated, drawn, no doubt, by curiosity and the chance to witness my poor mother's final collapse. Bonnie Marie and Wendell had arrived. Aunt Tillie and Aunt Augusta talked earnestly to a gesticulating Fearn. Irene and Mike sat stiffly on a bench, embarrassment exuding from their mute indrawn faces, while Uncle Ambrose steered his portable wheelchair along one side of the hall peering into open doorways. He saw me, waved, and propelled himself in my direction.

I glanced back at my mother. She hadn't moved. I stepped out into the hall and let the door sigh closed behind me. As it did, I heard the soft word, "Raymond." My mother speaking in her drugged sleep? Or a distortion of the sound made by the door and interpreted by my mind into a forlorn hope?

I hurried down the hall to join my family.

CHAPTER
23

"I don't know how you can do this to your own mother. They'll put her away for sure. She'll spend the rest of her life in a padded cell. Once these doctors get hold of you they never let go. Especially these nut doctors."

Fearn was in full spate and showed no sign of running down. She'd been arguing for twenty minutes, going over and over the same ground, after I told the group that my mother was staying in the hospital and would be seeing a psychiatrist in the morning. Wendell was dubious, but kept his doubts to himself, only once bemoaning the ruin of his reunion. Uncle Ambrose spotted a pretty young nurse and pursued her in his wheelchair, offering to show her his stump. Irene and Mike, relieved to find an excuse to leave, hustled him out to their car.

Aunt Tillie was the only one totally on my side. Except for David, of course, who'd been keeping Malachi and the other children amused with a game of Frisbee in the parking lot. But even with her support, even with Bonnie Marie's offer to stay at the hospital and take turns with me watching over my mother, the disapproval of the family was almost tangible. Illness and accident they could understand. A doctor could set a broken leg or give you medicine to cure an infection. They understood that operations were sometimes necessary, as with Uncle Ambrose's amputation or even Fearn's loudly regretted hysterectomy. But to turn a shattered mind over to the care of the "nut doctors" was disloyal and suspect. Aunt Augusta recommended prayer and the laying on of hands. She spoke of a healer who was holding tent meetings in the next county.

I shook my head stubbornly. "She's my mother, and it's up to me to decide what's best for her. There's no need for all of you to stay here. I can manage on my own."

"Well," said Wendell, ducking his head sheepishly, "it

is getting on for lunchtime. And we promised the kids they could all take a swim in the pool."

Bonnie Marie smiled at him. "Wendell does love his lunch," she said, patting him affectionately on the stomach. "Well," she said to me, "if you're sure you don't need us, we might as well carry on. But if anything happens, you just give us a call."

"Thanks, Bonnie Marie. I will."

Fearn flounced off, the skirt of her Sunday print polyester dress twitching angrily, as she announced to all within hearing, "I still think she's making a big mistake. But, of course, it's none of my business."

"For once, you're absolutely right," said Aunt Tillie.

They straggled across the waiting room and out into the bright day. I was glad to see them go, but once I was alone in the cool echoing space of the hospital, I was stricken with doubt. Had I done the right thing? Keeping my mother in the hospital seemed sensible, while taking her back to River House or even to her own house might set off another attack. On the other hand, even in her drugged, foggy state, she seemed afraid of something, possibly of being put away. Well, just one little talk with a psychiatrist didn't mean that she was going to be committed to an institution.

I sat down on one of the molded plastic chairs in the waiting room. Distant metallic rattles and stray wafts of steamy food smells told of lunch being taken around to the hospital's inmates. I realized I was hungry and looked around. The waiting room offered nothing but candy and soda machines. Unappetizing, and I'd come away without my shoulder bag. There didn't seem to be much reason for me to stick around. The doctor had said that my mother would probably sleep through the day and most of the night. She was safe, and I could safely leave her. But where would I go? Not to Wendell's certainly, where the rest of the family would be eating and buzzing over my mother's sad performance and my unpopular decision. Back out to River House? Not alone and with no way of getting there. And I wanted to be able to get back to the hospital later in the evening, just in case she woke up. I could go to my mother's house; it was just down the hill and three blocks away on Plum Street. But would she want me there, rummaging in her kitchen for something to eat, looking at the lonely furnishings of her life?

I decided I was being overly scrupulous. It was my home, too, the only home I'd known for nineteen years of my life. And if she still left the back door key on the ledge above the door, I would go in and make myself at home. Who knows, I might even find some hint, some insight to explain my mother's strange behavior.

I was halfway across the lobby when David and Malachi walked in. I'd thought they'd probably gone out to Wendell's with everyone else. David was carrying two large white paper bags.

"I thought you might want something to eat," he said. "It's only hamburgers. From the place across the highway."

"Let's go," I said. "We can eat them down at my mother's house. I was just on my way there."

I got back on the motorcycle with less apprehension than I had the first time. Malachi stowed the hamburgers and himself into the sidecar, and in two minutes we pulled into the driveway beside the familiar old frame house on Plum Street. The maple tree in the front yard was considerably bigger, spreading its welcome shade across the front of the house. But everything else seemed smaller, shrunken, and shabby. I led the way around to the back of the house where I was instantly greeted by my first sight of the result of my mother's flood phobia.

It was only an old rowboat adrift on a sea of uncut grass. She couldn't have thought it seaworthy. There were gaping holes in the bottom where grass sprouted through. If there had ever been oars, there were none now. I picked up a rusted fruitcake tin and shook it. There was something inside, probably the food Wendell told me she kept in the boat, but I couldn't get the lid off. I didn't really want to.

Malachi gave a yelp of joy and jumped into the boat. "I want to eat my lunch here," he cried. "Can I?"

"Why not?"

David handed him a hamburger, a package of french fries and a tall paper cup of soda. Then he and I sat down on the grass a short distance from the boat. While we ate, I gazed up at the back of the house and wandered off into memory.

"That's my room up there," I told David, pointing to a corner window on the second floor. "It has a little balcony on the side of the house where I used to sit at night and look at the stars."

As far as I could tell, through the screens on the window, the same ruffled yellow curtains still hung there as they had on the day I left. "It was a nice room. A nice house, even though it was always a bit gloomy inside. And it was too big for just the two of us. My mother used to talk about moving into an apartment and renting out the house, but she never did anything about it." As I remembered those old conversations, I remembered that there were a number of houses in the town that had belonged to my grandmother, small red brick apartment buildings that fringed the main shopping street, other frame houses like this one, and I supposed they all belonged to my mother now.

David spoke. "When I left home, it was to get away from just this kind of thing. Tucson is a lot different. I suppose New York is, too. I've never been there."

I understood him to mean not just the narrow tree-lined streets and the old houses that huddled under the trees, but the people—the meddlesome, quarrelsome, we-know-what's-best-for-you salt-of-the-earth people who lived in the houses, and I nodded. "Very different."

I imagined David and Malachi living in a simple cabin, maybe made of stone, on the edge of a clean sweeping desert. Each morning, they would get on the motorcycle; David would drop Malachi off at school and go on to his bookstore on a wide sunlit street. No trees to cast shadows in his path. I wondered if they had a dog.

"You mustn't let them get to you. You're doing the right thing. Your mother needs help." He'd finished his hamburger and I handed him my almost-full package of french fries. I wasn't hungry anymore.

"There used to be a swing," I told him. "Just rope and a piece of board hanging from that tree. I think my father must have put it up. It was a long time ago. And once I had a rocking horse."

Things I hadn't thought of for ages, trickling back into my mind. A blue velvet dress I loved but was allowed to wear only on Sundays, a pair of brown shoes I hated and which seemed never to wear out, the budgerigar my mother brought home that terrified me when it got loose and terrified me even more when it died because I'd wished it dead.

"I'm going inside," I said. "Want to come along?"

"If you want me to."

I would have gone without him, but I was glad of his company. Ten years is a long time and I didn't know what I would find in the house that might correspond to the dilapidated rowboat in the yard. We left Malachi playing in the rowboat and went up onto the small back porch. I stretched and groped above the door, and the key was there where it had always been. I used to have to stand on an upturned bucket to reach it those times I came home from school and my mother was out shopping or visiting or whatever it was she did with her days.

The key was grimy and touched with rust, but it worked. The back door swung open and we walked into a thick hot sweetish stench and a kitchen that hadn't been cleaned in months. There was garbage everywhere, spilling out of broken paper bags and strewing the floor with moldy bits of food. The sink was piled high with dirty dishes, and the huge white gas range, my mother's pride, was thickly coated with blackened grease. The round oak table, where in years past I'd labored over my homework, was cluttered with more dishes, sticky jam jars, crusted TV-dinner trays, and crumbs. And everywhere there were ants. Large, black, glistening, industrious thousands of ants.

I stood still, afraid of taking a step into the room and hearing the crunch underfoot of those shiny well-fed bodies. More afraid of a horde of them overrunning my bare sandaled feet. I wanted to think I'd walked into the wrong house, that this couldn't be my mother's kitchen. Not *my* mother who always kept house maniacally and never let a crumb escape her vigilance. But there was the table that I knew so well, and over the sink the framed faded print of Jesus suffering the little children. It used to puzzle me, that print, as I stood on a little wooden step stool reluctantly swishing dishes around in sudsy water. I thought it meant that children made poor Jesus feel bad and hurt all over, even though His face in the picture showed no sign of suffering and the kids gathered around Him looked like little pink and white angels. I truly believed that every bad thing I did gave Him and my mother a stab in the heart. She must have told me that, but I couldn't remember ever hearing the words.

David walked past me into the mess, not minding the

havoc his motorcycle boots wreaked among the milling ants.

"I guess we'd better clean this up," he said. "We can't let her come home to this. Where's the cleaning stuff?"

Mutely I pointed to a door in the far wall, a closet where in the old days brooms and mops hung neatly on hooks and shelves held every conceivable kind of cleaning preparation. David opened the door and stood studying the contents of the closet. When he turned around, he held a spray can.

"I guess we better start with this. Come on over here and I'll start spraying around the door. That's where they're coming in."

I couldn't move. The ants marched past my feet, ignoring me for the greater attraction of the strewn garbage. But any minute now, if I made the slightest move, they would swerve from their course and attack, first my feet, then creeping rapidly up my legs, invading my thighs and the soft secret places of my body. They would bite and chew and gnaw, their hundreds of tiny mouths carrying away minuscule bits of my flesh just as they had done with the dead kitten on the river bank. They would swarm all over me, into my mouth and ears, and quickly leave my eyes a leaking mass of jelly. I would fall among them, crushing some to be eaten by the rest, and soon there would be nothing left of me but clean bare bone. I couldn't breathe. My lungs burned as if somehow the quick ants had gotten inside and were gnawing at the soft pink tissue. My teeth clanged together as if they were a gate that could be slammed shut against the invaders. I felt myself swaying and ordered my muscles to clench against the fall.

"Jenny!"

The word echoed at me from a distance. And then I felt myself being jerked, tugged, lifted, and set down. When I opened my eyes, I was sitting on a chair next to the littered table. There were ants on the table. Just a few. The advance scouts, no doubt, checking out the surrounding territory against the day when the laboring legions had swept the floor clear of food. I drew my elbows into my sides and tucked my feet up onto a rung of the chair.

"Are you all right?" David hovered. "You looked like you were going to faint."

"I'm all right. Kill the bastards!" My words were an echo of Millie's on the river bank.

The smell of insecticide rose and covered the smell of rotting garbage. I watched the ranks of ants break and scatter, some of them running in maddened circles, others staggering under heavy loads they refused to relinquish even in death. David's boots trod among them as he wafted the hissing can here, there, everywhere. Ants rose on their hind legs, their jointed bodies arching backward until they toppled over and lay helpless and squirming. They took a long time to die.

I sat and watched the dying, reveling in it at the same time that it disgusted me. The ants were doing nothing but what they were meant to do, collecting food. The attack on me had been a product of my own imagination. But their determination, their single-minded dedication to the job at hand—even now a few of them were struggling to reestablish the food trail —was chilling. I wanted them dead, gone, out of my sight. And I hoped that no one ever pursued me with that antlike implacability.

At last, David's spray can hissed itself empty. He looked around at the writhing mass of dead and dying ants and then at me. His face was taut and his eyes clouded.

"Can you get a broom? And a dustpan? And maybe something to put all this in?"

I forced my feet down onto the floor. There were no ants between me and the closet. An old broom still hung on a hook there, its straws worn and scraggy. On another hook hung a dented black metal dustpan, and beside it an old mop whose gray stiffened strings reminded me of the gray hairs surrounding the Halloween witch's mask. The shelves held a few boxes and cans of cleaning supplies, nothing like the army my mother used to marshal against dirt and disorder, and apparently none of them had been used recently. On a lower shelf, I found an unopened box of plastic garbage bags.

David swept up the bodies and I held a bag open for him while he dumped them in. I found a pair of gardening gloves and helped him gather up the spilled garbage into the bulging plastic bags and stow it out in the yard. Then I began to wash the dishes while David mopped the floor. Soon the kitchen began to resemble the one I'd known so many years before.

"I'm sorry you got stuck with such a mess."

David shook his head. "Don't apologize. It looks like your mother's been in trouble for quite a while."

"I guess I shouldn't have left her. I guess I should have come back sooner. Wendell did write that she was doing strange things."

"No, Jenny. It's not your fault. She probably wouldn't have let anyone help her. She may even resent our cleaning up like this. But don't let it worry you. She'll be taken care of now."

I thought of the bag ladies on the streets of New York, how fiercely independent they seemed even when they were begging, and how adamantly they refused to be rescued from their own filth and squalor. Was that the road my mother was on? And how could I go away again and let it happen?

I glanced out the kitchen window. Malachi was still playing happily in the rowboat, chattering to himself and obviously miles away sailing the Spanish Main.

It was companionable, working side-by-side with David, and I allowed myself a brief fantasy of the two of us—the three of us—at home in Arizona cozily cleaning up after supper, tucking Malachi in bed, and having the whole evening before us. Before I could fill in the details, Malachi came in, tired of his game and thirsty.

"Can I have a drink of water? Yuck, this place stinks. Are we going where the swimming pool is?"

As David gave him a glass of water, I realized that the kitchen did, indeed, stink—of insecticide and the disinfectant that David had used to wash the floor. I wanted to see the rest of the house, but I wanted to see it alone. If there were any more messes, in the bedroom, for example, I didn't want David to leap in and start cleaning up. It wouldn't be right. It would be disloyal to my mother, although I was sure David would think nothing of it except that it was sad, and he certainly wouldn't gossip about it to the rest of the family. Still, whatever else there was to find in this house was between my mother and me.

"Why don't you go on over to Wendell's?" I said. "Malachi can swim and so can you. I'm going to stay here for a while and then go back up to the hospital."

"Let's go, Davey," said Malachi.

"Are you sure? Don't you want me to go through the house with you?"

"I'm sure. What could be worse than what we already found? Probably just a lot of dust."

"Is there a telephone?"

"It used to be in the hall. It probably still is."

"I don't like leaving you alone."

"Don't be silly. This isn't like River House. There are neighbors. And if anything happens, I'll call. I promise. But nothing's going to happen."

"Well, all right." He turned to leave, Malachi bobbing and leaping around him, clutching his hand and tugging him toward to door.

"I'll probably spend the night here," I said as an afterthought. "So I can be at the hospital first thing in the morning."

He stopped at the door. "Do you want me to come back? We can spend the night here, too."

"Better not," I said. "That would really set the tongues wagging. Not that I care, but things are difficult enough right now. Good-bye, David."

"I'll come back tomorrow."

"Okay. Fine. And thanks for . . ." I gestured around the kitchen.

He bobbed his head, almost shyly. "See you later," he said, and left.

I waited in the kitchen until I heard the roar of the motorcycle fade away down Plum Street. Then I pushed open the swinging door that led from the kitchen to the rest of the house.

CHAPTER
24

There was dust and some disorder, but not as much as I expected after the turmoil of the kitchen. My own room at the back of the house on the second floor was neater and cleaner than it had been when I lived in it. My old records were there —the Beatles, Bob Dylan, Joan Baez—and the clothes I'd left behind still hung in the closet, miniskirts and granny dresses, bell-bottomed slacks and that awful pink tulle prom gown. But the bookcase beside my bed reminded me that although many things had changed, some things remained constant. I took down a yellowing paperback copy of *Wuthering Heights*. It had been a favorite of mine. As I thumbed through it, its pages fell out. I gathered them up and put the book back on the shelf. Bittersweet romance on the moors held little appeal for me today.

I poked through the other rooms. The sewing room, just another small bedroom really, where skirts were lengthened or shortened, seams were let out or taken in, and sometimes whole dresses were stitched on the ancient foot-pedal Singer sewing machine. The machine was there, with a scrap of cloth clamped under its pressure foot, but the dust on its curved black body told me of a project long abandoned. I gave the wheel a shove and the needle went up and down. I'd never really learned how to operate the machine. But I had been a prisoner of the ironing board. It stood in its usual place and the iron propped up on it was the same one I'd slammed down onto handkerchiefs and pillowcases, blouses and tea towels. There was dust here, too, and the padding of the ironing board was scorched and split.

I wandered out of the sewing room and into my mother's bedroom. There had always been an unspoken rule that I did not ever enter that room without knocking. My mother had never been the sort to encourage confidences. I had never been permitted to sit on her bed and tell her of my dreams or woes. I had never seen her in a nightgown, but I did remember the robe she always put on before opening the door. It was a wine-colored quilted robe with a fringed belt. I wondered if she still had it and if I should take it and one of her own nightgowns up to the hospital. She wouldn't be happy if she had to talk to the psychiatrist in the morning wearing a wrinkled hospital gown.

I paused before the half-open door and my hand raised automatically to knock. I realized how silly that was and stopped before I completed the gesture. But silly or not, I entered the room with the same feeling of trespass I'd always felt as a child, as if there were drawers I shouldn't open, things I shouldn't know. The room was much as I remembered it, darkened by heavy drapes and smelling faintly of spice sachet and cedar. There was, in fact, a cedar chest at the foot of the bed. My mother had set great store by such things and had tried to interest me in a similar chest in which to keep linens for the time when I would marry. She called it a hope chest.

I'd never looked into her hope chest. Had all her hopes been realized when she married Raymond my father? Or were there still a few worn, bedraggled hopes lying at the bottom of the chest, waiting for the day they could spring out and ease her life?

I tiptoed across the room. Was I afraid that even in her drugged sleep in that hospital room she would hear me intruding on her privacy and wake and cry out, "Jenny! Stop! What on earth are you doing?" If she did, I refused to hear her. I lifted the lid of the cedar chest, cautiously, slowly, praying for it not to creak. The pungency of the wood billowed out at me, a clean, sharp fragrance that would keep more than moths away. Nothing frightening could live in that woodland odor. The first thing I saw was an ivory-colored woolen blanket. Of course. It was summer. She had put her heavy blanket away. I lifted it out and laid it on the bed. The next layer was a large paisley shawl, the kind that people used to drape over their pianos. We had never owned a piano. Had that been one of her unfulfilled hopes, to own a piano? I didn't even know if she played. I placed the shawl on top of the blanket and went on with my search.

A piece of velvet caught my eye. It was the color of the sky at twilight. I pulled it out. Oh, God! It was my dress, the blue one I'd loved so much and worn so seldom. How long ago? Why had it been hidden away here all these years? I held it against my cheek. Soft it was, softer than the young skin of the child who'd worn it. And then, because I didn't want to stain it with my tears, I held it away in my two hands and tried to guess how old it was, how old I was when it had been my greatest delight. Six or seven? It seemed very small with its gathered waist and its little lace collar, but I had never been a large child. I could have been eight years old. I could have worn it at the time Raymond my father disappeared from our lives.

I put the dress aside and went into the bathroom to wipe my eyes and blow my nose. No sense in crying over a child's dress. It had surprised me, that's all. I wondered what other surprises I would find in the cedar chest. Was it worth digging everything out if I was going to spend the afternoon in tears? But now that I had started, I knew I had to continue. There could be something in the chest that would tell me why my mother was lying up there in that hospital room. I went back to the bedroom and sat down on the floor in front of the chest.

A piece of unfinished crewel work, still clamped between wooden hoops, its needle threaded with chartreuse wool and slipped through the cloth in the middle of a stitch. It told me only that my mother embroidered neatly but had a poor sense of color, both things I already knew. I laid it aside. A wilted corsage in a plastic box. Mine? A book covered in pink leatherette, the front stamped in curving gold script "Our Baby Girl." I picked it up and held it, knowing, although I'd never seen it before, what I would find inside. Why had she never shown me this? Surely it was about me, and didn't that make it more mine than hers to hide away like this? Maybe, after the dates and vital statistics, there was some dreadful secret recorded. I opened it to the first page.

And found only what I had expected. My name, my birthdate, the name of the hospital, and the signatures of both my parents. So that was what Raymond my father's handwriting looked like, a swift scrawl overflowing the line meant to contain it. Beside it, my mother's name kept neatly to the space allowed, each prim, round letter carefully formed to make a legible whole. Printed on the page was a quaint illustration of a stork perched on a chimney top with a bundle dangling from its beak. No other information. I turned the page.

Here the first thing I saw was a photograph. An uncompromising, well-lit, head-on shot of an ugly, wizened creature, wrapped in a blanket and lying in a small crib. The eyes were screwed shut and the mouth pouted open. There seemed to be no hair on its head. Across the bottom of the picture was printed the name of the hospital, and handwritten in red ink the date and the words "Holland girl." I wasn't a beautiful baby. From the information recorded under the photograph, I learned that I had weighed five pounds and two ounces, and measured a little over fifteen inches. I was born a few minutes before midnight. I hadn't known any of this before, and now that I knew it, it seemed to apply to someone else, some other baby that grew up and lived a different life. Not me.

The next page was devoted to comments, and my mother had dutifully written in her neat round hand, "Jenny a good baby, never a bit of trouble since the moment she was born. On formula, but doesn't seem to need a lot. Dr. says this is all right since she is on the small side and I shouldn't worry. Raymond loves to play with her and can't wait for her to grow and talk and call him 'Daddy.' Mother comes to visit every day and wants us to come out and stay with her at River House so she can take care of us. But I tell her we are doing just fine, the three of us, and I like being close to the Dr.'s office just in case. Raymond is building a rocking horse even though I tell him it'll be a couple of years before she can use it."

A rocking horse! I rode it for years and loved it, but I never knew he'd built it. Was it still here in the house? I longed to touch something he had touched. Flipping through the book, then, past the obligatory pages where my mother had recorded weight gains, first tooth, crawling, walking, and my first birthday celebration, I found in a small white envelope pasted to the page a wisp of pale, fine hair and learned that my first word had been "car." On that page, my mother had written, "Jenny loves to go riding with Raymond in the Pontiac."

How strange to learn these things about myself, to know that the car of which Raymond my father was so proud was part of my life, too. And how utterly unremarkable. There was nothing here to give me the slightest clue to my mother's present mental condition. It could have been anyone's baby book, all the entries quite normal and ordinary. And again, I wondered why she had never shown it to me. Had she tried to erase all memory of Raymond from our lives after he died? Had his death wounded her so badly? Or had he done something to hurt her *before* he died, something so unforgivable that she felt she had to deny his very existence to herself, and to me?

The book obviously wasn't going to tell me that. I was about to put it aside to read again later, and perhaps to take back to New York with me, when the back cover flipped open and a photograph fell out into my lap.

Shock! The sudden chill, the quick thud of the heart and then its rapid, frightened skittering, the leaden weight in the stomach, and the prickling of the skin into premonitory bumps. All that, and more. It was not so much the photograph, that of a seven- or eight-year-old girl and a tall man, clearly father and daughter, certainly Raymond and me, but what had been

done to the photograph. The man's eyes had been poked ou
and other holes riddled his body, in the chest where his hear
would be, in the stomach, and at the place where his long leg
came together. The girl stood at his side, smiling and un
harmed.

I stared down at the photograph in my lap, unable to
touch it, to pick it up and hide it back in the book where it ha
lain mutilated all these years. Sightless, my father gazed up a
me. Sickened, I examined his wounds. Paper wounds, it's true
but nonetheless, a killing, awful, hate-filled piercing of his body
Why? What had made my mother stab and stab and stab agai
and then hide her murderous rage in the idyllic record of m
birth?

Should I show it to her and demand an explanation? No
That would be cruel and might send her further into the weir
world she inhabited. Could I show it to anyone else? Wendell
Bonnie Marie? Aunt Tillie? Again, no. If they knew anythin
about this, they would have told me by now. Fearn certainl
would have told me. David would be sympathetic but couldn'
possibly explain it. All I could do was show it to the psychiatris
in the morning and hope that it might help her help my mother
Oh, God, it was ugly!

I forced my fingers to pick it up. Holding it squeamishl
by the white border, I got up from the floor and went to he
writing desk. An envelope was what I needed. I found one i
the top drawer and slid the photograph into it, face down so a
I could see was the raised edges of the puncture holes. I neve
wanted to look at that eyeless face again.

The writing desk showed no sign of recent use. Lik
everything else, its surface was covered with a layer of dus
Besides a few envelopes and sheets of stationery, the top drawe
held a postcard from Wendell dating from the time he'd take
his family to Disneyworld (I'd gotten one, too), a book o
thirteen-cent postage stamps, an old-fashioned fountain pe
and a dried-up bottle of Waterman's blue-black ink, a blotte
advertising Sparkey's milk, and a small address book.

I skimmed through the address book, not expecting t
find anything. She obviously hadn't been writing any lette
lately. And indeed, most of the pages were blank. There wer
family addresses clustered here and there. That was all. On a
impulse, I turned to the page for the letter H. There were tw

ntries. One was my New York City address. She must have
otten it from Wendell. The other was a rural delivery route
umber for a person named Alva Holland.

CHAPTER

25

Who was Alva Holland? Man or woman? The name
ould be either. Young or old? A relative of some kind? And
so, why wasn't Alva Holland present at the reunion?

The questions circled in my mind as I walked the three
locks along Plum Street and up Rattlesnake Hill to the hospi-
l. From the top of the hill, I could look down on the river
inding past the town. There was the old bridge that swayed
alarmingly when you drove across it into the next state, cars
ll of high school kids going for something stronger than near
eer. Next to it, the high narrow railroad bridge. And there, a
ile farther downstream, was the new bridge, broad and firm
nd shining, built while I was away. The sun was moving down
e sky, its long golden fingers touching church steeples, that
dd brown glass building that Wendell had pointed out as the
wn's skyscraper, the courthouse tower, a Gothic monstrosity
ut dear and familiar to my eye. The heat of the day was over
nd the evening's cool quietude was settling in. I hadn't prayed
r years, but on the steps of the hospital, I muttered to myself,
Dear God, let her have peace of mind."

I went in the front entrance and identified myself to the
oung nurse at the visitors' desk. She knew me and, when I
oked closely, I remembered her. "Betty Sue? Betty Sue Wig-
ns?"

She nodded and smiled, pleased that I recalled her
ame. "It's Henshaw now. I married Billy Henshaw five years
go. He's on the police. Remember that time he let loose a
uckload of calfs into the Fourth of July parade? He's calmed
wn a lot since then."

I nodded and smiled, too, to show that I remembered Billy Henshaw had been the class clown, a large red-faced boy who laughed loudest at his own jokes. I'd hated and feared him.

"My mother," I whispered to Betty Sue. "I've come to see my mother."

"Well, it's not visiting hours yet," she whispered back, "but I don't think anyone'll mind if you just slide on back there. I hear she really gave them something to gabble about this morning. What brings you back to town, Jenny?"

My smile stayed in place and I ignored her question, murmuring, "Thank you, Betty Sue." I felt her watching me walk away and push through the heavy swinging doors into the main corridor of the hospital. She would tell her husband and her husband would tell his cronies and the cronies would tell their wives and soon the whole town would know that Elizabeth Holland had finally flipped out and isn't it funny that it happened just when her no-good daughter turned up? Must be some connection.

I shrugged off the gossip but found myself wondering if there could be some connection. If I'd stayed away, would she have gone on being just mildly flaky but not remarkably so, not enough to get her into this place and draw down on her the attention of the staff psychiatrist? But isn't it, after all, time she had such attention?

After a couple of wrong turns and an encounter with a pair of teenage boys with plaster casts on their legs drag-racing in their wheelchairs, I found her room. It was quiet, dim, and cool and she lay in the high bed unmoving. Her stiff gray curls had sprung loose from their pins and lay on the pillow in untidy spirals. Perhaps she'd let me brush her hair. I'd found a small suitcase and in it packed hairbrush and comb, toothbrush, nightgown, and a robe. Not the wine-colored robe I remembered, that one was nowhere to be seen, but a pretty flower-printed housecoat all pink and white and lavender. Her hands lay on top of the coverlet, speckled with liver spots, veins prominent, but still and relaxed. I touched one of them. She didn't move. I put the suitcase down beside the bed, pulled the visitor chair over, and sat down.

On the night stand, her untouched supper tray waited. I lifted the metal lid from the plate. A thin slice of meat swimming in brown gravy, a scoop of mashed potatoes, a pile of lima grayish string beans. The round-bellied teapot was barely warm to the touch. A square of green gelatin shimmied in a dessert dish.

"Eat it if you want it."

She was smiling at me. She hadn't moved, but her eyes were open and she seemed glad to see me.

"You should eat it," I told her. "I'll bet you haven't eaten all day. Not since breakfast."

"David is a nice boy. He makes a nice breakfast. You should marry him."

"He's not a boy, Ma. He's a man. And I think he has someone. At least, eat your Jell-O."

She shook her head, wagging it back and forth on the pillow. "Nobody. She ran away. He told me. And he likes you, Jenny. I told him you were ready to settle down. You are, aren't you? If you're not, you ought to be. And then you can go away with him, go right away, tonight, and be safe. He'll take care of you." Her hands had started plucking at the coverlet and her eyes were blinking rapidly against a rush of tears.

"Ma! Ma, don't worry about me!" I caught her fugitive hands in mine. "I can take care of myself. David's very nice. I like him a lot. But I don't think I want to marry him. I don't want to marry anyone."

She turned her head away and mumbled something into her pillow. It sounded like, ". . . my fault. I should have known."

What should she have known?

Anyway, it didn't matter. What mattered now was getting her off the subject of me and any marriages she had in mind for me, and onto what was *really* bothering her. "I brought you some things from home. A nightgown, a robe. Why don't you sit up and let me brush your hair?"

Her head whipped around and her eyes bored into my face. "You went into *my* house?" The words came out in a suppressed scream.

"Yes, I did."

"Who gave you permission? What right do you have?" She struggled to sit up, pulling her hands away from me and trembling with anger. "No one is allowed inside my house. No one!"

I thought she was embarrassed over the mess we'd

found in the kitchen and tried to reassure her. "It's all right, Ma. We cleaned it all up."

" 'We'!" she exploded. "Who's 'we'?"

"David and I."

"You let David into my house!" She sank back into the pillow and closed her eyes. Her whole body went limp. Her lips moved, but I had to strain to catch the words. ". . . what happens when you get old and sick. Strangers take over."

"Ma," I pleaded. "I'm not a stranger."

"Yes, you are," she moaned. "I don't know you."

"You kept my room the same. All my things are there." She shuddered. I thought I'd better change the subject, but before I could find a better one, she rolled away from me and pulled the coverlet over her head.

The room was quiet. My thoughts were clamoring inside my head and so, I supposed, were hers. But thoughts make no noise in a quiet room. I decided to wait and keep my thoughts to myself until she gave me some idea of what she was thinking. And when she did, I would simply agree with her, no matter what she said, no matter how unpleasant or bizarre. Everything I'd said so far seemed to drive her into a frenzy. That wasn't what I was here for. I'd never find out anything if we continued to talk at cross-purposes.

I picked up the suitcase, put it on the chair, and opened it. I laid the nightgown and robe across the foot of the bed. She didn't move. Near the door was a small chest of drawers. I took the supper tray from the night stand and carried it to the chest. It clinked slightly as I set it down.

"Jenny." Her voice came from under the coverlet. "Are you still here?"

"Yes, Ma."

"Will you brush my hair? I'd like that."

"Sure."

I went back to the bed. She tossed the coverlet aside and sat straight up, pulling the remaining pins out of her hair. I took the hairbrush from the suitcase and began to brush. She smiled dreamily.

"Jenny, let's go away, you and I. We'll go where they'll never find us. We'll have a nice little house, or maybe one of those new condominium apartments. We can go to Florida. I've always wanted to go to Florida."

"Sure, Ma." How could I agree to that? "But I have a job and an apartment in New York. Would you like to go there?" I tried to imagine my mother at home in the East Village, visiting me at work in Max's Secondhand Books. I couldn't see it.

"Maybe," she said, "for a little while. But I don't think I'd like New York. And you don't have to work, Jenny. I've got lots of money. We could travel if you wanted to. See the world. I've always wanted to see the world."

"Let's think about it, Ma." I continued to brush the stiffness out of her hair. Without its pins and hair spray, her hair fluffed out into a soft gray aureole.

"We could leave tomorrow. Wouldn't Wendell be surprised?"

Her shoulders were shaking and I realized she was giggling with childish delight. I decided that now, while she was enjoying the prospect of a joke on Wendell, I might get answers to a couple of questions.

"Ma, who's Alva Holland?"

She stopped giggling and sat very still. After a long moment, she spoke. "Why, she's Raymond's sister, of course."

It was that "of course" that prompted me to go on. If my mother was going to pretend there was nothing unusual in the question, I would certainly go along with the game. "Then she's my aunt?"

"Well, yes. Yes, I guess she is."

"Have I ever met her? I mean when I was a child?"

"No. No, I don't believe she ever came around. She's kind of shy."

There was a breathless hush in the room. My mother was waiting for the next question, carefully gauging her reply.

I stroked the hairbrush through her hair. "Was she invited to the reunion?"

"You'll have to ask Wendell that."

"Then Wendell knows her?"

"I'm not sure. Maybe, maybe not. She keeps pretty much to herself."

"Where?"

"What?"

"Where does she keep to herself?"

"I believe she lives on a farm somewhere. Yes, that's it.

Just a small farm." She sighed, a deep, sorrowing heave of relief dredged up from a well of secrets at long last shared. I decided to press on.

"Have you ever visited her, there on the farm?"

"Oh, yes. I believe I've been there once or twice."

"Is it a nice place?"

"Oh, no. No, it was just a little farmhouse, but that burned down and now they have a trailer."

A trailer! Donny! My mother's three-dollar watchman. And the trailer she'd given them after their house burned down.

"Alva has a son, hasn't she?"

"Yes, poor thing. He's not much of a blessing to her."

"His name is Donny and you hired him to watch River House. And you gave them the trailer, didn't you?"

She nodded. "It was nothing. It was the least I could do."

"If Alva's my aunt, then Donny is my cousin. Right?"

"Oh, my. I never thought about that. I guess he is."

"And what about the old man? Donny told me he lives with his mother and his grandfather."

She sighed again. "Well, yes. I guess he does. Oh, that boy! I felt sorry for him, but I told him never to tell anyone. He's not too bright."

We were getting there. I felt as if I were picking my way across a mine field. At any moment, I would ask a question that would set off an explosion. And a question was forming in my mind that would probably do exactly that. I wondered if I ought to save it until after the visit of the psychiatrist. There was something else niggling at my mind, too. Something she'd said that didn't sound quite right. I decided to go ahead and ask my question.

"That room in the attic, Ma. Someone's been living up there. Is it Donny?"

The explosion didn't come. Instead, there was a long silence. I put the hairbrush down and placed both my hands on her thin shoulders, trying to sense what emotions lay under her apparent calm. But I was no mind reader. At last she spoke.

"At River House, you mean?"

"Yes. In the turret room. Where you and Grandma always told me not to go."

"Oh, there." She twisted away from me and leaned back against her pillows. "Roll up my bed, Jenny. I believe I could eat some of my supper now."

I went to the foot of the bed and cranked until the bed was elevated to her satisfaction. Then I carried the tray back and placed it on her lap.

"I'm afraid everything is cold."

"I don't mind. Anything tastes good when you're hungry."

She removed the metal dish cover and began to eat rapidly. Gravy ran down her chin and flecks of mashed potato clung to her lips. She chewed and swallowed the cold bland-looking hospital food with little murmurs of enjoyment.

"You didn't tell me, Ma. Is it Donny who's been camping out in that room?"

"Oh, my goodness, no," she said between swallows. "Donny wouldn't. He's afraid of the house. Thinks it's haunted. He'd never go inside. But there are kids who would, kids driving around looking for a place to . . . you know. Or just to vandalize. They're more afraid of Donny than he is of the house. That's why I set him up as watchman. To keep the kids away. Maybe some of them got in and used that room." She wiped up the last smears of gravy on her plate with a piece of bread and popped it into her mouth. "That must be it. I don't know what kids are coming to these days."

"That's not it, Ma," I insisted. "Someone's been living up there. For a long time. If it's not Donny, who is it?"

She started in on her dessert. "They should have put bananas in. Remember how you used to love lime Jell-O with bananas?"

I remembered nothing of the kind. But I did remember that when my mother turned evasive, it was impossible to get any further information out of her. It was the tactic she'd used whenever I brought up the subject of my father, until finally I'd given up asking. I wasn't quite ready to give up now, but the door opened and a tall, raw-boned, red-haired nurse came into the room.

"Oh, I see you've already got a visitor." She surveyed me with just a hint of disapproval, but then turned her attention to my mother's supper tray. "And you've eaten up all your nice supper. That's good. I can bring you some hot tea if you'd like.'

My mother simpered like a good child and said, "Yes
thank you."

"You've got some other visitors waiting in the hall," th
nurse said as she picked up the tray. "I told them I'd have t
see if you were awake. Visiting hours are from seven to nine an
you're allowed only two at a time." She glanced pointedly a
me.

"It's all right," I said. "I was just leaving. I'll be bacl
in the morning."

As I went out the door, I heard my mother say to th
nurse, "That was my daughter. She brought me a nightgow
and robe. I'd like to put them on before I have any visitors.

It made me feel better to know that I'd done somethin
that pleased her. My mother had always been stingy with prais
and was far more likely to puncture any balloons of pride tha
she found floating over my head. But it wasn't enough just t
have brought her a change of clothes. Somehow I would hav
to bring her back from the land of lies and evasion in whic
she'd been living for . . . how long? Since my father died? Th
thought was hideous, and made more so by the realization tha
I'd left when I was too young and stupid and self-centered t
understand that anything was wrong with her. Well, maybe th
psychiatrist would help.

Down at the end of the corridor, I spotted Wendell an
Bonnie Marie sitting on a bench near the nurse's station. The
were deep in conversation and didn't notice me. I turned th
other way, following the corridor around the corner and bac
to the main entrance where Sunday evening visitors were ac
justing their faces to the appropriate degree of bland optimism
I made my way through the small crowd, my own face concea
ing a heaviness of spirit mingled with a determination to fin
out what it was that had drawn my mother slowly and inexora
bly to the brink of madness.

I decided I would pay a visit to Alva Holland's traile

CHAPTER
26

But first I went home. To my mother's house. I didn't see any point in hanging around the hospital, waiting for Bonnie Marie and Wendell to leave. And even if I did, I'd probably get no further with the questions that still lingered in my mind. I couldn't bring myself to confront my mother with the mutilated photograph—I hadn't even brought it with me—and I suspected that if I did show it to her, she would regard it distantly and spout some plausible but totally false story to explain its condition. Better to leave that to the psychiatrist.

I'd taken the back door key with me. The long twilight was casting purple shadows over the backyard as I let myself into the house. I reached for the light switch just inside the back door before stepping over the threshold, just in case the survivors of the ant war had decided to reestablish their supply line. They hadn't. The kitchen floor was bare and clean, just as we'd left it, and the place still smelled strongly of insecticide and disinfectant.

A bath would be good, and a change of clothing. Perhaps I could find in that museum of a room of mine something to wear that wouldn't be grotesquely juvenile and out-of-date. I passed through the kitchen and dining room into the hall and up the stairs. I'd lived in only two places, this house and my tiny apartment in New York. The apartment seemed suddenly far away and impermanent, too far away to get back to, or if I did get there, I would find someone else living in it. The house was exerting a pull on me, as if I'd never left it, and I had a sudden vision of living in it twenty years from now caring for a sick old mindless wreck of a woman. I shivered. It wouldn't happen that way, I told myself. My mother would straighten up. She'd be her old self again. (But what was her old self?) I'd stay with her as long as necessary, we'd patch up our quarrel, and then I'd leave. And this time, when I got back to New York, I'd *do* something with myself. No more Max's Second-hand Books, no more hiding. (Like mother, like daughter?) I'd get a better job and go to school at night and *learn* something.

Back in my old room again, I rummaged through the closet shoving aside the miniskirts and the granny dresses, looking for something I could wear today. I found a pair of navy blue slacks that didn't have legs a mile wide and a plain white shirt. In the dresser drawer I found clean underwear, white cotton briefs and a bra that would probably still fit. I also found my old high school yearbook, but I resisted the impulse to skim through its pages and put it aside for later.

I had to scrub out the pink bathtub before filling it. My mother had certainly relaxed her housekeeping standards. And on a shelf I found a half-filled bottle of the bath oil to which I'd been partial ten years ago. Why not? I dumped some into the hot rushing water and the bathroom filled with the scent of lemon verbena. Gratefully, I stripped off my clothes and when the bubbles crowded the top of the tub I sank into the steamy depths.

I don't know how long I lay there soaking. I think I must have drifted off into a doze or a deep daydream, because when the ringing started I thought it was a distant school bell and I would be late for school. When I realized it was the telephone, I leaped out of the tub shivering—the water had cooled and the bubbles had all evaporated—and wrapped myself in a towel. The telephone was in the downstairs hall, still clamoring. I could only think that it was the hospital calling, that my mother had gone over the edge, or had a stroke, or worse. I ran down the stairs, my wet feet sliding on the smooth oak treads, and snatched up the phone.

"Hello?" I produced a barely audible gasp.

"Lizzie," came the voice, "you've got to do something. He's out here and he won't go away. You promised you wouldn't let him bother us. I swear I'll shoot him if he doesn't leave."

"Who-who's this?" I stammered. The voice was hoarse and angry, a belligerent cawing in my ear.

"Don't play games, Lizzie. You know perfectly well who this is. You better get out here right away. If you don't, I'm not responsible."

I tried again. "Where are you calling from?"

"Dammit!" the voice screeched. "Where do you think I'm calling from? The gas station. And I have to get back before he does something stupid. Hurry up!"

"Wait! Wait!" I cried into the phone. "How do I get there?"

Silence. Then the voice again, this time still hoarse but reduced to a whisper. "You ain't Lizzie." And the line went dead.

I slumped down into the little phone chair, not caring how my damp towel might stain its needlepoint seat. Who? Who was this voice calling out of the night, for it was night and the hall in darkness except for the glow trickling through from the kitchen where I'd left the lights on. Who was calling on my mother to come quickly and do something about *him*? Who was *he*? And what could I do about it? The voice had threatened to shoot. Should I take the threat seriously and call the police? But what would I tell them? That someone had called my mother and threatened to shoot someone else, but I didn't know who or where? They would either laugh at me and do nothing, or go to the hospital and frighten my mother with their questions. No. She would never tell them anything. But she might tell me.

As I got up from the telephone chair, clutching the damp towel around me, I saw through the dining room window a pair of headlights flash into the driveway and abruptly go out. A car door slammed and running footsteps pounded around to the back of the house. I hesitated, feeling vulnerable in nothing but a towel and apprehensive about who would be rushing up to the house like that. More bad news? I had started for the stairs to find my clothes so I could decently answer the door, when the rapping came and a voice called my name. A familiar voice. David.

Thank God! I forgot the clothes and ran to the door. He stepped smiling into the kitchen, and I fell gratefully into his arms.

"Hey! What is this?" he said. "You're all wet."

"I was taking a bath."

"You sure were. You smell like a lemon."

I wanted to tell him everything but all I could manage was, "Oh, David. What are you doing here?"

He held me close and said, "Wendell asked me to drive your mother's car home. It was up in the church parking lot and he was afraid someone might steal it. Hey, you're shivering. Maybe you ought to get dressed. Not that this isn't kind of nice."

I pulled away from him, wishing the towel was as big as a tent, and felt my skin reddening in a flush that seemed to start at my toes. "I'm sorry," I muttered. "I'll be right back. Don't go away."

I raced away and up the stairs, the towel flapping wetly against my thighs. David called after me, "Don't be long. I've got some news."

News. What could he have to tell me more startling than what I had to tell him? I dressed quickly. The navy blue slacks and white shirt fit as well as they had ten years ago. I buckled on my sandals and ran a comb through my hair. Before I went downstairs, I slipped the envelope containing the mutilated photograph into my pocket. As an afterthought, I added my mother's address book. My mother's bedroom looked sad and lonely in the yellowish light from the overhead fixture. I turned it off and closed the door.

Back in the kitchen, we sat at the round oak table over cups of instant coffee made by David while I was upstairs dressing. The coffee was bitter, but I drank it anyway in hasty gulps between installments of my story. I told him first about the phone call; it was freshest in my mind and most disturbing. He could make nothing of it and agreed that my mother probably could *if* we wanted to take the chance of telling her about it.

"She might want to leave the hospital and go see what the caller wants," he warned.

Then I told him about my visit to the hospital and my mother's admission that there were relatives on my father's side living on a farm nearby and that Donny, the feeble-minded watchman, was one of them.

"Nice of her to look after them," was his only comment.

Finally I pulled the envelope from my pocket and handed it to him. "Look at that," I said. I couldn't bear to look myself, but I told him that I'd found it tucked away inside my baby book. A book I'd never seen before.

He stared at the photograph, turned it over and then

back again, and let out a long low whistle. "Creepy," he said. "She must have been very angry. But look, she wasn't angry at you."

"What should we do?" I asked him. "Should we go and tell her about the phone call? Ask her who it was?"

"We may not have to," he said. He leaned back in his chair, clasping his hands behind his head. His turquoise eyes examined my face as if gauging how much more I could handle. I felt a jolt of apprehension; maybe there were some family secrets that were best left undiscovered.

"I had a little talk with Bonnie Marie this afternoon. She's a nice woman. Really nice and sensible. The others were all splashing around in the pool, and we sat under a tree and talked. I told her how worried you are about your mother, and she's worried, too. She thinks that your mother's been fretting for years over something that happened a long time ago. And she told me what she thought that something was. She's never told anyone else.

"It seems that before Bonnie Marie married Wendell, she used to work in the County Clerk's office. After they got engaged, she kept right on working up until a week before the wedding. Well, things are usually kind of slow in the court-house and one day, just for something to do, she started looking up the vital statistics of the family she was marrying into. She said that at first all she wanted to do was find out how far back the family went. She knew it was an old family, probably as old as the town itself. And she knew there'd been stories about you and Wendell. This was about a year or so after you'd left. So she looked up your birth record just to be passing the time on a slow afternoon. Well, the records were kept in big ledgers then, one for each year, and she started thumbing through the pages, taking note of all the familiar names, people who were born in the same year and matching them up with what they were doing in that year. She told me she found you in Septem-ber and just started turning the pages backward toward the beginning of the year, picking out this name and that name, and when she got as far back as March, there it was again. The name *Holland*.

"Well, as far as she knew, she said, there weren't any other Hollands in town, except for your mother. But maybe there were years ago and they all left or died off. So she looked at the name of the baby. It was Donald Earl. She didn't know of any young man by that name. Then she looked at the names of the parents. Alva Beggs Holland and Raymond Earl Holland. She flipped back to September and there it was again. Raymond Earl Holland. Your father.

"She didn't know what to make of it, and being Bonnie Marie, she kept it to herself. It all happened a long time ago and for all she knew there could have been two of them, cousins with the same name, or your father could have been married to someone else and got divorced before he married your mother. She didn't find any record of a divorce, but it could have happened in another town. So she just put it away in the back of her mind and never spoke to a soul about it until today. Only she did say that after she got to know your mother and the brief acquaintance she had with your grandmother, she got to wondering if maybe Raymond had been one of those men with wives all over the place and if that was what your mother was brooding on. But she never asked and wasn't about to start up a lot of gossip over ancient history."

I sipped my bitter coffee. Bigamy? Raymond my father a bigamist? Poor silly Donny my brother? Half-brother? It didn't make sense. No! It couldn't be! Because what was it my mother had told me this afternoon? That Alva Holland was . . .

"It's not true!" I cried. "Alva Holland is my aunt. She's my father's sister. So Donny is . . . Donny is . . ."

I couldn't say it. But he had to be someone else's son. The records were wrong. It was a mistake. Bonnie Marie was lying. But why should she? Then she didn't remember correctly. It was some other name. I would go see Alva Holland and make her name Donny's father. I dug out the address book and opened it shakily to the H page.

"We'll find out," I whispered. "Here's the address. We'll go there right now."

David took the book and looked at the page. "Jenny," he said patiently, "this is only a rural route number. It's not a road. I don't know how to find it."

I snatched the book back. He was right. "Call the post office. They'll know."

"The post office is closed."

I remembered my conversation, if you could call it that, with Donny on the back porch. I'd asked him where he lived nd he'd replied, "On the farm," with a vague wave of his hand oward the area beyond River House.

"We'll drive out River Road and explore every lane and cowpath on the other side of River House. Donny told me the arm is out in that direction. We'll find it."

"Okay. Okay." He grabbed my hand as I was loping oward the back door. "Hold on, Jenny. What about that phone call? Did the voice sound like a woman?"

I tried to recall the hoarse words that had squawked angrily in my ear. "I don't know. It could have been."

"Could it have been Alva Holland?"

"We'll find out."

CHAPTER
27

We drove out River Road in darkness. I'd forgotten how bsolutely pitch black it could be on country roads at night, with only the headlights of the car to show us the sudden curves, the unexpected dips and bumps in the road. The trees losed in and shook their heavy branches at us, black against he black sky. There were no stars and the moon must have een busy elsewhere. It seemed that we'd been driving for ours, but when I looked at the lighted clock in the dashboard, t read nine-thirty. Only twenty minutes since we'd left my nother's house.

My mother's car, a sedate elderly Buick, smelled of range peel and old galoshes. I remembered how she used to at oranges, daintily on a china plate, peeling them with a earl-handled fruit knife, the rind falling away in a perfect piral. She would separate each segment with her fingers and ibble at it delicately. She always tried to remove the pips before ach bite, prodding the juicy flesh with the point of her knife. But if one made its way into her mouth, she would raise her apkin and behind its discreet cover, spit the seed into the palm of her other hand and from there brush it onto the plate. Very ladylike. I wondered how, and when, she ate oranges in the car. Perhaps I would take some to her at the hospital.

We drove without speaking, David concentrating on the twisting road and I awash in the memories that had been flooding my mind since my arrival at the reunion. When the lights of River House appeared on the right, I said, "Let's stop a minute. I want to get my bag. I'll need it in the morning."

He drove up the dirt drive and parked on the grass next to Aunt Tillie's Porsche. Apparently everyone had returned from Wendell's swimming party. The front porch light was on and country music wailed from the radio in the parlor.

David said, "I ought to see how Malachi's doing. I left him with Fearn."

We went into the house. Walter Proud and David's brother Mike were hunched over a checkerboard in the parlor. Walter looked up and smiled when he saw us. "How's your mother?" he asked.

There wasn't much I could say without launching into a long explanation, so I smiled back and said, "Okay."

David asked, "Where's Malachi?"

"Upstairs," said Walter. "Fearn's putting all the kids to bed."

Mike jumped one of Walter's red checkers and smirked, "Smart kid you got there, Davey-boy." He leered at David. "Must have inherited it from his mother."

David ignored him and started up the stairs.

Mike called after him, "Must have got that black hair from her, too. None of us got hair like that."

I felt my neck getting hot and my hands tingling. I wanted to slap his smug mouth. David just continued on up the stairs. Walter pushed a red checker forward and said, "Your move."

Mike was enjoying himself. "You're nothing but a squaw-man, Davey," he shouted. "And she left you holding the baby. Haw! Haw! Should have stuck to your own kind."

His laugh was lacerating, his scornful words obscene. But there was something else that enraged me, something about the checkerboard. It lay on the table, black and red, black and red. He shouldn't be touching it. No one should be touching it. No one would ever touch it again.

I rushed into the room, picked up the checkerboard and brought it down on his head. Red and black checkers went flying. One of them hit me in the eye. I felt the board crack in my hands, but I went on flailing at him with the two halves.

He laughed. He grabbed my wrists and roared with brutal, mocking, humiliating laughter. "You like him, don't you, kid?" he sneered. "You're just creaming your jeans for my freaky brother. Everybody can see it. Well, you're nothing but a freak yourself. You make a fine pair. Wild west hippie and big city chippy. How do you like that for a poem? A l-o-o-ve poem." He drawled the last words so that they sounded like an obscenity.

I struggled but he was stronger. He pulled me closer to him. I realized from his beery breath and bloodshot squinting eyes that he was drunk. It seemed like a year that he held my arms and peered accusingly into my face. I didn't want to yell and bring David running. I'd provoked Mike, so I had to deal with his anger. But it was Walter, kind, stolid Walter, who broke up the uneven struggle. He came between us and put a hand on Mike's shoulder.

"Looks like you won the game," he said. "You gonna give me another chance?"

Mike looked confused. The checkerboard was lying on the floor split in half. The checkers were scattered about on the blue oceanic carpet. At a glance from Walter, I stopped trying to twist away and stood very still. Mike said, "Sure."

Walter plucked Mike's hands away from my wrists and pressed him back into his chair. Mike sagged and shook his head blearily. I stooped to help Walter pick up the scattered checkers, but he said, "Maybe you can find us some Scotch tape, Jenny. I think we can put that board back together."

I fled. As I ran up the stairs, I heard Mike muttering, "Son of a bitch! *He* should have to live with the old man for a while. Put the one-legged old bastard on the back of his motorcycle and take him away. Drop him in the Grand Canyon for all I care."

Wendell's reunion was turning into a seething cauldron of long-hidden resentments. I opened the door to my grandmother's bedroom and flicked on the light. I should have locked it, but we'd left in such a hurry I didn't have a chance. If the gun was gone from its hiding place . . . but it wasn't. I ran my hand under the mattress and felt its reassuring steely hardness. Quickly, I took it to the window seat, where I sat and reloaded it according to Wendell's instructions. My shoulder bag was lying on the floor next to the chaise longue. I put the gun in the bag, relieved to have it out of sight but ready in case I needed it. I hoped I wouldn't, but the voice on the phone had spoken of shooting. David didn't have to know I was carrying it, unless something happened. And then he might be glad.

As I left the room, I glanced into the wide mirror that sat atop the ornate mahogany dresser. The mirror was flawed with age, but even allowing for that, I looked terrible. There were dark circles under my eyes, and my face looked pale and pinched. My hair hung in limp wisps around my cheeks. And the clothes, those ten-year-old schoolgirl clothes, made me feel infantile and helpless.

Nonsense. No one with a gun in her bag is helpless. And I wasn't entering a beauty contest. It didn't matter how I looked. Nevertheless, I pulled a lipstick out of my bag and laid a touch of color on my lips. It didn't help my face much, but it made me feel a little better. I left the room, closing the door behind me.

And came face-to-face with Fearn across the hall. She was just tiptoeing out of her own bedroom, a look of sheer exhaustion on her face. When she saw me, she raised a finger to her lips and whispered around it, "Ssh. I think they're sleeping. What a day!"

I gave her a sympathetic nod and started on my way downstairs to wait for David in the car. One thing I didn't want right now was to get involved in a wrangle with Fearn. But she put a hand on my arm and drew me back up the hall toward the room that Petey and Arlene had used the night before. "Don't go, Jenny," she whispered. "I want to show you something."

Footsteps sounded overhead. David was up there with Malachi, and a burst of noisy teenage horseplay indicated that Irene and Mike's boys were up there, too. Irene's voice floated down in exasperated scolding. From below, the radio moaned a nasal melancholy lament, and Uncle Ambrose called out for his hot milk. Mike cursed, and Walter said, "I'll go." Everything was normal.

Everything but Fearn's face. Her lips were stiff and

colorless and her eyes darted every which way as if searching for lurkers in the shadows.

"What is it?" I asked as I let her pull me along.

"You'll see. It's in this room."

I had enough on my mind without getting involved in any more of Fearn's crusades. I'd look at whatever it was she wanted to show me—probably some household offense committed by the defectors from the reunion—and be on my way. At least she'd found some other target for her fits of dudgeon. She pulled me right up to the door of the back bedroom, made sure I was standing exactly in the doorway, then reached across me, turned the knob and flung the door open.

"There!" she exclaimed. "What do you think of that?"

Lights blazed in the room. There was blood everywhere. Splattered on the walls, speckled on the ceiling, streaked in wavering trails across the floor. The white candlewick bedspread on the double bed was soaked with it. And in the middle of the bed lay a stained bedraggled heap.

"It's a chicken!" I blurted.

"A chicken," she echoed. "And that's not all. Look at the mirror."

I did as she commanded. The dresser could have been a twin to the one in my grandmother's room. Its mirror was wide and framed in heavily carved wood. But scrawled across the darkening glass of this one were the words "GET OUT," dried to a brownish crust. On the dresser itself, a milk glass vase held a bunch of strawflowers into which the chicken's head had been thrust. It stared at me stupidly, its beak open and its beady eyes fixed on whoever stood in the doorway.

I stepped across the threshold, leaving Fearn behind me in the hall. It was incredible to think that a chicken would contain so much blood. I peered at the feathery corpse on the bed. Apparently its neck had been wrung. I had a fleeting memory of my grandmother wringing a chicken's neck. She'd gripped it by its head and whirled the squawking creature around and around in the air until its body went flapping and flying across the yard. Then the headless chicken had run in aimless, erratic circles for what seemed an eternity, blood spurting from its neck, until finally it collapsed in a quivering heap. I hadn't eaten any of that chicken.

Something like that had happened here in this room.

Someone had brought the chicken here and wrung its neck and scrawled that message on the mirror. But who?

Fearn was babbling in the hall. "I knew someone had been here when we got back from Wendell's. I can sense things like that. Since my operation, I'm very sensitive. But everything seemed quiet. Petey and Arlene were gone. Their car was gone. I came up to see if they'd forgotten anything. And I found that. You can imagine what a shock it was."

"Didn't you tell anyone?"

"Well, of course. I told Walter. Showed it to him. No one else, though. Mike's been drinking beer all afternoon. He'd be no help. And Tillie's such a snob, I wouldn't give her the time of day. Let her find out for herself."

"Where is she now?" Fearn would survive the shock. She'd already resumed hostilities.

"Gone to bed with a good book. That's what she said. Said she'd had enough of this family soap opera and needed to refresh her mind with something truly tragic. I don't have to take insults like that."

It crossed my mind that Aunt Tillie had the right idea. But I couldn't say that to Fearn. Instead I asked her, "What did Walter say?"

"He said maybe we ought to do it. Get out, I mean. So, I guess we'll be leaving in the morning. I don't think I'll get a wink of sleep tonight wondering if it's going to be one of us next, instead of a chicken."

"Is that all?" I demanded. "Didn't either one of you try to find out who did it?"

She shrugged. "Walter looked around. But he didn't find anybody. He wanted to go back into town and get the police out here. But what good would that do? Just make more trouble for the family, and it'd be all over town by morning. Do you think that weird kid of Petey's could have done it? That Luke?"

"No," I said. "I don't think it was Luke."

I had a pretty good idea of who'd killed the chicken and been responsible for all the other strange events of the past few days. Donny Holland, despite his protestations of never having been inside the house, was just off balance enough to wring a chicken's neck and write messages in blood on the mirror. For reasons of her own, my mother had taken him under her protection, giving him a "job" as watchman. Maybe he took his job too seriously and was trying to frighten us all away. He'd told me he lived on a farm. But there was nothing to stop him from prowling around River House and making himself a hideaway in the turret room. For all I knew, he might be harboring some resentment at not having been invited to the reunion. Or his mother might have put him up to it; she'd be far more likely to be suffering from the snub than Donny, who seemed not even to know the family name or connection. Once we found Alva Holland, I was sure we'd find a few answers.

"What's going on here?"

I turned at the sound of David's voice. Fearn was trying to push the door closed against his shoulder.

"It's nothing," she insisted. "Nothing to worry about."

"No, it's all right, Fearn," I said. "Let him see. David's got as much right as the rest of us to know what's happened."

Petulantly, Fearn flung the door away from her, banging it against the wall. David peered into the room and sucked in a startled breath.

"It's only a chicken," I told him, warning him with a glance not to say anything about our search for the Holland farm.

He stepped into the room, carefully avoiding the wandering trails of blood on the floor. "Did a job, didn't they?" he commented. He stared at the message on the mirror, turned away from the gaping chicken's head among the strawflowers, and poked at the feathered heap on the bed. "I wonder how long it's been there."

"I found it when we came back from Wendell's about an hour ago," Fearn said. She leaned against the door jamb and groaned. "Ooooh, I think I'm going to be sick."

I wasn't feeling exactly well myself. The smell of blood was lodged in the back of my throat and a dull pain was gathering behind my eyes. David saved us both from disgrace.

"Look here," he said. "Jenny's told me about all the things that have been going on here. It's only reasonable to assume that whoever's been doing the other mischief did this, too."

"But who?" Fearn whimpered. "I can't take much more of this."

"Well, we know it wasn't any one of us," David explained. "We were all together at Wendell's all afternoon. And Aunt Elizabeth's in the hospital, so she couldn't have done it."

"What about her?" Fearn pointed a chubby finger at me. "She didn't come to Wendell's at all. She could have come out here and done it. Nobody's seen her since she left her poor mother at the mercy of those quacks. If you ask me, she's the one who needs to have her head examined."

"No! I didn't. I swear it." But even to my own ears, my protests sounded thin and insubstantial. Could I have done it? How much time had I really spent poring over the past in my mother's dusty bedroom? How long had I lain soaking in the bathtub before that strange telephone call had dragged me to my senses? Could I have lost a couple of hours in which I had somewhere found a live chicken and the means to transport both it and myself to River House and done . . . this? My mind had been leaping back and forth from the secrets of the past to the puzzles of the present. What if there'd been some kind of overload, a short circuit, and I'd been out doing things of which I had no memory? Or suppose there was another personality living inside me? I remembered the book I'd read about the girl, Sybil, who'd had something like sixteen different personalities. Could something like that be happening to me? This other person could have been sleeping all these years and awoke only on my return to my grandmother's house. The thought was terrifying . . . someone else using my body, my hands, my eyes, my mouth, to speak and act in ways that were totally alien to me and beyond my control. Fearn's voice brought me back to the bloodstained room and David's dear, sensible presence.

"Look at her!" she squawked. "If that isn't the face of guilt, I don't know what it is!"

David put his arm around me and his warmth made me realize how cold I'd suddenly become. "Don't be frightened," he said. "I know it isn't you. We'll find out who it is. Are you ready?"

I nodded, clutching my bag close to my body. I could feel the weight of the gun against my hip.

"Ready for what?" Fearn demanded. "What are you two up to?"

"We're going for a little ride," he told her. "I can't tell you where or what it's about right now, because we don't know. But once we *do* know, we'll tell you and everyone else. Just be patient."

"Patient!" Fearn exploded. "How can I be patient when we all might be killed in our beds! It's all right for you to go gallivanting all over the countryside. You don't have to stay here with a houseful of kids and a murdering maniac likely to drop by unannounced."

"Fearn," I tried to reason with her, "no one's been harmed. I know it's unpleasant and frightening, but whoever's been playing these tricks hasn't tried to hurt anyone. Apparently he just wants us all to go away."

"Well, I'm going." She stalked to the door and paused there, flushed with ill will and suspicion. "First thing in the morning. And Walter and I are going to stay up all night just to make sure that nothing else happens. I wish I'd never heard of a family reunion. This is one family that should stay as far apart from each other as possible. I told Wendell it wouldn't work, but he's a softhearted fool."

She clumped away down the stairs. I looked at David and whispered, "Donny?"

"Could be," he said. "With any luck, we'll find out."

He took my hand and led me out of the bloodied room, closing the door behind us. Once in the hall, I could breathe freely again, and the thickness in my throat subsided. The pain behind my eyes, however, remained like a leaden weight pressing on my brain. Fatigue, I supposed, or worry. I'd felt that way before. Years ago, before I'd got up the courage to leave my mother's house and make my own way. Never in the years since.

We went down the stairs. The house was quiet. Fearn had probably gone back to the kitchen to brew coffee for her all-night vigil. As we passed the parlor, Walter looked up from the broken checkerboard which he was trying to mend. The checkers had all been picked up and stacked in rows on the low marble-topped table.

"Found some tape in the kitchen," he said. "It's pretty dried out, but it might work."

Mike lay on the sofa, asleep.

"I'm sorry about the checkerboard," I said, wondering what there was about it that had set me off. It seemed just an ordinary checkerboard now, old and worn and broken.

Walter grinned. "He asked for it. I was tempted to do it myself. He cheats."

"Fearn tells me you're leaving in the morning."

"Well, I guess. That's pretty nasty upstairs. You saw it?"

I nodded.

"Don't want the kids to see it. Guess I'll clean it up."

"Don't," said David. "Let it be for a while. At least until we get back. We might have some news."

"You know who did it?" Walter asked.

"No," I said, "but there's someone we have to see. Maybe then we'll know."

Walter looked his question at me, but didn't ask it.

I answered it anyway. "I don't think there's any danger. David wouldn't leave Malachi here if there were."

Walter nodded. "I'll wait up for you anyway. Keep an eye on things."

CHAPTER 28

Back on River Road, we drove slowly with the dank night smell of the river seeping in the open windows. I watched my side of the road for a break in the vegetation that might indicate a lane or driveway leading to Alva Holland's farm. It couldn't be far. Donny had returned that morning in less than half an hour with his basket of tomatoes. But he'd gone through the woods on a familiar path, probably straight as the crow flies, in broad daylight, while we had to follow in darkness the twists and turns of the road that paralleled the winding course of the river, not knowing what we were looking for.

I searched my memory for a picture of what lay in this direction. There was only a hazy recollection of a ramshackle roadside stand where my mother had bought sweet corn and a dirty boy had thrown pebbles at me from behind a tree. A dirty boy! I must have made some sound as the connection fell into place, for David slowed the car still further.

"What is it?" he asked. "See something?"

"No. Keep going," I said, "but watch for a shack at the side of the road. It might not even be there anymore."

The dirty boy had been Donny. There was no doubt of it in my mind. Even then, my mother had known. But *what* had she known? Or had she been trying to find out? I could dredge up nothing more, no sound of words, no image of the person tending the stand, and no idea of whether this had happened before or after my father had died.

We traveled on in silence with only the constant purring of the car's engine forming a background for my thoughts. Not thoughts. No. There was nothing coherent about the tangled drift of my mind as the car jounced and bucketed along the pitted road. Faster! Faster! A screaming sense of urgency rebelled at our snaillike progress. We had to get there before . . . before what? At the same time, another voice cautioned. Back off! Go away! There are things here better left undisturbed. Overriding the conflict was curiosity. Alva Holland was my father's sister. What could she tell me about him? Would she look like him? Was the old man Donny'd spoken of my grandfather? I craved answers. I wanted to go back to my mother and tell her I knew all her secrets and they weren't so dreadful after all, not dreadful enough to send her to the brink of insanity. If only she had shared them with me, she could have saved herself. She could *still* save herself.

The pain in my head was gaining in strength. I groped in my bag for a tissue to blot away the wetness that had begun to seep from my eyes, and felt the reassuring hardness of Wendell's gun. Beside me, David was crouched over the steering wheel, staring into the stream of light cast by the headlights. I wiped my eyes and almost missed it. David hadn't seen it at all. We were past it before I realized what it was.

"Stop!" I cried. "Back up! There's something. . . ."

It was a rural mailbox, a gray metal cave sitting atop a tilted post. Its door hung open and the small metal flag on its side dangled uselessly downward. Beside the post, a rutted grass-grown track led into the thicket. I leaped out of the car and in the light spilling from the headlights' beams examined the mailbox for traces of a name. There were flecks of black paint but nothing that resembled a whole word or even a single letter. I closed the little metal door and it immediately fell open again. There were scuttlings in the dark interior of the box. I thought of spiders, scorpions, centipedes, and backed away. The flag on the side of the box fell off into the tall grass. It would never again stand upright to summon the mailman for an important letter to be picked up. How long since it had done so?

David had gotten out of the car and was prowling around on the other side of the road. He called to me, and I crossed behind the car making for his dark silhouette. The river seemed closer to the road here, the slope not quite so steep. I could hear water lapping at the shore, but could see only flat darkness in that direction. And then I heard David's boots knocking against something hollow and wooden.

"Is this what you're looking for?" he asked.

I went closer and saw what he had found. A couple of splintered boards lying on the ground, a weathered fruit crate, its bottom stove in, a broken Mason jar. That was all. If there had ever been more, it had long since been carried away and put to other uses.

"I don't know," I told him. "There's a road on the other side. Not a road really. Just a couple of wheel ruts going off into the woods. Looks like it hasn't been used for a long time."

"Should we try it?"

"Might as well."

We got back into the car and David backed it around until it nosed straight into the overgrown track. Slowly we edged forward. Branches scraped the top of the car and struck in through the open window to tug at my arm. I closed the window halfway. Once, David had to get out to remove a fallen tree limb from the path, while I sat listening to the night sounds of the forest. Distant screechings, nearby croakings, faint patterings of small clawed feet. Moths fluttered in the car's twin beams. I sat stiff and still, grateful for the safe cocoon of the car's metal body. David came back and we drove on.

At last we came to a clearing. The track ended abruptly at a patch of ground where nothing grew. In the center of the clearing something tall and squarish blotted out what we could see of the sky. David jockeyed the car around so its lights shone on the dark column, and we got out. The ground crunched underfoot. There was a faint acrid smell in the air. The night sounds all seemed far away, as if even the animals avoided this place.

David took my hand and we walked closer. I was grateful for his presence and his strength, but I walked with my other hand plunged inside my shoulder bag gripping the butt of Wendell's gun. The acrid smell grew stronger, like a fireplace long unused but never cleaned out.

"Watch it!" cried David.

He pulled me to a halt. Our next steps would have taken us tumbling into a pit. The headlights swept over the blackened area, but from where we stood we could just distinguish a drop of about four or five feet. There appeared to be a jumble of debris piled at the bottom, rising from there to a distorted mound on the other side of the tall structure.

"It's a chimney," said David. "This must have been a house that burned. Most of it collapsed into the cellar, but the chimney's still standing and I think part of the back wall is still in place."

I stared across the abyss, trying to see vacant doors and windows without much success. The car's lights didn't penetrate that far. But the chimney, now that David had identified it, revealed itself brick by brick until its top was lost in darkness.

"Well, there's no one living here. That's for sure," said David. "We might as well press on, if I can turn the car around and get us out of here."

"No, wait," I whispered. "This is the place. I'm sure of it. Donny told me his house burned down and my mother gave them a trailer to live in. It must be somewhere near here."

I strained my eyes against the darkness, searching for a glint of metal or the sheen of glass that would give us the location of the trailer.

"It would help if we had a flashlight. I'll see if there's one in the car."

David left me standing at the brink of the exposed cellar and ran back to the car. I began picking my way around the wreckage toward the chimney, realizing as I walked that the crunching underfoot came from shards of glass, windows that had shattered when the house burned. It must have been a terrifying sight. Flames leaping skyward in the lonely clearing, no hope of putting the fire out before the entire house was destroyed.

As I came around the bulk of the chimney, straying out of the glare of the headlights, I sensed rather than saw movement on the other side of the burned-out hulk.

"Who's there?" I called. My throat was suddenly constricted and the words were barely audible.

"Who's there?" came back at me. An echo? Or another voice mocking my fear?

I pressed up against the damp bricks of the chimney, feeling the softness of moss under my fingers. Sounds came to me. Tired creakings as the charred boards of the remaining wall swayed in the breeze, a faint chink as if a foot had dislodged a small stone in passing. A sigh.

"Donny?" I whispered into the night.

And "Donny" came whispering back. Or was it "Jenny"? I couldn't be sure. I clung to the mossy wall of the chimney, trembling but with every sense alert. Was that a flash of white through the trees beyond? I remembered the voice that had called me on the bank of the river while I crouched trembling on the rock. Then I hadn't been sure if it was real or a voice out of a dream calling inside my head. I hadn't told David about it because I wasn't sure. But there'd been a flash of something white through the trees then, too. Round and white, like Donny's pale moon face. I was about to call his name again, when I heard the car's door slam and David's footsteps come crunching over the glass-strewn earth.

"Jenny," he called, "where are you?"

"Over here." I kept my voice low, hoping he would do the same. "By the chimney."

He came around the pile of bricks, playing the strong beam of a flashlight before him. "I turned the lights off," he said. "Don't want to run the battery down."

"Ssh," I cautioned him. "I just saw something in the trees. A face, maybe. I don't know. It was just a flash of white."

"Where?"

I leaned away from the chimney and pointed vaguely in the direction of the trees behind the burned-out shell.

"Good," he said. "We're in luck. The moon's coming up. That must have been what you saw."

I looked over his shoulder and saw the moon's white face half-hidden by the restless treetops. Was that what I had seen? I thought it had been closer to the ground, about the height of a man. But I could have been mistaken. I could have been hearing things and seeing things. It wouldn't surprise me. Pretty soon, I'd be seeing Donny Holland under the bed. David was leading the way toward the woods at the back of the clearing, and I followed.

"There's a path here," he said.

It wasn't much of a path, just a narrow trail that wound between the trees, but it seemed to lead always in one direction, away from the river. We had to walk single file, David and the flashlight leading the way, I stumbling along behind. I wished I had worn some sturdy shoes; twigs and stones kept filtering into my sandals and I had to stop often and shake them out. I was sure we sounded like an army trampling through the undergrowth, and I wondered if any of it was poison ivy. I'd know in the morning.

Suddenly, we came out into a field. The light was surprising, even blinding after the dark of the forest, and I blinked under the gibbous moon now riding halfway up the sky. David turned off his flashlight. The field was studded with stubble; it must have been early corn, all harvested now. In the distance, about a mile away, a string of colored lights indicated the spread of commercial enterprise along the new highway. It looked pretty from here, warm and glowing and friendly, and I wished I were sitting safely in a plastic hamburger palace with David across the table from me, instead of standing in this cornfield on the brink of discovery.

The trailer was there. The path led across the stubbled cornfield in a straight line right up to the silvery shape of it. It looked like a clumsy spacecraft stranded in the middle of an alien landscape. There were darker shapes around it, outbuildings, no doubt, for corn and chickens and farm machinery. No need to wonder where Donny had found his sacrificial bird. Yellow light shone from the trailer's windows.

David turned to me. "What do you say, Jenny? Advance or retreat?"

"We've come this far," I answered. "If it's not Alva Holland's place, maybe they'll know where we can find her." But I was sure we'd found my father's sister.

We trudged along the path, easier going now with the moonlight showing us the way and no tangled forest to slow us down. As we drew closer to the trailer, a pungent green scent filled the air. It seemed to come from the left of the path where a darker area of rustling leaves rose up and spread into the distance. Donny's tomato vines.

The trailer was raised on cinder blocks. Its windows were open, but I heard no sound from within. We walked around to the side where two cinder block steps led up to a narrow door. David started up the steps but I held him back with a light touch on his arm. He understood and stepped aside. I mounted the steps and knocked at the flimsy door.

"Who's there?" came a voice from within. I couldn't tell if it was the voice I'd heard on the phone.

"Jenny Holland. I'm looking for my aunt Alva."

Silence.

I knocked again.

"Just a minute."

Faintly, I heard the slap of bare feet moving away from the door. Then one of the windows toward the back of the trailer went dark. The feet came back and the door opened a crack. Not enough for me to see who was on the other side of it, but enough for a single eye to stare at me in the narrow shaft of light. I let myself be examined. At last, the door swung open.

The woman who stood in the doorway was tall and thin. She wore a pair of men's bib overalls bleached to a pale streaky blue and a faded chambray work shirt with the sleeves rolled up. Her face and arms were brown and freckled, and her hair was braided into a silvery coronet. She stood and gazed down at me, her eyes the color of sleet. She didn't speak.

"Are you Alva Holland?" I tried not to stammer.

She took her time about answering. When she did, it wasn't helpful. "What if I am?"

"I'd like to talk to you."

She caught sight of David, standing a few steps away in the yard. "Who's he?" she asked.

"David Mears. A cousin."

She smiled then, without pleasure, showing strong white teeth between thin lips. "That's right," she said. "You folks are having a reunion." She drawled the word, making it sound like a ridiculous enterprise. "I heard."

"Can we come in?"

She stood back from the door, holding it open. "Help yourself."

I mounted the last step and walked into the trailer. David followed close behind. The woman looked him over frankly, as if he were a stud bull she was thinking of using to service her herd. He looked back just as candidly, then they both grinned and shook their heads. I felt, for that brief moment, like a child who'd blundered into a forbidden room and seen what she was not supposed to see. Then it passed. David put his arm around my shoulder and the woman slouched against the door as she closed it.

"*Are* you Alva Holland?" I asked again.

"Might as well admit it," she replied, "but don't start thinking it's gonna do *you* any good."

It was hard to tell how old she was. I'd thought of her as being a contemporary of my mother. And my father. But she seemed much younger. The overalls hung loosely on her tall frame and disguised whatever figure she might have. Her hands were roughened from farm work, but her face was smooth with the only lines radiating from her eyes, the result, no doubt, of squinting into the sun. Her coronet of hair, which I'd thought gray, was revealed in the lighted interior of the trailer as a pale ashy blond. The same color, I realized with a jolt, as my own.

"Did you call my mother today?" I asked.

"Don't have a telephone."

"From the gas station?"

"Got the truck filled up today."

I was getting tired of fencing and angry with the woman for evading my questions. And laughing at me while she was doing it. David felt my tension and intervened with a request to sit down.

"We walked up from River Road," he explained. "Left the car by that burned-out house and walked through the woods."

"What did you do that for?" she asked, pulling out a couple of ancient spindle back chairs from the dropleaf table where she'd obviously been sitting before we arrived. There was a half-empty cup of coffee on the table and the local newspaper folded open to the classified ads for farm auctions. "Easier to come by the highway. You could have driven right up to the door. Not that anybody does very much."

"We didn't know that. You're kind of hard to find."

She smiled at David, ignoring me. "Anybody needs to know where I am, knows where I am."

"Like my mother," I suggested.

"How about some coffee?" she said, addressing David.

"It's still hot. I was just having some when you came to call."

She got two mugs from a tiny cupboard and filled them with coffee from an aluminum pot sitting on a two-burner hot plate. She set them on the table, serving David first, and then sat down in her own chair and sipped from her mug. "Got no milk or sugar. Don't use 'em."

"Aunt Alva . . ." I began.

"Don't call me that!" She whipped the words at me so harshly I jumped and slopped hot coffee into my lap. "I didn't ask you to come here. I don't want you here. I told Lizzie I wanted nothing to do with her high and mighty family."

"But you don't understand," I protested. "My mother's in the hospital. When you called today, I answered the phone. You sounded like . . . you had trouble. I've got trouble, too. My mother does. I thought we could help each other."

She glared at me over her coffee mug, but she didn't deny the phone call. "What kind of trouble?" she demanded. "What's wrong with her?"

"I . . . I don't know. They're having a psychiatrist see her in the morning."

Alva snorted. "She's not crazy. Least ways, no more than she ought to be with the kind of life she's had. She's a good woman, your mother. Better than you deserve."

"Then help me. I need to understand why she does the things she does. The rowboat in the yard, the life preserver. Those are kind of strange things to do."

She shook her head stubbornly. "Not my place to tell you, even if I knew." Her hand inched toward the newspaper and I sensed she'd be glad if we went away and left her to whatever she was thinking of buying or selling.

"Please, Alva," I begged. "She's getting much worse. She took off her clothes in church this morning and then collapsed in front of the whole congregation."

I was embarrassed for my mother and felt foolish for telling this hard practical woman of her public weakness. Alva laughed. A hoarse, ripping, racketing string of barks sprang from her open mouth, and in the lamplight I could see the soft tissue quivering at the back of her throat. I hated her in that moment, and moved to get up from the chair and leave.

She held me back. My hand squirmed under hers. "Set tle down," she said. "I'm not laughing at Lizzie. Good Lord no. I'm thinking of all those Holy Joe faces gaping at her. Prunes and prisms." She chuckled. "Prunes and prisms. So that's why they've got her lined up for the nut doctor. Well, Lizzie always did have it in her to bust loose. Only she never could get out from under that grandmother of yours. Oh, she tried. But only so far. Like marrying Ray. But when he wanted her to go off with him, leave this town, she wouldn't do it. She waited too long." The silence grew, while Alva Holland gazed at a distant time.

"So he went alone," I prompted.

"Yeah."

"And died."

She nodded.

"How did he die, Alva?"

"The old man wants me." She got up and moved toward the back of the trailer where a faded chintz curtain hung from a wooden pole. She brushed through it without revealing what lay in the darkness beyond.

I hadn't heard anyone call her. But maybe they had some kind of signal arranged. Or maybe she just wanted to get away from my questions so she could prepare some answers. Her voice murmured through the curtain, but her words were indistinguishable, and there were soft patting sounds. I reached across the table for David's hand. He gripped mine and nodded.

"You're doing fine," he mouthed. "She's loosening up."

The wooden rings of the curtain clattered and she slipped through, pulling it closed behind her. I pulled my hands away from David's and wrapped them around the coffee mug. Alva returned to the table. I sipped at the coffee. It was lukewarm and bitter, tasting strongly of iron.

I must have grimaced at the taste. She noticed and apologized for the coffee. "It's the water," she said. "It comes from a well. It's good enough water, but it tastes like sin. You get used to it after a while."

I didn't know how to reopen the conversation and groped for a starting point. "Why do you live way out here?"

I was surprised at her answer.

"The old man likes it."

She hadn't struck me as a person who would dedicate her life to someone else's ease, and she seemed to feel the inadequacy of her reply, for she went on as if she'd never really considered the question before.

"I guess I like it, too. It's quiet, and I don't have to put up with fools too often."

That sounded more in character, but I wondered if she meant David and me. I didn't relish being called a fool, but I was willing to bear it if I could find out more about my mother. And Raymond my father.

"The old man," I began, "is he . . . ?"

"He's senile. And he's had a stroke. I don't want you bothering him."

"I won't," I assured her, "but is he my grandfather?"

"He sure is. But he hasn't set eyes on you since you were a pup. I think he forgot all about you years ago. Best not to remind him now." She began gathering up the coffee mugs. "Well, I'll say good night now. We get up early around here."

But I wasn't ready to leave. "Alva, when you called my mother, you said someone was out here bothering you. Who was it?"

"Did I?"

"You said you were going to shoot him if he didn't go away."

She produced her wide mirthless grin. "Manner of speaking. I never shot anyone in my life." She glanced at a deer rifle bracketed above one of the windows. "Although sometimes I feel like it."

Maybe it was a threat and maybe it wasn't. I hugged my shoulder bag and felt the outline of the gun through its soft leather.

"Who was it? Who was here, and what did you expect my mother to do about it?"

"Oh, hell," she said. "I may as well tell you. Seems like you won't scoot until you know it all. I got a son, see. He's not too bright and sometimes he gets a little riled up and I can't tell what he's going to do next."

"Donny," I murmured.

"Oh," she said. "You know him?"

"He came by River House. Brought me some tomatoes."

"So that's where they went. I was figuring on selling them down at the highway. There's a market buys a lot of my garden stuff."

"What about Donny?"

"Yeah. Well, Lizzie's the only one he'll listen to. Ever since he had his accident and she looked after him, he might as well be her kid. They understand each other."

"What accident?"

"When the house burned down. We barely got out alive and Donny got hurt pretty bad. He jumped out an upstairs window and broke both his legs and did something to his backbone. Lizzie got the best doctors and paid for all the operations. She practically lived at the hospital all the time he was there. I couldn't do it. I had the old man to look after and the farming to do. So Lizzie took care of Donny and he never forgot that. He's a terror when he gets upset, and he doesn't realize what he's doing or how strong he is. Once he got mad at me over some little thing—I can't even remember what it was—and tried to run me over with the tractor. Lizzie came out and talked to him and quietened him down like a lamb."

"But doesn't he live here?" I asked, amazed at how calmly she spoke of Donny's attempt to kill her.

"More or less," she replied. "He likes to live wild. Sometimes he sleeps in the barn or in the woods, but more often lately I think he's been camping out in one of those cabins behind River House. Lizzie made him watchman and he takes his job very seriously."

"Do you think he could have been living in the house?"

"Inside River House?" Alva brooded on the question. "I don't know. He's afraid of houses since the fire. But he might. If he thought Lizzie wanted him to, he might. Why?"

Her eyes had turned watchful and I wondered how much of what I knew was known to her. Did she, for instance, know about the turret room, and was she protecting Donny's secret haven from a world he couldn't begin to comprehend? I countered with another question of my own.

"How did the fire start?"

"Kerosene lamp," she said. "We didn't have the electric in the old place. We always thought Donny must have knocked it over. Accidentally. He's kind of clumsy."

"He told me my mother gave you this trailer. Is that true?"

"She did, indeed."

"Why?"

"Like I told you, Lizzie's a good woman. We didn't have a place to live, and the old man didn't want to leave the farm. She had the trailer hauled out the morning after the fire. We've been living in it ever since."

"How long is that?"

"Eight years, come September."

"And where is Donny now?" Involuntarily, I glanced toward the chintz curtain and wondered if he were hiding behind it listening to our conversation.

She shrugged. "Gone off, I guess. He was raising a ruckus in the chicken house, yelling his head off and chasing the hens all over the yard. I couldn't get him to stop, and that's when I called Lizzie. And got you instead."

"Well," said David, rising from his chair and looming like a bearded giant in the confined space of the trailer. "Thank you, Mrs. Holland."

"Miss," she corrected him.

"We've taken up a lot of your time," he went on, "and I'm sure Jenny feels much better about her mother's chances of coming through this illness. Probably just the strain of all the family getting together after all these years. We'll be going now."

Alva looked surprised, and I certainly wasn't ready to leave. I had plenty of questions left unanswered. Alva had turned out to be a gold mine of information. I wanted to show her my father's mutilated snapshot and ask her what she made of it. And I had made up my mind to tell her about the prowler at River House—the Halloween mask, the dead chicken on the bed, all of it, even my mother's wild shooting spree the night before—and have her confirm my suspicions that poor simple Donny was behind it all. But David was pulling out my chair and I had to get up or be dumped off.

"Come on, Jenny," he urged me. "It's time to go. Miss Holland has been very helpful. Good night. Thanks again."

He herded me toward the door, pulled it open and practically shoved me down the steps. I turned back once to see Alva staring after us, her gray eyes cold and impenetrable. There was no smile on her lips as the door swung closed behind us. I murmured a faint, "Good night," but I wasn't sure she heard me.

CHAPTER
29

"What's the big idea?" I demanded. "She would have told me anything I wanted to know. It's probably the first time in years that anybody's really listened to her. Do you think she can talk to Donny? She would have told me her whole life story."

We were retracing our steps toward the path through the cornfield, David swinging his flashlight in wide arcs around the property, flicking it off the outbuildings, the pickup truck, the garden plot where cabbages slept in the white moonlight.

"Ssh," he whispered. "How much of it was true?"

I stopped in my tracks to consider the implications of his question. He continued to swing the flashlight back and forth, stopping now and again to peer intently along its beam.

"What are you looking for?" I asked.

"Someone was listening outside the trailer. Every time I heard footsteps, your dear auntie Alva let loose a mouthful of words. Why do you think she tried to turf us out and then changed her mind? She knew who was out there and she didn't want us to see him."

"Must have been Donny."

"Yeah. Maybe." He took my hand and guided me onto the path through the stubble. "Come on. Let's get out of here."

I looked back once. The trailer squatted on its cinder blocks like an overgrown cocoon. All its lights were out. I imagined Alva standing at one of its darkened windows watching us find our way along the path.

We reached the car without seeing anyone. Donny must have hundreds of hiding places. He wouldn't be found unless he wanted to be. I wondered about his devotion to my mother. Was it enough to make him try to frighten the rest of us out of River House, believing in some obscure fashion that it was his duty as watchman? Was he even capable of planning such bizarre occurrences? I supposed he could have slashed my clothes without much planning. And even played the part of the "hairy old lady" and later peered through the kitchen window at me. That didn't take much intelligence. He could even have taken my ruined clothes and the razor to the cabin in some feeble attempt to conceal what he'd done. But where had he gotten those old trousers and shirts? The ones I thought might have belonged to Raymond my father? Could my mother, out of some notion of charity, have given them to him?

All the other episodes, except that of the dead chicken, had been the result of our own silliness or ineptitude. Luke had cut his hand because he was a pigheaded, unpleasant child. My mother had taken aim at drunken fantasies and shot up the quiet night thinking she'd seen a ghost. I'd heard voices calling me, but it was all in my imagination. Coming home had *not* been a good idea. And as for the occupant of that prisonlike room in the turret of River House, well, it had to be Donny. He must have been using it for years, sleeping there sometimes, finding his own kind of peace, and locking it up when he was away so no one would intrude on his secret place. Hadn't I found much the same kind of secret place in Max's Secondhand Books? And wouldn't it be best for all concerned if I simply took myself back there in the morning, leaving everyone's secrets intact? My mother could resume her role as Donny's guardian and village crackpot. Fearn could go back to Wilmington secure in the knowledge that I would not be around to corrupt her brother with my big-city wiles. And David? David had his own life and seemed to manage it very well without my assistance. There wasn't room for me on his motorcycle.

He jockeyed the car around the small clearing, its headlights exposing now the crumbling chimney, now the sagging back wall of the burned-out shell. It was a sobering sight, now that my mind was filled with the vision of a terrified Donny leaping from a second-story window with the flames raging behind him, to land in a pain-wracked heap on the ground below. We headed back along the overgrown track, and it wasn't until we were safely rolling along River Road that I asked David to explain himself.

"How did you know she was lying?"

"Not all of it," he said. "But she was sure trying to make out that Donny was responsible for everything that's happened. He's her son. Why should she do that? Why wasn't she protecting him?"

Since I'd already made up my mind that Donny was indeed the prowler who'd disrupted the reunion, I shrugged his questions off. "How should I know? Maybe she just wants to get rid of him. She's not exactly a motherly sort, and he must have been a terrible responsibility."

"But why now?" David persisted. "And in this way? Blaming him for something that could get him locked up as a dangerous lunatic."

"But she doesn't even *know* what's been going on at River House. You didn't give me a chance to mention it."

"She knows. Believe me. That's why she was so subtly offering Donny up as the culprit."

"But how could she? Who could have told her?"

"How about your mother? She and Alva seem to be pretty close. She could have nipped over to the trailer this morning before she did her big scene in church. Maybe it was something that happened then that set her off."

We drove along in silence for a while. Alva Holland had seemed to me to be direct, forthright and more than a bit ungracious. It was hard to accept David's view of her as a subtle and cunning manipulator. But maybe he was right. The Donny I'd talked to on the back porch seemed gentle and harmless, even a little frightened of being that close to River House. What was there about the house to frighten him? And if his fear was genuine, could he have overcome it to creep inside and slaughter a chicken in the bedroom? I couldn't even be sure that Donny could read and write. But someone had written "GET OUT" on the mirror. If it wasn't Donny, then who?

The lights of River House appeared in the distance.

"Do you want to stop?" asked David.

"No. I'll spend the night at my mother's place. I want to get to the hospital first thing in the morning, before she sees the psychiatrist."

We swept on by and I turned to watch the lights receding and then blinking out abruptly as we rounded a bend in the road.

"David," I said, "if she's trying to blame it all on

Donny, and he didn't do it, then she must be protecting some-one else."

"Exactly."

"Who?"

"Who do you think?"

"Someone who wants us all out of there. Someone who hates the family."

"Go on."

"Someone who's close to my mother and wants to keep things just the way they are."

"Try harder."

"Someone who's afraid my mother and I will patch up our quarrel. Someone who hates *me!* Someone who might even try to kill me!" I heard my voice rising in pitch and tried to quell the edge of hysteria that was tightening my throat and bringing back the pain in my head that had subsided over the past few hours.

"Hey! Hey!" said David. "That's far enough. Don't go overboard. Now, who do you think that someone could be?"

"Alva Holland?"

David turned the car off River Road and onto the high-way leading to town.

CHAPTER
30

Alva Holland. But why? It was strange enough to find out in one day that I had relatives I'd never known about, but to realize that one of them might be maliciously trying to break up the reunion, or worse, was unnerving. Alva's animosity could spring from the simple fact that she hadn't been invited or from the long years in which she'd been ignored by the Mear clan. She could hate me because of the inevitable comparison with her own son. Alva probably had never been considered one of the family, although it was inconceivable that Wendell was unaware of her existence. But if he knew, why had he never written to me about her and Donny? He certainly gossiped at length about everyone else. Maybe he *didn't* know.

There was little traffic on the highway and I remembered how the town closed down on Sunday nights. Everyone was supposed to be at home digesting Sunday dinner and the substance of the morning's sermons. We drove past the sprawling clutter lining the highway with only one pair of headlights behind us. The clock on the dashboard purred its way toward eleven. Still early by my city standards, but the middle of the night to most of the good citizens of my hometown. David was driving fast, a little over the speed limit, but I felt secure with him at the wheel, the two of us speeding through the night, for the moment suspended between the alarms of River House and the phantoms out of my mother's past. I could have gone on that way for miles, leaving it all behind me.

As we approached a bridge over a nameless creek that meandered down from the high timbered ground beyond the highway, the headlights behind us drew closer. David slowed the car and pulled into the right lane to allow the driver to pass. He didn't. Instead, he switched his headlights onto bright and followed us. David sped up again and flipped on the turn indicator to warn the driver that he intended to move back into the fast lane. Before he could do so, a horn blared deafeningly and the lights moved up on our left side. David swore and stamped down on the accelerator. The car leaped forward but the pursuing lights kept even with our rear window and began nudging us toward the bridge railing. I twisted in my seat and tried to see beyond the blazing lights. All I could make out was a high body and a glimmer of dark windshield.

Beside me, David fought the wheel and urged the car on to greater speed. The horn kept up its nerve-racking din and the lights inched forward until they merged with our own, casting a broad wavering white streak down the empty highway. The bridge railing flashed by and I realized it was a scant few inches from the side of our car. David hunched over the wheel, his eyes riveted on the road. I clung to the back of the seat peering over his shoulder through the side window hoping for a glimpse of whoever was trying to force us off the bridge. All I could see was a streak of dull red metal and the lower portion of a side window. The car bumped, lurched, and rolled down an incline.

228

I think I heard David yell, "Hold on!" Then there was nothing but noise.

The noise went away by degrees. I opened my eyes and looked out on blackness. Something was pressing against my chest. I was afraid to find out what it was, but somehow forced my hands to move. It was the diagonal strap of the seat belt holding me in place against the pull of gravity. It wasn't until that moment that I realized the car was tilted at a crazy angle, nose down and lying on its side. I looked out my window, up, really, and saw the arch of the bridge looming over us. I tried to find my voice but nothing would come until I remembered to breathe. Even then, it was a feeble whisper.

"David?"

No answer.

I reached over in the darkness and felt an arm, a thigh, his head was resting against the door. My hand came away wet. It was then I began to move. I pushed against the door on my side. It wouldn't budge. I felt for the lock button. It was down. I pulled it up and tried again. The door opened a crack but fell closed again as soon as I let up the pressure. I realized I'd have to give it a great heave. It wouldn't just swing open. It would have to be pushed all the way, or it would just slam down on me. I twisted around in the seat, relying on the seat belt to keep me from falling on David, brought my knees up under my chin, counted to three, and kicked the door hard with the soles of both feet. The door flew up and out, its hinges shrieking hideously. I stuck my legs through the opening, unbuckled the seat belt, and managed to squirm my way after them until I was sitting precariously on the side of the car with my legs dangling down into darkness. Not too far away, I heard the creek lapping its way peaceably to merge with the river. I didn't know what to do next.

David was hurt, unconscious, maybe even dead. I wanted to get him out of the car but didn't know how to do it. I didn't think I could drag him through the open door, and I might even do him some harm by trying it. As my eyes grew accustomed to the darkness, I saw the glint of white pebbles about three feet beneath me sloping away toward the creek bed. David had managed to get the car across the bridge, but apparently we'd gone through the guard rail on the other side and landed in the soft bank leading down to the creek. I could jump down from my perch on the side of the tilted car, climb back up to the highway, and go for help. But first, I groped behind me in the front seat to find my shoulder bag. If the driver who'd forced us off the road was waiting to finish the job, I'd be ready for him with Wendell's gun. I found the bag wedged under the front seat. I tugged it out and gave my funny bone a numbing thump against the dash. The glove compartment flew open and the flashlight practically fell into my tingling hand. I didn't drop it. The first piece of good luck I'd had since I got off the plane on Friday.

I flicked the light on and shone it on David's face. No good luck there. His skin was the color of eggshells except where it was streaked with blood that seemed to be coming from somewhere under his tangle of yellow hair. I couldn't get close enough to see if he was breathing. He didn't answer when I called his name again. I didn't want to leave him but maybe it wouldn't be for long, if I could find a phone or flag down a passing car. I twisted around and jumped.

The momentum carried me a few feet down the pebbly slope toward the creek, but I managed not to fall in. Then with the flashlight in one hand and the other plunged inside my bag gripping the butt of the gun, I started climbing. It wasn't a steep slope, but my sandals kept sliding on the pebbles. Once I fell and my knees hit gravel with a needle-sharp jolt. By the time I reached the road, I felt as if I'd scaled Mt. Everest. I shone the light back down the hill. The car looked like it was trying to burrow its way into the earth. It lay on its side nuzzling the exposed roots of a decaying tree that looked ready to topple over at any moment. I had to get David out of there before it did.

There was no traffic on the road. The nearest building was a corrugated metal shed that squatted under a lighted sign advertising "Neal's Furniture Outlet. Dinettes. Bedroom Suites. Free table lamp with purchase of complete living room." Neal didn't seem to be around, but maybe there'd be a public telephone somewhere on his premises. The driver of the red van or pickup or whatever it was had chosen an ideal stretch of highway for his dirty work. The area on either side of the bridge was relatively undeveloped. About half a mile down the road toward the town was a glow of lights. If I couldn't find a phone at Neal's, I'd just have to start walking.

I ran across the highway and through Neal's parking lot. The door to the metal shed was closed and locked. I hadn't really expected it to be open. In the front of the shed, a wide picture window glowed with a faint light. I peered in. The light came from a desk lamp just inside the window. It shone on a desk littered with furniture catalogs, order blanks, fabric swatches, and two telephones, one a beige push-button model, the other an old-fashioned black one with a blank circle where the dial should have been, probably the house phone. Beyond the desk, ranks of formica tables and cut velvet sofas receded into the gloom; along one wall an army of terrible ceramic cats sprouted fluted lampshades from between their ears. The free table lamps, no doubt. I longed to get my fingers on Neal's push-button phone, and the ceramic cats dispelled any pangs of conscience I might have had about breaking the picture window. I pulled Wendell's gun out of my bag, gripped it by the barrel and was about to slam it against the glass when I heard the distant howl of sirens, coming closer.

Guiltily I stuffed the gun back into my bag and ran out onto the highway swinging the flashlight in wild circles. There were rotating red lights coming from both directions. I hurried back to the place where we'd gone off the road. The sirens split the night with their clamor. The cars, five or six of them, including an ambulance, screeched into a circle surrounding me with their pulsing red lights and slamming doors. A platoon of Smokey Bear hats fanned out onto the bridge and down the slope. One of them, tall, broad, beefy, and polite came up to me.

"Are you the accident, ma'am?"

I nodded and pointed down the slope. If I opened my mouth, a torrent of giggles would pour out. Of course I was the accident. Didn't I look like one? Why else would I be standing at the side of the road waving a flashlight?

"Anyone else involved?"

I got the giggles under control. He was a nice man and he was here to help. He didn't deserve to be laughed at.

"David," I told him. My voice sounded squeaky between the clattering of my teeth. "He's still in the car. I think he's hurt."

My Smokey Bear shouted to the others, "She says there's a guy in the car. May be hurt. See can you get him out."

Searchlights began to play on the scene and a tow truck joined the circle of official cars. The two mechanics leaped out and ran down the slope, one of them muttering, "Must have been drunk or a damn fool."

I shook my head and groped for the right words.

"Are you all right, ma'am? You can go sit in the ambulance if you want." Smokey Bear was being kindly again.

I felt his eyes on me, checking me out for injuries. Until that moment, I hadn't thought about whether I'd been hurt. I didn't feel any pain and I'd been able to climb the slope and run back and forth on the road. But once he reminded me, I began to feel the bruises. A great sore place on my thigh, a fingernail broken down to the quick, a twinge in my shoulder that might or might not be serious. And the shakiness that left me feeling hollowed out and weak. I leaned against the nearest police car.

"I'll be all right," I whispered. "I want to see. . . ."

What I wanted to see was David when they brought him up. If he was dead, I wanted to know it right away. And if he wasn't, I wanted to know that, too, so I could stop the shaking and start offering up some kind of thanks.

From below the highway, there came the sound of men's voices counting in unison and then a grinding of weary metal. I could tell that my kindly guardian was torn between his duty to me and the desire to see what was going on down in the creek bed. I wanted to see, too. I pulled myself upright and tottered toward the rim of the road. Smokey Bear took my arm and escorted me as if we were entering hallowed premises.

"What's your name?" I asked him, just to be making conversation as we watched the men below trying to right the car.

"Sergeant Binns," he said. "Most folks just call me Bert."

The men from the tow truck had hooked a cable to the rear of the car. The cable pulled taut while the other men pushed and jiggled the car to work it loose from the soft earth. The car groaned and I thought of what my mother would say when she saw it. David was still in the car. I could just make out his slumped silhouette in the glare of the searchlights. He didn't move except to bounce slightly with every jolt the men gave the car in their attempts to free it. And with every jolt, I gripped Bert's arm harder and gritted my teeth.

"Easy, there," he soothed. "They're good boys. They'll get him loose any minute now."

I had my doubts. Good boys they may have been, but there didn't seem to be any way of getting the car upright without giving David some knocks that might worsen his injuries. I wanted to get down there myself and lower the car gently with my own hands without disturbing a hair of David's head.

Suddenly the tow truck gave a lurch, the men shouted a chorus of "Heave!" and the car floated off the incline like a feather in the breeze and came to rest on all four of its wheels halfway up the slope. The ambulance attendants were ready with a stretcher, and before I could run down to him, David was being hauled up to the road and slotted into the rear of the ambulance. I got in beside him, and so did Sergeant Bert Binns.

David was still pale and there was a sheen of moisture on his face that gave him a terrible waxy look. The streaks of blood were beginning to dry and no more seemed to be flowing from beneath his hair. I didn't know whether that was good or bad. I'd read somewhere that dead people don't bleed. The ambulance attendant covered him with a gray blanket and strapped him in. Would he have bothered to do that for a dead person? Hope and fear were making me dizzy and ill. When the ambulance rolled, I crumpled forward. The attendant shoved a plastic bucket between my feet. Bert Binns held my shoulders while I retched. I think I must have splattered his khaki trousers, but he never flinched. When it was all over, I tried to apologize, but he just handed me a damp towel and whisked the bucket away. I wiped my face, and then it was time to get out of the ambulance. We were back at the emergency entrance, and I thought it might be a good idea to ask Wendell to transfer the reunion from River House to the hospital. Not so far to go when the next thing went wrong. The giggles were lurking in the back of my throat again, but this time I recognized them for a reaction to the accident. I swallowed hard and they went away.

They rolled David away before I could say a word to him. A nurse pushed a wheelchair up behind me and pressed me into it. I protested, but not too hard. It was a relief to relax and let someone else take charge of me for a little while. She stuck a thermometer in my mouth and pressed her cool efficient fingertips to my wrist. Bert Binns beamed down at me and I tried out a weak smile in return. It felt like a silly crooked smirk because of the thermometer, but it served.

When the nurse finished recording that I was alive, Binns got out a notebook and a ballpoint pen. It was time to get down to business.

"Care to tell me what happened, ma'am? You can start with your name. And his."

"I'm Jenny Holland. And David is my cousin. David Mears."

Binns frowned at his notebook as he wrote, then looked down at me, puzzled.

"Don't recall seeing you around here much, ma'am. Although Holland and Mears are both familiar names in this town. Any relation to Mears' Sporting Goods?"

"Wendell is my cousin, too. I live in New York. David lives in Arizona. We're having a reunion."

"Right. Right. I see."

Whatever it was he saw couldn't have been very complimentary. His frown deepened and there was a definite chill in his next question.

"Whose car is it? Yours or his?"

"Neither. It's my mother's. Mrs. Elizabeth Holland of Plum Street."

He jotted the information down carefully and said, "Ah-ha!" I didn't like the obvious connection he was making. He didn't need to say that he knew my mother's reputation and now here was her equally crazy daughter, from New York no less, making life difficult with Sunday night car crashes. I decided to try a question of my own.

"How did you know we'd had an accident? I was trying to find a phone to call for help."

"We got a call."

"Who from?"

"Person who saw the accident."

"No one saw the accident except the person who caused it."

There was a momentary pause, then, "And who was that?"

"I don't know. There was a truck or a van that came up behind us and forced us off the road. I couldn't see the driver.

It happened very fast. He was trying to force us off the bridge, but David managed to get us to the other side before the car went off the road."

Disbelief. I read it on his broad, open face, in the hesitation of his ballpoint pen as he faltered in his note-taking.

"Now why would anybody want to do that?" he asked.

I couldn't answer him without going into everything that had happened at River House in the past few days. And I wasn't ready to do that. Sergeant Bert Binns would never believe it was anything more than overheated imagination.

I shrugged and said, "I don't know."

"How fast were you going?" His pen was poised again above his notebook and he was ready to take refuge behind numbers and facts.

"You'll have to ask David. We weren't speeding."

"That's funny. Call we got said this car was weaving up the highway doing about eighty. Said you guys shot past him and then zoomed over the edge. Almost knocked him off the road with your tail wind. How about that?"

"I don't think my mother's car can do eighty. Who made the call? Are you sure it was a man?"

"I didn't take the call. We just came right on out and found you."

"And I'm glad you did."

I couldn't think of anything else to say. And apparently Bert Binns was fresh out of questions for the moment. He stared at his notebook as if hoping it would flash some bright idea before his eyes. When it didn't, he closed it and stowed it back in his pocket along with his ballpoint pen. Then he sat down on one of the molded plastic chairs and closed his eyes.

"Bert," I called over to him.

"Uh-huh?"

"There *was* a truck. It was a red one. Kind of old. Probably a pickup."

"Yeah?"

"Do you know who has an old red pickup truck?"

"Lots of them around."

"If David dies, it's murder. Right?"

"Maybe."

"Then you'll have to find the truck."

"I guess."

"Even if he doesn't die, it's still attempted murder, isn't it?"

"Could be."

"If I tell you whose truck I think it was, would you go take a look at it?"

"I might could do that."

The trouble was, I wasn't *sure* it was Alva's truck that had tried to kill us. I'd seen a truck in her yard, but in the darkness it was just another dark shape, no color. And had it been Alva at the wheel, or Donny? And above all, why? Why would either one of them want David and me dead? It didn't make any sense at all. And even if Binns went to look at Alva's truck, what would he find? I couldn't remember whether the truck had rammed into us at any point. And an old truck would have lots of dents and scratches. Inconclusive. Maybe I ought to wait until David was able to talk. He might have seen the driver. If he had, our troubles would be over.

Bert Binns had opened his eyes and was looking at me expectantly. "Well?" he said.

The nurse trotted up in her soft white shoes. "Doctor wants to see you now," she said.

"How's David?" I asked her as she began to roll me away to the examining room.

"Got a bad bump, but he'll live," she said. "They're stitching him up now. Had to shave off all that crowning glory on one side. Now maybe he'll cut off the rest to match. Looks pretty peculiar otherwise. They'll X-ray his head just to be sure, but he'll be okay. How're you feeling?"

"Better. Much better," I told her, and then craned around for a last word with Sergeant Bert. "Talk to you some more later. And so will David."

"I'll wait," he said. He settled back down in the too small chair and closed his eyes again.

CHAPTER
31

They put me in a room next to my mother's. Her door was closed, but I remembered the number and spotted it as the nurse wheeled me by. There wasn't anything wrong with me except bruises and a tendency to get dizzy when I tried to stand up too fast. I could have walked home to my mother's house, but it was already well after midnight and I was bone-weary. When the doctor offered me a bed and a sedative, I grabbed it. Besides, David was somewhere in the hospital and I wanted more than reassurances that he would be all right. I wanted to see him.

The nurse brought me a white cotton hospital gown and helped me undress. She hung my clothes in a narrow closet and offered to put my shoulder bag with them. When I declined and shoved it under my pillow, she looked at me a little oddly and left the room abruptly. I couldn't explain that it was no reflection on her honesty, but simply that I didn't want to be separated from Wendell's gun. Not even by the few steps it would take to get from the bed to the closet. The driver of the truck must know by now that David and I had survived the crash. We'd be easy targets, each of us alone in a hospital room, David unconscious or groggy from his injury, me in a drugged sleep. When the nurse returned with a hypodermic syringe, I told her I'd changed my mind and would do very nicely, thank you, without the knockout needle. Her lips got thin but she didn't insist. All she said was, "If you want it later on, you can ring for it." She made it sound as if I could ring until the cows came home before she would give it to me.

Before she left, I asked her where David was.

"Sleeping," was all she would tell me. I hadn't made a friend.

Alone in the room, I settled down to do some serious

thinking. My thigh was tender and my shoulder ached, but those were only minor distractions. The big item on the agenda was whether someone was trying to kill me. And why. And who. After you live in the city long enough, you do kind of get the impression that "they" are out to get you. But it's impersonal, and you learn to live with it. There isn't any bullet (or switchblade or baseball bat or hand shoving you onto the subway track) with your name on it. If you happen to be in the wrong place at the wrong time, that's it. Blam! It's malevolent and frightening, but it's got nothing to do with your beautiful eyes or the way you wear your hair or what you had for breakfast. What it does is make you a little nervous.

When things started happening out at River House, I thought I'd brought some of that nervous apprehension with me. And the dreams I'd been having all seemed to warn me to stay away. Even now, I wondered if I hadn't come to the reunion, would it have been the ordinary family fried chicken bash that happens in country towns all summer long. But from the beginning, from the dead kitten on the river bank (and who had been responsible for *that?*), I'd had a growing sense that every succeeding bit of mischief was being enacted for my benefit. To scare me away or, if I wouldn't scare, to get rid of me by some other means. It seemed almost immodest, even megalomaniacal, to think of myself as the object of all this frenzied activity. Who, me? Insignificant little bookstore clerk? Absurd! And until the attempt to run us off the bridge, I'd been trying to view it as an absurd set of coincidences, silly pranks that went awry magnified by Fearn's hysteria and my own private, personal dream terrors.

But no longer. The red truck was real. And whoever had been behind the wheel really meant to harm me. Us. Suspicion was an ugly thing. I suspected Donny and Alva Holland, together or separately. I was even beginning to wonder if Wendell had engineered the whole thing simply to get even with me for my rejection of him ten years ago. And that *was* absurd. Wendell was much happier with Bonnie Marie than he ever would have been with me, and he seemed to know it despite his bravura attempts at playing the aging lothario. David, if I could find him and talk to him, might have some kind of answer. If only he'd been able to see the driver of the truck before we went off the road.

I got out of bed and quietly put my clothes back on. The knees of my slacks were gritty with dust from where I'd fallen in climbing up to the highway, and one of them was torn. My white shirt, clean only a few hours ago, was stained with David's blood and smelled of fearful perspiration. I took my shoulder bag from under the pillow, turned off the light, and peered out into the corridor.

It was dim and shadowy, with only a couple of night lights and a glow from the nurse's station at the far end for illumination. Most of the room doors were closed, and those that weren't were dark and unoccupied. I slid along, close to the wall, ready to duck into one of the empty rooms at the first sign of a white uniform. I'd no idea where David was. The hospital had five floors and he could be on any one of them. But the rooms on this floor were adjacent to the emergency room, and since both my mother and I had been quartered in this wing, the chances seemed pretty good that David was nearby. After eliminating the empty rooms, my mother's and my own, there were about eight or nine closed doors behind which David might be sleeping. But I didn't want to barge in on a wakeful patient or the nurse tending to someone's midnight agony. As I edged nearer the nurse's station, I saw a white nylon elbow resting on the desk and a hand twisting and untwisting a telephone cord. A little closer and I could hear a gentle murmur, not at all Florence Nightingale battling disease and festering wounds in the Crimea, more like midnight passion at General Hospital.

I left nursie to her telephone romance and opened the first door I came to, just a crack. A very old woman stared unblinking at a soundless television screen showing an old Three Stooges movie. She had a tube in her nose, another attached to her arm, and the room stank of urine. She didn't even look at me. I closed the door and went on to the next one. After a very fat man who slept sitting up and snuffling, a little boy with his arm in a cast who whimpered for his mother, and a lovely teenage girl lying flat on her back and looking every inch the Sleeping Beauty, I found David in a room just across the hall from a door marked "Linen Closet."

He, too, was sleeping, but when I turned on the bedside lamp I was relieved to see that his face had regained some color. They'd cleaned the blood away and his head was heavily bandaged. He also had some kind of strap arrangement across his shoulder and around his chest. I put my hand on his arm. He didn't move.

"David," I whispered. "Can you hear me?"

His breathing changed rhythm, but that was all.

"David. It's me. Jenny. I need to talk to you."

A sigh.

"David. Who was in the truck? Did you see who was driving?"

His eyelids flickered and I could see the twin chips of turquoise, but they were dulled and without recognition.

"Was it Alva in the truck?"

His lips moved and a bubble of saliva grew on them as he tried for words.

"I can't hear you," I persisted, feeling like the Grand Inquisitor demanding the impossible from a victim on the rack. "Was it Alva?"

"Not Alva." He sighed again and his eyes closed.

"Was it Donny? You've got to tell me."

His fingers curled and I placed my hand in his. His palm was smooth and dry, but there was no answering grip to my own.

"Not Donny." It was less than a whisper, merely a breathy movement of his lips.

"Then who was it? Did you see him? Would you recognize him? Was it Wendell?"

The questions tumbled out of my mouth, but I was not to get an answer to any of them. Not that night. David sank back into his deep slumber. His fingers relaxed and I drew my hand away. I wanted to do something for him, something to let him know I'd been there and was all right, and that he should just concentrate on getting better. I dug into my shoulder bag. Beneath Wendell's gun and the flashlight, I found a wrinkled scrap of paper and the stub of a pencil. I wrote, "David, you've helped more than you know. I'm off to find out whatever I can. Rest easy. See you in the morning. Love, Jenny."

I wondered about that "love," but I'd already written it and couldn't very well cross it out. And I wondered what else I could find out in the middle of the night, but I couldn't spend the rest of it in a hospital bed, relentlessly going over suspects in my mind and waiting for someone to creep in on me if I dozed off. Without a car, I couldn't go anywhere, even if I could drive it, and there wasn't much I could do on the telephone unless I wanted to wake up Wendell and get the whole tribe excited over the accident. Time enough for that in the morning.

What I could do was go back to my mother's house and see what a thorough search of her belongings might reveal. There was no doubt in my mind that my mother was involved in what was going on, either unwittingly or unwillingly, and it was that involvement that had pushed her beyond her frail resources.

I turned off David's lamp, bent to kiss his bandaged head but stopped at the last moment—I'm not sure why—and quietly left the room. Back in the corridor, I thought about the best way to leave without being seen. I could probably just walk right past the nurse if she was still pursuing romance on the phone, but I didn't feel like risking an argument with her if I disturbed the course of true love. Across the way, I noticed that my mother's door was slightly ajar and spilling out a faint light. If she was awake, and lucid, maybe she could help me. If not, the least I could do was tuck her in and kiss her good night, for old times' sake.

I pushed open the door. My mother was sitting up in bed. Bending over her, glass in hand, was a tall figure in bib overalls.

"Don't drink that!" I shouted, and rushed in to knock the glass to the floor.

CHAPTER

32

"It's only water, for God's sake! What's the matter with you?"

Alva Holland was wet and mad. The contents of the glass had spattered the front of her overalls, and the glass itself had shattered on the hard tile floor. She glared at me across my mother's bed. I glared back.

"What are you doing here?" I demanded.

"Visiting the sick, like the Bible tells us to do."

My mother tried to watch us both, her eyes flitting from one angry face to the other like anxious mayflies.

"You two know each other?" she murmured, polite as a hostess at a tea party. "Alva, this is Jenny. Jenny, this is Alva."

"We've met," Alva grated, snatching a towel from the rack on the side of the night stand and mopping at her clothes.

"Once at least," I acknowledged, "and maybe twice in one night."

"What's that supposed to mean?"

"Girls. Girls," my mother chided. "Keep your voices down. Alva, clean up that mess while I tell Jenny a few facts of life."

The tall woman subsided into a sullen silence and bent to pick up the broken pieces of glass. I waited, breathless, for my mother's revelations. At last, I was going to find out the truth.

"Jenny . . ." my mother began.

I nodded encouragingly.

"Go close the door. I thought I brought you up better than that."

Raging, I stomped to the door. She hadn't lost the knack of making me feel like an incompetent child. I considered walking right on through the door and out of the hospital and away. Forever. But the prospect of finally learning what it was that had warped my mother's life held me. I looked down the corridor. The nurse's fingers were still entwined lovingly with the telephone cord. Our racket hadn't penetrated her electronic dalliance. Good. I closed the door softly and went back to my mother's bedside, my face set in what I hoped was an expression of eager anticipation. On the other side of the bed, Alva had slumped in a chair still scowling and looking as if she'd just eaten half a sour wormy apple. My mother patted the bed and urged me to sit down. I perched at the end of the bed and waited.

"That really was just water," she said. "Did you think Alva was trying to poison me?"

Alva snorted. I shook my head. At this point, I didn't know what to think.

"That's the last thing in the world Alva would do. She

and I have been good friends for a long time. We were just talking and I got thirsty and she was kindly helping me to a drink. I think you ought to apologize."

I glanced across at Alva. She seemed ready to be mollified, and I'd do anything to get on with the story.

"I'm sorry, Alva."

"You should be," she grumped. But the scowl left her face and she took a pack of chewing gum from her pocket, unwrapped two sticks, and crammed them into her mouth without offering anyone else a sniff.

"That's better," said my mother and settled back into her pillow as if she were ready to tell us a bedtime story.

"Jenny, your father is dead."

I groaned and turned away. More lies, more fantasies, more confusion of an issue that was already so confused I'd just as soon forget it and pretend I'd never had a father.

"No, wait!" my mother cried. "I know I lied to you in the past. I had to, but I'm afraid I wasn't very good at it. You wouldn't have understood the truth. I wasn't too crazy about it myself. Fact of the matter is, I killed Raymond."

The room was suddenly quiet. Alva was staring at me. My mother lay back on her pillow, her eyes slitted, waiting for my reaction. I looked down at her hands lying still as cornered mice on the coverlet. Small, gnarled, liver-spotted hands. Hands that had cooked and sewed and prayed and killed. I couldn't take my eyes off them.

My mother's voice was low. "Now you know. Alva's always known. Your grandmother knew. And I know. Oh, dear God, how I know!"

Alva spoke up. "Aren't you going to ask her why, girl? It's important."

I raised my head. "Why, Ma?"

She countered with a question of her own. "How much do you remember of your father?"

"Not much. A few things." And I told her of my scanty memories—being tossed among the apple trees, his wide, bright Raymond smile, the snapshots in the family photo album. I didn't mention the mutilated picture I'd found in my baby book or the dream of the grinning blade-handed man who may or may not have been Raymond my father.

"It's just as well," she said. "Those are happy memories.

Raymond was handsome and could be kind and loving and lots of fun. But there was another side to him. He had a mean streak and liked to have his own way in everything. Anybody who crossed him was likely to get hurt. And that's how it happened, don't you see?"

I didn't see. "How what happened? I don't understand."

My mother sighed and looked to Alva for help. Alva produced a contortion between a nod and a shrug, as if relinquishing responsibility for anything else that was said.

"What I mean is, I got between Raymond and something he wanted and he turned nasty. I didn't mean to kill him. But if I hadn't done something, I believe he would have killed me. He had a gun, don't you see?"

This time I was beginning to see. "Did you shoot him?"

She nodded. "Bit him on the hand when he was trying to aim that thing at me. He dropped it. I picked it up. He made to kick me in the head. I shot him. Just like that." She looked at me shyly, to see how I was taking it. "All of this is news to you, isn't it?"

"News?" I echoed. "I guess so. Yes. Then what happened?"

"Well, your grandmother went and got Alva."

Alva's eyes lit up at the recollection. "First and last time the old lady ever spoke to me. We was living in Muley at the time. She pulled up in her big old black car and says to me, 'Get in.' So I got. I was just a dumb young thing or I might have said something back to her. She drove me out to River House and showed me what happened and said, 'You help Lizzie get rid of him.' So we did."

This time, I couldn't conceal my astonishment. "This happened at River House?" How could I not have sensed it? All those visits to my grandmother, the tranquil hours spent in her room, how could they not have been poisoned by the death of Raymond?

"Sure did," said Alva. "And we put him in the old well, like your grandma told us to do, and gave out that he'd run off to parts unknown. He'd been threatening to do that anyway. After that, Donny and the old man and me, we moved into the old farmhouse up the road and lived there until it burned down."

"But how could you? He was your brother."

Her eyes glittered. "I had my reasons."

"Was Donny one of them?"

"What do you know about that?"

"Only what's in the County Clerk's records. Names and birthdate. Donny's about six months older than I am."

"Dammit!" She leaped from her chair and began to pace the room. "He did it! He told me he was gonna, but I didn't know what he was talkin' about. He said he was gonna make it official so no one else would ever marry me and I would be his baby sister forever. Not that I would ever want to get married, not after *that*. But I might have. I just might have."

I was surprised to see tears glittering in the tall woman's eyes. My mother reached out to her as she lurched by the bed and caught her arm.

"That's enough, Alva. Enough talk about what's past and done."

She reached for my hand, too, and numbly I let her take it. Holding both of us, she talked earnestly to me.

"Now, Jenny. What I want you to do is leave. Go back to New York. Promise me you will. First thing in the morning. That's your home now. There's nothing for you here. And don't worry about me. I'll be all right. I know what I have to do now. And Alva will help me. Won't you, Alva?"

Alva nodded mutely, her eyes still shining over the grim line of her wide, thin lips. My mother released us both.

"That's settled then," she said and lay back on her pillow contentedly. "Jenny, roll down my bed. I want to go back to sleep."

I hadn't promised her anything, and I couldn't. She may have given me some answers about the past, answers I still couldn't comprehend and would need to think about, but there were questions about the present that needed to be settled.

"Ma, why did you let Wendell open up River House and hold the reunion there?"

She smiled. "Well, you know how Wendell is when he gets his heart set on something. He just wouldn't take no for an answer. And to tell you the truth, I didn't think anyone would show up. Least of all you."

"And who's been prowling around, cutting up my clothes and frightening all of us with Halloween masks?"

Alva smirked. "Aw, that was just me. I guess it was a

dumb idea, but I wanted to shake up that whole snot-nosed bunch. They're so stuck-up it makes me sick. But I'm real sorry about your clothes. They was pretty."

"Okay, one last question and then I'll go. Who ran David and me off the road tonight and almost killed us?"

A look passed between them, some message I couldn't fathom. Then Alva got up and said, "Wasn't none of us. I better be going."

"Wait," my mother commanded. And Alva waited, tapping her foot in its heavy work boot impatiently. "Where's David now?"

"Right across the hall. With stitches in his head and his shoulder all strapped up." Consternation blossomed on my mother's face. More than consternation. Fear. "He'll be okay," I reassured her. "I saw him a few minutes ago."

"What about you?"

"I'm fine. A few bruises, but nothing serious."

"You're sure?"

"Of course, I'm sure." I guess she would never believe that I was capable of looking after myself, even after ten years of doing exactly that with no help from her. "The doctor checked me out and they even gave me a room here, right next door."

"Good." She smiled, but there was little warmth in it. "At least I'll know where you are for a change. Now roll down my bed, and let's all get some sleep."

I didn't tell her that I had no intention of spending what was left of the night in the room next door. Alva left while I was cranking the bed down. I gave the crank a final twist, said, "Good night, Ma," and hurried after her.

I followed Alva as she strode down the corridor, past the nurse's station where the nurse slammed down the phone and shouted, "Hey!" but didn't pursue us. We swept on through the waiting area, Alva in the lead, me panting to catch up, and out into the parking lot. Sergeant Bert Binns had evidently given up his vigil, or maybe he'd just been waiting for someone to come and pick him up. I caught up with Alva in the parking lot, just as she was opening the door of a battered farm truck that shone a sullen murky red under the sodium vapor lamps.

"This your truck?" I asked her.

"Yeah. Want a ride?"

"You mind dropping me at my mother's house?"

"Hop in."

I hopped. It was strange, to say the least, to be riding home in the very truck that had run us off the road. I was as sure of that as I was of the broken springs that made the ride a misery to my bruised body and of the fact that Alva knew more than she was telling.

"We were just lucky we didn't go off the bridge and into the creek."

"Yeah. Creek's pretty full this time of year. We've had a lot of rain. You could have drowned."

"I saw the truck that pushed us off. It looked a lot like this one."

"Did it now?"

"David saw the driver. He said it wasn't you."

Alva drove like a man, punishing the gears and tromping the brake to a screeching halt at the stop sign on the crest of Rattlesnake Hill. We bumped down the hill and swung onto Plum Street in a turn that pressed me against the door. Alva said nothing.

"He said it wasn't Donny either."

"He say who it was?"

"No."

"Must have been some other truck. Just some kids out skylarking."

"I don't believe that. And neither do you."

She pulled into the driveway of my mother's house and cut the motor. Then she got out her pack of chewing gum and offered me a stick. When I declined, she unwrapped one for herself, spit her chewed wad into the wrapper, threw it on the floor of the truck, and started chewing on the fresh stick.

"Trying to stop smoking," she said. And then she turned to me, resting one arm on the steering wheel and raising an overalled knee to sit sideways on the worn seat. "Listen to me, Jenny Holland. I don't bear you any malice. What happened all those years ago wasn't your fault. You were just a kid and you didn't know what was going on. But if anything happens now, it *will* be your fault. Not through anything you've done, but just because of your being here. Do what your mother says. Go back where you came from. Don't even set foot in

River House again. Get Wendell or somebody to pick up your stuff and hightail it out to the airport first thing in the morning. That way, everything'll get calmed down again."

"But Alva, I still don't understand. And I can't go away until I know my mother's not going to be locked up in an institution."

"Did she seem crazy to you tonight?"

"No. But she's worried about something."

"She's worried about you. And the only way to relieve her mind is for you to get out. The one thing that's kept her going all these years was knowing you were well out of it. She used to tell me about the postcards you sent Wendell. She was so proud of you with your good job and all your fancy friends. Now all she wants is for you to go back. Is that so hard to do?"

It was time for a little honesty on my part. I hadn't thought about Wendell's showing those postcards to my mother. Or maybe I had. Maybe that was why I'd written such glowing fables about my life in New York. I knew Wendell would pass the news on. And now it was time to set the record straight.

"Alva," I said, "I have no wonderful job. I work in a secondhand bookstore in a crummy neighborhood. I live in a very small apartment in an old tenement building. And I have no friends, fancy or otherwise, except maybe Max, the old man I work for. I haven't done so well with my life, and I thought maybe I could figure out why if I came back home and took a good look at where I started out."

"Ah," said Alva, "I think maybe we won't tell your mother any of that. I think we have to let her hang on to something nice."

"But isn't that what she's been doing all these years? Hanging on to an illusion?"

"Well, yes and no. And anyway, what else could she have done? She was strong enough for some things, but not strong enough to stand up to your grandmother. Hardly anybody was. When the thing happened with Raymond, she did exactly what your grandmother told her to do. That old woman was a dragon, let me tell you."

"She was always good to me."

"That's because she used you against your mother. But

you were too young to know about that. Lizzie was so tickled when you up and left town and wouldn't even stay with the old lady when she offered."

"You mean she wanted me to go?"

"What else?"

I couldn't believe it. To this day, I remembered her dire warnings about what happened to young girls who left home. No respectable girl would dream of it, and those who actually did it were little better than tramps. In fact, that's what most of them turned out to be. Streetwalkers, I think she said, diseased and filthy. Her final words to me echoed down the years, biting and cruel. "If you leave, don't ever come back." Well, I had come back, and now here was Alva telling me that my mother had craftily engineered our quarrel precisely so that I would leave.

"Why didn't she just tell me to go?"

"Would you have gone? Without asking questions?"

"I don't know. But I'm asking questions now."

"Yeah. You sure are." She twisted back around in her seat and started up the engine. "Well, I'd best be getting back out to the farm. The old man don't sleep too well and he gets cranky if I'm not there."

"Alva, what would happen if I opened up that old well?"

"I wouldn't do that if I were you. Not unless you want your ma to spend the rest of her life in jail. Not to mention me. Good night, Jenny. I don't want to be rude, but I hope I never set eyes on you again."

"Good night, Alva."

I got out of the truck and stood in the driveway watching it back out and trundle off down Plum Street, still positive it was the same one that had forced us off the road.

CHAPTER
33

The red truck sounded terrible. It rattled and shook so hard it seemed that parts would start flying off it any moment. And, indeed, even as I watched, a fender fell off with a loud clank and landed rocking in the road. I picked it up and tried to put it back on.

There was no one in the truck, but its engine growled and its horn blared and I was afraid it would run driverless through the town, mowing down people and destroying everything in its path. I had to get in. And then I *was* in and we were moving. I put my hands on the steering wheel. It twisted and whirled despite all I could do to hold it steady. I felt with my foot for the brake pedal. There was nothing there. The floor of the truck was carpeted with chewing gum and my feet were stuck in it.

Churches whizzed by. A whole street full of churches. In front of each one, a knot of people dressed for a funeral. The truck tooted its horn at them mockingly. I knew that the funerals were for Raymond my father.

We roared through the ramshackle streets of Muley. From the porches, people waved and a voice cried out, "Guess she knows where she belongs." I tried to wave back, but the steering wheel had bent itself around my hands and I couldn't free them.

The truck skidded to a halt under a tree. The tree was immense and had apples the size of basketballs hanging from its branches. I was outside the truck when the apples started falling on it. The truck disappeared under a mound of the giant apples and I was standing on a sheet of clear ice over a deep circular hole in the ground. The sides of the hole were covered with white subway tile and it was lit from below. Raymond my father smiled up at me. The ice began to melt.

I knew I was dreaming. There was no reason to be afraid. Just like the ice, the dream would melt away and I would wake up safe and it would be morning. The ice dissolved and I fell past Raymond's wide white smile into a blinding light and the sound of a train rushing toward me.

I woke up. Sunlight streamed in the window through the yellow ruffled curtains. I lay fully clothed on the bed in my childhood room, feeling that I'd forgotten something. There was no clock in the room. There used to be one, a Baby Ben wind-up alarm clock that woke me for school, but it was gone. I sat up, groggy and aching, and tried to guess from the angle of the sunlight what time it was. Not early. In fact, late if I meant to be at the hospital with my mother when she talked to the psychiatrist.

I stumbled into the bathroom and splashed cold water on my face. My clothes were a mess, wrinkled and dirty. Back to the schoolgirl's closet to find something else. It felt strange, going through those outdated skirts and dresses, like going back in time, or worse yet, never having grown out of those years. I found an inoffensive blue shirtwaist dress, a little short, but not remarkably so, and remembered it was one my mother had bought for me and I'd hated because it was so plain and *long*. I put it on, ran a comb through my hair, and ran down to the kitchen.

The electric clock on the stove said it was almost ten-thirty. No time for breakfast. I left by the back door, locking it and putting the key back in its hiding place above the door.

Ten minutes later, I was looking at an empty hospital bed. My mother had flown the coop.

"But where did she go?" I asked the nurse, not the same one who held telephone marathons at midnight. "She didn't come home."

"I didn't ask her. The doctor said it was all right for her to leave, and she asked me to call a taxi. That's all I know."

"Did she see Doctor Marks?"

The nurse nodded. "First thing this morning."

"Can I see Doctor Marks?"

"Well, I don't know about that. She's very busy." But after this small show of the power of positive nursing, she led me down yet another corridor to a dingy corner of the old building where a new sign on the battered door announced the presence of the psychiatric department.

The nurse knocked on the door and a voice within called out, "The doctor is in."

The nurse gave me a look that declared, "The doctor is weird," and walked away, leaving it up to me to open the door or not as I chose. I opened it.

The room was small and the doctor was long, thin and sad-faced, stopping just short of ugly. She lay sprawled on a couch, not the customary leather-covered psychiatric model, but a beat-up bloated yellow monster leaking its stuffing and sprouting a wild assortment of colorful throw pillows. Her feet, in canvas espadrilles, were propped on one arm of the couch and her head, a frizzy mass of reddish curls, rested on the other. In between, she wore a purple T-shirt that read, "What do women *really* want?" in acid green and a pair of baggy fuschia jeans. She looked like home.

And she sounded like home, too, when she said, "Is this business or pleasure? If it's pleasure, I'll get up." Her hoarse voice and wiseass intonation were straight off the streets of Manhattan and I felt a sudden pang of homesickness.

"I'm here about my mother," I said. "Mrs. Holland."

"Oh, yeah. Quite a lady. She's gonna work on my hot line when she feels better."

"You let her go?"

"Well, I couldn't keep her here, could I? She doesn't need to stay, and she didn't want to. She's gonna come in twice a week and see what we can do together."

"She won't come." I couldn't see my mother baring her soul to this very undoctorlike person. Underneath her life preserver and her admission of murder, my mother was a very conventional person. Or so I thought.

"Sure she will. We had a nice long talk already. In fact, she thinks you could use some help."

"Me!"

"Yeah, well. You know what mothers are like."

"What did she tell you?"

"Harrumph, as they say. I really ought to be steepling my fingers and stroking my goatee. That's what shrinks do in the movies, isn't it? You know I can't tell you that."

She swung her long legs off the couch and stood up. She must have been close to six feet tall and when she laid her long arm across my shoulder, I felt like I was being nuzzled by a friendly giraffe.

"What I can tell you," she said, "is that your mother is under a good deal of stress right now, but she seems to know what's causing it and feels that she can work it out. I think you ought to trust her."

I wanted to shout, "How can you trust someone who killed your father?" but I still couldn't quite believe it and even if it were true, it was up to my mother to tell this weird doctor, if she hadn't already.

"Did she say where she was going?"

The doctor shook her head. "Something about setting her house in order, cleaning the bats out of her belfry. She seemed very happy. Very purposeful."

"Well, thanks." There wasn't anything else to say. I headed for the door.

The doctor said, "You're welcome," and drifted back to her couch. "Your mother told me you were leaving today. Give my regards to East Broadway. There's a great Szechuan restaurant there."

She sounded wistful, but I wasn't in the mood to exchange New York reminiscences. So my mother was setting her house in order and cleaning the bats out of her belfry. That sounded just like her. But did she mean mental bats, or literally cleaning out the horrible prisonlike room at the top of River House? Since she hadn't come home, I was willing to bet that she'd gone out to River House to do whatever it was she was feeling so purposeful about. And, despite Alva's warning, I intended to follow her out there and make sure she didn't do anything drastic. Like tell the family what she'd told me.

But first I had to see David.

I was beginning to know the hospital almost as well as I knew Max's Secondhand Books. I found David's room after only one wrong turn. Nurses and porters went about their business. Doctors hurried by. No one questioned my right to roam the corridors. I felt almost invisible.

David was sitting up in bed. The door to his room was open and I walked right in.

"Jenny," he croaked in a voice rippled with pain. "Thank God you're all right. They told me you left in the middle of the night. Just walked right out."

"Well, it's true. But here I am back again. How are you?"

"My head feels like a bomb went off in it, but otherwise fine. The police were here this morning wanting to know if I'd been drinking or taking dope."

"I told them about the truck."

"So did I. I don't think they liked it much."

"Do you remember talking to me last night?"

"No."

"You told me it wasn't Alva or Donny driving the truck. Do you remember who it was?"

He shook his head slightly and then winced.

"Alva has a red truck," I told him. "A beat-up old rattletrap farm truck." Briefly I recalled trying to drive it in my dream.

David closed his eyes. "I'm trying to picture it," he said. "There was one person in the truck. No one in the passenger seat. I was looking up for just a second, right before we went off. I was yelling at him to get over. I saw an eye, hooded like a snake's eye. No hair. Either bald or cut very short. That's all."

"Was it a man?"

"I think so. But no one I'd ever seen before. And I wouldn't swear I'd recognize him again. Oh, yeah. He was smiling, a terrible gaptoothed grin, like he was enjoying himself. What a way to get your kicks!"

"Alva thinks it was someone out joy riding."

"Could be." He threw me a puzzled look. "You saw her again last night?"

I nodded. "She came in to see my mother."

I didn't want to take the time to tell him all that I'd learned. I wasn't even sure I *should* tell him. It was really between me and my mother. And Alva. I had to get out to River House and see what my mother was up to. And then maybe I would take her advice: pack up my stuff and go back to New York. Wendell's reunion seemed to be over almost before it had begun.

"I'm going out to River House now," I told him. "What should I do about Malachi?"

"I don't know," he said. "I can't drive the bike for a while. Could you keep an eye on him?"

"Ummm."

"He's a good kid. Not much of a bother."

"No, it's not that. It's just that I don't know if I'll be staying . . . at River House or at my mother's."

"Well, maybe Wendell can . . ."

"No, no. It's all right. He can stay with me wherever I stay. There's plenty of room at my mother's. And you can stay there, too, when you get out."

"Thanks. Maybe someone could bring him in this afternoon? He'd love to see his old man being treated like a helpless baby. Be sure and tell him I'm okay, though. By the way, what happened to the car? Can it be fixed?"

"I don't know. It looked a mess, but maybe it can be patched up. Another thing I'll have to check up on. That, and a talk with Sergeant Bert Binns to make sure he didn't just forget about trying to find out who was driving that truck."

I bent over him to say good-bye, and this time I *did* kiss him on the bandage. It felt rough and warm against my lips. He put a hand to my face and raised his own. His lips were smoother and warmer than the bandage on his head, and his beard tickled. I backed away.

"So long, David. I'll see you later."

I hurried out the front entrance of the hospital where my old friend, Betty Sue Wiggins, now Henshaw, presided behind the tall wooden barrier of the information desk. "Morning, there, Jenny," she called out. "I hear you had a little crackup last night. My Billy was out there pulling your boyfriend out of the wreck, but he didn't know it was you until he came to pick up Bert Binns later on. Kind of spoils the reunion, don't it? Why don't you come on out and visit tomorrow? We both get our days off on Tuesday."

I waved to her but didn't answer. That's the way news travels in a small town. Everybody knows everybody else and you don't even have to read the newspaper to find out what's going on. In fact, most people know more than the newspaper prints, although it's inclined to be a bit on the imaginative, not to say scandalous, side. I could imagine what a visit with the Henshaws would be like, both of them probing none too subtly for tidbits of gossip to pass along.

Out in front of the hospital, at one side of the sweeping circular drive, a lone taxicab waited. It was an old Checker cab, painted apple-green, and I imagined it was one that had been retired from the New York City street wars and put out to pasture in this quiet backwater. The driver was dozing behind the wheel.

"How much for a trip out River Road?" I asked him. "It's about twelve miles. I'll tell you how to get there."

"Seven dollars," he said after a cavernous yawn. "And I know how to get there. Been out there and back once already this morning."

I got in. The spacious back seat had been covered in terry cloth printed with huge yellow flowers on an apple-green background. The back of the front seat was plastered with evangelical slogans. The one right behind the driver read, "I'm only the copilot. Jesus is the pilot." Somehow, it didn't reassure me the way it was supposed to. I wasn't sure that Jesus could pass a motor vehicle examination.

But the driver seemed to know what he was doing. We swept down Rattlesnake Hill with scarcely a bump and eased onto the highway going out of town.

"You going out to that River House place, ain't you?" he asked, not waiting for an answer. "Took old Miz Holland out there this morning. Heard she got took strange in church and started speaking in tongues. Told her she ought to come on out to my church where she'd be highly regarded for such an accomplishment, 'stead of carted off to the hospital. Said she might just do that. You any relation of hers?"

"She's my mother." I stared at the back of his creased red neck, willing him to shut up. We had twelve miles to go and I didn't want to travel it with a running commentary on my family.

"A fine woman. A fine woman." I saw him eyeing me in the rearview mirror. "You mind if I play a little music?"

"Go right ahead."

The car radio must have been on with the volume turned down. All he did was twist a knob and the cab filled with a dolorous country ballad.

"That too loud for you?" he shouted.

"Yes!" I shouted back.

He lowered the volume and we drove on for a while listening to Waylon Jennings moaning about a good-hearted woman.

There was traffic on the road this morning: huge trailer trucks rumbling steadily along, Greyhound buses heading in both directions, station wagons full of children, and a battered red farm truck filled with a load of pig corn. I looked closely as we passed it; the driver was a round-faced young man with lank black hair and a bad case of acne. Where were they all last night when just one of them could have meant the difference between crashing down the hill and getting safely home? I started watching the side of the road for a glimpse in daylight of the place where it had happened.

The driver saved me the trouble.

"Terrible accident along here last night," he announced over the music. "Couple of folks like to got killed. One of 'em might not make it, so I hear. Got trapped in the wreckage and about bled to death. Car got totaled. God works in mysterious ways."

He waited for my reply, eyeing me once again in the rearview mirror. I recognized the ploy. He knew who I was and had exaggerated the accident in the hope that I would correct him and give him the true details, which he could then pass on to his next passenger. I refused to bite.

"Indeed He does," I answered.

"That's where it happened," he said, jerking his head to the other side of the road. "Heard they was a couple of druggies from out of state. Must have been flying high. Pretty hard to go off a straight stretch of road like this."

I peered out the window and caught a glimpse of the broken guardrail before we rolled onto the bridge. It didn't look like much had happened there. If the driver hadn't been poking around for information, I'd have asked him to stop and gone to take a look for myself in daylight. There might be tire tracks or something to prove that there had been a truck behind us in the night.

We drove on and after four or five songs about jail and love, faithless women and love, drinking and love, and the pitfalls of life in the big city for a country boy, we pulled into the lane leading up to River House. I handed the driver a ten-dollar bill and told him to keep the change.

As I got out, the driver said, "Thank you, Miss. I'm sure glad you didn't get hurt bad. Anytime you want to come around to my church and offer up thanks, you'd be welcome. Here's my card. Praise the Lord."

I glanced at the card. The driver, it seemed, was a

preacher on Sundays and drove the cab the rest of the week. There were telephone numbers for both occupations and an address for the Zion Four-Square Church of Christ Evangelist. His name was Reverend Gideon Daniels. He smiled at me and said, "I'll pray for your friend."

I shoved the card into my shoulder bag, felt the hardness of the gun that still rested there, and said, "You do that."

On the porch of River House a row of suitcases waited. I ran past them and into the front hall, calling, "Ma! Ma, are you here?"

"Is that you, Wendell?" came Fearn's voice from upstairs.

"No. It's me. Jenny." I ran up the stairs two at a time and poked my head into Fearn's bedroom. "Is my mother here?"

She looked up from brushing Millie's hair, gave her a shove and said, "Get on downstairs, but don't go outside."

Millie sidled out of the room giving me a wall-eyed stare as she went.

"About time you showed up," Fearn muttered. She plopped herself down on the bed, drooping with fatigue. Her eyes were dark-ringed and her hair an untidy mess of apricot-colored spikes. "You missed all the fun. If you could call it that."

"What happened?" There couldn't have been any more visitations from the prowler. Not after Alva had admitted that she was the culprit.

"Somebody tried to set the place on fire. A darn good thing Walter and me stayed up all night, otherwise we'd all be burned to a crisp this morning."

"But that's impossible," I cried.

"Oh, yes? There's a five-gallon can of gasoline out in the yard that calls you a liar. Where were you anyway? You were supposed to come back and do something about that dead chicken."

I'd forgotten about the chicken. Had Alva done that, too? And had she come back here after she'd left me at my mother's house and tried to burn the place down? I couldn't believe it, but then so many unbelievable things were happening, it was beginning to be the norm. "Is my mother here?" I asked again.

"She was. But when me and Walter told her about the firebug, she lit off across the fields like her own tail was on fire. Didn't even stop to ask how we all were or what we intended to do about it."

"How are you?" I obliged, "and what do you intend to do?"

"I'm mad as sin, and I intend to leave here just as soon as Wendell gets here to drive us to the airport. Irene and Mike and that crowd left already. They're supposed to stop at Wendell's and tell him to get on out and pick us up. Walter's out patrolling the grounds so nothing else happens before we can get away. So much for Wendell's reunion. It was a dumb idea, anyway."

"What about Aunt Tillie?"

"I don't know. She took off in that fancy red car of hers about an hour ago. Didn't say where she was going."

"And Malachi? Where's he?"

She huffed to her feet and stomped over to the dresser where she glared into the mirror and applied the hairbrush to her tangled mop. "He's around someplace. I can't be responsible for everybody's kids. I got enough to do looking after my own. He's got a father, hasn't he?"

I didn't think now was the right time to tell Fearn about the accident. She'd have to find out sooner or later, but sooner would only make her madder. "I'll go find him," I said.

Fearn leered at me in the mirror. "You two got a thing going, haven't you? You and David? Is that where you spent the night? At some motel with him? Did he come back with you? Do you think he'll marry you?"

I left the bedroom while Fearn was still spouting questions and tugging at her sticky overworked hair. The hall was quiet. Dust motes swam in the colored rays of light from the leaded glass window on the landing. Across the way was my grandmother's room, and further down the hall the door behind which the dead chicken was undoubtedly beginning to rot. I thought I could smell it. David and Malachi had been using a room on the floor above. I went up the stairs quietly, loath to disturb the stillness that was settling once more on the old house. Soon we'd all be gone. Then whoever'd been distressed by our presence could settle down, too. Maybe it was best not to find out too much. I'd learned things about my mother that explained some of the puzzles of my childhood, but raised others I hadn't known existed. Alva and Donny, for example. Alva I could accept as my aunt, the sister of Raymond my father. But what was I to make of Donny? If he was both cousin and brother, as the county records suggested and Alva didn't deny, then my father was a different person from the one I'd cherished in my memory all these years. Different and frightening. I wasn't sure I wanted to look too closely at the difference.

On the third floor, the bedroom doors all hung open. Two of the rooms were deserted, the beds left tumbled and a lone dirty sock wadded under a chair. In the last room, David's saddlebags crouched on the floor. Both the beds were neatly made. Malachi's bright woven blanket was folded across the foot of one of them, and on it lay an exotically costumed Katchina doll. If David hadn't driven me out to Alva's farm last night, he would have been here this morning, probably getting ready to travel on somewhere else or back to Arizona with Malachi in the sidecar. The reunion hadn't been so wonderful for them either, with David's brothers making it clear that a half-Indian bastard child was a questionable addition to the family. There was a small pine dresser in the room, and on it rested Malachi's child-sized motorcycle helmet. I put my hand on top of it and wondered what it would be like to be a third member of the motorcycle team. The helmet told me nothing. I took my hand away and left the room. Malachi must have been downstairs.

The stairs to the attic caught my eye, narrow and shadowy even in the bright morning. Just on the off chance that he might have been exploring up there, I called his name. There was no answer, only the heavy, hot stillness that seemed to be descending all over River House now that we were being driven out. I thought of the turret room and the filthy pallet on the floor. When we were gone, would a face look down from that tiny window, smiling at our defeat? Whose face?

I fled back down to the second floor and burst into my grandmother's room.

"What did you do?" I cried to the Delectable Mountains quilt, to the window seat, to the family album in its place on the night table. "What did you make my mother do? Couldn't you have let her go?"

Tears fell without warning, great streams of tears that ran and splashed as I tore about the room, pummeling the bed, knocking into the furniture, pulling pages from the album. As quickly as it had come, the seizure passed. I slumped onto the window seat panting and wiped my face on the sleeve of my dress. It was pointless. I couldn't reach her now. Not this way. Not ever. There was no way to change the past. I reached down to pick up the torn pages of the album. My grandmother's wedding picture had been ripped in half.

"What on earth's going on in here?"

Fearn stood in the open doorway, a look of sheer panic on her face.

"Nothing. I'm sorry. I got upset."

"You scared the wits out of me. I thought it was . . ." She stopped and stared around the disordered room. "Is Malachi with you?"

"No."

"Well, maybe he's upstairs."

"He's not."

"Where is he, then? He's not with Billy and Millie. They haven't seen him."

I looked at her.

"Well, don't blame me!" she cried. "I can't keep track of everything."

CHAPTER 34

Wendell arrived around noon and joined the search. We'd been all over the house and barn by then, including the turret room which came as a shock to Fearn and Walter when I pulled down the ladder that led to its trapdoor.

"I had no idea!" Fearn exclaimed at the top of the ladder. "And will you look at this filth! Disgusting!"

"Makes a pretty good hiding place," said Walter

thoughtfully as he climbed down after taking a thorough look around. "But there's nobody up there now."

Walter had put the gasoline can in the barn to get it away from the house, but he showed it to me when we were there looking for Malachi. He also showed me a note that he'd found under the can when he moved it. It was on a torn scrap of brown wrapping paper, printed in pencil in wavering block letters, and it read, "Leave or burn. There's more where this came from." He hadn't shown it to Fearn or anyone else because they were all leaving anyway and he didn't want to give Fearn something else to worry about. He gave the note to me in case, as he said, I might want to pass it on later. What he meant was, don't call the police unless you have to and only after Fearn and I are safely back in Wilmington. I put the note in my shoulder bag.

Then he told me that he and Fearn had stayed up all night to keep an eye on things. Everyone else had gone to bed. They were sitting in the front parlor, feeling drowsy, with the lights out except for a night light in the hall. About two-thirty by the mantel clock, Fearn heard a car coming along River Road. They thought it was David and I returning, but the car didn't drive up to the house and they couldn't tell if it had stopped in the road or gone on by. Everything was quiet for about fifteen or twenty minutes. Then Fearn, whose hearing was acute, said she heard someone walking around the side of the house. They went out to the kitchen and watched through the window, but couldn't see anything. Then they both heard a clanking sound. Walter ran out the back door, stumbled over the gasoline can, and went sprawling. By the time he got back on his feet, whoever'd been there was gone and he heard a car engine starting up in the road. He ran down the drive, but when he got to the road, all he could see was taillights disappearing around the bend. He and Fearn spent the rest of the night on the front porch.

I asked him if the car could have been a truck, but he couldn't be sure. All he was sure of was that when morning came, the gasoline can was still there and Fearn was determined to leave. She'd told the whole story to Irene and Mike as soon as they got up, and they'd gathered up their kids, belongings, and Uncle Ambrose and cleared out, denouncing reunions in general, their own family most particularly, and River House as the target of some local lunatic whose further antics they were well content to do without. As Mike had succinctly put it, "Let's get the hell out of here before that wacko does something right for a change."

After Wendell arrived, we looked up and down the river bank, as far as the rock in the stream. Wendell and I checked each of the old cabins behind the house, while Walter scouted the apple orchard and the family cemetery.

"Maybe he just went off on his own," said Fearn. We were back in the kitchen by then, trying to think of where to look next. "He seems to be the kind of kid who would do that. Comes from not having a mother to make him toe the line."

Billy and Millie, quiet for once, were sitting on the floor building something with Lego blocks. Fearn shrieked at them, "I thought I told you kids to put that stuff away! Pack it up now. We're leaving."

"Maybe we should stay awhile," said Walter. "At least until Malachi turns up."

Fearn's round jaw jutted stubbornly. "We're all packed. Wendell's here with the car. The plane leaves at two-thirty. I'm not spending another night in this house."

Walter sighed and bent to help the children put their blocks away.

"Did anyone see him this morning?" I asked.

"I gave him his breakfast," said Fearn. "I don't know why I have to be the chief cook around here for other people's kids."

Wendell, who'd been staring out the back door, lost in thought, muttered over his shoulder, "Didn't you tell them, Jenny?"

Before I could answer, Fearn demanded, "Tell us what? Something else has happened, hasn't it? That settles it. We're leaving. This minute. Walter, get that luggage out to the car."

Walter ignored her. He straightened up with the box of blocks in his hands and came over to me.

"What happened, Jenny?"

"David's in the hospital. We had an accident."

"On the motorcycle?"

"No. In my mother's car. How did you hear about it, Wendell?"

"Bert Binns called me this morning. He's an old bowling buddy of mine. Wanted to know if I knew anything about anybody who had a red truck and a grudge against the family. You and David in particular. I had to tell him I didn't." Wendell's face was broad and bland, innocence shining like a beacon in his close-set eyes. I wondered if he was covering up knowledge about red trucks, dead chickens, Alva and Donny, and people who came calling at night with five-gallon gasoline cans.

It hadn't occurred to me before, but Wendell was in an ideal position to influence my mother. Had been for years. He claimed that his sporting goods business was prospering, but maybe that was just fine and boisterous talk. I knew he'd had a hand in the settlement of my grandmother's estate; he'd sent me her jewelry with an official-looking letter that I'd scarcely bothered to read. As I recalled, everything else went to my mother on the condition that she never leave town. I'd thrown the letter away, thinking it a strange condition and one which need not have been made. My mother wasn't likely to go seeking adventure.

But suppose Wendell, wanting to expand his business, had his eye on my mother's property. I'd no idea what that property was or if she'd made a will or who was likely to inherit. But Wendell would know; he'd have no trouble finding out through his good old buddy network. Could he have orchestrated the whole incredible series of events hoping to worsen my mother's condition and have himself declared trustee or guardian or whatever the doctors and lawyers between them decided was necessary? And just by the way, wouldn't it suit his purposes to discredit me or even arrange an accident for me? Wendell wasn't nearly the simple country boy he liked people to think.

Fearn's reaction to the news of our car accident was predictably unpredictable. She threw her arms around me and cried, "Oh, Jenny! How awful! And poor David! Is he hurt bad? And what about you? Are you all right?"

I slipped out of her sisterly grip, reassuring her that outside of a few bruises, I was, indeed, all right. "But I'm worried about Malachi," I reminded her. "Did anyone see him after breakfast?"

"I seen him." Millie tugged at my sleeve, her small face eager for attention.

"None of your fibs now, young lady," Fearn scolded. "This is serious."

"I ain't fibbin'," Millie whined. "I did too see him. I went up to his bedroom with him. He showed me some funny-looking doll he had. He said it was magic. But he couldn't make it do anything."

"That's nonsense," said Fearn. "Boys don't have dolls."

"Honest he did. It was all dressed up in a Indian costume." Millie was pleading with me to believe her. It crossed my mind that Millie was a pretty nice little girl and Fearn was doing the best she could to turn her into a sniveling devious brat. But that wasn't really any of my business. I believed her, and said so.

"There's a Katchina doll on his bed."

Millie's face shone. "That's what he said. I didn't like it. It didn't cry or talk or anything. I got a Baby Wet-the-Bed for my birthday. She cries and wets and gets spots on her bottom." At this last, she giggled and put her hand over her mouth.

"What happened then?" I asked her.

"That's all. He showed me the doll and I said, 'Make it do something,' and he couldn't, so I went downstairs."

"Did he stay in his room?"

She stared at me and began nibbling a strand of her hair.

"What time was it?"

But again she had nothing to say.

Fearn shook her. "Speak up, Miss. You wanted to tell stories. Don't stop now."

Millie started crying. Fearn slapped her and told her to stop. Millie threw herself down on the floor and howled. If she knew anything more about Malachi's whereabouts, we'd never find out. Fearn jerked her to her feet and dragged her, screaming, from the room. Walter looked as if he might follow, but changed his mind. We all listened to Millie's cries receding up the stairs.

"Well," I said, "maybe he went with Aunt Tillie. Or with my mother."

Walter shook his head. "We were all right here when Tillie left. She said she'd be back but she didn't know when. And your mother went off by herself. I asked her if she wanted me to go with her, but she said no, she had something to do and she had to do it alone." He took Billy's hand and led him toward the door. "Guess I better go see what Fearn's up to."

I had a pretty good idea of where my mother had gone. Alva's trailer could be reached on foot by following the route that Donny used through the woods and fields that separated the farm from River House. I wondered whether I ought to try to find my way there, but I didn't want to leave the house without knowing where Malachi was. Wendell, I noticed, was fairly subdued, leaning against the refrigerator, his crossed arms resting on the slope of his belly.

There was one thing I could do, and Wendell could help me. Although I was inclined to believe my mother's latest story of how Raymond had died, there was still a shred of doubt in my mind. If it were true and it became known, it could mean an agonizing public trial for her. But wasn't it better to get it all out in the open where it could no longer torment her? And what sentence could the law inflict on her more punishing than the one she'd passed on herself? Surely they wouldn't lock her away for the few remaining years of her life. And, if I were totally honest, I had to admit that I wanted to know positively and without doubt that she had told me the truth at last. I had the means to make sure. Whatever the consequences, I had to do it.

"Wendell," I said, "can you get Ralph Dean Otwell out here? I've got a job for him."

Wendell blinked and licked his lips. "The Monkey Man? You think the kid's up on the roof?"

"No. I want him to open up the old well."

"What for? It's been sealed up for years. He couldn't have fallen in."

"I'll tell you what for after Ralph Dean goes down and comes back up."

"No need to be so mysterious. Ralph Dean'll have to know what he's looking for."

"No, he won't. If it's there, he'll know. And if it's not, well, none of us will be any wiser."

Wendell sighed. "This reunion's already a disaster, so I might as well top it all off by having the Monkey Man pull a dead body out of the well. I'll see if I can find him and send him on out."

I froze. Wendell knew! He must have known all along. This was confirmation of my mother's story! But if he knew, why had he kept quiet about it? And why had he insisted on holding the reunion here where memories would intrude and upset my mother's fragile balance?

"What are you talking about?" I asked, dreading the answer. "What dead body?"

"Oh, shoot, girl. Why do you have to take everything so serious? I don't know what you're looking for down in that well. I hope you find buried treasure. All I meant was, things has been going so bad out here, it wouldn't surprise me none if old Ralph Dean *did* haul up a corpse. If you don't want to tell me what you've got in mind, that's your business. But I'll tell you gladly, I wish I'd never got involved in this whole reunion business."

"Why did you?"

"Well, it wasn't my idea."

"Whose?"

"Well, I'm not supposed to tell. But now that it's all falling apart, I don't suppose it matters if I tell you. It was your mother who wanted it. She talked me into it. Said she wanted to patch up her differences with you, and the only way she could think to get you back home was if the invitation was for everybody, not just you. And wouldn't it be nice anyway to get the whole family together before the old folks die off? And what could be better than to have it at River House where there was room for everyone to stay awhile? And, like I say, she talked me into it. It seemed like a good idea. But now I just don't understand why she wanted to get everybody together out here, and then try to scare them away. It's just plain crazy."

"You think she's behind it all?"

"Who else?"

"But she was in the hospital last night. She couldn't have been creeping around with a gas can in the middle of the night. And besides, her car's been wrecked. And that's another thing. I'm sure she wasn't the one who ran us off the road."

"Maybe she's got friends."

I was about to tell him that I knew about her friend Alva Holland, when Fearn marched into the kitchen lugging her big white plastic pocketbook and an overnight case.

"We're ready to go," she announced. "Good-bye, Jenny. Looks like you're the last one left. Sure you don't want to come with us?"

I could have gone. It would have taken me about two

minutes to pack my bag. But Malachi was still missing and David, from the look of him, would be in the hospital for another week or so. I couldn't leave. Besides, I wanted to be here when my mother came back. She'd provided some answers, but they only raised more questions. I shook my head and said, "No, thanks."

Fearn primmed up her lips and shrugged as if to say she'd given up wasting words on me. She turned and marched out of the room, a round, righteous figure, bedeviled by events she couldn't control. I felt sad for her, sadder for Millie and Billy and poor patient Walter. Wendell slouched after her, his usual blustering ebullience quenched.

"I'll be back, Jenny. I'll come right back."

"Don't forget to send Ralph Dean out."

"You really want to do that? Open up that well?"

"I really do."

"Well, all right."

And he was gone. I slumped down in a kitchen chair, my bag lying heavily across my lap, and listened to the faint sounds of their departure. Millie howled piteously once, followed by Fearn's scolding tones and the slamming of the car door. More car doors slammed. Wendell gunned the engine and tooted the horn. I couldn't hear the soft slur of the tires on the dirt lane, but after a while I knew they were gone and I was alone in River House.

It wasn't so bad. It was quiet. I sat on in the kitchen, letting the heat of the summer afternoon soak into my body. My bruises ached and I prodded the big one on my thigh, bringing it into sharper relief. It felt good, a good pain. It meant I was alive and feeling. The house towered around me, all those rooms, empty now but once full of life. Funny thing, though. In all my life, no one had lived in it but my grandmother. Alone. It had never occurred to me to wonder how it had been for her, living so isolated with no one to talk to, except my mother who came to visit and whisper over cups of tea in this very kitchen. And me, before I went away.

Before I went away. My mother told me that my father had died in this house, and I had to believe her, didn't I? I tried to envision the scene as she had so sketchily described it to me: the two of them struggling, he with a gun in his hand (and was he smiling his wide white Raymond smile?), she biting him fiercely on that hand, wresting the gun away from him, and then shooting him. How many times? Once? Twice? More? And where? In the head? The heart? Messily in the stomach?

And where was my grandmother while this was going on? Where was I? In what room of the house did it happen?

And why did she do it?

My imagination couldn't bring me the answers. The story was simple, as simple as all the other lies she'd told me. But was it true? It could have happened. When I read the newspapers in the city, I am often amazed at the ease with which people take the lives of others. Could my mother have killed Raymond my father as easily as those news reports tell us it happens? One minute alive, the next minute dead. I couldn't believe it. I didn't want to believe it. I wanted it to be another of her lies, the lies that made it possible for me to hope that one day I would look up from some ordinary task and see him smiling down at me.

I stretched in the kitchen chair and got up. Maybe if I went from room to room in the silent deserted house and listened with all my might, I would hear the echo of that shot reverberating down the years. A ghost shot.

I laughed at myself softly. It sounded loud and a little mad in the quiet kitchen, and I clapped my hands over my ears. My shoulder bag swung and bumped against my hip, reminding me of the gun I had been carrying around with me for two days now. If I could contemplate aiming and firing it at someone, why should I doubt that my mother had actually done the same when she was not much older than I?

But she would not have done it in the kitchen. If she had, how could she and my grandmother have spent so many hours there calmly gossiping and sipping their tea?

I wandered into the dining room. Not here, either. The table and chairs, the sideboard, the china closet twinkled in the sunlight streaming through the tall windows. This was the brightest room in the house with its gleaming chandelier, its polished wood and the triple panes of the bay window looking out across the sun-drenched side yard to the stand of willows beyond. I lingered for only a moment, long enough to catch a fleeting memory of a Christmas dinner with my grandmother at the head of the table, my father at the foot, and my mother and me between. He was laughing. The rest of us were not.

It could have happened in the parlor, in that dim, velvety room where only days ago I'd crumpled and knocked my head on the sofa arm. In my own mind, I'd attributed my fainting spell to fatigue and nervous anticipation. I didn't even like to think of it as fainting, just a freakish kind of blackout. It had never happened before and wouldn't happen again. But what if it had been caused by some kind of signal from the past, a vacuum created by a violent act that drained my senses and sent me toppling?

I walked into the parlor warily, my footsteps lost in the thick pile of the swirling blue carpet. At the first sign of dizziness, I was ready to run back out into the safety of the hall. Even the silence was muffled here and the sound of my own breathing was lost in the thick, heavy air. The heat was more noticeable in this room, moist and intense, as if it had collected throughout the summer in the wine-colored cushions and drapes. I had the faintly unpleasant sensation of being inside a living organism, of being somehow unborn. But I did not feel dizzy, and I received no telltale echoes from the past.

What I did begin to feel was foolish. There were other things I should be doing and not groping through the house in search of omens. I should be doing my best to figure out where Malachi had gone. But we'd already searched everywhere with no luck. He was a pretty self-reliant little boy, but he was just that—a *little* boy. And I'd promised David I would look after him. Maybe, if I just stayed in one place, here at River House, he would turn up. It hadn't worked for Raymond my father, but, of course, there was a perfectly good reason for that. He was dead. I guess I'd always known that was true even though I'd mistrusted my mother's lies about how he had died. And that mistrust had led me to hope that he was somewhere, still alive, and because he was my daddy would find me where I waited for him in Max's Secondhand Books. Now I knew he would never come.

But Malachi was alive and well, if a bit irresponsible for going off on his own, and had nowhere to return but here. His nonappearance was making me edgy, a mixture of worry over his safety, anger at his thoughtlessness, and the sheer dumb helplessness of not knowing what to do next. I itched to do something, anything, to relieve the tension. And there was that awful dead chicken mess in the room upstairs. I really ought to clean that up before it got too putrid to face. No more listening for ghost shots in ancient rooms and making myself as crazy as my mother. I gathered up some cleaning supplies from the kitchen and headed purposefully up the stairs.

The stench was already pretty bad in the back bedroom. Someone had thoughtfully closed the windows and the heat had done its work. I put my bag on the dresser, next to the staring chicken head, and groped in it for a scarf. I found a faded bandanna handkerchief, one I sometimes used to tie around my head gypsy-fashion. This time I tied it around my face. I glanced in the mirror and snickered; I looked like an outlaw about to rob the town bank. Then my eyes focused on the dried chicken blood smeared on the glass. "GET OUT" was printed across my reflected image. I stopped laughing.

Avoiding the smears of blood on the floor, I opened both windows and turned to survey the damage and decide where to begin. The bedspread obviously couldn't be saved, and there was no way I was going to pick up that chicken corpse and carry it away. I decided to burn everything that was beyond redemption in the backyard. A cleansing bonfire with a barbecued chicken at the center of it. Okay. Joking about it made it easier to do.

Gingerly I plucked the chicken head out of the vase of strawflowers, holding it with two fingers clamped on its limp red comb, and tossed it onto the bed. Then I bundled the whole ugly mess up in the bedspread and tossed it into the corner. It was a shame about the bedspread, not really an antique, but a nice old candlewick spread that had a lot of years left in it. The braided rug was badly splattered but probably could be cleaned. I rolled it up and put it aside for Wendell to deal with.

The hard part came next, cleaning the bloodstains off the floor, the walls, the furniture—everywhere it had splattered. I filled a bucket with cold water and began sponging the hardwood floor first so I wouldn't have to worry about walking on blood. It was a tedious job. Even where the blood had gathered in pools, it had coagulated and dried, and I had to soak it and scrub at it to get it off. Gradually, the water in the bucket turned a muddy pink.

While I worked, my thoughts wandered over the events precipitated by my homecoming. Would any of it have happened, I wondered, if I had not accepted Wendell's invitation?

What was it all supposed to achieve? I could see no sane reason for inviting everyone to a reunion and then frightening them all away. But that seems to have been what my mother, with Alva's help, was up to. And, except for me, she had succeeded. I wanted to know why.

The silence in the house, my own thoughts, and the soft rhythmic swiping of the sponge on the floor boards had thrown me into a soporific mood. Nothing existed outside the room, the job at hand, and the questions inside my head. So when the shot came, distant, muffled and unreal, like the sound of a television program in the next apartment, I didn't immediately realize what it was I had heard. Then, when realization came, my first thought was that I had heard the echo through the years of the shot that had killed my father, that it had happened in this room, and that through some odd twist of time, it was his blood I was cleaning off the floor.

I sat back on my heels, pulled the kerchief away from my face, and listened. The silence persisted. There were no other shots. Had I imagined it? Or were there hunters across the river, the sound of their kill carrying for miles in the still, hot afternoon? The floor was almost clean. There was still a narrow trail of blood circling the foot of the bed and a few scattered specks near the window. When I finished the floor, I would change the water and see what I could do about cleaning the wallpaper. I squeezed out the sponge, bent to my work, and heard the screen door below creak open and closed.

It could have been my mother. Or Malachi. I was tempted to call out their names. It could have been Alva or Donny. I heard no other sound, and I kept quiet myself. Waiting. Then, after a long time—how long I couldn't judge—there was a footstep. And another. The stairs groaned and the footsteps sounded slowly and regularly on the treads, step, pause, step, pause, with a whisper of ragged breathing between each step. I stayed crouched on the floor, gripping the stained sponge, staring at the open door. The footsteps ceased as they reached the top of the stairs, but the ragged breathing continued. Then they started up again, shuffling, limping by the irregular rhythm of it, coming along the hall. And Donny's awkward gait sprang to mind. I waited for him to appear in the doorway.

But he didn't. Instead, the step, pause, step, pause went

up the narrow flight of stairs to the third floor. I listened to them passing by on the other side of the wall where the stairway rose between this room and the one that had been occupied by Fearn and Walter. I pictured Donny clumsily hauling himself up the stairs, one step at a time, favoring his lame leg, his big floppy hands gripping the wooden railing. And I almost went to see if I could help him. But then I remembered that in all likelihood, he was responsible for the mess I was cleaning up. Donny didn't frighten me. I felt sorry for him. And as far as I was concerned, he could spend the rest of his sad miserable existence in the foul nest he'd made for himself at the top of the house, if that's what pleased him. The footsteps thumped overhead and then faded as the step, pause rhythm took him up to the attic.

Good, I thought. I didn't particularly want to see Donny. I wasn't going to go up there and ask him where my mother was, or if he'd just heard a shot, or whether he was in the habit of driving his mother's truck into the sides of other folks' cars in the middle of Sunday night. Nosirree, I wasn't going to do any of that.

But I tossed the sponge into the bucket, dried my hands on a clean piece of rag, and went out into the hall and listened some more. Everything was quiet. There might have been no one in the house but me. Downstairs, the mantel clock chimed three times. I set my foot on the first stair riser going up.

And several things happened at once.

The screen door slammed and there was a sudden commotion down below. In the midst of it, I recognized Malachi's excited piping and Donny's hoarse croak.

Malachi was yelling, "I saw him! I saw him come in here!"

And Donny was protesting, "I ain't supposed to be in the house. She won't like it."

At the same time, from the attic, an agonized shriek plummeted down. Barely human, yet it sprang from a human throat. Quivering, rising and falling, it howled of aching loneliness and despair. It howled my mother's name. Again and again, it howled, "L-i-i-z-z-e-e-e-e!"

I ran. Up the stairs, stumbling over my own feet, almost sprawling onto the third-floor landing, and up again until I stood panting in the hot hazy attic where the ladder to the turret room waited for me to ascend.

The voice had quietened to a wracking moan, so filled with anguish that it twisted in my gut and turned my legs to stone. Yet I had to see who was making that awful sound. I forced myself to move. The sun was shining in the small turret window and spilling through the open trapdoor bathing the ladder in a shaft of light. Mechanically I moved toward the ladder, forcing my hands to grip the sides, my foot to step upon the first rung. And the second. The moaning continued, interspersed with a thin, high-pitched babbling that made no sense at all.

I rose toward the sound, fighting off waves of nausea. Sweat leaked from every pore in my body, and a dull throbbing pain began to bang away behind my eyes. A step up, and then another step up. I hauled my reluctant body, rung by rung, up the ladder, resisting the urge to turn and run and hide myself away in a dark, soft, warm place where no one would ever find me. When I reached the trapdoor, I crouched on the ladder and let only my eyes rise above the level of the floor.

The tenant of the turret room lay curled on the pallet, face to the wall. All I could see was the thin curve of a back and the meager haunches, dressed in a stained white T-shirt and faded jeans. And the feet, bare, calloused and dirty, tucked under the curve of the body like a pair of naked nurslings seeking warmth and shelter. On one of them, a trickle of blood gleamed wetly and there was a dark blotch on the leg of the jeans just below a ragged hole. The sight was pitiable, and the moaning and babbling, which went on without any awareness of an audience, wrung my heart. I hoisted myself further through the trapdoor until I was sitting on the floor with my legs dangling down the ladder.

"Who are you?" I whispered.

The moaning stopped, and the body stiffened in its fetal crouch.

"I'm sorry. I didn't mean to startle you." The words clung to my lips and I had to force them out.

As I sat trembling on the edge of the trapdoor, the sun passed away from the small window and the light in the turret room changed from golden to gray. The head on the pallet raised itself and began to turn toward me. I saw a watery blue eye, shrouded in folds of unhealthy pale and wrinkled skin; a beaky nose; a high, domed forehead curving back to a fringe of wispy no-color hair. The eye stared at me over a bony shoulder.

And then the body scrambled until it was squatting on the pallet, its long arms wrapped around the spires of its knees. The sad, ravaged face, only a few feet from my own, swayed rhythmically from side to side as the blue eyes gazed hungrily at me. God knows how long we sat like that, staring at each other, but at last one of us spoke. It was he, and when I heard his voice, I recognized the harsh, metallic tones that had called to me on the river bank while I crouched terrified on the rock.

"Jenny. I knew you'd come. You had to. I've been waiting so long."

And then he smiled. The thin lips parted over stained and broken teeth in a wide, hideous grin.

"She tried to keep you away from me, but I always knew you'd come back to your loving daddy."

CHAPTER
35

It had been raining all day, but it was Mother's Day so we all had to go out to Grandma's after church. Daddy never went to church, but I had to go to Sunday school and learn all about how Jesus loves me and the Good Samaritan and Lot's wife turning into a pillar of salt 'cause she didn't do what she was told and stuff like that.

When we got to Grandma's it was still raining, so I couldn't play outside and it was boring with nothing to do but listen to the grown-ups talk. Daddy played checkers with me for a while but then I spilled them on the floor when he won and he wouldn't play anymore. Grandma wanted me to sit on her lap, but I didn't like sitting on laps unless it was Daddy's. Anyway, she smelled funny and she always wanted me to drink tea from her cup. Mama would look mad when she did that, but she never said anything. Except later she would tell me how you could get germs drinking from other people's cups.

So after a while, I went upstairs. Grandma didn't mind

if I went in her room and looked at the old magazines she had in the window seat. But after a few minutes of that, I couldn't sit still anymore. The rain was splashing on the windows, and I couldn't even see down to the road, let alone down to the river. So there was no point in watching for boats to go by. I went out of Grandma's room and on up to the third floor.

There was nothing up there but some more bedrooms where nobody slept anymore. Sometimes Grandma would tell me of the days when she was a girl and the whole house would be full of visiting relatives and friends and there'd be parties and reunions and weddings and funerals and I don't know what all. Nothing like that had ever happened that I could remember. O'course, I couldn't remember back too far. I'd be nine in September, but that was a long ways away and maybe I'd have something nice to remember by then. Something to tell stories about when I grew up.

It was boring on the third floor, so I went on up to the attic. It wasn't so boring up there. It was a little bit dark and creepy, and there were funny noises that I hoped came from the rain banging away on the roof. And there was lots of interesting junk piled around that I could play with. Grandma never told me *not* to go in the attic. I don't think she knew that I ever went up there. But I did. The last time was when I found the little room at the top of the ladder. I never would have found it except I was lying down on an old blanket on the floor, sort of daydreaming about how I was a lost princess and didn't belong to this family at all and soon my real family would come and take me away, and I was just kind of staring up at the ceiling. And that's when I saw this piece of rope hanging down. Well, of course, I had to find out what it was. I could barely reach it standing on a chair. But I reached it and pulled it and the ladder came down.

So this time, I went right to the ladder and pulled it down and went up into my secret lost princess room way at the top of the castle. The last time, I'd carried up the blanket and an old chair and a raggedy old doll with a broken china face. This time I took a long purple dress from one of the trunks and a lace tablecloth with a big hole in it, but that was all right because I could put my head through it and wear it for a princess cape.

I hadn't even got my princess clothes on when I heard

them calling me. I didn't answer. My blue velvet Sunday dress was on the floor and I was standing there in my underwear just getting ready to put on the purple princess gown. I heard my name again, getting closer. It wasn't Grandma or Mama. It was Daddy calling.

I didn't mind so much if Daddy found out about my secret room. Daddy used to like to play games and carry me on his shoulders and throw me up in the air. But he didn't do that so much anymore. Mama said I was getting too big. Maybe he could be the prince who finds the lost princess and takes her back to his own land and they live happily ever after. When he called again, I answered. Then I quick put the dress on and put the tablecloth over my head so I would look like a bride. The dress had a whole lot of hooks and eyes that I couldn't get hooked, and it trailed down on the floor so I couldn't walk without holding it up.

When he poked his head through the trapdoor, he looked at me and whistled.

"Is that my little ugly duckling turned into a beautiful princess?" he said.

I knew Daddy would like to play the game. "Are you the handsome prince come to rescue me from the tower?"

"That's me," he said, and came on up into the secret room. "This sure beats listening to those two carrying on like a couple of nesting hens. I guess you got pretty bored with it, too."

I put my hands over my mouth so I wouldn't giggle.

"Well," he said, "what happens next, now that you're the princess and I'm the prince?"

I took my hands away long enough to say, "I guess we have to get married."

He smiled at me. Daddy had a big smile and his teeth were so big and white and his hair so smooth and blond and his face was always nice and brown from being outdoors a lot. He was the handsomest man in the world.

"Oh, ho," he said. "You know what that means, don't you?"

I shook my head.

"It means you have to take off all your princess clothes and let me look at you."

"But I just put them on." I liked the feeling of the long

purple dress against my legs. It was smooth and cool and not a bit like wearing short dresses and knee socks. It made me feel all grown-up.

"Well, you can put them on again later. You have to do it, otherwise you can't be a princess. How else will I know if you're perfect? You might have a wart on your backside."

I really did giggle then. Daddy was so funny. "You *know* I haven't got a wart there where you said."

"No, I don't. You might have sat on a frog."

"Did not."

"Well, show me."

"Oh, all right."

So I took off the lace tablecloth and the long purple gown.

"Take off the rest of it, too."

I was wearing a white cotton undershirt and white panties with little blue flowers on them. I didn't know which one I was supposed to take off first. A princess ought to know things like that. But Daddy was nice and he helped me. He pulled the shirt up and over my head and folded it and put it on the chair.

"That's better," he said. "Now, all you have to do is step right out of these."

I still had on my white sandals that I polished that morning before church, and when he pulled down my panties and I tried to step out of them, they got caught on one of the buckles and I had to hop around like a crippled bird. Another thing a princess wouldn't do. I felt pretty dumb. But Daddy made me feel better.

"Oh, you are a pretty little thing," he said. "If I didn't know better, I'd say you weren't my daughter at all but a fairy princess from a distant star."

"Oh, Daddy! Do you want me to take my shoes off, too?"

He hugged me then and picked me up and whirled around with me so I had to hang on tight and wrap my legs around him. He felt so good and strong and smelled so nice. I pushed my nose against his cheek so I could smell him better, and gave him a big kiss.

"You love your Daddy, don't you?" he said.

I kissed him again.

"And Daddy loves you. You know that, don't you?"

278

I nodded my head, still pressed against his cheek.

"Well, you're going to do something for Daddy to show how much you love him. You'd like that, wouldn't you?"

"What is it?"

"Oh, it's like hugging and kissing, but nicer."

I couldn't imagine what was nicer than hugging and kissing, and I would hug him and kiss him a thousand times if that's what he wanted. He put me down then and told me to lie down on the blanket.

He was wearing his Sunday suit. Not the jacket of it, but the vest and shirt and tie and the trousers that Mama had pressed for him that morning. When he started taking them off, I got a funny feeling in my stomach like something was crawling around inside me and making me feel all hot and woozy. I bent over so I wouldn't have to look at him and started unbuckling my shoes.

"Look!" he said. "I have a present for the princess."

I didn't want to look, but he took my face in his two hands and lifted it up so I had to. He was kneeling on the floor. His bare thighs were covered with shining golden hairs and on one of them there was an ugly puckered scar.

I touched it and said, "Daddy, you're not perfect."

He laughed out loud at that. "That's what your mother keeps telling me. Don't you start doing it, too."

He started stroking and petting me, then, just like he'd do when he came to tuck me in bed at night. Only this time I didn't have my pajamas on and it felt tickly when his hands went over the bare skin on my chest and belly. Then he put his fingers there where Mama always told me never to touch. I yelped.

"Ssh, ssh," he said. "You sound like a little bird. This isn't gonna hurt. And besides, princesses never cry."

I was still trying not to look at him. I closed my eyes, but they kept popping open because there was this weird-looking thing growing on him that I never saw before and I was trying to figure out what it was. I thought maybe it was one of those tumors that Grandma and Mama were always talking about that made people die. Maybe Daddy was gonna die. That made me feel so bad that I put my arms around his neck and hugged him hard.

And he said, "Okay, little princess. Here goes!"

Ooooh, how it hurt! I kept trying to get away from the hurt, but he held me and flopped down on top of me so I couldn't move. It wasn't a good game anymore. I guess I was crying, but I didn't care 'cause I didn't want to be a princess if that's what princesses had to do. And Daddy sure wasn't a prince, 'cause he was making funny groaning noises and I didn't think princes ever sounded like that.

And then there was a scream, and Mama yelled, "Raymond!" and Daddy yelled, "Lizzie!" and I closed my eyes while they yelled at each other. Just when I thought the yelling would never stop, there was a loud bang, and Daddy said, "Jesus Christ!"

I don't remember what happened next.

CHAPTER
36

"I came back. I didn't know. I thought you were dead. I just remembered . . . what you did. To me."

I gripped the edge of the trapdoor to keep from falling. He squatted on the filthy pallet, nodding and grinning. Blood from his injured leg added to the stains on the gray sheet.

"You were sure a pretty little girl," he croaked. "And now you're a pretty woman. When Lizzie told me you were coming, I thought I wouldn't recognize you after all these years. But I did. The minute I set eyes on you. Bet you drive the men crazy. You married, Jenny? You got kids?"

"No." Beyond that single word, I didn't trust myself to speak. I'd found Raymond my father. My long search was over. The memory that had been lurking in my dreams of River House, the act of violation that had been sealed away in my mind was now exposed. But what was I to do with it? It had driven me from my home. It had kept me for almost ten years in the safe haven of Max's Secondhand Books. It had gotten between me and all the men who'd drifted in and out of my

Macy's three-quarter bed. And it had probably drawn me back here to face this man and do what I must. But what was it?

"Why?" I asked him.

His face turned ugly and he clenched his fists in helpless rage. "It's Lizzie," he snarled. "She wants me to get out. She says she's tired of the whole thing. Now, I ask you, what would I do if I left this place? It wasn't my idea. It was her and that mother of hers. But I took care of the old lady, all right. Pushed her right down that ladder one night. I listened to her screaming and hollering all night long. She didn't shut up until daylight. I'll do it to Lizzie, too, if she don't stop trying to shove me out." He smiled his awful Raymond smile at me and reached for me with his thin white hands. "Now that you're back, I don't need her anymore. You can bring me my food and my smokes. You'll do that for your daddy, won't you, Jenny? You can even live right here in the house. I been thinking about that a lot, Jenny. You and me, just like when you were little."

The revulsion that I'd been trying to keep in check rose like a flame feeding on dry tinder. No wonder my mother was teetering on the edge of insanity if she'd been tending this monster all these years. I shrank away from his clutching hands and reached for the ladder with my feet.

"I'll get something to fix up your leg. It's bleeding."

"No. Wait," he said. He was quick. Before I could lower myself through the trapdoor, he'd gripped my arms and pulled me all the way into the turret room. I sprawled on the dusty floor, shuddering from his touch.

"I want to talk to you. Lizzie won't talk to me, except to tell me to leave. She says she'll starve me out, but she won't. She's too softhearted for that. Lizzie always was a poor weak thing. She couldn't even shoot straight when she wanted to kill me." He laughed hideously at the memory of my mother's incompetence.

"She did shoot at you, then?"

"She sure did. But she missed. The first time and the second time. Third time's supposed to be charmed, but she only winged me."

"Third time?"

"Just now. When I was trying to get back here. She was laying for me in the woods behind Alva's place. Got hold of Alva's rifle and started screaming she was gonna kill me for sure this time. I don't know what's got into that woman. She used to be just as nice and biddable as sweet cream."

"And the second time?"

"The other night. When you folks were all out in front singing. It reminded me of the good old days, so I put my old Navy uniform on and went to see if I could talk some sense into her. I thought she'd listen to me if I could get her thinking about how it was when we first got together. But she started shooting at me before I could say boo. She can't throw me out now." His voice whined with self-pity and there were tears gathering in the corners of his eyes. "Where would I go?" he moaned. "What would I do?"

"Why didn't you leave years ago? Why didn't you just get out of our lives after . . . after she tried to shoot you the first time?" I still couldn't bring myself to speak of what I had remembered.

"I couldn't. I offered to, but she wouldn't let me."

"Who? My mother?"

"Not her. The old lady. She locked me in up here." He laughed again bitterly. "Said if I liked playing house so much I could just spend the rest of my life in this playhouse. They took you away and I never saw you from that day until this reunion, except what I saw from that little window when you and Lizzie would come to visit. Didn't you ever know that I watched you from the window? Didn't you ever know I was up here?"

Did I? Perhaps I did, and didn't want to know it. All those dreams about the old house must have meant I knew something. I didn't understand how I could have forgotten what he'd done to me, but if I could forget that, there could be whole chunks of my life that were still buried away.

"Want a cigarette?" He was rummaging in a crumpled pack of Camels and I remembered how he used to tell me stories about the camel on the front and the desert town on the back. I shook my head. He lit a bent cigarette with an old Zippo lighter (which I also remembered) and reached for the coffee can that served as his ashtray.

"Gotta get some more cigarettes," he said. "You bring me some, you hear?"

"I'll go get them now," I said, edging toward the trap-door.

"Not now!"

He scuttled over to crouch between me and the room's only exit. "How do I know you'll come back? There's a lot you don't understand yet. I gotta make you understand. Lizzie's no good to me anymore. She leaves the door unlocked. I don't mind at night. I like to go walking around at night. I look at people and they never know I'm there. But she's supposed to lock it up in the daytime. And she won't. She's even started trying to lock me *out*. But I fooled her. She gave an extra key to Alva and I stole it from her. I've got all the keys for the house. So now when she tries to lock me out, I can get in. But I can't lock the door behind me. And now somebody's taken the lock away. You'll get a new one, won't you, Jenny? You'll lock me in?"

"Why? Why do you want to be locked in up here?"

"Don't ask me that!" He dropped his head onto his knees and pounded the floor with his fists. "Don't you ever ask me that!" he shouted. "Just do it! You hear?"

"Okay, okay."

"Okay. You're a good girl, Jenny." His head came up and he was smiling again. He'd crushed his cigarette out during his spasm of anger, and now he was trying to light it again but it wouldn't draw. He flipped it into the coffee can. "Sometimes," he said, "I pick the butts apart and roll my own in newspaper. She don't like me to smoke up here. She's afraid I'm gonna burn the house down, like I did the other one."

"You burned Alva's house?"

"Yep. That was when Lizzie first started talking about throwing me out. I had to show her that I meant to stay." He chuckled. "That kept her in line for a good long time."

"But you could have killed someone. Donny was hurt."

"Yeah. Too bad. Alva's never been much of a sister to me. And that kid of hers is a born loser. Not too bright upstairs. Not like you. I can tell you're smart. It's gonna be real nice having you around, Jenny. Come over here and give your daddy a big kiss."

He reached for me again, and again I shrank away.

"Wait a minute," I said. My mouth had gone dry and my head was hurting. I kept trying to think of some way to convince him to let me go, but all the things he'd done were buzzing in my mind like a swarm of angry bees. "That was you in the truck, wasn't it? You ran us off the road last night. David's in the hospital and my mother's car is a wreck."

He sighed heavily and got to his feet. From where I crouched on the floor he looked tall and very dangerous. His eyes glinted at me from beneath hooded lids and his long-taloned fingers clutched the air.

"Didn't your mother teach you not to go gallivanting around at night with strange men? I guess you learned it now. I catch you doing it again, I'll have to lock you in up here. But you behave yourself and we'll get along just fine."

"But David's not a stranger. He's part of the family."

"He's a man, ain't he? I don't want you fooling around with men. You're my little girl and that's the way it's gonna be. From now on."

He reached for me yet again, but this time I slithered away from his grasping fingers and made it back to the trap-door. With my feet scrabbling for the rungs of the ladder, I babbled up at him, "I'll get you something to eat now, Daddy. I'll be back in ten minutes. A sandwich and a beer. I'll be right back."

I slid rather than climbed down the ladder and landed with a jolt on the attic floor. I stood there shaking and waiting to see if he would follow me. If he did, I would run. Out of the house, out of this world, out of this life that had turned so ugly. There was always the river, deep and forgetful.

He didn't follow me. The howling started up again. But this time I could distinguish the words.

"Jenny, come back," he keened, over and over. "Jenny, come back. Don't leave me. I want you."

I ran.

CHAPTER
37

Down in the kitchen, Malachi and Donny were eating tomato sandwiches with tall glasses of Sparkey's milk. I couldn't let them see my agitation, and Malachi's small face reminded me of my promise to David. There would be no forgetfulness in the river, not while there were claims on me that had to be honored. Donny lurched up from the table when he saw me.

"He said it was okay if I comed in. I told him she wouldn't like it none."

"It's all right, Donny. Relax. Eat your sandwich."

He sat back down and stuffed half a sandwich into his mouth. Malachi looked at me solemnly over his glass of milk.

"Where've you been?" I asked him.

"Outside. Where's David? I want to talk to him."

"You can talk to me."

Malachi shook his head and took another swallow of milk. Donny chewed his sandwich hugely and mumbled around the shreds of tomato that sprouted on his lips.

"We was tracking the old man," he said. "I took the kid to the burned-up house and the old man come by, so we followed him."

Malachi shrugged at this betrayal of their secret. "I wanted to tell David. He'd know what to do."

"About what?" I couldn't bring myself to tell him that his father was in the hospital. I'd have to sooner or later, but I couldn't find the right words.

Malachi stared down at the half-consumed sandwich on his plate.

Donny swallowed and spoke. "He whacked her. She shot at him and he whacked her down, and then he came here."

He nodded wisely over this information. "He came in the house, he did. We seen him. She didn't get up."

There were tears on Malachi's cheeks. A few of them fell onto his sandwich before he brushed them away with the back of his small brown hand. Dear God, I thought, my father killed my mother and this child saw it. I sat down in a chair next to Malachi and put my arm around his shoulders. His small body felt stiff and unyielding and he turned his face away.

"Where is she?" I asked, keeping my voice soft and unalarmed. "Where did it happen?"

Donny's big head bobbed with excitement and he waved a loose-jointed paw into the vague distance. "Out back," he cried. "In the woods. My ma's there, too. She didn't see me. She'd whack me good if she seen me."

"Can you take me there?"

Donny grinned happily, but Malachi squirmed out of his chair and ran to the back door.

"I don't want to go back there. I hate this place. I want to go home."

I wanted to go home, too, but first I had to follow Donny back to where my mother had been "whacked down" and find out if Raymond had finally ended her long misery. But I wouldn't take Malachi back there if he didn't want to go, and I couldn't leave him alone. I didn't want to stay in River House a minute longer than necessary, but before I left I had to make sure that the man upstairs was incapable of inflicting any more damage on anyone. We had no transportation and no telephone. A child, a child-man, and a woman who'd been living a childish dream for most of her life. The dream was over now. I'd found Raymond my father and the reality was worse than any of the nightmares that had plagued my sleeping brain with inklings of the truth. The truth shall set you free, shall it? Not in this case. My mother had known the truth and it had tied her for twenty years to keeping and serving a dark secret. I'd denied the truth, blanked it out of my consciousness, but it hadn't make me any more free than she was. I had scurried between Max's Books and my dingy apartment, always on the lookout for a mythical smile and an ancient green car. There really had been nothing else in my life.

But now there would be, once I found the way to deal

with the man upstairs and my mother, if she were still alive.

"Hey! What's *he* doing?"

Malachi had gone to the kitchen window and was peering out into the backyard. I followed him.

Ralph Dean Otwell had backed his truck up to the old well and was winching away at the concrete plug. There was no need to open up the well now. My mother had told the last of her lies. We'd find no moldering Raymond bones at the bottom of the well. But Ralph Dean worked fast. The concrete plug came out of the ground with a grinding of winch gears and dangled at the end of the hook at the back of the truck. Ralph Dean himself was down on all fours peering down the well shaft.

By the time I got outside, he was carrying one of his extension ladders to the well. On his head, he wore a miner's helmet with its lamp glowing feebly in the bright sunshine.

"You don't have to go down there, Ralph Dean," I told him.

"It's okay, ma'am. Mr. Mears told me to, so I guess I will."

"Well, I changed my mind. Would you please cover it up again?"

"I can't do that, ma'am. Mr. Mears already paid me for the job. Besides, I got nothing else to do this afternoon. Be different if it was October or so and the leaves was coming down. Then I'd be real busy cleaning gutters and I wouldn't likely have time for this. What all you folks looking for down there?"

Ralph Dean was honest and polite and, like everyone else in this town, curious.

"Nothing. Nothing at all. I found what I was looking for."

"Well, if it's all the same to you," he set his ladder into the open well mouth, "if it's all the same to you, I'll just take a quick trip down there and come right back up. Just so Mr. Mears gets what he paid for."

The ladder went down and down. Ralph Dean adjusted the extensions and it went down some more. At last he seemed satisfied that the end of the ladder rested on solid bottom. He threw a rock down and listened for a splash. There was none.

"Don't seem to be much water down there. Well, here

goes nothing." He stepped onto the ladder and grinned at me, a tall, rangy man with hollow stubbled cheeks and dirt under his ragged fingernails. "If I find any coins or such what d'you want me to do with 'em?"

"You can keep them, Ralph Dean."

He saluted smartly and began to descend. I watched his plaid shirt disappear. As his head sank below the level of the ground, the light on his helmet grew brighter, then it, too, disappeared. There was nothing else to see. Malachi stood beside me, aching to go closer and peer down the shaft, but I kept my hand on his shoulder. Donny hung back, fascinated but fearful, looking as if he might go haring off into his beloved woods at any moment.

"We got a well," he whispered. "I never been down it."

A cloud moved across the face of the sun and a breeze off the river rustled the long dry grass. For no reason at all—it wasn't cold—I shivered. It must have been the silence at the well mouth and the thought of the long, dark, dank trip that Ralph Dean was taking into the depths of the earth. I found myself willing him to reappear, grinning shyly and chinking a few tarnished quarters in his horny hand.

I glanced over my shoulder at the upper floors of the house, but the turret room was at the front and there was no lean white face leering gaptoothed down at me from any of the back windows. I'd left the trapdoor open but somehow I didn't think that Raymond would take advantage of his freedom to escape. He'd grown to love his prison. Still, it might be wise to lock the door.

"Malachi," I said, "whatever happened to that padlock I gave you yesterday?" And was it only yesterday that he and David had set off happily to go fishing? It seemed like years ago.

"Got it," he said, plunging his small hand into the back pocket of his jeans. He pulled it out and dangled it with one finger thrust through its shining steel loop. "I didn't close it," he told me seriously, " 'cause then I couldn't get it open again. I got no key."

"May I have it back now, please?"

He handed it to me. It was warm from its closeness to his young body. As soon as Ralph Dean comes up, I thought, and closes up the well, I'll lock the trapdoor and go with Donny to find my mother. Maybe Ralph Dean will stay and keep an eye on Malachi. I edged a little closer to the well mouth, still keeping a hand on Malachi's shoulder and wondering what was taking Ralph Dean so long. I hoped that for his trouble he would find a treasure trove of old silver coins.

A sepulchral groan arose, echoing, from the bottom of the well. Donny stiffened, then ran, lurching on his bad leg, for the shelter of the trees that bordered the yard. Malachi watched him go, then looked up at me, his eyes questioning.

"Stay here," I whispered.

I crept up to the gaping hole in the ground and dropped to my knees. Behind me, I sensed Malachi edging closer, as curious as I was about the sound we'd heard. Perhaps Ralph Dean had hurt himself and needed help in climbing up. The groan came again, and the ladder shook. I leaned over the edge and peered down the shaft. Far below, the light bobbed and wavered. In its beam, I saw the dark sides of the well shaft, uneven and patchy with strange growths. Remembering what you might find when lifting up a mossy rock in the forest, my flesh tingled at the thought of the crawling pallid creatures that lived in dark places. There was an odor, too. A sweetish, musty smell that floated above the well mouth and lodged sickeningly at the back of my throat.

"Are you all right?" I called down the shaft, realizing as the words left my mouth how stupid they sounded. If he wasn't all right, what could I do? Go down the shaft and help him? I shuddered.

"I'm comin' up now, ma'am." His voice echoed dully and, it seemed to me, thick with revulsion. But that could have been the echo effect of the shaft or my own imagination projecting my feelings onto him. For all I knew, Ralph Dean explored old wells for fun and possible profit every chance he could get.

The light on his helmet was coming closer and I could hear the tread of his heavy work boots on every rung of the ladder. I got to my feet and backed away from the well, dragging Malachi with me. Ralph Dean's face appeared at the top of the ladder. It seemed no different than when he had gone down, but there was something odd about his eyes. He reached up with one hand and switched off his miner's lamp.

"I think you better get the police out here, ma'am," he said. "If you like, I can run into town and fetch old Bert Binns."

"What for?" I asked, astounded. "There's nothing down there. My father . . ." I broke off and shot a swift glance at the house. It slumbered quietly in the heat of the afternoon, a nice house, an old house, full of family memories.

"There's something down there," said Ralph Dean. He was trying to choose his words carefully, but the effort was too much for him. "There's bones down there," he blurted.

"But there can't be!" I cried. "My mother lied! My father is alive! His body isn't in the well!"

Ralph Dean slowly shook his head from side to side. For the first time, I noticed that there were drops of sweat beading his forehead and trickling down his thin cheeks.

"Small bones, I mean. Little ones. Lots of them."

And slowly, reluctantly, with infinite sadness spreading over his craggy features, he drew his other arm out of the well shaft and deposited on the ground at my feet a small perfect human skull.

Then he leaned away from me and vomited apologetically into the grass.

CHAPTER
38

How long we stood there, I can't tell. Things seemed to move in slow motion. Ralph Dean clambered out of the well, wiping his mouth on his plaid shirt sleeve, and stood gazing at his boots, waiting for me to tell him what to do. The sunlight glinted on the skull, showing up brownish stains on the yellowed ivory of the bone. As Ralph Dean had said, it was small. I glanced at Malachi who had become as still as a statue, or as one of his ancestors waiting patiently for a hunted animal to appear. Yes, I thought, about that small. The skull of a child.

Finding my voice at last, I whispered, "A lot, you say? How many?"

And Ralph Dean answered from far away, "Four or five. Maybe more. I couldn't rightly tell. They're all jumbled up. I didn't want to disturb them too much."

"How," I began, although I must have had an inkling of the answer, "how did they get there?"

Ralph Dean shrugged. "Been there a long time. You want me to go now?"

I nodded. Better to get it over with quickly. Oh, Raymond, a voice within me wept, what kind of a man are you? My grandmother, my mother, what you did to me. And now this. There was no doubt in my mind how those pitiful remains came to be at the bottom of the shaft. I might have been among them if my mother hadn't come in time.

"Yes," I said. "Go now. Go quickly. And take Malachi with you. Drop him off at Wendell's house. And hurry back."

"Best I leave the ladder there. They'll be needing it."

He walked stiff-legged to his truck, making a wide detour around the small skull lying in the grass. With a great show of muscle, he removed the concrete well cover from the winch hook at the back of the truck and laid it gently on the ground. Then, evidently feeling his manhood restored, he leaped into the cab of the truck and gunned the motor.

I nudged Malachi. "Go with him," I said.

"Don't want to. You'll be here alone."

I glanced toward the trees. Donny was lurking there uncertainly, staring in our direction.

"I'm not alone. Donny's over there."

"Same thing," said Malachi. "I'll stay here and wait for David."

I knew it was a bad time to tell Malachi about the accident, but it was the only thing I could think of that would make him leave.

"Malachi, your father can't come here. If you go with Ralph Dean, Bonnie Marie will take you to him."

"Where is he?" His turquoise eyes, replicas of David's, narrowed suspiciously in his small brown face.

"In the hospital. But he's all right. We had an accident."

"On the bike?"

"No. In a car. He hurt his head. But I saw him this morning. He wants you to visit him. He asked for you."

"You really want me to go?"

"I do."

"Well, all right." He started scuffling toward the truck. "But I'm coming back. I left all my stuff upstairs."

I followed him to the truck and watched as he struggled with the heavy door and climbed into the high seat. If I ever have a child, I thought, I'd want him to be just like this one. If I ever . . . but the unlikelihood struck me with a bruising force. The possibility that any child of mine would inherit through me the genes that had made a monster of my father sent a cold wave of repulsion through me. Never! I waved at Malachi who waved back at me through the open window of the truck. He said something, but the noise of the engine drowned it out and the truck bumped its way across the rough ground of the yard. As it turned the corner of the house, I thought I saw him blow me a kiss. I could have been wrong. Then they were gone.

Alone in the yard, I walked back to the well and stood for a moment staring down into its depths. There was nothing to see but blackness. Four or five, Ralph Dean had said. Four or five little girls. And what was it Aunt Tillie had said the other night on the river bank? Raymond had been accused of trying to rape a little girl? But he hadn't been guilty, or at least not that time. Aunt Tillie had clammed up then. I wondered where she had gone and what she would be willing to tell me now.

Under the trees, Donny was waving both his floppy hands in the air and uttering hoarse, croaking cries.

"Donny!" I called out to him. "Come here."

He came sidling across the yard, exaggerating his uneven gait, until he reached a point midway between the house and the trees. He would come no closer to the well, so I went to him. He seemed distressed.

"Where's the kid?" he cried. "Where'd he go? He's my friend."

"He'll be back. He went to see his father."

"What's that there?" Donny was staring at the skull in the grass.

"It's nothing," I told him. "Nothing you need to worry about. Donny, I need your help."

He stared at me.

"I want you to come into the house with me."

He started shaking his head.

"You've been in before. I saw you in the kitchen, remember?"

"You gonna tell her? She don't want me goin' in the

house." His mouth trembled and he wrapped his long arms across his chest as if trying to protect himself from unknown dangers.

"I won't tell her. All I want you to do is stand at the bottom of the stairs and not let anyone come down. You can do that, can't you? You're big and strong."

"You mean *him?*" He turned his pink moon face toward the top of River House.

"You know about him?"

"Course I know about him. That's what she makes me watch the house for. If he comes out, I'm to run to the phone at the gas station and call her up and tell her. Only now he whacked her down so I don't know if I should call her. I know how to use the phone."

"Do you know who he is?"

"My ma says he's a dirty old man."

The words, so often a joke, rang evilly true. I fingered the padlock, which I had thrust into the pocket of my dress, and hoped that I'd be able to close the trapdoor and lock it before anything else went wrong.

"My ma said once that he was my daddy, but she was drunk and crying at the time, so I don't know if she meant it. She sure don't like him much. Maybe she made a mistake."

"Maybe she did. Will you come into the house now and help me?"

"I guess."

We walked across the grass. Donny made an odd ally. My brother, if I care to look at the relationship closely enough, but he didn't seem to know it. Although from his sometimes oblique, sometimes direct, method of communication, it was hard to tell exactly what he did know. But I knew, and that was something else I'd have to deal with once the business of Raymond was over. I wondered how long it would take Ralph Dean to get back here with the police. I wondered about my mother, whether she were alive or dead. But if I could believe Donny, Alva was with her and would do what was necessary. We walked up onto the back porch.

The kitchen was just as we'd left it, milk glasses and sandwich plates on the table. Donny snatched up a crust of bread from one of the plates and stuffed it into his mouth. We passed through the dining room where the chandelier twinkled and the mahogany glowed and on into the hall. There was no sound in the house but our footsteps and Donny's chomping on his crust of bread. At the foot of the stairs, I stopped and looked through the wide archway into the front parlor. It was dim, as usual, and pulsing with wine velvet upholstery and oceanic blue carpet, but there was no one there. If it were mine, I decided, I would clear it out and lighten it and make it less stifling and repellent. But it wasn't mine, and I had other things to do. I set my foot on the first riser of the stairway.

"Stay here," I whispered to Donny. "If he comes down, stop him. Don't let him get away. Even if you have to sit on him."

Donny nodded and chortled.

I went on up the stairs, treading softly in my old flat sandals. In the second-floor hallway, I paused and listened. Still no sound from above. Could he have come down and gone out the front way while we were in the back waiting for the horrors of the well to be revealed?

Remembering the strength in his thin hands when he hauled me away from the trapdoor and sent me sprawling across the floor of the turret room, I tiptoed down the hall and retrieved my shoulder bag from the dresser in the back bedroom. The smell of rotten meat came heavily from the bundle in the corner, and I thought of him gleefully wringing the chicken's neck and watching it flap headless around the room.

With the bag hanging from my shoulder, I climbed the narrow stairs to the third floor. Still no sound from above. Up again, to the hot murky attic, to the place where my childhood had been destroyed and the rest of my life made a lonely wasteland. This time I didn't shake; I suffered no nausea or dizziness. This time I knew what there was to know.

I went straight to the ladder and climbed high enough to reach the edge of the door. All I had to do was swing it up into place and slip the padlock through its hasp. I started to do that, but stopped midway and let the door swing back. I had to be sure he was in the room before I locked it. There'd been no sound, no cry, no moan or howl to warn me of his presence.

I climbed farther and thrust my head through the opening. He was there all right, lying flat on his back on the pallet. He seemed to be asleep, although from my angle of vision I couldn't see whether his eyes were closed. Hoping he hadn't noticed me, I started back down the ladder, ready now to close the door and lock it for the last time. But his voice stopped me.

"Jenny," he called, softly now and seductively. "Jenny, come up here."

I looked back through the door. He was sitting on the pallet, a gun in his hand.

"No," I breathed, and my hand fumbled with the flap of my shoulder bag.

"Yes," he insisted. "I need you. I want you." The gun was aimed unwaveringly at my head.

"We opened up the well," I told him. "The police are coming."

"I know that. I watched you. That's why I need you. If you're up here with me, they won't be able to take me away. Because I'll kill you if they try. Now get up here."

His voice had changed to a peremptory bark. While he was talking, I was groping in my bag for Wendell's revolver. It wasn't there. I looked closely at the gun in his hand.

"That's right," he said. "Women shouldn't fool around with guns. You're careless with them. Leave them lying around for other folks to pick up. And you can't shoot straight. Look at your mother. Tried three times and missed. She doesn't get another chance. Now get up here before I blow your pretty head off."

I got. I slithered through the trapdoor, keeping well away from him. He sat back on the pallet and smiled at me. The trapdoor hung open between us like a yawning grave. The gun stared.

"Take your clothes off," he ordered.

"What!"

"You heard me. You're my little princess, aren't you? And I'm your handsome prince. And we're going to live happily ever after. But first you have to take your clothes off so I can see if you're perfect."

It was a ghastly replay of the scene in this room so many years ago. I wondered if he'd used the same script on the little girls whose bones lay tumbled together at the bottom of the well. Innocence, I thought. What was it? Was there any in the world? For now I saw that in innocently playing a game, I'd led him on. I *had* wanted him for myself, *all* for myself. I had loved him. But I hadn't known. Oh, truly I hadn't known. What does any little girl know? Except that she loves her father and wants him to love her. Oh, no! I wouldn't bear the guilt for what he had become. Most men are fathers, and most fathers love their daughters without doing what he had done. His pattern had been set long before I was born. Look at Alva. She couldn't have been more than twelve or thirteen when Donny was born. God knows what forces had shaped my father, but it wasn't my fault. *IT WASN'T MY FAULT!*

He was coming toward me then, limping on his wounded leg, the gun pointed straight at my heart.

"Guess I'll have to help you," he said. "Remember how I helped you before? You were such a pretty little thing. I'm glad you didn't grow too tall. You still look like a little girl."

His left hand gripped the front of my dress and pulled. Buttons spattered on the floor. His right hand rested on my shoulder, the gun pressed against my head. He reached into my dress and passed his hand over my breasts. I looked up into his face. His eyes were closed and his mouth was working, muttering words I couldn't hear.

Quickly I twisted my head toward my shoulder and bit the hand that held the gun. I bit hard and tasted blood. He screamed and leaped away from me, dropping the gun on the floor behind me. I whirled around and picked it up. When I straightened, he was coming at me, rage in his eyes, froth on his snarling mouth. I fired. Once.

I couldn't see whether or where I'd hit him. He stumbled backward and fell through the trapdoor. There was a slithering, ripping sound and then a soft thud. I looked down through the trapdoor. He was lying at the foot of the ladder, curled as if in sleep, with blood pooling on the floor in the curve of his body.

One of my mother's lies had come true.

CHAPTER
39

I heard the sound of an engine and looked out the small turret window. Aunt Tillie's red Porsche was nosing up the drive. It angled onto the lawn and stopped. Aunt Tillie leaped out and ran around to open the other door. She bent to help someone out. When she got him to his feet, I saw that he was a very old man who walked with the aid of two canes. She led him to the porch and they disappeared from my view.

I had to go downstairs. I had to descend the ladder and step over my dead father. It was one of the hardest things I'd ever done, but I did it. I stood for a moment looking down at him. There was no doubt that he was dead. His eyes stared without seeing and no sign of breath disturbed him where he lay. His right hand bore the marks of my teeth. My mouth filled with a bitter taste and I turned away.

At the foot of the stairs, Donny gabbled excitedly, while Aunt Tillie tried to calm him. The old man looked sternly at me as I came slowly down the stairs, the gun still in my hand. I stopped midway down the stairs and clung to the banister.

"I've just killed my father," I told them.

"Oh, God!" cried Tillie. "We're too late!"

Donny goggled up at me, then sat down on the bottom step and burst into tears.

Tillie threw her arms around me and murmured, "You poor child."

The old man reached for the gun and I gave it to him gladly. Tillie herded us all into the kitchen where I collapsed gratefully onto a hard kitchen chair. She bustled around with the coffeepot and cups, cautioning me not to say a word until I'd had some coffee with a large shot of brandy in it. The old man sat patiently in his chair, his wise eyes regarding me with a mixture of pity and curiosity. I didn't know who he was. I didn't want to know. I just wanted to get finished with the business at hand and go somewhere and sleep and sleep and sleep.

"I didn't know, Jenny. I honestly didn't know," Tillie began, "until I got the bright idea of looking up Chief Hawthorne."

"It's Mister Hawthorne now," the old man said. "I'm retired."

"But you weren't retired when Ray Holland disappeared."

"No," he agreed. "I was on the job then."

Tillie leaned across the table and spoke earnestly to me. "So I thought, if anybody knows anything about what happened back then, it would have to be Chief Hawthorne. It took me a while to find him. And it took me even longer to convince him to come with me and open up old wounds. But when I told him what had been going on here, and that I thought someone's life might be in danger, he agreed to come. It's all yours, Chief."

The old man smiled slightly. "If you won't call me Mister, why don't you call me Andy? It sounds less official that way. And that's what this is, strictly unofficial."

He took a sip of his coffee and shifted himself to a more comfortable position in his chair. "Arthritis," he said, "the plague of old bones. Well, anyway, Jenny. Your aunt said you'd been hurting over things you didn't understand. I wasn't sure that you needed to understand them. Best let sleeping dogs lie, and all that. But after what's happened here today, I guess you ought to know. Years ago—you're too young to remember—there was a string of missing girls. Most of 'em Muley kids and all of 'em about eight or nine years old. Some of 'em we didn't know about right away. The Muley folks tend to keep to themselves and they didn't trust the police much. Still don't, for that matter. But one mother came to us with a story that someone had seen her girl getting into a green Pontiac. Now green Pontiacs weren't all that common, but they weren't exactly rare. Your daddy had one. So we decided to keep an eye on Ray Holland as well as on a few other guys.

"Now, Muley kids are strange—hell, all kids are strange sometimes—they'll run off and stay away and drive their poor folks crazy. And then one day they'll turn up, all piefaced and innocent and wondering what the fuss is all about. It's boys mostly that do it, but girls do too sometimes."

"I know," I whispered, thinking of my poor mother after I'd left town.

"Well, now. One night we got a call from a girl's mother who said some guy'd tried to force her daughter into a green car down by the freight yards. The girl wasn't supposed to play down there, but she was a wild little thing, joy riding on the freight trains, shoplifting in the dime store, that sort of thing. And she was only nine years old. Seems she always carried a hunting knife in a sheath on her belt, and when the guy tried to shove her into the car, she whipped out the knife and stabbed him in the thigh. It's a wonder she told her mother about it, but I guess she was really scared.

"Well, we went right over to Ray Holland's house and there was his green Pontiac in the garage, and there was Ray sitting in his chair reading the paper. Your mother was there and she swore that he hadn't left the house all evening. We'd brought the girl along to see if she could identify him, but she said it was dark and she was scared and she never got a good look at the guy's face. And we couldn't very well ask your father to take off his pants and let us see if he had a stab wound in his thigh."

"He did," I said, remembering the flash of memory I'd had in the turret room—my small finger touching the puckered scar.

Andy Hawthorne continued. "Shortly after that, Ray Holland sold his car and bought some other kind of car; I forget now what it was. We got no more reports of girls getting into green cars, but every once in a while, once or twice a year, a Muley girl would disappear. And every time we talked to Ray Holland about it, he was as smooth and innocent as banana pie and your mother always backed him up. Finally, your grandmother threatened us with lawyers if we didn't stop hounding him and blackening the family's good name in the town.

"Then one day, the gossip was all about how Ray Holland had left his wife and young daughter and run off somewhere. And a few months later, the word was out that he had died, no one was sure where or how. No more Muley girls disappeared, at least none that we heard about, so by and by we forgot about it.

"But that wasn't the end of it. Not for me. About a year after I retired—that'd be close to ten years ago—I ran into your grandmother in the bank one day. She said good morning, as polite as can be, and asked me if I'd be kind enough to take a short ride with her in her car. She had something to tell me that I'd be interested to hear.

"And that was when she told me that I'd been right about Ray Holland all along. She told me she was sorry for obstructing justice, those were her very words, but she couldn't afford to be branded in the town as related to a child rapist and murderer. But she said that she'd made sure that justice was served. I tried to find out what she meant, but she just smiled and told me not to worry about it and enjoy my retirement. I asked her if she knew where the girls' bodies were so at least the families could give them a Christian burial. But she just shook her head and said she was sure their souls were with the angels. A few months later, she was dead herself."

"They're in the well," I whispered.

"What is?" asked Aunt Tillie.

"The bodies. The girls. We opened the well and found them."

"Well," said Andy Hawthorne, "I'm right glad I don't have to be the one to break the news. This has been bad enough. But suppose you tell me something now, Miss Jenny. What did you mean when you came down the stairs? How could you have killed your father? I thought he died years ago. Matter of fact, I always suspected your grandmother had something to do with his disappearing like that."

"My grandmother's justice," I reminded him. "She kept him locked in an attic room. When she died the responsibility passed on to my mother. He tried to . . . to do something to me. I shot him."

"Oh, my God!" Aunt Tillie sighed. "I never dreamed— I knew there was something peculiar going on—but I never dreamed it was this. I think I'll go back to Chicago and stay there. It's safer. Did anybody go for the police?"

"Ralph Dean Otwell. He should be getting back soon."

And soon they came. The police cars, the ambulances, the newspaper reporters, even the television camera crews. It was all gruesome and public. The questions, the pictures. There was no way the family could keep this secret. My mother, thank God, was safely back in the hospital where Alva had taken her after my father had knocked her down with a fallen tree limb. She was unconscious and being watched around the clock, but there was hope for her.

Sergeant Bert Binns took personal charge of me and listened sympathetically as I poured out the whole story. I didn't go out to watch the excavation of the well—that would have been too heartbreaking—but I did watch them carry Raymond my father out of River House. He was, by then, anonymously shrouded in heavy green plastic, but as the stretcher went by I whispered, "I'm sorry, Daddy." Who or what I was sorry for was tumbled in my mind with visions of a handsome brown smiling face and a small girl who flew into the air and knew she would come down safely.

Wendell turned up, for once deprived of all his bluster. "I can't believe it," he repeated over and over again. "I can't believe it. Your poor mother. All these years, and I never knew. Never even guessed." He threw his burly arm around my shoulder and I didn't flinch. There was nothing but cousinly sympathy in the gesture. "Jenny," he asked, "why do you suppose your ma wanted you and all the family to congregate at River House?"

It was a question I'd been pondering. "I think," I told him, "I think she wanted someone to help her, but didn't know how to go about asking for help. She must have figured that if everyone were here, sooner or later someone would stumble across her secret and do something about it. I don't think she wanted it to be me. She kept telling me to go back to New York. But I'm glad I had to face him at the end. Not that I shot him, but that I finally saw him as he was. I could have gone on hiding from my memories all my life."

I felt the tears coming and tried to hold them back but couldn't. I wept on Wendell's shoulder while he held me awkwardly and murmured, "There, there, Jenny-girl." I wept for all the empty years, both mine and my mother's; I wept at last for my dead father, who really died long years ago; and I wept for tomorrow because I didn't know what would happen next.

Wendell handed me a clean handkerchief and after I dampened it thoroughly, I asked him to take me to the hospital. We left while the operations in the backyard were still in progress. Andy Hawthorne wanted to keep an eye on things—it was a case from his term as chief of police—and Aunt Tillie was sitting on the front porch waiting to take him home.

"I think I'll be heading back to Chicago," she said. "I'm not superstitious, but I don't want to spend another night in this house."

I stood on the battered front lawn and looked up at River House. It was no longer the house of my dreams, stark and menacing in the moonlight, with a consuming fire breaking out of that small turret window to destroy everything I loved. It was an old shabby relic of times gone by, probably of some value, but not to me. I hoped my mother would sell it and everything in it.

"I don't think anyone will sleep here tonight," I told Aunt Tillie. I went to her and kissed her soft dry cheek. "Good-bye. Come and see me in New York."

"I will. Unless I have to track you down in Arizona." She winked and I smiled. "Don't lose touch," she called after me. "Take care of yourself."

At the hospital, my fifth visit in two days, I found Alva hovering over my mother in the same room she'd had before. There was a bandage around my mother's head.

"Ssh!" Alva cautioned me, a finger to her lips. "She's sleeping now. She fell down in the woods and hit her head on a rock."

"No more lies, Alva. I know who hit her and why and there's nothing to worry about anymore. He's dead."

My mother's eyes opened under the bandage and she echoed my last words. "Dead? He's dead? Raymond is dead?"

"I killed him. Just like you told me you had done. The police are out there now. We opened up the old well."

"Oh, no!" she groaned and her eyes fell closed again. "Now the whole town will know."

Alva shook her roughly by the shoulder and growled, "Don't be a fool, Lizzie. It doesn't matter anymore who knows. They'll buzz about it for a while like flies around a dead river rat, and then they'll find something else to buzz over. Anyway, you don't have to stay here now. You can pack up and go wherever you like."

She opened her eyes and probed my face, knowing the answer even before she asked the question.

"Will you stay here, Jenny? Will you stay home with me now?"

Sadly, I shook my head. "I'll stay until you're well and until David can ride his motorcycle. I told him I'd look after Malachi. And I guess I'll have to stay until they hold a hearing on Raymond's death. Both Wendell and Bert Binns think it'll be just a formality, no chance of my going to jail. Especially after I told them that he killed Grandma. I guess you'll have to speak up, too. Why didn't you do it then? You could have had him arrested and lived a normal life all these years."

My mother turned her face to the wall. "She wouldn't have wanted me to do that. She always told me that he was my punishment for being headstrong enough to marry him in the first place. She wanted you to be let in on the secret and share the burden of taking care of him. That's why I was so glad you ran off. What she didn't realize was that we were just as much prisoners as he was. Now I'm free. And I don't know what to do with my freedom."

"Take it slow," I told her. "Doctor Marks said you were going to help her with her hot line. That's a start."

"Yes." She turned back to me and smiled. "I can't believe she's really a doctor. She's so nice. And funny. I found myself telling her things I never told anyone before. Not even Alva."

"Then she must be good at her job."

I left my mother and Alva chattering gleefully about what the town would say when the news broke, and went across the hall to David's room. Malachi was there, perched on the foot of the bed. They were playing poker with a tattered deck of cards, using tongue depressors for their stakes.

"I win!" Malachi cried, laying down a full house and gathering up a pile of sticks.

"Jenny," said David. "What's going on? Malachi told me about following a strange old man. How's your mother? If you only knew how I hate being cooped up in this room. Did they ever find out anything about that truck?"

"It's all over," I told him, with a cautionary glance at Malachi. "It's a long story and I think I'll save it until we have more time. Here comes your supper."

The nurse who came in with his supper tray frowned at both Malachi and me and said, "You really shouldn't be here."

David grinned at her, grabbed my hand, and said, "But I was just about to ask this lady to marry me."

I tried to pull away. The nurse smiled and said, "Well, I certainly don't want to interrupt a proposal." She slid the tray onto the bed table, wheeled it into position, smirked at both of us and left, closing the door behind her.

"I can't, David," I began.

"Hush, hush," he said. "I didn't mean right this minute. What do you think, Malachi?"

"It's okay by me." He was squatting on the floor, building a teepee with the tongue depressors he'd won.

I didn't know how I felt. Hollow, quavery, uncertain, elated, grateful, and frightened. All at once, all mixed up together. What could I bring to this man, or any man? A legacy of destruction and a soul grown old and cold before its time.

"You don't know . . ." I stammered. "I can't marry . . . not you . . . not anyone."

"Hush, hush," he said again. "I know what I'm doing. Let me lead the way just until you feel sure. You can trust me. I know that's hard for you to believe, but it's true. Malachi likes you, and you already know the bookstore business so I can put you right to work. See how underhanded my purposes are?"

I laughed. It wasn't much of a laugh but it was the first real one in days and days. But his mention of the book business reminded me of Max's Secondhand Books. That was all I had to go back to when I left here. And somehow, suddenly, it wasn't enough. It had served as my shelter for almost ten years. It had been more than a shelter; it had been every bit as much a prison for me as that turret room had been for Raymond my father. Would I willingly go back there even while I was encouraging my mother to seek the freedom she'd never known?

"I'll come with you," I whispered, "for a visit. We'll see how it works out."

He pulled me onto the bed beside him and stroked my hair. I was suddenly conscious of looking a mess, my hair uncombed, the safety pin that Tillie'd given me to hold my dress together, and an almost unbearable weariness. I sank back against the pillow and sighed. His voice was a gentle whisper against my ear.

"You haven't said something important. Neither have I."

I looked into his face, questioning.

"I love you, Jenny."

"And I . . . I hope . . . I think . . . I could love you, David."

I realized I'd never said that to anyone before. And I vowed silently to make it be true.

"When are we going home?" piped Malachi from the floor.

"Soon, kid. Very soon," said David.

"I won't have to travel on that motorcycle, will I?" I asked.

"No, we'll have it shipped and take a plane."

"Oh, rats," said Malachi.

David smiled, and so did I. "Eat your supper," I said.

Murder & Intrigue
FROM THE WITTY AND MASTERFUL
CHARLOTTE MACLEOD